Sweet November

ORLA
KELLY
PUBLISHING

Siobhán Curran

This book is dedicated to the memory of three beautiful women.

Three generations of women from the same family tree who left this world before we in this world were ready to let them go...

Kate O'Shea

B. 1898   D. 1923

Kathleen Doyle (nee O'Shea)

B. 1945   D. 2013

Margaret Curran

B. 1959   D. 2013

SYNOPSIS

This is the story of an Irish artist, Kate O' Shea who is coming to terms with the fact that her marriage isn't the relationship she had dreamed about as a young girl. The attempts she makes to get things back on track, only to be hit by a devastating blow along the way. It recounts Kate's journey through bereavement, attempting to reclaim some kind of life for herself.

The story takes her across Europe to her spiritual home in Western Crete. It briefly reaches into the past touching the tragedy of World War Two and its effect on this Mediterranean island. It fast forwards to modern day soulful painting in a stunningly beautiful location. The journey includes a three-month sabbatical in America before it brings her full circle back to where she started from!

Kate bravely confronts every fear and emotion buried deep in her sub-conscious only to emerge as a stronger more powerful version of herself.

A whole new world begins to open up for her. A world better than anything she could ever have dreamed of for herself or does it...?

Contents

INTRODUCTION

Eleni Mitsotakis was lying on her bed looking out to sea, to the view she was lucky enough to have had for the last seventy years of her life.

She knew she hadn't long left.

She wasn't afraid.

In fact, she welcomed death. She would finally be with her beloved Dimitris and her beautiful daughter Maria. All three of them together, at last…

Eleni had a long and healthy life. She had been exactly where she had wanted to be – on her beloved and beautiful peninsula in Western Crete. All bare rock and steep cliffs. Wild and desolate and so familiar to her.

She smiled to herself. She considered herself so lucky to have spent her whole life on the peninsula. Her happy childhood, her brief passionate marriage, the dark days of war and occupation, the bittersweet years of motherhood and last but not least, the happy times as a grandmother. She had seen Crete through the good times and the bad times. She was grateful for all her life's experiences, both the agonies and the ecstasies. The wisdom of old age told her she would never have appreciated the good times without the challenges of the bad.

Crete had brought her the first great love of her life, her husband Dimitris, the gift of their beautiful daughter Maria. And it had brought her grandson Yiannis to her, he was with her still.

Eleni watched him with great fondness and love in her heart. He was a good, kind man and she was very proud of him. Sometimes when she looked at him, it was like looking at her husband, Dimitris, all over again. He had inherited his grandfather's good looks. He had the same dark intense eyes, the same strong physique and comfortableness in his own skin, the same even temperament and a heart full of love and passion. Not to mention the pride he had in his Cretan heritage and his roots on the peninsula.

Hadn't he come back? After all the years, hadn't he come back to Crete, where he truly belonged? She had been so sure she had lost him to the mainland and Athens years before. Deep down she knew he had moved back to Crete to take care of her, even though he pretended otherwise. It gladdened her heart when she thought about the last two years. There was no doubt they had been wonderful. As wonderful as when Yiannis had grown up on the peninsula, she reflected. Only this time it was him looking out for her, not the other way around.

Yiannis moved to the bed and took her hand in his, dwarfing her by his powerful physical presence.

"Is there anything you want, Mama?"

He had always called her 'Mama' ever since he had come to live with her as a child. Eleni looked at him tenderly and shook her head, "Nothing. Thank you, Yiannis. Just sit with me a while?"

As she held his hand in hers, Eleni couldn't but think of her beloved husband again. She lay back on her pillows, smiled and sighed quietly. She could still remember the first time she had ever seen him. Closing her eyes, it was as real to her now as if it had only happened yesterday…

It was the end of August, baking hot and everyone had trekked the long pilgrimage to the tiny church of Agios Ioannis, out on the edge of the peninsula, miles and miles from anywhere. Once a year, it was a mecca for all the villagers who were scattered in every direction along the peninsula. Supposedly a holy day, but in true Cretan style it ended up more of a social gathering than a religious one.

As soon as the ceremonies were finished, the festivities began with great gusto. It was a chance for them to meet with neighbours and friends from the other villages. An opportunity to socialise, eat and drink a little, sing the old Cretan songs, dance, and laugh till the early hours of the morning. Eleni's people knew how to party. For as long as she could remember, her parents had brought her there. Now, being the youngest, she was the only one of her siblings still at home. The only one left to go with them. One by one, all her brothers and sisters had left the peninsula and moved on to the bigger towns and cities. Some had even gone to the mainland. Eleni could never imagine leaving her beloved peninsula. She loved it too much.

The tiny church in the most isolated part of the peninsula was surrounded by rugged terrain on all sides. To the west she could see the entire breath-taking Bay of Kissamos and to the east the view was clear the whole way to the city of Chania and the headland beyond. It had to be the most stunning vista in the world. Awe inspiring, Eleni thought fondly. It could soften the hardest of hearts and quiet the busiest of minds.

The searing August heat had given way to a beautiful balmy evening. Eleni left her parents and neighbours underneath the shade of a plane tree in the churchyard and went in search of her friends. All the adults could talk about these days was the possibility of war in Europe and the Nazis. Boring! Boring! Boring! thought Eleni. At seventeen she only wanted to laugh and gossip and flirt with boys. To see who had come this year. To see if there were any new faces. Eleni was a beautiful spirited young woman and way more mature than friends her own age. Already she was turning heads in the village, with her raven black hair, vivid blue eyes and feminine curves. She enjoyed all the attention of course, but she hadn't seen anyone who took her fancy – not yet anyway. At least at the festival there was certain to be more boys to look at or flirt with, she thought mischievously.

She spotted her friends on that glorious August evening, grouped together at the far wall, away from the church and the prying eyes of parents, giggling and laughing and every so often glancing towards the group of boys standing next to them. One quick sweep of her eyes told Eleni she had no interest in any of them. They were all so young and immature, she thought dismissively. Way too young for her.

However, as her eyes moved a little further along she saw a much more interesting group altogether. A small gathering of young men were talking quietly amongst themselves. Eleni didn't think she knew any of them, but something about one of the men aroused her curiosity. He had his back to her, but she could tell by the way he stood he was confident and sure of himself. He was well over six foot, with a strong muscular body. A man in comparison to the other boys. He had a strong side profile anytime he turned his head, and his hair was as black as coal.

She stared at him quite unintentionally, temporarily distracted by his confident stance. He must have felt her eyes on him because ever so slowly he turned around, looking straight at her and smiled. Eleni caught her breath and quickly looked away. He was magnificent, she thought, so handsome with his short dark hair, dark eyes and full moustache. He was wearing the knee-high traditional boots, baggy trousers and dark shirt common to Cretan men. When she dared look up again, he was still watching her, smiling. Their eyes locked for a few moments before she looked away again. In that instant, she was hooked. Something instinctively told her he was the one. She just knew it.

He spent the rest of the evening casually leaning against the wall, chatting to his friends and every so often looking in her direction. There were lots of furtive looks and smiles that night, Eleni, uncharacteristically giggly and secretly hoping she was being watched. She welcomed any attention from him. It made her feel very feminine and very beautiful.

Before the evening was over she had learned his name, Dimitris Mitsotakis. He was from the next village to her own. He had recently returned from the army. He was twenty-one years old, four years older than her. Dimitris Mitsotakis was going to figure in her future somehow. Of that, she was determined.

That night, as was the custom, Eleni slept in the churchyard alongside her watchful parents, all her friends doing likewise with their own parents. Everyone had come prepared, throwing blankets on the ground, sleeping beneath the stars. It was the tradition. Her mind however was a different matter. She didn't sleep a wink, her thoughts on other very pleasant things... such as thinking about Dimitris all night long. How he had smiled at her and caught her eye, many times. How she hoped against hope that he was as interested in her as she was in him. She gladly whiled away the night hours, in blissful admiration of Dimitris Mitsotakis.

The next morning, she passed by him in the courtyard of the church and their eyes locked again. This time, she boldly held his gaze and smiled.

"Kalimera," he greeted her, smiling and stopping for just an instant before he passed along.

"Kalimera," she returned his greeting, blushing in spite of herself. Up close, he had the most intense black eyes she had ever seen, and his gaze skimmed over her appreciatively. Now she was fairly sure he was interested. She was positive of it. How her heart soared!

Once the festivities and ceremonies were over at Agios Ioannis, they all slowly trekked the return journey to their villages. Eleni, who was with her parents, desperately skimmed the crowds to try to catch sight of him, but to no avail. It was as if he had disappeared into thin air.

Once home, she spent hours preoccupied, wondering about him. What was to happen next? Since she had seen and exchanged the minimal of pleasantries with Dimitris, she knew he was the one for her. She was desperate to see him again. How could she arrange it? Did he know her name and where she was from? A million questions flitted through her brain. Mulling it over and over in her head, Eleni tried to think of an excuse to go to his village, to initiate some kind of contact between them. She knew she had to be careful, but she just had to see him again.

However, she needn't have worried as less than a week later, a respected person approached her father and she could sense there was some excitement afoot, such was the air of expectation in the house. The man, considered a matchmaker, had come to propose a possible meeting between herself and Dimitris.

Eleni's heart nearly burst with happiness that day. What joy! Dimitris was orchestrating things from afar. He was interested! She was right! It was a dream come true.

Eleni was truly ecstatic, her parents somewhat reticent. She was their last child and favoured in a way. She was too young, they protested, only seventeen. But headstrong and impatient Eleni knew how to manipulate her parents, especially her doting papa. She worked on them tirelessly until they relented. And Eleni finally got her way. But she was no fool and knew things had to be done in the proper fashion. So, they agreed she could meet him, but only with someone else present.

At first Eleni and Dimitris were shy together, but bit by bit, they discovered they had a lot in common. They both loved the peninsula and Crete.

Both had a strong sense of family and loyalty. And whenever they were able to snatch a few kisses or private moments together, they also discovered a simmering passion underneath all the propriety. Quite quickly they became betrothed and a little more than a year after they first met, they married once Eleni turned eighteen.

She would never forget her wedding day. It was forever etched on her heart. All of them, family, friends and neighbours in high spirits, laughing excitedly as they made the short procession from her house to the church. Herself and Dimitris barely able to contain themselves, both feeling so lucky they were marrying for love.

Little did they know it at the time, but it was to be one of the last truly happy days on the peninsula...

Everyone joined in the celebrations in the village square. Eating and drinking, dancing and singing songs. They drank to the health of Dimitris and Eleni, until the early hours of the morning. It seemed as if everyone was so happy that night. The new bride and groom were the happiest of them all. And their wedding night was the perfect end to a perfect day. It could still make Eleni's heart skip a beat when she thought about it seventy years later. Dimitris was the most passionate, gentle lover. And she matched his passion with every kiss and caress. It was as if they had been made for each other. Eleni vowed then, that she would love him with all her heart until the day she died.

She left her village and moved the short distance to a little stone cottage by the sea. They were to live with Dimitris' mother, Anastasia, who was a widow. She was a kind gentle woman whose one wish, was for her only child to be happy with his new bride. Dimitris' father had died years before in a fishing accident.

Eleni and Dimitris settled into married life, happy to be living together as husband and wife. Times were hard, but it seemed as if everybody was poor back then. There may not have been much to go around but at least they had the loving comfort of each other's arms at night. Their days were taken up tending the small patch of land, feeding the hens, milking the few sheep and goats or foraging for mountain greens and looking after the olive grove in hope of a good harvest. Now and again, Dimitris went fishing to supplement the meagre food supplies. And Eleni loved nothing more than to create simple tasty meals for her husband and mother-in-law using produce from the garden or whatever was to hand.

Besides looking after his own place, Dimitris would do odd jobs whenever he could for their neighbours. A skilled craftsman, he could turn his hand to almost anything and occasionally, they came looking for him from the surrounding villages. He would often arrive home with extra eggs, or honey or something home-baked, something from the homes of their resourceful neighbours. Very rarely did money change hands and it all helped to keep the three of them fed and clothed. Dimitris made sure they never went hungry.

Eleni had lived all her young life on the peninsula and had always been happy there. When her friends had talked about moving on to the mainland or the cities, she knew it wasn't for her. It lifted her heart to be by the sea and feel the gentle wind in her hair or walk the cliffs and view the awesome scenery surrounding her every day. And now that she had found her perfect love, she had no desire to be anywhere other than where he was – on their beautiful peninsula. It was all she had ever dreamed of.

Nevertheless, they were barely married a couple of months when all the talk in the village and beyond was of the Italians and the Germans and trouble on the mainland. They were all shocked. It seemed like the big war was inching closer and closer. Many of Dimitris' friends had already left to join the Greek army. Eleni pleaded with him not to go. She could see he was torn between defending his country and providing for the three of them. He gave in to her this time, and they watched events unfold from afar, taking pride in the initial success of the Greek army.

But who would ever forget that fateful day in May 1941? All of them stood frozen in the fields. It was the day they watched in horror as hundreds of 'umbrellas' fell to the ground further east for as far as the eye could see – a life changing day for everyone. The Germans were parachuting into Crete. They knew instinctively it was the start of the war for them. It's what they had all dreaded. The war had finally come to Crete from the sky.

Almost without speaking, the men left the fields. They went and collected whatever weapons they could lay their hands on. Old hunting guns, knives, shovels, pots, sticks, whatever was to hand, and they left the villages, to seek out the enemy and defend their island. Sadly, to no great avail. The might of the German Army crushed their efforts and thus began a reign of terror in Crete. Even now, Eleni shook her head in disbelief as she remembered the beginning of a very sad time for her beloved island.

All of a sudden, they were propelled into a war not of their making. Not one of them had asked for this, but they would resist it with all their might. They were, after all, proud Cretans.

Eleni knew in her heart of hearts, that Dimitris joining the resistance was inevitable now. She couldn't stop him. In fact, she didn't want to stop him. It wasn't something either of them had to think about. Defend their beautiful island? The birthplace of their fathers and forefathers?

Along with the other men, Dimitris took to leaving home in the dead of night, for days and sometimes weeks at a time. The men were never sure when they would see their families again, but they never failed to defend Crete and help the allies hiding throughout the island. They trekked over mountains and through valleys. Sleeping wherever they could lay their heads safely, providing safe passage or hideouts in the mountains for the needy. All of them living with the uncertainty and the fear. It seemed to Eleni that the worst of times had brought out the very best in her people. They got to know who could and couldn't be trusted.

Sometimes when Dimitris returned home, he would tell her of the terrible things he had seen or heard about. Other times he would return and say nothing at all, trying to protect her from the horrors he had witnessed. The spirit of resistance was so deeply embedded in them all, it wasn't a choice. It was a deep-seated knowing of the right thing to do. Defend Crete to the death.

She was very proud of him, of them all. Very proud of what he was doing for Crete and Greece. All she could do was support him as best she could and provide loving comfort when he returned home. Eleni and Anastasia like all women helped whenever and wherever, keeping the home fires burning, carrying secret messages and going without themselves so the allies could eat or be clothed. Always with their eyes and ears open to help their men. Of course, it didn't stop her worrying sick when he was gone and praying for his safe return. Every moment they had together became so much more precious.

Eleni became pregnant during this tumultuous time. Dimitris was overjoyed that out of so much sadness and death, they were creating a new life together. He said it spurred him on, even more, to fight for a free and liberated Crete. The last time Dimitris left, he held her tightly in his arms, whispering that he would be back before the birth. "I'll stay for a while then, until the baby is big and strong," he said kissing her deeply with great love and passion, gently placing his hands on her large swollen stomach.

Eleni knew in her heart of hearts that day, before anybody ever came with the news. She had the feeling earlier in the day that someone had walked over her grave. It had chilled her to the very bone, but she had hoped and prayed she was wrong. When they finally came to the house to break the news, Eleni was distraught with grief. Inconsolable that Dimitris, the love and light of her life, had been killed while fighting for their liberty. The father of her unborn child. Gone. It was almost more than she could bear. Her heart felt like it had been ripped from her chest and smashed into tiny pieces and the shock propelled her into an early labour. Anastasia managed to get her through the birth, even though she herself was broken-hearted for her only son. And Maria Anastasia Eleni Mitsotakis, their beautiful baby daughter, came into the world the same day her father was killed defending Crete from the Germans.

In those early heart-numbing days of grief, the only thing that kept Eleni going, was the tiny helpless bundle in her arms, dependent on her mother for survival. She had to feed her, bathe her, clothe her and love her. She was her sole responsibility. Anaesthetized by the pain of Dimitris' death, Eleni dug deep, and vowed that she would protect her daughter, do anything she could to survive the war, support the resistance and deceive the Germans, without putting any of their lives at risk of course. Her father and mother begged her to move back to the village with Maria, so they could look after them both, but Eleni categorically refused. She would never leave Dimitris' mother now. They had become very close since the upheaval of war, and particularly since Maria's birth. Besides, there was no way she would ever leave her beautiful stone house by the sea. It was where she felt closest to Dimitris. It was where they had lived and loved together.

It seemed as if Dimitris' death heralded a very black time in the history of Crete. The Germans had gained a strong foothold on the island and ruled viciously for over four years. They bullied their way from one end of the island to the other, perpetrating misery wherever they went. For the Cretans, everyday life was difficult, very difficult, full of hardship, hunger and fear. Maria was always fed but her mother and grandmother got used to going without. Food was always scarce and medicines almost impossible to come by. Curfews were rigidly imposed, and everyone lived in a state of high alert, never knowing where the next onslaught would come from. Fear and suspicion were palpable in the air. Life was as hard as it could get. And yet, the incredible fighting spirit of resistance and defiance in the Cretans was stronger than it had ever been.

The Germans may have controlled the land, but they would never control the hearts and minds of her people. All of them helped each other and the allies, thwarting the efforts of the occupation at every opportunity. The price was high of course. Reprisals of unspeakable cruelty were carried out. Living on the peninsula helped them in a way, it was a little more isolated than other areas and thankfully the road connections weren't great, so they were sometimes spared the full brunt of German cruelty. They heard the horror stories of people's animals being confiscated or killed. Of men and women on the island being used as forced labour. Or whole villages and valleys wiped out further eastwards. People were brutally tortured and shot. Eleni and Anastasia, never put Maria's life in danger, not once. They went without themselves so that someone on the run could eat. Eleni made sure that every piece of Dimitris clothing was put to good use. They kept their heads down, quietly helping. It was little Maria who instilled in them the strength to keep going. She was the spit of her father. Every time either of the war weary women looked at her, they saw a husband or a son. They both longed for a better life for her. They yearned for her to grow up knowing something other than hardship, hate and death.

Endless days followed endless days. Months merged together. Seasons passed and passed again and somewhere the war turned. Almost four years from the day they saw the first parachute, the Germans finally surrendered in the city of Chania, their last enclave. It was hard to comprehend after the drudgery of four years. They could finally grieve for all the husbands, fathers, sons and brothers who had never come home, alongside the innocents who were slaughtered just because…

Maria was three years old when the war ended, and they had been able to shield her from the worst. Thankfully she was too young and innocent to have any conscious memory of it. Eleni and Anastasia celebrated as best they could, but like most people, it was hard to be festive when so much had been taken away from them.

Despite their lingering grief, they continued to pour whatever love and affection they had into Maria, a beautiful child in every way. She was happy from the moment she got up in the morning, until she collapsed asleep at night full of innocent wonder at normal daily activities. Everything was a delight to behold. She filled her mother's and her grandmothers' lives with unparalleled joy. Singing and laughter could be heard from the stone cottage again. Unintentionally, Maria helped them both through the grieving process and made them want to live again.

Even though Eleni was a very beautiful young widow, she had no intention of ever marrying again. She was more than content living in their stone cottage on the peninsula with Maria and Anastasia, tending their small plot.

Nonetheless by the 1950s, they realised they were three women living on their own and they needed some small income to supplement their lives. The world and Crete were changing at a furious pace and things that would never have been contemplated before became a distinct possibility. They needed money. It was agreed that Eleni would be the one to look for a job. She was a bright young woman, who had finished all her schooling before she married Dimitris. She could have worked anywhere, at anything but she opted to stay on the peninsula, to be near Maria at all times. Besides, it was too awkward to be trying to get to the city to look for work.

So, Eleni approached her father. He already owned a small coffee house, and she knew he was thinking about expanding and opening a taverna. It would be ideal. She could indulge her passion for food and cooking at the taverna while at the same time earning a little extra, maybe even doing the books. And if ever there was any problem, Maria could go with her. In fact, her grandparents would insist on it. They already complained they didn't see enough of her.

It turned out to be a perfect arrangement. When Maria was gone to school in the mornings Eleni would cycle or walk the distance to the next village. There, she would prepare and bake some food for use in the taverna, do a little bookkeeping or whatever was required. Then, in the evenings she would return home, where Anastasia and Maria would be waiting for her. They would tend the garden together; go foraging for herbs or play games with Maria in the olive grove. Anastasia was the most wonderful homemaker and the cottage ran like clockwork. She even had the time to handcraft beautiful clothes for them and embroider elaborate table linen for the house.

Both women worked hard at creating a stable, happy home for Maria and she grew into a beautiful strong-willed young girl, who spread joy to all she came in contact with. She loved everyone but held a special love for her mother and her grandparents. She was a delight to be around, always finding the good in everyone and everything. Days were finally filled with gaiety and good humour, and a new sense of fun permeated the stone cottage. The fifties in Crete and life was reasonably good. People were finally beginning to put the war behind them. The wounds were healing, albeit slowly. They would never forget but at least they could live their daily lives without fear, death and hardship.

Eleni stirred in the bed and opened her eyes. Her grandson was still by her side.

"Were you thinking of the old times again, Mama? You were smiling in your sleep."

"I was thinking of your mother, Yiannis, and what a beautiful woman she was."

"I'll get you a drink of water and you can tell me all about her," he smiled at her.

When he lifted her forward to take a sip of water, he was reminded just how weak and frail she had become, and a wave of sadness hit him again. He knew she hadn't long left.

"When your mother brought your father home here from the city, I knew she would marry him. They were so in love. Anyone could see it. They reminded me of your grandfather and me. I told her to follow her heart, Yiannis. And she did. It brought her to your father. You too Yiannis, always follow your heart, no matter where it leads you…"

She lay back again on the pillows and closed her eyes. Smiling away to herself, thinking about Maria and her true love, Yiorgas Theodorakis, her grandson's father.

Yiannis took his grandmother's hand in his again and sat with her. He stayed like that, for the rest of the evening until daylight gave way to dusk. She didn't speak again. She lay there, smiling. And gradually he could feel her hand slip from his. Then he knew. He just knew she had slipped away.

How typical of his grandmother to leave them just after the sun had set, he thought. As if the sun was setting on her life. He kissed her on her forehead gently and with great love. She had been like a mother to him. He felt both sadness and gratitude. Privileged to have known such a strong woman. A woman who had never felt a moment's bitterness despite the hand life had dealt her. He walked out of her bedroom and called her friends and neighbours to say their goodbyes. He walked the few metres to the sea, and in his own way said goodbye to his grandmother.

PART 1

Chapter One

Kate O'Shea was at Dublin Airport with her daughter Molly, who was there to see her off…

"Mam, are you sure you have everything you need?"

"Yes, I've been making lists since Christmas. If it's not in my bag, I don't need it."

"Two months Mam! Are you sure you'll be ok? Can I go out for a week, please? You might get tired of being on your own," Molly pleaded

"No. I have to do this for myself, Molly, and more importantly by myself," Kate said sounding a lot more confident than she felt inside. "Besides, I have a load of painting to do, don't forget that bit. I won't have a minute to spare. Come on, no fussing now, you know I'll be ok."

"I know, Mam. We're all really proud of you. We'll just miss you so much."

Kate smiled. Not a real happy smile but a smile of acceptance and resignation. By 'we're all' Kate knew that Molly meant herself and her brother David, relatives, friends, neighbours even – the whole shooting gallery! They had been there, the whole way with her, the entire journey through the bereavement. Hovering in the background, waiting to support her. Sure, weren't most of them flying out for the exhibition at Halloween? How was that for support?

"I'll miss you all too pet, but hey, lucky me, I'll be painting in the sun."

Molly looked at her mother lovingly and with huge admiration. They had all got such a shock when her Dad died nearly two years ago but her mother had been bereft, so lost for such a long time afterwards, her brother and herself had begun to despair. But, she had pulled herself up by the bootstraps and put herself back together. And now here she was on the brink of flying to the sun for two months, to paint for an exhibition she had organised herself. How cool was that?

Molly found herself so emotional that her voice cracked.

"I'm so proud of you, Mam."

"Don't start me off too, Molly. Look I'll ring you and David every other day, just like we arranged. I have to go now, or I'll miss my flight. I love you two so much." She kissed Molly tenderly and set off for security, before she started to cry herself.

"Ring when you get there!" Molly called after her.

And she watched as this tall, dark, elegant lady moved away from her. She was a brilliant mum to herself and David. She had loved them both unconditionally for as long as Molly could remember. Then she had let them go gradually in their teens, always respecting their views even when she didn't agree with them. Now that herself and her brother were both in their twenties, the three of them were more like friends than parent and children. And of course, she was always available for a bit of wise counselling if needed. She looks more like someone in their early thirties than early forties, thought Molly. All the weight she lost, she had nearly put back on. Maybe she was a little thin in the face but hopefully after the summer she'd be fully back to her old self.

They both gave one final wave as Kate disappeared through security, and Molly set off home.

Once Kate negotiated the baggage checks, avoided the endless shopping and finally boarded the plane, little niggles and mixed feelings had started to seep in about the impending trip. On the one hand, if she allowed it, she was a teeny bit excited about the prospect of the two months ahead and what they were for – a solo art exhibition later in the year. But on the other hand, she felt more than a little apprehensive about how she would handle it all – the memories, the emotions, the angst, and separation from her nearest and dearest. Two months away from everyone on her own. Two months alone, completely alone! Longer than she had ever been away on her own before, especially now... Most especially now. But it was a done deal. At this stage, she had no choice, unless she wanted to pull out of the exhibition. And that wasn't her style. There was no going back. She had to do it and what's more she knew at some deep subconscious level, she wanted to do it. It was the final challenge she needed.

The plane was packed full of excited smiling holidaymakers, all going for a bit of summer sun. That was herself and Paul only a couple of years ago, Kate thought abjectly. Closing her eyes, she lay back and tried to relax for the four-hour flight. She dozed, flicked through a few magazines and people-watched for a while but found it difficult to settle on any one thing. Bigger doubts were beginning to creep into her mind as the plane winged its way eastwards. Maybe she was mad! Maybe she should have stayed in Ireland. Maybe this was just a bridge too far. Maybe. Maybe. Maybe…

Four hours later when the plane finally touched down, Kate felt no frisson of excitement as she would have done on arriving in Crete. Her emotions had taken a nose dive on the plane journey. She had half expected it. For God's sake she had even prepared for it. Now, suddenly, she felt weighed down by what she was about to do.

Two months.

On her own.

No visitors.

No one except herself.

"Me Myself and I yet again," groaned Kate.

All alone by choice, no counsellors, no therapists, no family, no friends. No one to hold my hand or wipe my tears, she thought miserably. She had chosen this.

At the end of a horrible couple of years, she knew she needed to do it. The exhibition of course, was a major factor in her travelling to Crete, probably the only factor. Her spur of the moment email last year, wasn't quite making her feel like it was a great idea now. But being on her own, painting in a soulful place would surely be good for her, wouldn't it? Emotions are funny things and right now hers were all over the place. Any other time, being in Crete would have been a happy and exciting prospect. Right now, it seemed more like a chore, something that had to be done. Another box to be ticked on the journey to being better – whatever that meant.

Now I've done that. What next? she thought. As she drifted off in her thoughts, she could feel an ocean of tears well up behind her eyes.

Shit! Kate despaired. She was fed up of crying. She thought she had become better in the past twelve months. In fact, she knew she was a lot better. She had cried a whole river of tears the first year, improved hugely the next, but now here she was again, out of the blue, back to square one!

Help! she almost screamed in frustration. It had to be that this was her first time back in Crete.

She briefly thought about the last time she had been in the same airport. She had been collecting Paul then. It had been just the two of them, eager and a little apprehensive. Their first holiday in maybe twenty years without one or other of their children. A supposed new beginning for them. Before that, it had either been holiday with the children, or not at all. But once the kids had started to blaze their own trails, it had reverted to the way it started – just Kate and Paul. And, despite everything, despite the underlying tension that had crept into the marriage, they had had a good holiday. For two weeks they had relaxed, swam, explored, and made a real effort to reconnect for the first time in ages. What a difference a couple of years can make.

Now, she was in the same beautiful place, only this Kate was so different to the Kate who had been there two years previously. She had definitely been to the school of hard knocks. As she went to collect her bag from the carousel, she dreaded the next few hours and days. The thing that she had first loved about the place was now the one thing that would make it all the more difficult for her to bear. Chania was a small beautiful city. And after some years visiting the area, she, or rather they had got to know a small circle of people. Now she would have to go through it all again – the offers of sympathy, the awkwardness, people not knowing what to say.

Before she had time to get her bearings a familiar warm voice greeted her and enveloped her in a big bear hug.

"*Kalispera*, Kate!"

"*Kalispera*, Costas. How are you?" She smiled in recognition as she hugged him back. Costas, the car rental guy, had become a good friend over the years, and he was waiting for her as she exited the airport. He was a man of few words but anything he said was heartfelt.

"Good, good!" he beamed at her, "And you?"

"OK. I'm ok," Kate shrugged.

"You know Kate, if you need anything, anything at all… you have my number," he said eventually as he released her.

"I know, Costas. *Efkharisto.* Thank you."

And Kate knew that if she did need anything, Costas and his family would drop everything to help her out. That's just the way they were. Cretan hospitality at its best.

As soon as the car details were sorted, Kate finally set off on the last leg of her journey.

A journey that used to be so uplifting, passed now in a blur of self-re-crimination. Driving the road towards the city, she failed to see the majestic mountains towering beside her, revealing the stunning beauty that is Souda Bay, one of the deepest natural harbours in Europe. Neither did she notice the huge military ships cruising the water below – deadly and exciting all at the same time. The sky was a vivid intense blue and the strong summer sunlight glistened off the aquamarine water as she passed by. Things that she yearned for so much in Ireland didn't even enter her consciousness, so lost was she in thought. A little nearer the city she missed the first glimpses of the old port, clearly visible between the plane trees. The port with its distinctive Egyptian lighthouse standing to attention at harbour's end. Its long arm extended into the sea, as if somehow protecting its city, a city full of exotic flat roofed houses, baking in the summer heat. Kate drove on past the open-air cinema, a place she had always frequented in the past. The prospect of going to the cinema outdoors had always excited her, given that she knew it would never happen in Ireland. She had always checked out what was show-ing as she passed through the city, (though that was generally a secondary consideration.) Regardless, Kate would have found an excuse to go, loving the whole experience. Sitting outdoors on a hot sticky night. Waiting for darkness. City noises in the background. The big screen to entertain.

She continued past the magnificent old city, hands gripping the wheel oblivious to the beautiful stone buildings on every side. Houses with peeling paint in need of attention sat alongside buildings that were skillfully restored to their former glory. Ancient elegant doorways with sculpted architraves stood side by side with modern day cafes and shops. A little further along the grand old market building stood centre stage, dividing the old and new city. All the bits came effortlessly together making Chania the most beautiful atmospheric city, now floated absentmindedly through her consciousness.

Kate left the hustle and bustle of the city behind and drove along the road further west. Still deep in concentration she missed the small sandy beaches dotted along the coastal route, each spectacular. The sea crashing to shore was so near she could have reached out to touch it. And of course, she didn't see the tiny whitewashed orthodox church perched like a miniature dolls house, at the end of some pier. Neither did she notice the small island of *Agios Theodorou* plonked in the ocean just off shore at busy *Platanias*, as if it had only broken away from the mainland moments before.

All the familiar landmarks, she would have mentally ticked off in her head before, building up her excitement at being back in Crete. No, today it was all very different. All Kate wanted to do was get to her destination. Quite quickly she left *Platanias*, its treasures hidden by shop after shop on the strip, peddling their wares for the season. The pinks and purples of the bougainvillea tumbled over pretty stone walls and formed a guard of honour as she made her way further into the countryside of Western Crete. Once Kate was nearing her destination she made a quick stop for water It felt like it had been a very long journey and it wasn't over just yet.

Ten minutes later, she took a sharp right towards the sea and with enormous relief she finally pulled up outside the house, not even glancing at the stunning vista in front of her.

An hour later, with the car unpacked, Kate finally let out a long sigh. It was like she had been holding her breath for the whole journey. She had most definitely arrived.

'What an anti- climax!' she sighed in frustration.

And now that she was there, without Paul, Kate could feel the tears she had held in check for most of the journey, seek a much-needed release. First, they trickled silently down her cheeks, but they gradually morphed into great big noisy sobs. She let them come, finally sliding to the floor in the kitchen with her arms wrapped around her knees. She cried and cried until she literally could cry no more. Kate stumbled to the bedroom, grabbed a blanket and not caring, curled herself into a ball on the musty bed. Exhausted as much from the emotional journey as from the physical one, she fell into a fitful sleep.

When she woke an hour later still tired and drained, all she could think was; Now I've done it. Here I am for the next two months, all on my own. What a terrible mistake I've made! She suddenly felt overwhelmed by Paul's absence. Even though she had been there many times without him, she felt no sense of achievement. No sense of purpose that she had made this long journey, this pilgrimage to paint. All she felt was a great big gaping hole where she thought her heart should be.

Robotically, Kate busied herself with the house, lifting shutters, opening windows and doors to let fresh air blow through. Furniture had to be moved, a bed to be made and water and electricity turned on. A quick hoover, a dust around and it was just about presentable. She poured herself a glass of water and sat out on the patio to take it all in. The real heat of the day had diminished, and she knew the sun would soon be setting. Kate looked bleakly at the sea and mountains in front of her. It was hard to fully appreciate their beauty.

"Maybe tomorrow…" she grimaced doubtfully.

A few faces she knew strolled by and waved from a distance. They didn't intrude, as if somehow sensing her melancholy. Kate wished she had something a lot stronger than the glass of water in her hand. Actually, as she unpacked the car earlier, she had found plastic bottles of olive oil and wine that Costas must have left for her.

Typical. He had said nothing, just left bottles on the back seat. It was a custom he had started years before, soon after they began hiring the car from him. Kate knew from experience that the best olive oil and wine in Crete always came in recycled plastic water bottles.

Ten minutes later, wine in hand and back on the patio, she was ready for some serious wallowing. As she sipped the potent liquid she allowed herself drift off in thought again. If only I could turn back the clock. If only I could change things…

Chapter Two

TWO YEARS EARLIER

Kate was parked outside the airport, waiting for her husband Paul. She had travelled to Crete a month ahead of him, working on some art work for a small local fair she had been asked to take part in. She had loved every minute of her time alone in Crete. But finally, with all the painting stuff out of the way, she was ready for company, ready to be sociable again. She was looking forward to seeing Paul. They had spoken only a few times on the phone since she left Ireland and waiting at the airport, Kate realised she had missed him. Theirs may not have been the marriage made in heaven Kate dreamt about as a little girl, but she kept reminding herself she had a lot to be thankful for. Paul was a good man.

All of a sudden, she saw him, grimace on his face, bag slung over his shoulder, sauntering out of the airport looking around for her. He dropped his bag, put his arms around her and kissed her affectionately. "I've missed you, Kate," he said matter of factly.

"Me too," she smiled back at him, "me too."

They spent the car journey catching up on all the news and talking about what Molly and David were up to.

"So, are you all set for the show or fair, whatever it's called?" Paul asked distractedly, glancing at his phone when they were back inside the house.

"Pretty much except for a few minor details," she replied.

"Like?"

"Like getting someone to put up my paintings. I assumed the shop would handle all that. But they rang during the week and asked who was doing it for me. I have to make a few more calls. It's nearly sorted but I might have to go to the shop for a couple of days beforehand, that's all," Kate tensed. anticipating his irritation.

"Major details more like," Paul replied tartly. He was a rules and regulations man and didn't like it when her creative life spilled over into his. She knew he would perceive this as an intrusion into his holiday.

"Anyway, where are these priceless works of art?" he mocked in a lighter tone.

"In the spare room." Kate shook off her annoyance, unable to contain her excitement now.

"I'll get them. Stay where you are. I want to set them up for you."

When they were all set up in exhibition mode, Paul was actually surprised he liked them so much. They were good, very good. In fact, probably the best she had ever done. But then again, he had never been a lover of modern art or any art for that matter.

"Well?" She asked excitedly.

"They're good Kate, very good," he answered honestly. "It was a good decision for you to accept the invitation and come out early. Well done!"

High praise indeed from her nearest and dearest.

"Make sure they're priced high enough though, "he continued. The clinical Paul she had been subconsciously waiting for, kicked in.

He may have been wishy washy about the whole art thing, but her paintings sold well which was good for them financially. But even he could tell it had moved to another level, more than just colourful. The paintings looked dramatic and the colours were intense. Definitely not for the faint hearted. He hoped it wouldn't put off any buyers.

Kate was well aware her abstract style wasn't everyone's cup of tea, but she was passionate about what she was doing, and it came across in her work.

"So, when exactly is the show?"

"It's opening the night before we fly home, so you could say it's perfectly timed. I don't fancy being here wondering if people will like the paintings or not. And I've decided to call my section of the show *New Beginnings*." Kate looked at Paul meaningfully. "To maybe signify a new phase in our lives. What do you think?" She was referring to the fact that the spotlight was on the marriage now and how they were both trying to make things work. Trying to see if they could get it back on track.

"Fine." Paul gave a non-committal shrug and Kate as always found it hard to read where he was at in his head. He blew hot and cold a lot and sometimes she tired of trying to second guess him.

"There are just a few housekeeping things to do and then it's holiday time for us," Kate exclaimed on a more positive upbeat note. It was the start of their holiday and she was dammed if she was going to let any negativity between them invade her head space.

She wasn't to know then that *New Beginnings* would take on a whole other meaning within a couple of weeks.

They quickly fell into a pleasurable routine of sunbathing, swimming, eating-out, with a small bit of exploring thrown in. Paul was tired after the school year and Kate had painted almost non-stop for nearly a month. Now all they both wanted was to relax. They were happy to let the Cretan sun take over and recharge the batteries. They travelled a little but generally were lazy – very, very lazy.

Before they knew it, two weeks had slipped by and all of a sudden it was the day of the show.

Paul had been so helpful around the show and so supportive of her that Kate was hopeful things might work out. It still wasn't perfect, but hey, what marriage was?

All the finer details had been taken care of, Paul had insisted on doing things she normally would have. He had organised the transportation of all her paintings to the city the day before, carefully listened to her lay-out instructions. And all Kate really had to do was show up on time.

The small show of four artists' work was being launched in a craft shop's exhibition area. The craft shop was only one street away from the harbour in the city. Four foreigners – Kate, a couple of Norwegians and an English girl, who had some connection with the area had all been invited to show their work. Each artist could submit a maximum of ten pieces of named artwork, along with their individual artistic statements and that was it, essentially.

They were also asked to give invitations to friends or family. Not knowing that many people in the area, Kate asked almost all of her neighbours at the complex, Costas the car rental guy and his family, Dimitri from the art shop, Sophia the owner of her favourite restaurant, and a few others she had crossed paths with over the years. She had no idea if any of them would turn up or not, but they had all seemed delighted to be asked.

Kate treated herself to a new dress in the city. She wasn't big into making a fuss over make-up, hair and stuff, so she just showered, applied some eyeliner and lip gloss. With her tanned skin and happy disposition, she looked stunning. She was so excited heading along the cobbled streets on her way to the shop that Paul kept looking over at her and grinning. Her excitement was infectious.

"Look, in case I forget to tell you later, I'm proud of you," he said holding her in his arms and kissing her before they went in to the shop.

"Thanks Paul, for all the help and support." They had both worked hard at things over the last two weeks.

Kate slowly inhaled the warm night air and closed her eyes. She wanted to capture the moment forever. She had to be one of the luckiest people in the world. A mother to two beautiful children. A good man for a husband. A passion in her life that helped pay the bills and if that wasn't enough, they were the proud owners of their own magical place in the sun. Life could hardly get any better.

The show was a roaring success. There was a lot of people there she didn't know but all the people she asked had turned up, so they formed their own little sub-group. A good mix of foreigners and Greeks and there was a great buzz all night. Kate got very positive feedback about her paintings, and with the wine flowing and an abundance of delicious finger food, it was a very relaxed and enjoyable evening.

The hours flew by and before Kate knew it, people had started to leave. It was time for them to go. The paintings would stay up for a month. A local guy had hung all her work and he would take them down once it was over and store them for her until she was back in October. Imagine Paul had arranged all that for her!

There was at least one red sticker on one of her paintings when she was leaving but she never got a chance to find out who had bought it. They said their goodbyes and wandered back to the car in silence. Kate was reliving every moment of the night in her head. She was tired but so, so happy! They had a busy day ahead of them the next day, but what a night it had been! It had to be up there with the best.

Years earlier when Kate and Paul got together you could almost have written the script. Childhood friends, they started going out in school. They were on again, off again for a good few years until they married very suddenly straight out of college. Kate had discovered she was pregnant and living together wasn't really an option in the eighties in rural Ireland and conservative Paul was super sensitive to what people might think.

He was tall and athletic, the sporty type, deceptively self-assured and popular with almost everyone. Free-spirited Kate may not have appeared as self-assured as Paul, but nonetheless she was a great communicator and happy to let him hog the limelight when they were out together. She was vivacious and had a great sense of fun. An extremely creative and talented woman, all five foot eight inches of her. On a personal level they got on as well as anyone else they knew. Initially it may have been a case of opposites attract but before either of them could figure out what they wanted out of life, they had walked down the aisle, complete with mortgage pending and baby on the way. People would never have guessed it, but Kate was the strong one in the relationship. Paul on the other hand was basically insecure even though he gave off the vibe of super confidence.

Despite his public persona Paul relied on Kate enormously. She was quietly confident with a strong belief in herself. Not to mention the fact that she was tall, dark and curvy, had amazing almond shaped green eyes and had no idea of how beautiful she was. It all resulted from growing up in a home where she was affectionately referred to as a 'fine strapping' girl. Kate knew that that roughly translated as a fine 'big' girl. It didn't bother her in the least; she accepted her body exactly as it was. Kisses and hugs were the order of the day in her parent's house and everybody was perfect as they were. Maybe she had been big in her teens but by her early twenties, after following two small kids around for a couple of years, Kate had morphed into a beautiful, voluptuous woman.

The young newly-weds bought themselves an old house a mile from their home town. The early years were spent working hard, trying to establish their respective careers, and before long a daughter and son had arrived on the scene. Three years into marriage they found themselves with two beautiful children, Molly and David, a big renovation project as their home and very little money. Paul had only recently been made permanent in his teaching job and Kate had decided to put her own career as an artist on hold in order to stay at home with the children. It gave Paul free rein to concentrate on his career. Whatever time and energy Kate had went to the kids and their house. And even though she found she could dabble a bit with her own work at home, she couldn't devote the time she longed to on her painting.

Life was no bed of roses for any young couple with two babies, a mortgage and one income but they were generally hard-working and survived on little once the bills were paid. Paul was driven and worked very hard in school whereas relaxed Kate, having been denied a formal expressive outlet went on to make her home her own personal work of art. She spent any spare time she had either occupied in the house or with David and Molly creating many happy memories. No surprise that playtime with Kate involved endless creativity and lots of fun!

The years passed slowly and gradually things became a little easier for them, financially. Paul was appointed principal of the secondary school they had both attended. The kids were growing up, becoming more independent and a little less demanding, and the years and years of work and love she had poured into the house had finally paid off. They had a home they were both proud of. Inside there were open-plan yet cosy family friendly spaces, three substantial ensuite bedrooms, along with imaginative nooks and crannies kept from the original building. The house was in a beautiful location with green rolling hills and pine trees the view out every window, and they were still within walking distance of town.

Kate found that she finally had a little more time to indulge her passion for painting. Unlike her college friends she had never wanted to teach art, only to be able to paint. She set about turning the old stone outhouse that came with the property into a proper artist's studio for herself. For years she had been idly daydreaming about the perfect studio in her head. Very deliberately, she remodelled the stone shed. She created great wall space for painting, maximised the light with skylights, and incorporated an indispensable wet area into her new studio. And still she managed to keep a lot of the original stone as a feature. The shed was structurally sound, so the renovations were mainly cosmetic. Her biggest expenses were putting in skylights, a toilet and plastering a couple of the walls.

As soon as it was possible, Kate began to paint from her new studio and almost immediately began selling, ploughing whatever money she made back into the studio. After two years of dogged determination and hard graft, it was complete. Kate had created a beautiful light and bright open space for herself. The piece de résistance was a working potbellied stove she found in an old junk yard. It ensured the studio stayed cosy and warm all year round.

Every spare minute Kate had, she was to be found in her new studio, freely indulging her passion for painting. She'd drop David and Molly to school, head straight home and pick up where she had left off the day before. Sometimes, unbeknownst to Paul there were sick days from school when herself Molly and David would lose track of time, playing and messing and having fun in the studio.

When Kate left Art College she threw out every rule she had ever learned about painting. She mixed materials and paints she was told should never go together. In Kate's mind there was no such thing as shouldn't or can't – no rules and it all led to a very unorthodox and unique style making her work instantly recognisable. The finished product was sometimes as much of a revelation to Kate as to the casual onlooker. Her paintings were bright, colourful and fun. And from her first solo exhibition, Kate never looked back. Over the years, she became sought after to exhibit, making quite a name for herself locally.

Occasionally the studio doubled up for a girls' night out or rather a girls' night in! Many was the great evening herself and her friends spent there sharing food or a bottle of wine and laughing the night away. It was always warm and cosy and even had a pull-out couch for anyone who wanted to stay.

All in all, more than ten years into the marriage, life was pretty ok. The children were happy and healthy, they had a beautiful cosy home, Kate could bury herself in her painting and Paul was fulfilled in his job. They appeared a typical Irish family. Life wasn't all sweetness and light of course. They continued to have their ups and downs like every other couple, but they stuck with it. David and Molly seemed well adjusted and independent. And since Kate was bringing in extra money through painting sales and commissions, they were able to afford to take the children on foreign holidays and indulge in a few treats…

Around this time Kate's adored Gran died leaving her a sizeable inheritance. Forty thousand euro. It wasn't enough to go mad on, but plenty to do something nice for herself and the family. If she bought a car, she knew it would drop in value almost immediately. Anyway she wasn't into cars. It wasn't enough to buy a house, not in Ireland. Maybe a nice mobile home by the sea… But her heart wasn't really in that. A flash of inspiration finally hit Kate. It occurred to her how she could actually spend the inheritance, she got so excited she could hardly contain herself. It was as obvious as the nose on her face!

Kate's other passion in life, besides her children and painting, was Greece and anything to do with Greece. But it had been locked away in her soul since the eighties.

From the time she had spent idyllic college summers with the girls' island hopping across the Greek islands, she had fallen head over heels in love with the country. She fondly remembered them living on fresh juices and take-away souvlaki by day. Cleaning rooms or bartending to earn the few drachmas to survive, and then partying the nights away. Moving from island to island on a whim, when work or the latest romance ended. Hilariously, in a moment of madness herself and the girls had all ended up with the same tiny heart-shaped tattoo on their upper thighs. Permanent enough to satisfy their rebellious sides and small and discreet enough to be kept well out of sight of disapproving parents.

They were always only a heartbeat away from Greek hospitality and culture. They had lost track of the countless 'name days' toasted in people's homes or the sweet sticky liquid they had downed with the locals in celebration of a myriad of occasions. She loved the friendliness and warmth of the people wherever they went. Not to mention the incredible scenery, amazing sunsets and fabulous beaches, whitewashed houses with their vibrantly coloured shutters, cobbled winding backstreets on the islands, cruising on the ferries in the perfect climate. She could go on forever. For God's sake, even the quirky Greek alphabet got her excited. You either loved it or hated it and Kate truly loved it. Breathtakingly beautiful, hidden away, buried deep in her subconscious, waiting for its moment to re-emerge.

Years before when they had travelled with the children to other, more popular destinations around Europe, there was always something missing as far as Kate was concerned. It took her a few years and a few holidays to figure out why. She finally realised it wasn't Greece. And once she had the opportunity to do something positive with Gran's money. Kate knew that no matter what it took, she would find a haven for them in her beloved spiritual home.

After a bit of research, a chat with a girl at the bank and a somewhat fraught exchange with Paul, she was able to top up and extend their mortgage, just a bit, to make it all possible. And then, the nice part began. Budget in hand, she started to look for the ideal holiday home. One property search holiday later and it seemed to Kate she had found the perfect place.

A three-bedroomed townhouse in a small complex in Crete. All the houses were centered around a large swimming pool and over time would be in beautiful mature gardens. Each house had its own veranda and they were ingeniously designed so that they all had incredible views of the sea and mountains. The complex was only a stone's throw from the city and yet still in the country. And it was only five minutes from the beach. It almost sounded too good to be true. But she convinced Paul to check it out with her on the family holiday.

It was exactly as described. In fact, it probably surpassed her expectations. The complex wasn't quite finished, but Kate could see the potential. Standing on site, twenty houses almost complete. All they could see that day was the vibrant blue Mediterranean and a rugged mountainous peninsula in front. The sun was beaming down on them. Sea. Mountains. Blue sky. Picture postcard perfect. Humbled by the beauty of nature all around her, Kate could feel the excitement bubbling up inside.

"Well, what do you think?" asked Paul.

She was speechless, overwhelmed by what was laid out before her.

"This is it," she mumbled, barely trusting herself to speak.

Wild and beautiful, it reminded her a little of Connemara back home. Paul smiled indulgently at her. He thought so too. It was a good sound investment he reckoned and the figures all stacked up.

With figures the last thing on her mind, Kate looked behind only to be greeted by another miracle of nature. The magnificent White Mountains of Crete. The *Lefka Ori*. Higher than anything she had ever seen before, dominating the whole landscape right behind and she hadn't seen them until that moment.

Wow! That definitely seals it! she thought.

They retired to a little taverna by the sea to discuss things with the estate agent and even though they didn't buy there and then, she knew they would.

Chapter Three

THE ACCIDENT

After the excitement of the show and a memorable holiday in the sun, Kate and Paul gradually eased themselves back into life in Ireland. They revelled in that lazy invincible feeling after a holiday abroad, still benefitting from the sun on their bones and a feeling of deep, deep relaxation. Even though they were physically back, they didn't quite feel mentally back, particularly Kate who had been away for six whole weeks. She was on a high and reluctant to give up that post-holiday, warm fuzzy feeling she had. Family and friends had to be caught up with. She just had to regale them all with the stories back from Crete, especially about the paintings and the show. How she loved that!

It was on the way to pick up their son from the airport that the accident happened. David was flying in from a summer spent in New York. Paul was driving, as he usually did when they were together, unless he'd had a few drinks of course, then he was quite happy to hand over to her. True to his character he was a careful driver, never going too fast or taking stupid chances, but he hadn't much of a chance that day.

They were driving along both absorbed in their own head space, occasionally talking about this and that, mainly how nice it would be to catch up with David. All of a sudden, a car came flying out of a side road, straight onto the main road they were travelling along. Kate only registered it at the very last minute.

Paul cursed loudly and slammed the brakes.

After that, it was as if everything went into a horrible slow motion…

There was an endless screeching sound as the tyres skidded along the road. A weird image as the two of them tensed their bodies and braced themselves for impact. The inevitable smashing of one car into the other. A loud crunch of metal, glass breaking and then nothing.

For a split second, absolutely nothing, only deathly silence.

The very next instant, a fully alert Kate could hear the rhythmic sound of Paul breathing very strangely, as if he was snoring or something.

Why was he snoring, she thought.

She tried to sit upright in her seat, half afraid to move yet aware that something bad had happened. Only in hindsight did she realise she must have gone into some kind of shock, or an altered state of awareness. She was functioning on auto-pilot, feeling nothing only the survival instinct kick in.

"Paul, Paul are you ok?" she shouted.

Nothing back.

Again. "Paul? Paul, are you ok? I'm ok, Paul. Are you alright?"

Nothing. Only the sound of snoring.

What was he doing snoring, she wondered. Could he have passed out? She was afraid to look over at him, of what she might see.

Hours later or maybe it was only minutes, she wasn't sure, she heard the sound of cars, of doors slamming. There was shouting and people's voices in the distance but she couldn't make out what they were saying. Kate still sat frozen. She couldn't move. She was afraid to. Out of the corner of her eye, she thought Paul seemed bent over the wheel of the car. And he was still snoring.

An eternity seemed to pass.

Sirens in the distance.

Out of nowhere somebody reached their hand in through Kate's half open window and stroked her face.

"Are you ok, love?" a kind voice asked.

The human touch, a warm hand on her face released a steady stream of silent tears down Kate's face but still she couldn't speak. Still rigid. Frozen.

More voices and then eventually the car door was opened for her. Hands led her out wrapping blankets around her and taking her to a nearby ambulance.

"I'm ok. I'm ok. Please just look after Paul, my husband." She heard a voice quiver.

"Is that his name? Paul?" someone asked.

Kate nodded and whispered, "Yes Paul, Paul Murphy..."

"We have to check you out, love. We'll get to your husband."

The doors closed, and the ambulance started to move off. Despite the blankets, Kate was shivering uncontrollably.

She was on her own with the paramedic. They must be putting Paul into another ambulance, she thought. She felt small and vulnerable and helpless.

When they got to the hospital, they took her to a small sterile room and kept asking her ridiculous questions about any soreness or pain. Probably to ascertain whether she was injured or not. Somebody answered the questions, but she didn't think it was her. She felt as if it was all happening to somebody else. She heard someone ask about Paul again and was told they were bringing him in.

After what seemed like hours, David came flying in the door, visibly upset. Her knuckles white, she clung onto him so tightly thinking she never wanted to let him go. For once she wished she was the child and not the mother.

He just held her and kept saying, "It's fine, Mum. You're ok. Molly's on her way."

They stayed like that for what seemed like an eternity until Molly arrived, red and teary-eyed followed by her boyfriend, Jack.

"Are you ok, Mum?" sobbed Molly and then she started to cry again.

Intermittently, they all asked about Paul, but nobody seemed to have any news of him.

They were a sorrowful bunch.

Kate insisted she was alright, but at the same time on tender hooks waiting for news of Paul. Molly and David were trying to comfort her, but also like her they were wondering why it was taking so long to get any news of their dad.

Nurses were taking her pulse and blood pressure and God knows what else, checking her out she supposed. Someone brought in tea for them all, but it lay untouched on a tray and still they waited for news of Paul.

Eventually a doctor came into the room all official and uncomfortable looking. She looked around at them all sympathetically and her eyes finally rested on Kate.

"Mrs. Murphy?" she spoke softly, and their eyes met as she walked over to Kate. "We did everything we could. I'm sorry to have to tell you this… Your husband didn't survive the accident. I'm afraid he died while we were trying to save him."

Silence.

Time stood still then for a long moment. Kate could hear a ringing in her ears. It felt like she was moving to another place. She could see all the people in the room, Molly, David, herself all looking in shock at the doctor.

Then she heard a desperate voice pleading, "But I'm not Mrs. Murphy, I'm Kate O'Shea. There's been a terrible mistake!"

She was grasping at straws now, but David and Molly were so distraught beside her, she knew that something was terribly, terribly wrong. Everything played out slowly in front of her. David was sobbing great big sobs. Jack was holding Molly, who in turn was holding her hand. And then she caught a glimpse of her own face in a mirror, frozen in horror. She heard someone scream out in desperation and realised it was her voice.

"No! No! Not Paul. Please God not Paul!"

Back in the room and in her body, she broke down in convulsions. The pain was unbearable. Each of them were now gripped by the full unimaginable horror of what had happened. Their Dad. Paul. Her husband. Dead. How could that be? They had only been going to the airport.

One by one, Paul's family started to arrive and the realisation of what had happened slowly dawned on them all.

It was horrible. Like being in a nightmare unable to wake up. A horror movie and they were the main characters.

At some point someone from Paul's family took over. All three of them, Kate Molly and David were incapable at that stage.

Maybe minutes later, Kate had no idea how long, they were brought to see him. Just the three of them.

Real and surreal all at the one time. Kate felt weirdly removed from the whole awful scene. And yet there was no denying his still body, lying on the table. It still felt like it was happening to someone else.

How could this have happened?

They had woken up in the same bed only a few hours earlier.

Now he was still... so still. Eerily still. They each tried to say a few words, but Kate found that she just couldn't, only kiss him and tell him that she was so sorry and that she really did love him.

How she got home that day, she'll never know.

And the nightmare was only beginning.

Kate went into some kind of trance over the next few days. She switched in and out of autopilot. People spoke to her and asked her things and she answered them, but she felt like someone else was doing the answering.

She knew in her logical brain that Paul was dead, but she didn't believe it. She couldn't quite grasp it. She was acting out a part and she knew that soon this terrible dream or nightmare would be over, and things would go back to the way they had been. Wouldn't they? He'd walk in the door again and they could go back to trying to fix things?

She had to be there for Molly and David and that's the most she could manage. Whatever about accepting things for herself, she just couldn't get her head around Molly and David's grief, their beloved dad. Every time she looked at one or the other of them, they were bereft. It was almost more than she could bear.

Paul was a good father to his children, no matter what was going on between them. He always had time for them regardless of what meeting or event he was going to. And he was always going somewhere. That was the nature of his job. He had that special knack of really talking *to* them but not talking *at* them. A unique and special relationship with both. He may have been the disciplinarian in the house, but he always tried to do it in the most loving way. They could talk to him and even managed to remain on speaking terms during the turbulent teenage years.

Molly their first born, his little princess, a real Daddy's little girl. He doted on her from the moment of her birth, yet he was able to parent her so well.

Then, when David came along, Kate knew he was secretly delighted, even though he never said it.

He would have a son to kick football with, play hurling with, or go for a pint with later on in life. All things he had done with his own father. He treated them both exactly the same and they grew up respecting him in so many ways.

How would she ever be able to fill the void in their lives?

Before any of them could even begin to get their heads around what had happened, people had started to call to the house to sympathise.

'For God's sake he wasn't dead twenty-four hours!' she wanted to scream. They hadn't even released his body.

Kate was numb. Apart from the hospital she hadn't cried at all. She could feel nothing. She was in some alien place, this zone of no-mans-land in her head, where her body went through the motions. Nothing could hurt her here because she felt nothing.

Molly and David, she supported as much as she could. They hugged and held each other. Kate longed to sit them on her knee and tell them it would all be ok, like she had when they were small. Like when she used to wipe their tears and comfort them in her bed when they had a bad dream or sit them on her knee and cuddle them when they had fallen and cut a hand or a knee or something else. But she couldn't fix it this time. They were adults and there was only so much she could do for them.

When Paul's body was brought home, it jolted her back into a temporary reality. Kate was confronted once again by her husband's dead body. And even though she asked for them to have time alone with him, once again, she couldn't think of anything to say, so she just wearily said sorry and goodbye.

And all of a sudden, their lives were taken over, and the ritual that is the Irish funeral began. They had been through this before when Kate's parents died, both within the same year. But somehow that had been a natural progression. They were elderly and had lived full, happy and healthy lives. This was very different. There was nothing normal about this. It was wrong, unnatural and very unfair.

She had often heard people say before, that the ritual is what gets you through the days of the funeral. The shaking of hands, the sympathising, people's feelings of inadequacy, the church, the burial.

She never would have believed it, but the days passed in a blur, an emotional rollercoaster and they all survived. Somebody was organising things in the background, telling her what to wear or when to eat. Food appeared magically out of nowhere and she didn't think she had cooked it. When they lowered Paul's body into the ground in the graveyard, she felt her legs go a bit shaky, but David and Molly were on either side of her and their presence alone gave her the strength to keep going. Afterwards she stayed at the hotel for the post burial meal for as long as was deemed respectful to all, and then she escaped home, only to rehash it all again in her head. At least they had gotten through the funeral.

Kate had slept very little over the few days and was completely exhausted, but every time she closed her eyes, her mind started to go at full throttle. All the what if's, what if she had been driving instead of Paul, what if they had gone on the motorway and not used the old road, what if it was all her fault and Paul had been distracted by their latest row. On and on it went until she nearly drove herself demented. She was lucky to sleep an hour, maybe two if she was really fortunate.

But the worst thing, the worst thing always, was waking up. Even after one hour of sleep, just for an instant – for one split second, she'd forget what had happened and think that everything was ok, that everything was normal and that nothing had happened. Then with a sinking sensation in the pit of her stomach, the God-awful truth would come back to her and she'd feel the terrible dread again. Instinctively Kate would reach out to his side of the bed to double check, but it was always cold now, really cold. Paul was gone. Dead. It was all horribly true.

How was she supposed to get herself out of bed? And why would she even want to? The funeral got her up the first few days. Then it was Molly and David but after two weeks they both had to return to work and college respectively. Kate's friend, Jane had taken a month off work to be with her so that kept her going for another couple of weeks.

A terrible heavy energy settled on her. Every second of every minute of every day she thought about Paul. She was consumed not only by grief for the man she had spent over twenty years of her life with, but also by guilt. Guilt that it was mainly her questioning the state of their relationship. Guilt that she had tried to mould Paul to fit the type of relationship her heart had longed for. Guilt that she had wanted more for herself. Paul had known of course. It had been the main reason for the holiday together in Crete. An attempt to get things back on track. Why had she not left well enough alone? Said nothing to Paul. Let things continue as they had been. It hadn't been that bad. All she had done was fill the last few weeks of his life with frustration for both of them. In her quest for a better life for herself, she ended up feeling selfish and guilty. If she could only have him back, she'd erase all the doubts from her mind. They'd be fine. She'd make sure of it.

When Molly and David were both gone, her grief intensified again. She became full of fear, fearful for them. For their safety on the roads. Thinking they were going to be killed. Thinking that some awful negative energy had settled on their house and it was all her fault. She kept ringing them to make sure they were ok and if they were out driving she was doubly worried. Jane tried to get her into some kind of routine. The house was scrubbed from top to bottom. People called intermittently. Presses were organised and washed and cleared out. And washed again. She refused to go near Paul's wardrobe though. Or her studio. She couldn't.

No proper sleep routine was in place even though she tried almost everything. Herbal remedies, medication, old wives' tales, reading, anything but she still dreaded going to bed and most of all she hated waking up. Jane tried hard to make sure she ate properly and regularly, to keep her strength up. In those first few weeks she kept waiting for his key to turn in the door and for him to walk in as if nothing had happened. Very soon they had limped to the memorial service one month after the loss but that just rehashed all the feelings and emotions stronger than ever before. But she had survived it. She continued to remain obsessed about him and how they had been struggling. She had taken to going to bed a little earlier, in the hopes that she could think about him and then make herself dream about him. She half hoped he'd miraculously appear and forgive her. It didn't work.

Before Jane left to go back to work, they had gone into her studio, organising all of Kate's paints brushes and canvasses. I must have the cleanest house and garden in the whole country, she thought to herself, I'm turning into one of those obsessively clean housewives. And yet as they scrubbed and tidied the studio there was something oddly comforting and familiar about the smell of the turps and paints.

By the time Jane actually left, Kate was sleeping about four hours a night, if she was lucky. And a steady stream of her friends and neighbours were always popping in to say hello or with something they had made. She knew they were all trying to keep an eye on her, watching out for her.

Chapter Four

PUTTING HERSELF BACK TOGETHER
TWO YEARS AGO UP TO THE PRESENT TIME

For the very first time since Paul died, Kate was wholly and completely on her own. She had often felt alone in the marriage, but this was a strange kind of aloneness. The house was eerily silent and all of a sudden, the reality of his death hit her like a juggernaut.

He was never coming back.

Before when he was at work or away at meetings, she had thrived on the quiet calm atmosphere of her home and studio. This was very different, a lonely aloneness and every single day became an endurance test. Kate had never felt so utterly alone and yet there were never as many people passing through her life and her house. There was always someone popping in and out, with this and that, asking her to go here and there with them. Sometimes she found it comforting, and at other times it irritated her so much so that she didn't even answer the door. She suspected her friends or neighbours were reporting back to Molly or David, because if she didn't answer the door, lo and behold, ten minutes later she had a phone call from one or the other. Ringing for a chat, they said.

Truth be told, all she wanted to do was curl up in a ball, block the whole world out and cry and cry and cry. They took to daily check-up calls. Molly and David would call, one in the morning and one in the evening and after a while she came to organise her days around the calls. She didn't want to burden her children with the depth of her emotions, the despair and anger she was feeling. There was so much they could never know. She knew they were concerned about her. She was even concerned about her. How could she keep telling Molly and David the same thing? That she was utterly devastated. She had never felt so lonely in her life, nor so guilty.

They assumed she was completely heartbroken for Paul, for their Dad. Grieving for her soulmate. How wrong could people be? She was heartsick alright but more from her feelings of guilt than anything else. How could she tell them things she could hardly admit to herself? That they had married because she got pregnant. That their marriage had been a sham and not the happy ever after they wanted to believe in. And that Paul had left her on her own now in the cruellest of ways, compounding her sense of guilt and anger. The feelings kept eating away at her. Why couldn't they both have been killed in the crash? Then she wouldn't have to go through the misery day in, day out. Then of course there was the obvious questions that kept gnawing away at her.

Why hadn't she left him?

Why hadn't she made the break years before?

Why hadn't she done the decent thing when she realised she wasn't in love with him, instead of burying herself in her painting? Then she could have grieved honestly for the father of her children and the good man he was. Kate hated the perception of herself as the heartbroken widow. She was a strong independent woman.

Why had she stayed in a marriage that wasn't working? Kate's grief and guilt were so deeply intertwined and embedded in each new day that she became powerless to help herself. She see-sawed her way through the next couple of months, barely able to drag herself out of the bed in the mornings. Breakfast didn't exist. A quick cup of coffee and she was fine. She hated eating on her own anyway. Kate had always tried to get Paul to sit to meals with her, even though he was permanently rushing here or there. She had insisted on sitting to the table for every meal when the kids were small and tried to continue it after they were both gone. She had always made the effort, setting the table properly. Dinner usually included a glass of wine for herself, even if she regularly ended up like Shirley Valentine, on her own talking to the walls.

Kate began to neglect herself. She took no interest in her appearance, made no effort with her clothes and started only wearing tracksuits. She didn't go shopping anymore and had visibly lost weight. The tall Amazonian Kate was a shadow of her former self. She was still striking and had curves in all the right places, whereas before she was voluptuous and had a continual healthy glow about her, she had become pale and her face a little gaunt. For the weekends, when Molly and David were home, she made some kind of effort but other than that, she was just going through the motions. She knew it. They all knew it. Putting in time. The first Christmas was a nightmare. Kate hated every minute of it. Only for Molly and David, there would have been no tree, or presents. They insisted on keeping up the traditions.

Post-Christmas it was Paul's birthday. Another reason to feel guilty, facilitating her continuing downward spiral. Another reason for her to opt out and put off getting back to any kind of normality.

By the time six months had passed since the accident, Molly sat her down for a serious chat.

"Mam, how do you think you're coping on your own?" she asked gently.

Kate sighed deeply. She was no fool and knew she was struggling.

"Look Moll, I'm finding it so hard. I want to protect you and David, but I have all these thoughts and feelings inside me and I don't know what to do with them. They just keep going around and around in my head. I can't focus on anything. I feel a bit unhinged at times. People keep saying what a wonderful man Paul was, and he was but… I don't know! I wonder am I depressed? I just can't bring myself to paint. It seems like I've lost my appetite for life." That was the longest speech Kate had strung together in six months.

"Well what about Crete, Mam? Would you like to go for a couple of weeks? Just you and me? For a break, maybe?"

Kate's reaction was so vehement, Molly was taken aback.

"I couldn't bring myself to go there. In fact, I've decided I'm going to sell it. I just want to get rid of it now. As soon as possible!"

Where had that come from? It was like she was punishing herself.

"But Mam, you love Crete. You've always loved Crete. We all love it. Please don't do anything rash. At least talk to me and David about it first."

Kate didn't really know why she had said that. True enough, it had popped into her mind recently but to actually go and sell it? She was sorry when she saw how her reaction had upset Molly.

"Look, this is me at the moment. I'm all over the place. One minute I try to be upbeat, the next minute I'm down in the dumps again. I don't know myself anymore. I'm lost somewhere in all the sadness and grief. I feel like I'm drowning in it all. I think I might need to go and talk to somebody."

A single tear ran down Kate's cheek.

Molly took her mother's hand in hers. She loved her so much and it was upsetting to see her like this.

"Mam, I think that's a great idea. Have you anybody in mind?"

"Well, I might have," Kate shrugged. "I've heard of this really good lady who lives just outside town and she's supposed to be excellent and very discreet. She does all kinds of counselling not just bereavement. And they say you're never likely to meet anyone else there you know. I wouldn't mind trying her."

"Well you know what they say, there's no time like the present. Have you a number?" Molly smiled at her mother and gently placed her phone into her hand.

Kate was a little taken aback. She hadn't expected Moll to jump on it straight away. She had the number tucked away in her purse. A good friend and neighbour had given her the card a few weeks before. For some reason she'd kept it in her bag. Then very strangely, the previous week, it seemed as if every time she opened her bag the card kept falling out. Before she could change her mind, Kate took a deep breath, punched in the numbers and within five minutes had booked herself an appointment for the following week. When she clicked off at the end of the call, she actually felt like she was taking a positive step forward – for the first time in six months. At least she was doing something, and Molly was delighted at the outcome.

The following week, Kate was quite nervous when it came to the time for her appointment. Her initial feeling of positivity at booking had only lasted for the rest of that particular day. And even though she had been tempted to cancel several times since, she knew deep down that she wanted to take control of her life again. She was sick and tired of drifting unconsciously along as if she was living some random person's life. She would like to be in charge again. She needed some kind of plan. She needed to find a new way of being Kate. Kate on her own, without all the guilt and self-loathing she was feeling.

Once seated in the counsellor's room, Kate let out a long sigh. The room was pleasant enough with a candle lighting and a beautiful scent of lavender wafting through the air. She figured the counsellor, whose name was Anne, was roughly the same age as herself. She appeared kind and gentle and immediately put Kate at her ease. They started to talk in general; first about why Kate felt she was there and then, with no warning, Kate broke down. She completely lost control. Crying and sobbing like a baby for the first half hour or so. The counsellor was happy to sit with her, handing out the tissues, saying nothing. Then miraculously, when the crying subsided, Kate started to talk like she had never talked before. Mainly about Paul and their relationship, but also about other stuff. The fear and upset at finding herself pregnant at nineteen. Paul's reaction. Childhood memories of her own. It was like a dam had opened and once she started, she found it very hard to stop.

At the end of the first session, Anne suggested that she would try and help her on several fronts and that if Kate was agreeable she would pencil her in once a week for a while, and they could see after that. Her only goal for the first week was to do something nice and report back to Anne at the next session. Just *one* thing. It could be anything at all. Kate was to choose.

Kate left that evening, feeling for the second time in a week that she was about to take control of her life again. That same night she slept for four hours straight which was a slight improvement for her. Granted she may have lain awake for the rest of the night but to get four hours continuous sleep was something like a little miracle for Kate. Mind you, the rest of the week reverted back to the normal pattern of sleep, but she latched onto her miracle as a small sign of hope.

Kate couldn't think what to do for herself that week. She racked her brain to try and imagine something nice but to no avail. Most things she thought of generally involved another person. She hit a blank. Then quite unexpectedly as she was walking along the street on her way home one day, she saw a most unusual plant in the greengrocer's window. It was a striking vivid pink colour with an intense orange centre. Very exotic looking and really eye-catching. Quite spontaneously Kate popped into the shop and bought the plant. She brought it home and gave it pride of place on the kitchen table. She had no choice but to admire its beautiful colours every day. Her admiration didn't last long of course. But for a few minutes every day, it was worth it.

The next week it was a book she thought she'd like. Mind you she didn't read it, but she had liked the title of it. Then she treated herself to a manicure and then a ceramic dish she bought at a little craft shop. Before she knew it, a month had passed, and she began to feel like there was the possibility of light at the end of the tunnel. Anne was helping her to work through the feelings of grief and guilt. Molly and David still rang to see how it was all going, checking up to see was she doing her weekly tasks. They were supportive of her and she felt glad of their support. Obviously, the counselling sessions were about more than just treating herself, but there were some things she just couldn't tell her two children.

Bit by bit, with the help of Anne, Kate started to set herself bigger challenges and goals, other than a once-a-week treat. She continued to talk through the sessions, unravelling her thoughts and emotions, layer by painful layer.

After another month Anne put her in contact with Mary, a massage therapist she knew personally, and another dimension was added to Kate's life. Every other week she went for a full body massage and after the first disastrous session (she cried the whole time) she began to look forward to the total relaxation and switch off she got from her massage therapist. Of course, Mary was more than just a massage therapist. She was one of those rare, gentle souls who come along once in a lifetime, who inspire by their mere physical presence and ability to fully listen.

Kate and Mary soon became good friends and a massage meant lots of chatter once the session was over.

Meanwhile at counselling, the goals being set were becoming bigger and bigger and the boundaries pushed out little by little. Kate now had a new routine in place at home. Anne had her meditating for five minutes every morning to start her day. Mealtimes always included a lighted candle now and a silent wish of gratitude and appreciation for the food she was eating. Nothing holy-holy, just a simple, silent blessing for the food. She was reading again, positive uplifting books about people changing their lives and she was regularly keeping a diary of how she was feeling. Trying to get it all down onto paper could be pretty tricky but it did help.

Occasionally music could be heard blaring from Kate's. All these changes didn't happen overnight or with ease. Each change that happened was like cutting a new tooth, a certain amount of pain was involved. But Kate doggedly stuck to the new routine and changes were happening, albeit small changes but changes nonetheless. She had even decided to take up yoga.

Eventually Anne tackled the painting issue head on.

"And when do you think you will pick up a brush again, Kate?" she asked about four months after first seeing her. She had judged that on account of the way things were going in other areas of Kate's life, she could push her a little more.

"I suppose it's time," was all Kate said. It was her livelihood after all, her source of income and there had been lots of e-mails and phone queries she had ignored since Paul's death.

So, the very next morning, Kate got up early, went through her usual routine and once she had finished her breakfast she made her way outside to the studio. When she opened the door, the place smelt musty and it looked dusty and a bit cobwebby. It had been months since she had last set foot in there – the day herself and Jane had cleaned it out. Underneath the musty smell she also registered the faint smell of turpentine and oil paints.

"Well, nothing for it only a bit of elbow grease and a duster," she said aloud, trying to be cheerful.

So, Kate set about clearing away the cobwebs and wiping the place down. After about twenty minutes of clearing, she stubbed her toe off an old board thrown on the floor and she nearly fell over, knocking over a few tubes of paint as she tried to balance herself. In the very next second, Kate was literally consumed by the most ferocious anger she had ever in her life experienced. Her whole body stiffened and tensed, she clenched her fists tightly. The anger rose up from somewhere deep within and seemed to flow all by itself into her arms and legs. She caught the nearest tube of paint to her and flung it with such strength across the room that she surprised even herself. She grabbed a few more and they followed suit and then more and more…

Teeth clenched, she lashed out at the nearest canvas she could find and flung that too. Then she kicked left and right, whatever was in her way. She was in a right strop, shouting obscenities as she rained tube after tube, canvas after canvas, and brush after brush. Whatever she could lay her hands on. Whatever was in the way of her arms or feet.

"It's not fuckin fair!

You bastard, Paul!

Why did you leave me all on my own? You know how hard I tried!

I know you hated my paintings.

I know I could have left you.

I should have died that day too.

What's all this counselling crap? A load of shite!

Do you know how hard it is?

Do you know how guilty I feel??"

On and on it went, for a long time.

"I hate being on my own all the time.

For fucks sake, who lights candles when they're having their breakfast?

Why do I feel so guilty that I survived, and you didn't?"

"Molly and David are broken-hearted after you." She threw and fired and kicked and shouted and roared until she collapsed into a sobbing mess on the floor, exhausted from all the exertions.

"Why couldn't I have left well enough alone? We weren't that bad. We weren't!" she whimpered in between the sobs

Christ, she hadn't seen that coming.

It seemed as if hours had passed when she picked herself up from the floor and looked around in bewilderment. It was as if someone had wrecked her studio. The place looked like a war zone. This was a total breakdown for her. Definitely not her finest hour. She hadn't realised it was possible to experience such anger. If it was a case of one step forward and two steps backwards, then these were definitely her backward steps.

Kate didn't go to counselling for the next few weeks. She felt a little lost again and slightly embarrassed by what had transpired in the studio, assuming the whole counselling thing just wasn't working for her. When she rang Anne to tell her that she wouldn't be continuing her sessions after the incident, Anne appeared quite excited and positive about it all. She talked about a breakthrough and Kate really getting in touch with her feelings around the bereavement and the guilt.

Kate's counselling resumed without any more delay and she progressed more and more rapidly. A couple of weeks later she had another go at getting the studio up and running and this time it went ahead without any major blips. She started to paint again, regularly, on a small scale.

And Anne challenged her yet again to do something with regard to painting that would really push her outside her comfort zone. Kate racked her brains to think of something she could do. And then one night while she was lying awake in bed, it came to her. Excitedly, she went downstairs to the computer. She looked up her contacts, wrote a short e-mail and hit the send button before she could change her mind.

"That's done it now," she said to herself, with an excited sick feeling in her stomach. "There's no going back."

She didn't sleep a wink that night thinking about what she may have put in place.

Anne was delighted when she filled her in.

"A major solo exhibition in Crete, and all initiated by yourself! That's fantastic, Kate! Well done. When are we talking about?"

"It's not for sure yet. They have to get back to me yet. I'll let you know."

Kate didn't have to wait too long. Within the next fortnight she had an e-mail back from Isabella, her contact in Crete. There was a slot available for an exhibition the following year at the end of October. They would be delighted to host her first solo exhibition in a couple of years. Would she be interested in taking the slot?

"Yes, please," Kate had replied immediately. "Book me in."

Because she had been part of a group show in Crete, she didn't have to go through a lot of the usual red tape. It was only a matter of forwarding her artistic records and her way was clear. Just the minor matter of the paintings and how she would work that out. But it was a long time away, more than a whole year and there was no need to concern herself about that just yet.

When Kate told her family and friends what she had done, it was no surprise that their reactions were all positive and supportive. Molly and David, without a moment's hesitation said they were going to Crete for the exhibition. Jane, her best friend was going too. All her college friends who happened to be art teachers said it would be perfectly timed at the Halloween Break, with a bit of luck they'd have the week off, so they could all go too. Her local arty friends thought it was the most brilliant idea and wanted to book flights straight away. Mary her massage therapist, wrote it into her diary so as to leave herself free that week, she was definitely going. And so, on and on it snowballed, Kate was buoyed up by all the support and enthusiasm. Where they would all stay she had no idea, but it would all work out. She felt quite excited at the prospect and she had a whole year to organise it.

In the meantime, Paul's one-year anniversary was looming large, so she put the exhibition firmly to the back of her mind. Part of Kate dreaded the anniversary. The days leading up to it, were particularly busy organising this and that, making sure all their family and friends knew about the service, sorting out food and a few other things. It shouldn't have been too hard. But it was. Why was she dreading it? The day turned out to be excruciatingly painful for her. Exactly as she had anticipated. Everything went off without a hitch, but all the old memories and emotions came flooding back. They all started talking about the exhibition and how great it was that she had booked it. It just didn't seem right or appropriate to Kate. Really, who was she to be organising exhibitions for herself? A bit selfish when Paul was lying dead in the graveyard. If only they knew…

Every person who was at the anniversary had a link to herself or Paul and it seemed as if every time she turned around she was confronted by another sad memory or feeling. There was no escaping it. She stayed as long as she possibly could but eventually she called Molly and David aside and told them she needed to get away. So, with no fuss, she retired to her bedroom, had a little cry and calmly wrote into her diary about how she was feeling. She really wanted the day to be over and get on with things. Her emotional rollercoaster lasted only a few days this time, but at least she had supports and crutches in place. Candles, music, diary, treats, massages, etc. She pulled them all out and got the routine back on track. She was learning a new way of being. In a way she was reinventing her life, a life on her own, without any pretence.

Things continued to flow for Kate. Some of the things she was doing were more of a delight now than part of any routine. She enjoyed the simple pleasure of eating on her own. She was back painting regularly, loving her massages, meeting her therapist but not as frequently as before. Other things were still difficult for her. Sleeping on her own all the time was a continual challenge. Well she'd just have to get used to it.

David's graduation was a huge occasion for them. He missed Paul terribly that day. But they got through it, speaking fondly of him, all the time. Knowing that he would have loved it too and been so proud of David. A bitter sweet day.

Their second Christmas without Paul came and went without too much fuss. This time Kate was prepared. She had bought everybody in her circle a present. A lot of thought had gone into the gifts. She knew she was very lucky to have a great support system around her. All her family and friends were on this journey with her. They only wanted to help in any way they could and now she wanted to acknowledge their support with a small gift for each and every one. And she reckoned after that, the best she could do, was to show them that she was ok and would survive.

With the help of Molly and David, she hosted a New Year's party. A sort of moving on for herself and everyone else. It wasn't easy, but for the first time in eighteen months, Kate knew she would be fine. She could and would build a new life for herself. It may not have been the one she would have chosen, but at least she was getting on with it, adapting.

So, another Christmas had come and gone. It was a new year and now she had a new focus. The exhibition in Crete. There were things to be organised. Her flight and car had to be booked.

The days were moving a little quicker now. Life had certainly sped up, and she was still practising her mindfulness techniques, trying to be fully present in every passing moment. Nights were still the hardest but she was hopeful that with time, they would improve too.

She discussed the logistics of the exhibition in Crete with her therapist, deciding that the best thing to do was to go out for July and August and do all the painting. Her intention was to have forty canvasses for the exhibition. That's the maximum the gallery could hold. It may have been a bit ambitious...She decided she'd aim for forty and see how she went. After all she had managed ten in four weeks before...easily. So, Kate went online, ordered her canvasses and paints from her contact, Dimitri in Crete. He e-mailed back quickly, delighted with such a large order. He had heard she was doing a solo exhibition and he offered to prepare all the canvasses for her beforehand. Brilliant! That would take hours off her workload. She could start painting on the canvasses as soon as she arrived. Lady Luck was shining on her.

She had had a decent spell of feeling good in herself and was hoping that it would last right through the summer. There was no reason why it shouldn't.

She was seeing her therapist less frequently but at one of her last sessions before she was to depart for Crete, Anne had tried to prepare her for some of the emotions and feelings Kate might face once there and her strategy for coping. With that done, and before Kate knew it, it was the last day in June and she was on her way to Dublin Airport for her two months painting holiday in Crete.

Chapter Five

PAINTING IN CRETE

Kate stretched lazily on waking the next day and wondered why the room was so bright and the sounds and smells were so unfamiliar. It took her a few moments to remember where she was. In Crete. She was in Crete! And she noted with surprise and dare she say it, with delight even, she had shaken off the darkness and gloom. In fact, her mood was decidedly more positive. Upbeat even.

Hopefully, the day before had been a blip. She put it down to the travel, her first time back in Crete in two years, and the final realisation that Paul would never be anywhere with her again. Kate exhaled.

Ok, so she had worked hard on this in counselling. She had half expected the meltdown of yesterday but today was a new day and she felt a lot better. She needed to put all her strategies and supports in place again.

Same strategies. Different country.

"Onwards and upwards," she murmured aloud to herself optimistically. She was on day one, of two months of a painting holiday and she had to make every day count if she was to complete her mammoth task. Kate was moving on with her life. She knew that, and somehow immersing herself in all this creativity was going to help. She had no idea how, but just that it would.

So, she started the morning as she intended to start every other morning. She walked out onto the veranda and slowly inhaled her first morning in Crete for a long, long time.

The sky was bright and clear and blue as it normally was, not a cloud to be seen. One of Kate's favourite things about painting in Crete was the incredible light. Pure, clear, mind-altering light. Everywhere and everything looked fresh and vibrant. No greyness to cast shadow over the day, or make the sky sit on the ground. It was early and already she could feel the warm glow of the sun on her face. She had forgotten how good it was to see and feel the sun on her body. She missed it so much in Ireland.

The promise of a beautiful day hung in the air. The complex was very silent. Most people were probably still in their beds. Kate delighted in the opportunity to sit quietly at the patio table and close her eyes for a few moments. She felt the gentlest of breezes caress her face. The waves on the beach were rhythmically crashing ashore, easily audible from her vantage point. The early birds were chirping loudly, enthusiastically going about their business and the odd cricket had started off its daily mantra. Its sound so distinctive she'd recognise it anywhere. Far off in the distance she could hear the muffled noise of a car engine and almost immediately she heard the sound of a shutter or two being pulled up. People had begun to stir.

Opening her eyes Kate looked straight out in front at the Aegean Sea, the bluest blue you could ever see and near enough to make her think about diving in.

'Later,' she smiled to herself. She slowly turned her head towards the mountains of the peninsula. They were so clear she could see as far as the little fishing village. And even further today, higher up to the tiny village tucked away in the hills, visible only by the whitewashed houses.

Wow! It lifted her heart just to be able to take in the vista that was laid out before her. How spectacularly beautiful it was. Kate had forgotten how she adored this time of morning. It was calm and peaceful. Nobody about. Just herself and the sea and the mountains.

'Perfect time for yoga,' she thought cheerfully.

So, she rolled out her mat and spent twenty blissful minutes practising her poses. Once she was finished, her stomach had started to rumble, a clear sign it was time to shop for food.

Kate set off in the car, down the road to the nearest village supermarket, where she knew they stocked good quality local produce. She had always found it a joy to shop for food in Crete. It was generally fresh and locally sourced. A taste test was always actively encouraged, in fact it was nearly obligatory. And the best bit had to be the fresh fruit and vegetable section of the shops. Nothing imported here. Everything was seasonal, loose, in its natural state, and often with leaves still intact. You could pick up any of the items, smell them and feel them before you purchased. Plastic and prepacked were a definite no-no. Produce sometimes may not have been the most visually appealing, but boy did it make up for in taste, what it lacked in appearance. And the best thing for Kate was that most of it was grown with no chemicals or sprays to prolong its shelf life. When something was out of season, it was out of season. There was most definitely a time for everything. She knew better than to expect to be eating pomegranates in July!

Kate happily selected all the food she wanted, making a conscious effort to shop for just one person. She sighed quietly to herself. Bags of fresh oranges were placed into the trolley, a huge water melon to juice, delicious fresh cherries to snack on, the makings of a Greek salad – plump ripe tomatoes, red onion and cucumber, dark green mountain herbs that still had the dew on them, plenty of water to quench her thirst in the heat of the day, a couple of bottles of wine and a few other bits and pieces to nibble on. Passing by the deli section she was lucky enough to see the girl putting out the famous local dip made from yogurt, cucumber and garlic, so naturally she purchased a tub. A few other sundries and she was good to go. She could hardly believe her bill at the check-out, a little over thirty euros for a trolley bursting full of the freshest fruit and veg! And the wine had been the most expensive part of that…

Right next door to the supermarket, Kate popped into the natural products shop and watched in wonder as her jar of honey was filled from a large barrel that had come directly from the owner's hives. She bought a little feta cheese for the Greek salad and then tasted all the olives for the proprietor, thrilled when he threw in a bag of her favourites to welcome her back to Crete.

Kate stopped at the bakery on the way home and sipped an ice-cold coffee in the shade, waiting for the girl to bring her a spinach pie. How she loved the spinach pies! They were so tasty. Freshly made every morning. Spinach leaves and feta cheese with a hint of fennel all wrapped in filo pastry and baked in the oven. The ultimate fast food. Mouth-wateringly delicious. But you had to be up early to get one, they were often sold out by eleven. This one didn't make it home!

Armed with her food supplies, Kate returned to the house. She laughed to herself, thinking that shopping for food in Crete was almost a social outing. With the coffee and the chat, she had probably been gone three hours. Not for the first time that day she noted that she was feeling good. Thankfully, the day before was a dim and distant memory and she happily unpacked all the shopping and made a fresh juice. A morning swim would be perfect and a quick glance out the window, told her she would have the pool to herself.

An hour later, refreshed and invigorated, she was waiting patiently for her canvasses to be delivered. She couldn't start the painting until they arrived, but that was probably just as well as she needed to get organised and set up her creative workspace. The most likely place to paint was the large patio that wrapped around the house. The fresh air and fantastic light would be a much better option than one of the upstairs bedrooms. Just as she had that sorted, the doorbell rang and there was Dimitri, from the art shop, perfectly on time with her big delivery. When Kate saw all the art materials, she couldn't help but feel the creative juices stirring deep inside her.

"No, I know I didn't think it yesterday, but this is the right thing for me to do," she affirmed quietly to herself.

She chatted to Dimitri for a short while and he reassured her that if she thought of anything else she needed, he would deliver it to her straight away.

Once he was gone, she took out her phone and rang Molly. Typical Molly all excited to hear from her mother. Kate gave her a quick fill-in on how horrendous the previous day had been and was thrilled to be able to tell her that she was much better. They chatted for a while, and said their goodbyes, Kate promising to call David the next day exactly as had been arranged.

Kate went straight to the task in hand. She got busy sorting all her canvasses, brushes according to size, and paints according to colour. Then she methodically laid out all the tools and equipment she thought she would need for the painting project. Two hours had passed before she knew where she was, and her stomach reminded her it was time for a snack. She rustled up a Greek salad, ate heartily and was straight back to business.

She needed some kind of a plan or timetable, she figured, something to get her on the right track. To make sure she was allowing enough time for everything, including and most importantly herself. Anne, her counsellor had taught her so many self-help strategies over the past year, so Kate was soon scribbling in her notebook. She was very focussed on painting, so naturally most of the time was given over to just that but she was generous in her time slots, allowing lots of flexibility. The last thing she wanted was a rigid routine that would turn her painting challenge into a chore. Deliberating for about an hour or so, she came up with a rough lay-out for her days.

TIMETABLE

8AM	Get up/Yoga. Lie-in? Water/ Juice coffee?
9AM	Swim/Shower
10AM	Paint
12PM	Snack/Juice/Paint
2PM	Break/Lunch. Walk/Drive/Snooze or whatever shows up. Swim? Beach?
4PM	Paint
6PM	Snack/Juice
6.30	Paint
8PM	Beach, sunset (Definitely)
9PM	Dinner (out- maybe? Maybe not. Definitely yes)
11PM	Bed – Approx, very approx.

That looks pretty good to me, Kate thought to herself. A quick calculation and she reckoned if she followed it rigidly (which of course she wasn't going to do) she'd be painting for zillions of hours. If she was flexible she would paint for around four hundred hours. And if she was really nice to herself she would paint for less. Whatever way you looked at it, it was a lot of painting time. And it should be enough to achieve what she wanted.

She'd start the routine the following day and stick with it for a while to see how it was going. It could always be re-adjusted, if it didn't suit her.

Pleased with her days work, Kate retired to the patio, for a cool drink. The sun had moved quite a way across the sky, so it would be the perfect time to wander to the beach for a swim and sunset. With a bikini under her sundress and a towel slung over her shoulder, she sauntered the couple of minutes to the sea. Nobody ever walked quickly in Crete as far as Kate could see. They meandered or strolled or sauntered slowly, slowly, slowly… Always slowly on Greek time.

When she reached the promenade at the beach, Kate stood quietly for a few minutes facing the sea to fully take in the beautiful scenery she hadn't seen for over two years. The peninsula off to the left was still sitting majestically in the sea just as she remembered. Why had she thought it would be any different, she laughed to herself. And she felt her heart swell as she looked in awe and wonder at the unspoiled, almost deserted beach and sea before her, right on her doorstep!

The horizon and island to her right completed the panorama. The last of the tourists were leaving the beach and she would have had it all to herself except for one or two Greek families. The sea had calmed considerably since the morning. The waves were quietly lapping the shore and the water was like a still lake with a sheer satin cover. The speed at which the sea could change from crashing waves and dangerous undercurrents to quiet waters with gentle lapping fascinated Kate.

Once in the sea, the salt water cooled and refreshed her. She lay back, closed her eyes and bobbed around for twenty minutes or so, listening to all the old familiar beach sounds. It had been too long… She could hear children's voices nearby, the rhythmic sound of beach bats and a ball, the low murmur of conversation on the breeze, the sound of laughter and people splashing about. All this, and the warm evening sun lulled Kate into a deep sense of relaxation. And for the third time that day she affirmed to herself that she was alive and well, and glad to be in Crete.

Once dried, she made her way up onto the promenade and positioned herself on one of the many wooden benches facing west for sunset. Exactly as she had remembered, the sun was sitting directly above the mountains of the peninsula, poised to set any time. She found it hard to get her head around the fact that it was actually the earth moving and not the sun. For the last ten minutes before sunset, the sun seemed to speed up and you could literally see it dropping down, down, down and all of a sudden, it was gone. It disappeared behind the mountains. Another day over. Almost immediately the light and atmosphere of the day changed. A softness came into the evening, the heat of the day diminished and everywhere looked and felt differently. Early diners were out and about strolling the promenade looking for somewhere nice to eat while a few stragglers like herself were only packing up to leave the beach. The time between full daylight and night light was another of her favourite times. It was as if the day was slowing down even further, making way for a different night rhythm to take over.

Back at the house, Kate showered and changed. She was feeling pretty peckish. It had been a long time since that Greek salad. It had been a lovely first day, so it was definitely time for a bit of socialising. She was half dreading it, but another part of her wanted to catch up with her Greek friends, particularly Sophia who was the owner of her favourite Cretan restaurant.

Almost an hour later she pulled up outside the restaurant. She could see Sophia from the car, doing what she always did best – effortlessly meeting and greeting the customers in her own unique way. It made Kate smile to see her in full flow. Sophia had a kind word for all, and amazingly always remembered really small details about her regulars that endeared her to them. Everybody loved her. She was a beautiful, kind woman from the mainland who had moved to Crete and opened the restaurant around the same time Kate had bought the house. She was also an artist, so that had further cemented a bond between them.

Her restaurant was untypically Greek. It was more of a bar than a taverna with a great big patio for diners, serving great local food with a twist, simple yet delicious. And Sophia loved music so there was often some local musician quietly strumming in the corner adding to the atmosphere. Trees seemed to grow up naturally through the floor tiles and interesting pieces of the islands gastronomic history were scattered here and there around the patio. There was an old baker's oven from the last century and the antique olive press Sophia had procured from a local factory when they were upgrading. Over the years the restaurant had built up quite a reputation for itself and people came from far and wide to sample the scrumptious menu and listen to the music.

Sophia squealed with delight when she saw Kate mounting the steps from the road. She hugged her so tightly, Kate could hardly breathe.

"Oh my God! Kate! How are you? I've missed you so much!" she gushed. And then as if suddenly remembering, she lowered her tone and took Kate's hands "I'm sorry about your husband. We were all so shocked here. Isabella told me…" Isabella was the lady who had organised the last art show she had been involved in.

Kate instantly felt emotional and could feel tears behind her eyes, but she heard herself saying truthfully with a sigh, "Me too, Sophia, me too. Paul was a good man, the best. But it's time for me to move on now, get my life back on track. That's partly what I'm doing in Crete." She started to tell her about the exhibition, but Sophia already knew. Chania was a small city and news travelled quickly, especially amongst the even smaller art circle. Sophia seated her at one of the smaller, more intimate tables and took off to get her order. Kate let out a sigh of relief. Thank God that was over. She had found it pretty difficult. Another box ticked.

"All part of the process," she murmured to herself.

Very soon Kate was tucking into her delicious food.

She had ordered an unusual fiery starter made from pomegranates, walnuts and spices served with a local dip and razor thin slices of homemade pita bread. Deliciously divine!

For her main course she had the equally tasty *souvlaki* and house salad, washed down with a glass of their own white wine from the barrel. Kate spent a very pleasant couple of hours refuelling and catching up with Sophia, who would sit with her every time there was a lull. To round off the meal dessert and a glass of the potent *raki* were complimentary, in the usual Cretan tradition. Kate was nicely tired by then and more than ready for bed. She paid her bill, said her goodbyes, and left for home promising she'd see them soon.

She would be spending a lot of time there this holiday she thought to herself as she set her alarm for the morning and climbed wearily into bed.

"What a lovely first day it had been," she smiled as her head hit the pillow and she allowed sleep to overtake her. Kate slept soundly until her alarm went off the next morning at eight am.

Eight hours straight sleep, was her first thought. It hadn't happened for so long, it was a minor miracle. Actually, it was more like a major miracle!

Another good day hopefully, Kate thought to herself as she dressed and set about putting the new plan into action. She stuck to the plan pretty well that day and really got into the painting. She started a book she had put on her Kindle, sunbathed for a while and by sunset that evening, she had one painting nearly complete.

And so it continued. Before she knew it, a week had passed.

And life fell into a relaxing routine, all of her own making, more or less as she had set out on the first day. The days were filled with lots of painting, punctuated by breaks, walks, swims, delicious snacks and meals out, etc. Pure bliss.

Apart from the first day, she was finding the painting process a little difficult. There always seemed to be some emotion surfacing during the day, nagging at her, begging to be acknowledged. She took to keeping a journal beside her as she worked so she could keep track of what was going on inside her. Looking back over her paintings, she was able to pinpoint each one by emotion. That was the day I was feeling happy or that was the day I was feeling sad or that was the day I was feeling angry… and so on. By days end she would bring her journal to the beach with her and read over what she had written and reflect.

In a way, it was funny, because a couple of weeks in, when she would wake up in the morning her first thought would be, I wonder what the feeling will be today.

The weeks were starting to fly. Time seemed to have sped up. She ate out nearly every night, mainly in Sophia's or sometimes at the nearest taverna on the beach a stone's throw from the house. It was quite beautiful sitting at the beach taverna, drinking her freshly squeezed juice or wine, tucking into stuffed tomatoes, zucchini flowers, or something else equally delicious while the waves were crashing to shore almost to her feet. The beautiful mountainous peninsula provided the backdrop.

Two weeks flew by, then three, and another problem surfaced. The physical act of painting at the complex was a big distraction. Not to Kate, but to others there. It was sometimes quite difficult to paint at all. Apart from the emotions surfacing, now there were always people at the complex unwittingly distracting her or being distracted by her. It was unintentional of course but nonetheless getting harder and harder for Kate to work. Her patio was very open, and she was a naturally friendly person. Anybody passing by who was interested in what she was doing stopped to chat and ask questions, maybe offer an opinion. People were just being people. You couldn't blame them for that. Her paintings were big, bold and colourful and demanded attention. People seemed to like them. The only problem was, all the talk and chat really slowed things down and interrupted her flow. Fine, if she had no deadline to meet or target to reach. But her time in Crete painting was precious and she really needed to maximise its potential.

She had fifteen paintings finished and stored in the bedroom, but she had hoped to be further along. Kate had come on a mission and if things continued as they were she would never get finished. It was more than a little frustrating! She needed to do something about it. She didn't particularly want to move inside to one of the spare bedrooms out of the fresh air and amazing light, but something was going to have to change.

On her fourth week in Crete, her English friends Denis and Claire arrived for a holiday at the complex. Kate graciously accepted the sympathy they offered on Paul's untimely death. Kate confided in them how hard it was becoming to paint, how people, meaning only the best, were actually interrupting her painting flow.

"What you need now is to be somewhere very quiet and peaceful, so you can complete with no distractions," suggested Claire.

"Yes, but where? I thought we were in that place," Kate retorted

"Why don't you ask Sophia does she know of anywhere suitable you could rent? Put the feelers out and see what comes back to you."

"That's a good idea," said Kate, "but I don't know if I'm ready for that just yet. The logistics of it would be huge and anyway, I don't really want to leave the complex or the area, even though it's becoming very difficult to paint." And she wasn't ready, but everything seemed to be pointing to the fact that she might have to move sooner rather than later. She couldn't imagine anywhere being as beautiful as where her house was, not to mention the massive operation it would be. Firstly to find somewhere and then move all the paintings materials…

Where would she go? How would she manage?

She didn't want to leave her beautiful paradise in the sun, but Kate knew Claire was right. Complete quiet was what she needed. She'd give it another couple of days and see.

As she set off for her break that day, Kate continued to mull things over in her head. She was driving along quite distractedly when all of a sudden, she found herself at the beautiful German cemetery

Kate vaguely knew that the cemetery had been a place of great significance during World War Two and The Battle for Crete. The graveyard was a place she had visited many times in the past and never, ever tired of. She set off up the stone steps towards the garden. It was a beautiful place to visit she thought, almost a meditation garden with its rows upon rows of neatly manicured memorials set in a still meadow, the only background noise the birds singing and the crickets loud chirping.

Kate surveyed the view from the high vantage point of the graveyard in admiration. She could see down to the old airstrip, an airstrip that was used for the invasion of Crete. Her eye then continued out towards the sea, past the fishing villages and on towards the mountains of the peninsula. What a view! Amazing to see it from a different vantage point, other than her patio or the beach.

Out of this world, she thought, if only I could find a place as peaceful as this for the next few weeks, I'd be sorted. And she made a silent wish that somehow, something would happen to resolve things.

It was hot, so Kate sat under the shade of a tree, idly listening to the crickets, thinking things over in her head, wondering how she could make this work. An hour or so later, no resolution found, but feeling differently inside, she set off home with renewed fire in her belly.

As Kate resumed painting. She felt the energy bursting forth from within, flowing through her arms and she felt as if she couldn't get the paint onto the canvas fast enough.

How things can change so quickly!

Working rapidly now and with determination, she was muttering in a low voice. "For Christ's sake, I can't paint here. What am I supposed to do now?" Kate was almost flinging paint onto the canvas. "This is ridiculous. What am I doing here? I'm feeling really angry now. Why am I so angry? I feel like packing up and going home."

On it went like that and continued for the rest of the evening. A bit of a tirade. Not anything like her day at the studio in Ireland but nonetheless, a bit of a rant. She painted furiously all afternoon and finished ahead of schedule for that day. She had completed one entire painting. Pounding down to the beach that evening, all fired up still, notebook in hand, she plonked herself on a bench on the promenade. She wrote and wrote in her journal, oblivious to the passers-by. She was lost in her thoughts and feelings of frustration and anger, lost in all the emotional baggage once again.

Much later, out of the blue, she heard a vaguely familiar Greek voice nearby. Not realising she was being addressed she continued her vigorous writing. She heard the voice again, louder, and this time she was sure she heard her name. Head up, Kate found herself staring into the most intense black eyes she had ever seen. Despite the warm evening Kate felt a tiny shiver. A tall man, with well-defined features, was standing there looking at her curiously, as if waiting. There was something vaguely familiar about him and Kate struggled to put him into context. She had definitely seen him somewhere before.

"I'm Yiannis," he said politely. "I don't know if you remember me. I hung your paintings in Chania two years ago." He held his hand out towards her.

That was it! Now she remembered. He was the guy Paul had gotten to store her paintings after the last exhibition. She had met him briefly at the time. Kate gathered herself and shook his hand.

"I'm Kate," she replied curtly, still in the flow of her personal writing. He was an interruption to her journaling and she felt vaguely annoyed. They exchanged a few pleasantries.

"Actually, I've come looking for you," he continued. "I heard you were back. I called to your home and was on my way home, but I saw you sitting here and…" his voice trailed away. And then he continued, "I'm sorry about your husband. He was a very nice man."

Kate groaned inwardly, she really didn't want to do this now. "Yeah thanks. Life sucks sometimes, doesn't it?" she said a little crossly.

Yiannis looked a bit uncomfortable but continued on, "I have some money for you, from the exhibition two years ago. I really want to give it to you. You know the paintings that sold? Isabella is away and asked me to pass it on if I could."

"You mean some paintings actually sold. Well there's a turn up for the books!" Kate replied sarcastically still clearly annoyed. Why did she say that? Nothing could have been further from the truth.

"They all sold. Here's the money," he said matter of factly, his eyes holding hers with an expression she couldn't read. And he was holding an envelope towards her.

Something in Kate flashed with anger. Who was this stupid man bringing up things that belonged in the past?

"I don't want it. What am I going to do with it? Give it to charity or something but don't give it to me," she barked at him.

Yiannis appeared at a loss to know what to do next. "Well, I can't keep it," he said. "You need to sort it out." And he looked in the direction of the road as if planning an escape.

Kate, didn't know why she was being so testy and unpleasant, particularly to someone she didn't even know. Her anger suddenly dissipated. She pulled herself together and tried to apologise.

"Look Yiannis, I'm sorry for being snappy. I'm a bit all over the place at the moment. All the painting I'm doing seems to be affecting me. Today is the worst day yet. I'm not normally like this," she appeared contrite.

"It's fine. There's no need to apologise." He looked a little relieved. "I can't pretend to know how it is for you, but I'm guessing it can't be easy," he added.

"Yes, but it's two years on now. Actually, I was really good in Ireland until I came back to Crete painting. All the old feelings seem to be surfacing again," Kate groaned clearly frustrated.

"It must be hard letting go of someone you loved so much."

And then for some strange reason, Kate poured it all out to Yiannis, sitting there on a bench, on the promenade. All the work she had done on herself in Ireland, why she was there painting, her limitations at the complex, how angry she had felt that day. On and on she went until eventually she realised she had been ranting for a long, long time. So, she stopped and apologised again. They both laughed, then Kate noticed that Yiannis was looking at her thoughtfully.

"Actually, I think I might be able to help you. Rather, we might both be able to help each other. Could you come with me for an hour or so? I have something to show you."

Kate's sense of curiosity was aroused immediately and with no hesitation or reluctance she agreed to go with him. She followed him to a jeep parked beside them at the promenade, with a beautiful golden retriever sitting quietly in the back.

"Hey boy, what's your name? Aren't you beautiful?" Kate patted him affectionately.

"Meet Zorba, my faithful companion," Yiannis laughed and Zorba wagged his tail, excited to be the centre of attention.

"Actually, Zorba is part of my plan. Hop in and I'll explain on the way," he added.

Kate noticed he drove a black jeep, one that looks like a roomy car at the front and has lots of trailer space behind to carry stuff.

As they drove west, Kate was thinking to herself she knew nothing about this man. Except of course, he hung paintings for exhibitions, that Paul had known him, and he had a dog. And of course, that he had sat there and listened good-naturedly to her while she had ranted and raved for a long while.

Once they left the promenade, they continued west passing through a few small villages. Kate was vaguely aware of him talking in the background, but she was looking out the window, taking it all in. They passed through a small sleepy fishing village and then continued on out towards the peninsula. The jeep started to climb, up steep corkscrew roads, rising high above the sea. The higher they went, the more amazing the views became. She could see all the villages eastwards – all the way to Chania in the far distance. She almost had the sense they were leaving the civilised world behind and heading towards oblivion. They finally drove through a small rural village, turning sharply in the square before the jeep climbed some more and then seemed to descend. They were on a dirt track, skirting close to the high steep cliff walls beside them. There was only room for one car here.

Yiannis drove around another cliff bend and then the road stopped dead – just disappeared. They had arrived into a clearing, with a gradual slope to the sea. They were looking down on a tiny cove, cliffs on either side from the clearing to the water. It was like a mini-gorge, a very private place. Kate could see a small boat pulled onto the tiny beach, sitting underneath a lone tree. Picture post card stuff. She was so mesmerised by the gorge and the cove, she hadn't taken in the two stone buildings, one to her left and one to her right. The buildings were both at an angle, almost diagonally facing the water, and yet snugly set back into the cliffs. They seemed to balance each other perfectly in size. Kate recognised them as the traditional stone houses of Crete but clearly, they had been renovated. The stone looked newly finished and they both had larger windows than would have been customary for these kinds of houses. Kate could make out a shaded veranda at the end of each house, directly facing the sea. She was intrigued.

Yiannis had stopped the jeep and Zorba was out, barking excitedly. Kate looked at him a little uncertainly.

"Where are we?" she asked with growing excitement.

"Welcome to my Cretan home," he smiled at her.

"Oh my God! You live here?"

"Yes. Come on, I'll show you."

"It's amazing," was all Kate could say, still looking around trying to absorb it all. It was quiet and peaceful and so, so beautiful. The sea. The houses. The cove. The setting.

The light was fading fast and Yiannis was walking towards one of the cottages.

"This is what I want to show you."

She followed him into the cottage. She thought it might be a bit dark because of the cliff behind but even at dusk she found the exact opposite to be true. It was light and bright and airy, due in part to the large glass windows and white painted walls. They had entered a very large room opened up all the way to the wooden beams of the ceiling. Skylights had been cleverly installed. There was a large bench in the middle of the room, and on it lay a very large, very beautiful ancient door, something you might see on one of the old Venetian houses in the city. A much larger and more beautiful version of her own reproduction front door. Two of the walls were shelved and filled with work tools. There was an impressive stone arch at one end that opened to a kitchen area, and she could see a closed door in the kitchen leading on to some other room. The main area was probably a workshop Kate guessed, but yet it looked way too nice to be used as a workshop. Yiannis walked through a doorway at the other end. They were now in a slightly smaller room. It was equally light, bright and airy. No workshop here just a huge glass window, high ceilings, lots of white wall space, exposed stone and a small couch.

"What do you think?" he asked, looking expectantly at her.

"*It's really nice,*" she replied not sure what she was supposed to say. In fact, it was more than very nice. It was an awesome space. But she still wasn't sure what he had in mind.

"Could you paint here? The glass slides into the wall and there's mosquito nets to pull down and shutters so you can have as much air as you like blowing through, and as much light as you need, or none at all. And outside is a shaded terrace, looking out at the water with somewhere to sit or paint or whatever…"

71

The light was fading fast now, and Kate could barely make out the sea and the boat. She was speechless. She didn't know what to say. The penny was finally dropping. He was offering her a quiet space to paint. Suddenly, she could see all the possibilities so clearly, and her face lit up like a Christmas tree.

"So, is that it? I can rent this from you. Is that what you mean?" she asked excitedly.

"Well, not exactly rent. I thought we could help each other out. I explained it on the way." Now it was his turn to look puzzled. Kate had been completely lost in her own thoughts on the journey and obviously took in nothing he had said.

He patiently explained again. "Next week I'm going to Athens for a few weeks. I need someone to look after Zorba and you need a painting space. Would you be interested?"

"Am I what?" Kate gushed back. "It's perfect for me, just perfect. And I'd be delighted to look after Zorba. Thank you so much! I'm thrilled." She patted Zorba who was sitting beside them.

Kate surveyed the space again. It was the perfect size and would easily accommodate her large paintings. She could picture herself there, happily painting looking out on the sea in blissful contentment. No distractions she hoped. The window opened back for air, which would be perfect for the August temperatures. The sofa in the corner of the room she suspected opened into a sofa bed. Another small door led to a kitchenette area complete with sink and leading off from that there was a beautiful shower-room and toilet. It was like a self-contained modern apartment.

But the highlight for Kate, after the perfect painting space of course, had to be the shaded veranda directly adjacent to the sea, accessible from the room she was to paint in. She could imagine herself there, lazily swaying in the hammock, lost in dreamy thought, reading a book, or doing yoga and then walking the few metres to the sea for a swim. It couldn't have been more perfect if she had ordered it. Her face must have shown her excitement because Yiannis was now openly grinning at her

"I guess you're pretty happy so?"

"Ecstatic!" beamed Kate

They walked across the yard to the second house ironing out the finer details as they went. He had volunteered to pick up all her paintings, finished and unfinished, along with the blank canvasses the day before he left, and she would bring the paint brushes and other smaller art materials. She was very welcome to use the main house as her base for the duration. It was up to her. She needn't feel she had to come and go between the complex and here. He wanted her to treat it as her own, to do with, as she pleased. He wouldn't be there. And all she had to do was feed and look after Zorba. How easy was that? There had to be a downside… She wondered what he normally did when he was going away somewhere. Surely, he had a friend or neighbour he could call on.

It must have been all that ranting at the promenade that swung it, she laughed quietly to herself.

All in all, Kate was more than pleased. It was the perfect solution for her, away from the distractions of the complex, in a stunningly beautiful and peaceful location.

Now, she thought there was every possibility she would get to finish all forty of her paintings for the exhibition in October. And, if that wasn't enough, he had also agreed to hang the whole exhibition and keep all the paintings until then.

They wandered into the main house. For the second time that evening Kate was rendered speechless as they entered the second stone cottage. The outside, like the other cottage was beautifully crafted cut stone, skilfully restored. Inside though it looked like a very contemporary modern space, like something out of a glossy magazine, and yet it felt very homely. She hadn't expected it. Yiannis turned on the lights. They were in a large living area with high ceilings and exposed beams. Again, it was light and bright and airy. Some of the walls were painted white on the inside and some were left in their natural state with the stone exposed. The overall feeling was of spaciousness and minimal clutter.

At one end of the room stood a stone fireplace, original she guessed. At the other end under a stone arch was a cream cottage style kitchen. The centre of the room was dominated by two large brightly coloured, comfy looking sofas angled towards the stone fireplace. Small beautiful artwork was dotted here and there, originals she guessed from a very quick look. Discreet lighting throughout and recessed shelving, completed the room. It was dark now, so she couldn't see outside, but there had to be amazing views of the sea from inside. The interior doors looked like they were the antiques and had obviously been carefully refurbished along with everything else. The place was almost a contradiction. There was a lovely cosy feel to it while at the same time it was modern and contemporary. It had been very tastefully restored.

Kate walked slowly around the room, touching everything as she went, marvelling at how perfectly the old and the new fitted together.

"Wow!" was all she could say. It was like something you could only dream about. She shrugged her shoulders at Yiannis as if to say, how is it possible to have such a spectacular room? It was amazing!

Kate was such a captive and appreciative audience, he continued to show her the rest of the house. The bathroom was an enormous wet area, beautifully tiled, in varying shades of blue and green and aquamarine, with tiny shiny complementary tiles dotted randomly throughout. A modern power shower completed the wet area and a huge roll top bath with old-fashioned taps dominated the other end of the room. It was well placed near the window to maximise the views. It looked like he had used the services of a very clever interior designer.

Yiannis had moved on ahead to another door.

"I have to tell you something before I show you the bedroom, there's something here you will recognise."

Curiously, Kate followed him down a step into another huge room. A white space. White walls, white bed, grey sofa, blue window frames and then lots of colourful accessories. But immediately her eye was drawn to the space over the large bed. Dominating, in all its glory and vibrancy, was her painting from the show of two years ago, New Beginnings, the main painting and the largest. It had found a perfect home. She instinctively put her hand to her mouth and her breath caught in her throat. Kate was momentarily frozen to the spot. A range of emotions flickered across her face and coursed through her body. Sadness for a time gone by never to come again, joy that the painting looked so great, and pride that someone had liked her work enough to buy it and put it in such a beautiful home. Even though people were buying her paintings for years, Kate seldom got to see them in their final resting place. She hadn't expected this.

"Oh my God. You bought it. I wondered who had…" she whispered.

"I loved it the first time I saw it. It's perfect there, don't you think?" Yiannis replied softly.

The vibrant fun colours of the painting complimented the stark white-ness of the room and picked up on the colourful accessories thrown around. He was right. It was perfect.

Yiannis could see the emotions flash across her face. "I'm sorry. Was it too much?"

"No!" Kate answered him honestly. "It makes me a little sad because it reminds me of the time it was painted, but I also feel so proud that it's found its place in such a beautiful home."

In the space of approximately two hours, Kate had gone from a torrent of rage to the exciting prospect of painting in the most scenically beautiful and soulful place she had ever seen. And then she had been confronted full on by her past in the form of this painting hanging in a stranger's house. How bizarre!

It was only that afternoon she had been in the German Graveyard wish-ing for a solution to her problem. The universe had answered her prayer. Now here she was, with just that, and lots more besides.

How quickly things can change, she thought to herself. In the blink of an eye. But of course, she knew that.

It seemed that her home for the rest of the holiday would be in a beau-tifully restored Cretan stone house, in a place of spectacular natural beauty. And all she had to do was foster Zorba, the beautiful golden retriever for a few weeks. The solution to all her problems. She could finally see light at the end of the tunnel. The paintings would all be completed, she knew that now. She could clearly visualise the exhibition. She could see it in her mind's eye.

"I can't thank you enough. It's all working out perfectly." She was grinning broadly at Yiannis now.

By the time he dropped her home that night, things were all sorted. All the arrangements were in place. She was feeling excited. The day before Yiannis left for Athens, he would come and collect all the canvasses and art materials. She would follow the next day with whatever she wanted to bring with her and move into her new painting studio. It was all very simple really. In the meantime, for the next few days, she'd continue painting at the complex, interruptions and all. Everything was falling into place. She couldn't wait to tell Claire and Denis. They'd never believe she had found a solution so quickly.

And so, about a week later, at the end of the first week in August, Yiannis was in touch to let her know he was leaving the following evening. He knew she was returning to Ireland on the last day of August, so she'd have about three weeks in paradise, all going well. Typically in the previous couple of days, things had gone really well painting-wise at the complex. Yiannis arrived the following morning, picked up all the canvasses and she followed on later. She had no desire to be in his space for too long before he left. He was still there when she arrived at the cottage but was almost ready to leave. They exchanged mobile numbers.

"Don't forget to ring or text if there's any problem," he reminded her. As he was leaving for the airport, he kissed her on both cheeks, in typical Greek fashion and Kate knew at once that she had been elevated to the status of friend, which was very nice indeed. She had just acquired another new friend in Crete.

Chapter Six

FORTY FABULOUS PAINTINGS

Kate listened as Yiannis' jeep receded into the distance and looking around her excitedly, gave a big 'yahoo' and a jump for joy.

"How lucky am I?" she laughed out loud.

It was late in the evening, shortly before sunset and with the sun at a low angle in the sky, shining from behind the cottages, it made the place look almost mystical or magical. She couldn't wait to get going and organise herself and her new studio. Yiannis had left her four timber laths to hold her paintings upright. Each lath had ten grooves, to securely slot in ten paintings, without them touching off each other. An ingenious simple solution. It was how he transported other stuff in the jeep and it worked perfectly for the paintings. She already had twenty finished and left in the other room. Only twenty to go.

Would she get them done in three weeks? They were primed and ready, and she was more than hopeful.

Kate worked quickly and quietly to organise her space. She kept Zorba close by, at all times, at least until he got used to her, determined to keep up her end of the bargain seeing as she was solely responsible for him. He was a beautiful dog, obedient and friendly and very easy to like. He followed her around the first evening once she called him, so much so, that after a while she found herself talking to him as if he was an old friend. Kate decided to use the main house as little as possible. In fairness to Yiannis, he had given her free rein, but it was his space and the studio was more than adequate for her needs. With its shower room and toilet, kitchen and sofa bed, not to mention all the painting area, it really was perfect. Once all her bits were in from the car, and arranged all around, it was starting to look a bit more homely. All ready for the following day.

It was a balmy evening, so she set off for a short walk with Zorba to explore a little and get her bearings. They walked out along the dirt track and followed a pathway up the hill, along the cliff top. They were very high up. "The cottage had to be right out on the peninsula," she murmured as she faced eastwards. In one direction, down below she could see the nearest village, only a stone's throw away, with its lights flickering to life. Turning the other direction, she was looking out onto the Aegean Sea, not very clear now as the light was fading, but it looked beautiful and peaceful.

She had run out of superlatives to describe how truly magnificent the place was. She closed her eyes and breathed in the balmy night air. An hour from starting, herself and Zorba were back at base, having walked to the nearby village and back. It was dark, so after sending the same text to Molly and David promising them the usual daily reports, she opened a bottle of wine and settled down with a book. Zorba lay at her feet, happy to be petted every now and again. She lazily turned in for the night around eleven pm, tired after her busy and exciting day. She wondered had Yiannis reached Athens as she drifted off to sleep.

Waking early the next day, the first thing that struck Kate was the absolute peace and quiet – the complete stillness. She had thought the complex was quiet! There was literally no sound at all, only the odd bird quietly singing. It wasn't long after sunrise, so she decided to go for a short walk. By the time she got to the door, Zorba was by her side. He had slept at the end of her bed all night long. They went out the dirt track and up the hill as they had done the night before. The world was still asleep. They sat at the top of the cliff looking out to sea. The sun a fiery ball of orange and pink lay low on the horizon and the morning was hazy, so early in the day. A cock crowed back towards the village and the birds had begun to chirp a little more enthusiastically.

What a rare privilege, she thought, to be out so early and get to see and hear the world waking up.

There was no need for Kate to have any new routine for her new location. Things flowed. Her first attempt at painting was a dream. So focused, so quiet it was easy to be fully absorbed by what she was doing. She kept her journal near at hand, intermittently making an entry.

Lost in her world of painting on that first morning, Zorba began to bark and took off out into the yard. She heard a voice outside and followed out, only to be met by a man on a bicycle. Definitely Greek, she thought, probably in his early sixties, grey hair, brown eyes, with that weather-beaten look about him.

He smiled greeting her, "*Kalimera*," and handed her a warm bag with a delicious smell wafting from it and another bag full of oranges. Kate was puzzled and without thinking took the bags from him. The aroma of fresh bread reminded her how hungry she was.

"Yiannis asked me to bring you these every morning while you are here," explained the man.

"Every morning?" Kate repeated in disbelief.

"Yes, every morning," laughed the man as he started to move off on his bicycle.

How kind, thought Kate and she shrugged her shoulders and laughed too.

"Wait! What is your name?" she called out after him as he started to cycle out the track.

"Nikos."

"Thank you very much, Nikos. *Efkharisto poli!*" she shouted at the receding figure on the bicycle.

"*Parakalo!*" He waved in reply as he made his way back out the dirt track.

Imagine that, Kate laughed to herself.

People would never cease to amaze her. How thoughtful!

"That's great. Breakfast is sorted," she called out to Zorba.

After the surprise of the first morning, the days settled into their own gentle rhythm. She generally rose around sunrise and sometimes was lucky enough to have a clear view of the sun rising from her vantage point on the cliff top. An early morning swim in the sea, some yoga, a bite to eat and she felt ready for the day. She managed to catch a couple of hours painting before Nikos would arrive with breakfast. She looked forward to her daily chats with him and gradually she heard all about his wife Katerina. How they had no children. He told her how he had lived all his life in the next house along the dirt track back towards the village. That he knew Yiannis as a young boy and again when he moved back from Athens. That he was like a son to the two of them. He regularly admired Kate's paintings and asked questions about the exhibition in Chania in October. The two of them got on very well, sharing a cup of coffee every morning. Occasionally he would bring her something his wife had cooked, along with the oranges and bread. When Nikos left, Kate would be back at painting immediately and keep going until her body reminded her it was time to eat again.

The days passed blissfully by. The new studio worked wonderfully for her. It was so well thought out, it maximised the light but still remained cool and shady in the August heat. The moving glass windows worked perfectly too, open during the day and closed with shutters against balmy night air and mosquitos. The air-conditioning was an excellent back-up plan if needed.

Kate was painting like she had never painted before and loving her retreat in the sun. Funnily, she felt no desire to socialise. Her daily visits from Nikos fulfilled that aspect of her life. Apart from one or two trips to the village and Sophia's she was very content and happy to stay put at the beautiful stone studio with Zorba.

He was a special dog. She loved his company. He shadowed her everywhere now. Slept every night at the foot of her bed, swam with her, and went walking with her. She talked to him now like they were best friends. Sometimes it seemed it was more of a case of him looking after her than the other way around.

As good as she had intended, Kate kept her use of the main house to a minimum. On the few occasions she was there, she felt like an intruder, like she was reading someone's private diary without their permission.

Once inside though, it was hard to resist not looking for little clues about Yiannis' life. She knew so little about him. She had found him to be very kind, thoughtful and generous and, even though she was living at his house temporarily, she found herself curious about him and his personal life. There were only a few photos around, one with him and a frail looking elderly lady. Then other photos, it seemed were of the same five or six people, at different stages of their lives. There were two beautiful old wedding photographs, one really old photo of a young man on his own. It looked like Yiannis, but Kate knew the photo was way too old for that. It was generally the same few people over and over again. There were lots of books on the shelves and around the living room. All in Greek, so she wasn't able to make out what they were about. Some had pictures of impressive looking buildings in them. Others were all writing, novels she guessed.

All in all, the house seemed very male. Somewhere at the back of her mind Kate had a feeling Yiannis had been involved with one of the other artists two years ago and that's why he had hung all the paintings. She couldn't remember how she knew that. But there was no obvious evidence of a woman, or a woman's touch about now. He was tidy or else got someone to clean the house for him. He had left the place immaculate too...much tidier than the first night she visited. Funny the thoughts that go through a person's mind, she laughed to herself as she wandered through his house. Kate couldn't resist a peep at her painting in the bedroom. She had to admit it looked great where it was. His room was really beautiful too, with the fabulous veranda facing the sea. The colours were very male with the greys, blues and whites contrasted by the colourful painting. Definitely like something out of a magazine. Somehow, she'd be surprised if there wasn't a woman in his life.

The days passed by now, in their own unique rhythm, full of creativity, relaxation and peacefulness. Not only did her paintings come easily but she felt her whole body relax and unwind more and more. Time had flown and before she knew it, she was into the last week in August and her paintings, all forty of them, were finally complete.

Kate had them all neatly stacked on the laths and she was very happy with the finished canvasses. Forty paintings and if she said so herself they were pretty good... maybe even fabulous. Well, they were fabulous to her. "Forty Fabulous Paintings," she laughed to herself. She carefully laid them out in groups of ten, to scrutinise them further. Some were textured, so they'd take longer to dry. Some were not textured which was fine too. Journal in hand, she surveyed them all for a final time.

She named each and every one and clearly remembered what she had been feeling while working on them. They were like babies to her. Forty babies. Each one she had given birth to. And just like childbirth, some had been painful, and some had not.

Kate was hugely proud of herself. She had done it! Two months painting was at an end, and she felt great. In fact, she felt awesome. Only that day as she finished the last painting she felt like an enormous weight had been lifted from her. It seemed like a lifetime ago since she had painted at the complex. All she had to do was tie up any loose ends regarding the paintings, clean up after herself and leave the house as if she had never been there.

There had been a few texts over and back between herself and Yiannis, so she knew he wouldn't be back until the day after she left for Ireland. She was reluctant to leave her Cretan paradise too soon, knowing she would never have this opportunity again. She cleaned her house at the complex, shutting it down as she normally would have. She packed her bag, said her goodbyes there, and headed back to the stone cottage for the last couple of days. She wanted to see what it would be like, to be there, relaxing with no agenda. It was a great plan and she knew it wouldn't make any difference to anyone.

When Nikos called on the last day, she showed him all the paintings. He really liked the whole abstract thing, so she got him to pick out his favourite.

"If you want it, it's yours Nikos," Kate said to him. "Let me put it in the exhibition, but afterwards it will be for you. No one can buy it." She could tell he was touched. Similarly, she had been very touched by his kindness to her. For Zorba she had bought a small silver medallion with his name inscribed on it and attached it to his collar.

Now Yiannis. What could she get for him to repay his kindness? That was a tough one. He already had a painting and besides a painting couldn't even begin to express her gratitude for what he had done for her. She'd have to think about that a lot.

She sat down on the last night to have a celebratory glass of wine, and to try and compose a thank you letter to him. She had so much to say. A frustrating hour and about a thousand scrapped pages later she was finished.

Yiannis,

I don't really know where or how to start thanking you for all that you have done for me in the last month. Your home is so beautiful. I love its peacefulness and solitude, not to mention its magnificent location. It was exactly what I needed and as you will see, I hit my target and got my forty paintings finished. I know it wouldn't have happened if I was still at the complex. You helped me more than you will ever know. Maybe in October you will allow me to thank you in some small way.

I can't believe you organised for the fresh bread and oranges to be delivered every day, it was very thoughtful of you. I'm thrilled to have a new friend for life in Nikos... If I forget to mention it, will you please make sure himself and Katerina come to the exhibition.

And Zorba... what can I say about Zorba that you don't already know. I have fallen totally and completely in love with him. I think he was minding me, not the other way around. He truly is an amazing dog. I love him to bits and will miss him terribly when I leave here.

From the bottom of my heart Yiannis thank you so much. I don't know how I can ever repay your kindness

With much gratitude,

Kate.

P.S. I will text or ring you soon about October.

Zorba knew something was up that last day because he was very much out of sorts as if somehow sensing something was afoot. And when Nikos came to pick him up, he howled and whined like a baby. Kate couldn't bear it. She hugged them both and walked away to have a good cry for herself. The place and Nikos and Zorba had really stolen her heart. She would most likely never be there again, and it wouldn't be the same meeting them in October. She had had such an amazing time, almost unbelievable. Painting had been a joy and had come very easily to her. Just before she left, she closed her eyes and slowly inhaled her last breath of air from this little piece of heaven on earth.

Three hours later Kate took her seat on the plane to Dublin. She sat back, shook her head and smiled secretly to herself. Imagine, the two months were over. What a productive time she had painting. She could honestly say she felt better now than she had ever felt in her life before. Hard to believe, given her first night in Crete two months ago. But she had worked through every emotion on the spectrum and felt she had come out the other end. While she was painting, it seemed like she was going through something at a very deep, subconscious level. The resilience of the human spirit never ceased to amaze her. She looked out the window as the plane became airborne and took in her last view of Chania and the peninsula for seven weeks. She smiled quietly to herself, leaving her home from home. She would be back for the exhibition before she knew it.

Chapter Seven

THE PURPLE DRESS

When Kate landed back in Ireland, she tapped into a whirlwind of social engagements. She had been away for so long and missed by so many people they all wanted to catch up with her. Naturally, her priority was Molly and David. She had missed them both so much. She stayed with Molly in Dublin for a few days en route home so that they could really catch up, and David lived near enough to come and go.

Kate delighted in filling them in about her adventures in Crete. They may have heard some of it before, but they got to hear it all again. A blow by blow account of her two months painting. The good days and the bad. They listened agog as she described Yiannis' stone cottage, Zorba, Nikos and the incredible unspoiled beauty of the area and the kindness bestowed on her. They had picked up some of it from phone conversations but there was nothing like getting it from the 'horse's mouth' so to speak. Kate was looking fantastic and exuded such a sense of utter contentment that Molly and David were thrilled. They had never seen her looking so well.

"Wow, Mam can we go there at Halloween?" asked Molly in excitement.

"What does this guy do?" demanded David.

"Would you believe David, I don't really know? A bit of building, I think. He hangs exhibitions. Nikos told me he had some big job in the city but left that and moved to Crete. I know very little about him, except the odd thing I picked up from Nikos." Kate shrugged her shoulders. "And to answer your question Molly, I'm not sure if it's a good idea to go at Halloween. I'm guessing he's a private person. It's a very private place. I think you'd want to be invited. We couldn't arrive there unannounced."

"Jesus Mam! He could have been an axe murderer for all you knew!" David piped up, as protective of her as ever.

"Yes, but he wasn't, was he? He was a very nice, thoughtful man," responded Kate.

"And he was gone all the time you were there?" quizzed Molly.

"Yes, sure that's why I was there. He had things to do in the city, catch up with old friends he said."

"Mmm!" said Molly thoughtfully.

Kate didn't know why, but she actually felt a bit defensive of Yiannis. Why were they questioning his integrity? She certainly hadn't.

"Anyway, you'll both meet him at Halloween," she continued on as if to close the subject.

They continued chatting about Crete and making plans for Halloween. Molly and Jack were going. David was going on his own, even though he had a new girlfriend.

Kate spent a lovely few days, catching up with her two children. She enjoyed their company so much. They had both turned into mature, kind adults and she felt really proud of them. And Paul would have been too, she smiled to herself.

Paul's second anniversary came and went without much emotional turmoil. Kate was amazed how time seemed to help things along. They were all reconciled in their own way to the fact that he wouldn't ever be back. She felt she had come to terms with the fact that things hadn't been perfect between them. And hopefully had forgiven herself that their last few weeks had been a stress, she felt mainly because of her. They marked the day with a small get together. Kate was in a good place and had more of a sense of gratitude for having had more than twenty years with a good man. Not to mention the fact that she felt so blessed to have Molly and David.

The following few weeks were about touching base with friends and neighbours. Once they were all satisfied that she had survived the two months intact and wasn't in any way fragile, they latched onto anything they could, to slag her about – in typical Irish fashion. A get-together with her college friends typified this! Kate met up with the girls she had island-hopped across Greece with, for one of their frequent and cherished reunions.

"So, tell us about this Greek Adonis. He loaned you his house and didn't expect anything in return!?" her friend Aoife enquired mischievously.

"Yeah right, and I'm Santa Claus," laughed Colette

"What does he look like?"

"Typically Greek, dark hair, brown eyes, sallow skin," Kate replied matter of factly, frowning a little as if trying to pull up a mental image of him

"So, was he nice?"

"Do you fancy him?" They bombarded her with all their questions.

"Girls, give me a break. I hardly met him. I was just staying at his house. His beautiful house might I add. He was a few hundred miles away."

And that line of questioning soon dried up as the girls felt it wasn't going anywhere. And they rapidly moved onto another topic, their upcoming trip to Crete. They were all excited. They had been there many times before and had loved it. This time most of them would be staying in the beautiful old Venetian harbour, as they had done many times before.

"Will you book it for us, Kate?"

"What about that hotel we stayed in before?"

"That's right. Remember the year we went with you to buy the house?"

"Yes, the October after you saw it."

"The place that was one street back from the harbour, with the big high ceilings and beautiful wooden floors?"

"Like something from a time gone by!" they all chorused together and laughed heartily at the memory of Kate's mantra about the beautiful hotel.

"That was a great holiday. Remember the night we went on the tear with the estate agents? That was a howl," announced Marie.

And they all laughed again at the great memories.

"Last time we went to buy a holiday home. This time an exhibition. What next, Kate?" Aoife giggled suggestively.

"Who knows" laughed Kate. "Let's hope another exhibition and maybe next time they'll ask me instead of vice versa!"

And they continued talking long into the night in hopeful anticipation of a great trip.

It was going to take some organising to book them all flights and accommodation. All in all, five different groups of people were travelling. At this stage of their lives they all knew each other, but naturally some wanted to be together more than others. She knew them all so well and knew who to put with whom. And to be honest if she didn't get it perfectly right, they were all mature and worldly enough to be adults and go with the flow. It took about a week on the internet to book the flights and accommodation. Because of the abundance of small boutique hotels in the harbour area, she was spoiled for choice. By Halloween, the tourist season was more or less over so there was full availability everywhere. Mind you there always seemed to be a buzz around the harbour no matter what time of the year it was.

Unfortunately, the flights weren't quite as easy to book. Precisely because the tourist season was over, direct flights from Dublin to Chania Airport were finished for the year, so they had to fly via Athens. Two flights and a lot of people to organise, but by mid-September she had finally got everything sorted. At least they would have a place to stay and flights to and from Crete. How they enjoyed it after that was up to themselves, even if she did feel a small amount of responsibility. After all they were going because of her.

The weeks were flying, and Kate could feel a growing excitement inside her. She couldn't wait. She kept counting down the weeks, like a child waiting for Christmas. Only seven weeks. Only six weeks. Only five weeks. Then, only four weeks.

Molly kept asking her what she was going to wear for the exhibition and to be honest, Kate hadn't the foggiest. She hadn't thought about that. She was one of those people who naturally seemed to dress well. Born with a sense of style, she had always liked clothes but was never obsessed about them. If she saw something she liked she bought it, no fuss. She didn't collect shoes or bags or tops like others did. Her wardrobe generally had a few nice pieces that she liked to wear and made her feel good. No, lingerie was Kate's thing. She had been that way for as long as she could remember, even as a teenager. As soon as she started to develop curves her mother took her on a shopping trip to the city and introduced her to the delights of under-wear as opposed to outerwear. Kate in turn introduced Molly to one of the joys of being a woman. On shopping trips with the girls, Kate could always be found browsing in the lingerie shop. She loved the beautiful, luxurious fabrics, holding them and feeling them, the satins and silks, the pretty hand sewn lace or soft feminine cottons. And when she put them on, she mar-velled how they made her feel about herself – sensuous from the inside out.

But nothing would do her Molly but a shopping trip to Dublin to orga-nise an outfit for Kate. Molly loved clothes, and nothing pleased her more than organising people's wardrobes or giving advice on clothes to anyone who would listen. She probably could have been a personal shopper.

Kate and her friend Jane had arranged to meet Molly in Grafton Street, one of the main shopping streets in Dublin. They met in one of the little cafes on a side street and had an early lunch to plan the day. Untypically though, Molly seemed quite distracted and not her usual focused shopping self. Usually it was launch attack on all the shops on her list, but today there was no list and seemingly no plan. Kate was more than a little puzzled.

"Molly, what are you up to? You're not your usual focused self. Jane, have you ever seen Molly like this? What are you up to?" she laughed suspiciously

Molly looked a little sheepish. "Look Mam, I've seen a dress on the in-ternet and I think it would be perfect for you."

"That's fine, Moll. Can I see it too?"

"I can go one better than that. I can bring you to the place where the dress is made," announced Molly.

"Perfect, let's go then and look at it."

"Ok but I have to tell you…" Molly's voice trailed off as if she was about to say something and then thought better of it.

Jane smiled to herself and said nothing.

"What are they up to?" wondered Kate. "Well come on then, let's go then and see this dress."

Molly led the way. They all strolled away from the Grafton Street area at a leisurely pace. Kate wasn't quite sure where they were leading her but didn't really mind either.

Less than ten minutes later they arrived into one of Dublin's fashionable Georgian squares. You couldn't but be impressed by the rows of grandiose red brick houses with their magnificent front doors, all symmetrically angled around a green park.

"Here we are," Molly smiled brightly as she stopped outside one of the more beautifully kept houses. For a moment Kate was puzzled. That is of course until she read the plaque on the door.

"Oh my God! O'Brien designs. A designer, Molly? Are you crazy? I can't afford anything in there," Kate blurted straight away.

"At least look before you make any assumptions," Molly pleaded

"Well, we're here now so we may as well go in," Jane suggested diplomatically.

Jane was saying very little. Kate suspecting at this stage, there was a plan and her friend had been in on it, all along. They walked up the steps to the elegant front door and rang the bell. From the way they were received, it seemed to Kate as though they had been expected.

Once inside, Kate caught her breath at the elegance and sumptuousness of her surroundings. As soon as the door was closed to Dublin city traffic, a sense of peace and quiet permeated the air. Kate could just about make out the low strains of classical music in the background and a delicate fragrance wafting in the air. Nothing overpowering but subtle enough for them all to notice. Everywhere they looked, they seemed to be surrounded by works of art, beautiful crystal displayed on bespoke furniture, full length mirrors reflected the gleaming chandeliers and glass lamps, dramatically vibrant hats carefully positioned here and there. The backdrop of soft creams and whites all over highlighted the beauty and style everywhere. It was hard to fully take it in, such was the assault on their senses. They had never been surrounded by so many beautiful things.

'What a perfect setting to showcase creativity!' Kate thought admiringly.

All three were discreetly ushered across the tiled floor and up the magnificent staircase to a luxuriously carpeted room where the Louise O'Brien clothes collection could be viewed and tried on.

Molly was so excited at this stage she could hardly contain herself. She spoke to the lady in charge, who left the room and almost immediately returned with a vision of lace on her arm.

"This is the dress you requested. Would you like to try it on?" she said, looking directly at Kate.

Kate gasped at the intense colour of the dress. Purple! Her favourite colour! She couldn't resist reaching out to stroke the fabric. And as she had guessed, it was soft and delicate to the touch. There was intricate detail in the lace and tiny hand-stitched beads when you looked closely. Every inch of it seemed to have been exquisitely hand sewn. It truly was a work of art. Kate felt drawn to the dress, compelled to try it on. Molly has chosen well, she thought.

Once in the dressing room, the dress fell over Kate's curves, like a glove. It had a v-neckline, front and back which was softened by scalloped edges, revealing a hint of her cleavage. Stopping just above the knee, it felt very comfortable and very luxurious on. Kate hated any type of formal clothes and this dress hit the perfect balance of understated elegance. It really was a tribute to Miss O'Brien's genius that she could design a dress that was very elegant and still looked cool and very hip, thought Kate as she whirled around in front of the mirror. She liked it. She really, really liked it. Nervously she walked out to show Molly and Jane.

"Well?"

They both looked at her in silence.

"Well?" she asked for a second time

"Mam, you look amazing," Kate thought Molly was going to cry. "I've never seen anything look so beautiful on anyone before. And sexy!"

"Molly! I'm not trying to look sexy. I just want to look nice for the exhibition," answered Kate a little embarrassed by Molly's gushing compliments.

"You could never look 'just nice' if you tried," quipped Jane. "You always look stunning."

Jane and Molly looked on in admiration.

Kate complimented the dress perfectly and vice versa. She still had her golden Cretan tan. With her tall curvy figure, it looked like the dress had been made with her in mind. She was totally seduced by the design, the craftsmanship and the fabric and the artist in her silently saluted the artist in Louise O'Brien. No wonder she was at the top of her game. She was wearing a work of art.

"You have to buy it, Kate. It looks like it was made for you," Jane said matter of factly.

Kate, excited now herself was almost convinced. She made her way to the dressing room to take off the dress and see how much it was. She wanted to buy it. Badly. But she knew it would be expensive. She really, really loved it. But she nearly fainted with shock when she saw the price. She was so disappointed. Well, unfortunately that was that. There was no way she would pay that for a dress. No way. What a pity.

Kate tried to discreetly tell the others that it was too expensive, but she hadn't bargained for the persuasive powers of her daughter Molly, backed up by her good friend, Jane. She always had a plan up her sleeve.

"Look Mam, I know it's expensive but why don't you use the money from the last exhibition. The money you had forgotten about, and only got this summer?"

Jane followed it up with, "You deserve this, Kate. The dress was made for you. Aren't you always saying you can't put a value on a work of art? Well this dress is a work of art and your name is on it."

On and on they went in the same vein, gradually weakening her resolve. True, she had finally taken the envelope Yiannis had handed her on the promenade months before. It was tucked away at the bottom of her handbag and there was a lot of money in it. Kate had hurriedly grabbed it this morning before she left home, meaning to leave some of the money behind. She was wrestling with her strong moral principles when Molly landed the final blow. Clearly delighted with herself she beamed at Kate and Jane

"Mam, I know what you can do. This is money you didn't know you had, right? So, buy the dress with some of the money and then we'll go straight to the Goal or Trócaire or Gorta office, whichever charity you like, with the rest of the money, and then everybody's happy!"

And there it was, the perfect solution.

Kate knew when she was beaten. She could have her dress and Molly was right, the donation would ease her conscience.

"Oh Moll," she laughed, "let's do this before I change my mind."

Kate bought her beautiful purple lace dress. True to her word, she went straight to her favourite charity's office. It was win-win all round. And then they all went to Brown Thomas' to buy matching lingerie and a few other bits and pieces. A successful days shopping was complete. On the train home, Kate was continually smiling to herself. She couldn't wait to get inside her front door, to feel the fabric of the dress and try it on again. She was so excited.

Soon enough September had turned into October and there were only three weeks to go to Halloween. She gave Yiannis a quick call, to confirm details about the exhibition and the paintings. He sounded relaxed and very comfortable on the phone. She asked after Zorba, Nikos and Katerina and they chatted for a while. She told him about her friends from Ireland travelling to the exhibition. She made arrangements to contact him in Crete a few days before the opening night, so they could agree a layout for the paintings. He raved about the paintings and mentioned how Nikos was so chuffed with his canvas. He had already booked his lift to the exhibition for himself and his wife. They continued chatting for another while, Kate jokingly suggesting to him that he think of some way she could repay him for all his hospitality and kindness, as she hung up.

The last couple of weeks before they left Ireland were taken up with planning an itinerary for all the holidaymakers. A week spent in Crete alone would be enough for anyone, but there were other beautiful things she wanted to try and arrange for them.

Kate had her case packed a week before departure. All that is, except for her perfect purple dress. She left it hanging until the very last minute. She loved looking at it, touching it and feeling it as it hung in her wardrobe. The fabric was so exquisite it was hard to stop herself from reaching out. Only Jane and Molly had seen it and for some reason she didn't want to show it to anyone else until the exhibition. And she had warned them not to tell anyone what she had paid for it.

She suddenly had a terrible thought – What if my case goes missing en route? And then the logical part of her brain answered back, your case has never gone missing before. Why would that happen now?

So, six days before the exhibition, a happy group of travellers found themselves at Dublin Airport boarding a flight to Athens. Their spirits were high, and they talked and chatted excitedly on the four-hour flight. A quick stopover in Athens and this time they boarded an internal flight for the short trip to Crete. They were on the last leg of their journey.

Almost two months after she had left Crete, Kate was back again in her home from home, eagerly breathing in the Cretan air as she stepped out of the plane. It was great to be back. And hugely exciting for her this time.

PART 2

Chapter Eight

YIANNIS

Yiannis Theodorakis was very much his own man.

In his forties, he was living a contented life, back to his roots in Crete. He was conceived out of the great love between his mother, Maria Mitsotakis and his father, Yiorgas Theodorakis.

His mother hailed from a loving home in Western Crete, and his father came from a prominent business family in Athens. They met in the sixties when a young Yiorgas was sent to Crete for his military service and Maria, his mother was working in an office near the old port in Chania. The young couple embarked on a passionate affair and Yiannis was the resulting love child. Eighteen months after first meeting the love of her life, Maria Mitsotakis left Crete with a new husband and a new baby – their beautiful son Yiannis. They settled with their infant son, in a modest suburb of Athens and though they lived through politically turbulent times, they were happy. The love and passion they felt for each other was evident for all to see.

Yiorgas joined other members of his family in the city to help with the construction company his father had started. It was the sixties, and tourism was starting to take off, big time in Greece. Young enthusiastic Yiorgas saw a niche in the market for his particular style, construction, with a strong emphasis on renovation. Yiorgas became the creative brain behind the business and it flourished under his father's shrewd guidance.

Maria was happy to stay at home and look after their young son. Both of them were clearly devoted to young Yiannis and each other. From humble beginnings, things improved rapidly for the Theodorakis family. So much so, that a year after moving to the city, Maria could think about the possibility of going to college in Athens, sometime in the future; something she had only ever dreamed about before.

Unfortunately, when Yiannis was barely two years old, tragedy struck. His mother and father were killed in a collision on the mainland. They had just left their young son in Crete, while they continued to a business conference in Northern Greece.

Athens and the peninsula were united in their grief, shockwaves reverberated throughout. Eleni Mitsotakis who had lost her husband during the occupation had been struck by heartbreak again. Her only daughter and son-in-law cruelly taken from her. *Life was unfair*, they said, *so unfair*. How could a person be asked to endure so much grief in one life-time, they wondered.

The only saving grace was that young Yiannis was not in the car with his parents. In reality, it was the only thing that kept Eleni going. Her two-year-old grandson, in her care, totally oblivious to the tragedy unfolding around him. She had been down this road before, this strong spirited lady. And once again she dug deep. She found that out of the tragic loss of her daughter, she now had her young innocent grandchild to care for. And at two years of age, Yiannis was totally dependent on his grandmother. Just like with Maria, it was what got her up in the mornings, what gave her the strength to carry on. She poured whatever love and energy she had left, into the care of her grandson.

And so, young Yiannis spent his formative years on the peninsula in the loving care of his grandmother. His earliest memories were of a happy, caring home in Western Crete. Long hot days spent in glorious freedom, roaming the countryside around the village and swimming in the sea at his grandmother's cottage. He loved to help her tend the vegetables and feed the animals or wander the hills to collect the mountain greens. He meandered his way home from school, along dirt tracks and country roads. He played in the olive groves with his friends and he loved sometimes being taken to the monastery on special days. He knew everyone, and everyone knew him. Life was one big long adventure on the peninsula and the days seemed to stretch out endlessly ahead of him.

Eleni lavished as much love on him as she could in an effort to compensate for the losses he had suffered in his young life. Losses they had all suffered. She taught him so many things. Eleni Mitsotakis knew more about life and loss than anyone should ever have to know. But rather than taint

Yiannis' mind with the sadness of loss and death, she filled his head with the beautiful stories of how she had met his grandfather and the great love they had shared. She told him how his mother and father had met, how they had fallen deeply in love too. He knew his grandfather had been killed during the war and he had often heard the stories about the occupation and how his grandfather had fought for the liberation of Crete. And he heard the sad story of how Dimitris Mitsotakis, had been killed the day his own mother was born. It made him very proud of his Cretan roots.

Eleni taught Yiannis about honesty, determination, loyalty a sense of fairness and above all, a great sense of fun. She instilled in him, great respect for his Cretan heritage. She taught him to be proud and independent spirited. All these strong characteristics balanced by her great love, gentleness and sensitivity. She was an amazing selfless woman and young Yiannis soon came to regard her as his mother.

By the time he was thirteen years old, Yiannis' life was turned upside down once again. His father's family in Athens sent for him. It was all part of some grand plan, some preordained scheme that had been worked out between the families' years previously. Even though she herself was heartbroken, Eleni made it sound wonderful for Yiannis, like an exciting magical adventure in the city. He was to attend private school in Athens and then be groomed to take some active part in his late father's successful family business. Being his father's only son, and the eldest Theodorakis grandson, it seemed it was his duty to someday take over the reins of the company.

What a shock it was for the young carefree Yiannis, to go from roaming the Cretan countryside to finding himself in a strict private school regime. Initially he found it difficult to cope. He literally went from a free, loving home to rules and regulations for everything – mealtimes, bedtime, study time, even family time. It wasn't the Cretan way. But Yiannis was a smart kid and found that by throwing himself into his studies. Finding something, anything that he liked, life was just that bit more bearable. His family in Athens were good people but they didn't know him and seemed distant and formal when they were together. How he longed for his life back in Crete. Even though he wrote regularly to his grandmother and tried to visit as often as he could, it wasn't easy for a boy who wasn't in any way independent. He had very little control over his own life. At first, he lived for, and was lucky to get a few weeks in Crete at the holidays. He could never say he was happy or unhappy in Athens, he just got on with it.

The years passed slowly by and very gradually his life in the city became the norm. But Yiannis never forgot the happy childhood spent in Crete. The freedom of his youth and the strength of his grandmother's love stayed with him throughout his life in Athens. And when he turned eighteen and finished school, it was no surprise to anyone that he opted to do his military service in Crete – exactly as his father had before him. Every spare moment Yiannis had, he took the bus to the village and hitched or walked the rest of the way to his grandmother's cottage. Eleni was thrilled to be able to truly reconnect with her grandson again after all the years. She had missed him so much. She was older now, but still healthy and active and loved to see him coming. After all he was her only grandchild and the light of her life. Yiannis got to meet with most of the old school friends and delighted in actively participating in village life again. This short interlude reignited Yiannis' love for Crete and for his grandmother. Deep down though he knew he was on borrowed time. His company career in Athens beckoned. The eighteen months of military service passed quickly, too quickly, and before he knew it, he was on his way back to Athens to take his rightful place in his father's company, for which he had been carefully groomed. It was his duty and responsibility. That much had been instilled into him. As Yiannis left Crete, he promised his grandmother he would visit often.

This time the years passed rapidly for Yiannis. He was busy learning every aspect of the business in Athens. Just like his father before him, he showed a real talent for the business. He had new innovative ideas aplenty and progressed quickly through the ranks of the company. He showed himself to be a natural born leader with a real flair for construction. No surprise then that he was most passionate about the specialised renovation side of the company. Yiannis would have loved to study architecture after school but a college education was deemed 'surplus to requirements' for a young man who had a thriving business to step into. He was a quick learner and appeared to have an innate ability to get along with everyone he crossed paths with. Despite his young age he had this inexplicable aura about him, people naturally gravitated towards him, without knowing exactly why. Returning to Crete became a choice for Yiannis and he did so as often as he could. But generally, it was a flying visit. Some or other work crisis in Athens always had to be seen to. Something that couldn't wait… He became torn between the sophisticated city life he was living or taking time-out in Crete. Gradually, much to his grandmother's dismay, the visits became less and less frequent. They didn't stop but became a rare occurrence.

By the time he was thirty, Yiannis Theodorakis was at the top of his game, heading up one of Athens most successful construction companies. Amazingly, he was still considered the new kid in town even though he had given years at the helm of the company. He appeared to have the Midas touch. Everything he touched, was a success. He had a real talent for turning projects around. Under Yiannis' management the company would invest heavily, bring all the experts on board and bring regeneration into areas previously abandoned. He specialised in taking on listed buildings, some of the priceless heritage of Athens. He would put all the right people in place, pump in money and regenerate a monument, a building, a landmark of some cultural or historical significance. And Athens was full of buildings in need of very specialised renovation. Yiannis Theodorakis was the man for the job and everybody in Athens knew it. He also had a reputation as a fair-minded person. He was honourable, honest and had a real passion for what he was doing; lovingly restoring old projects and bringing them back to their former glory. He was well respected in the business community and everybody liked him it seemed. All through his thirties, Yiannis worked very hard. His job was stressful. He loved being on site, actually getting his hands dirty, but regrettably for him the official side of the company started to take up his time – meeting with and attracting potential investors. More and more he was sucked into the people-pleasing side of the business, making sure the money kept rolling in. And away from the part he loved, getting his hands dirty on site.

Yiannis compensated by living the high life on Athens social scene. Seduced by all the trappings that go hand in hand with being the head of a very successful, very prosperous company, he was seen in all the right places. He frequented all the popular restaurants and nightclubs. Overindulged, he got used to having a beautiful woman in tow, driving a top of the range car, having an impressive apartment, the list was endless. Anything money could buy, he had. In a city of over five million people, he was considered to be one of Athens most eligible bachelors. He worked hard and partied harder. It seemed as if everything came to him with ease, he was living the dream.

And yet, in the brief moments he had time to stop and think, he felt an emptiness in his life. His grandmother had raised him to live by his own moral compass and Yiannis most definitely had the feeling he was surrounded by people-pleasers. When had his life changed, he wasn't quite sure. He was also feeling a subtle pressure now from within his father's family to marry and produce an heir. Duty and responsibility and all that. How he had come to hate those words! Yiannis had many relationships, but they generally fizzled out after a short while.

On the odd occasion he would escape to Crete to his grandmother's haven of tranquillity, she'd fuss over him and tell him he was working too hard and way too stressed. Tease him that he should find a nice Cretan girl to settle down with. At the back of all the joking she would always urge him to be true to himself. She would constantly say, *Follow your heart Yiannis. Always!* He usually had the feeling after he visited that she was the only person with her feet firmly on the ground.

The years rolled on and Yiannis continued to become more disillusioned and discontent in Athens. Business was booming, but deep down, he wasn't happy. He could see through the superficiality of the fast-paced life he was living. All the pieces didn't fit for him. And still he couldn't motivate himself to make a change. The part of his job that he loved and had a real flair for, he seldom got to do. But the social aspect of his life he didn't much care for, was all that seemed to matter to some people. Eligible girls were paraded through his life as if he was supposed to pick or choose one. He wasn't a fool. He could see through their plans. Certain people were attracted only to his perceived wealth and power. It was hard to know who his genuine friends were.

By the time he hit forty, Yiannis knew he had some serious re-evaluating to do. He ached for something deep down in his soul and yet couldn't name what that something was. Yiannis Theodorakis was lost.

He really didn't know what he wanted. Pressure was building from within the family. Even Alex his long-term girlfriend was dropping not so subtle hints. Maybe marriage was the answer, but he wasn't so sure. He needed to do something about changing his life but knew it would be difficult to leave the existence he knew behind. To give up all the power and wealth that went with his job. To turn his back on his comfortable life in Athens.

And then two things happened in quick succession that were truly life changing moments for him. Following his routine annual check-up, his doctor told him, rather heartlessly, that the prospect of him ever fathering children was very unlikely indeed, because of his low sperm count. Yiannis was devastated. It wasn't part of his immediate plan, but he had taken for granted that it would happen sometime in the future. Precisely because he had been an only son, he knew he would have liked to have a family of his own one day. So now it looked like it was going to be only him, unless he married Alex. It was a lot to get his head around. And of course, once he was told he couldn't, he realised, he wanted it more than anything else in the world. How ironic! A beautiful woman ready to commit, more money than he could ever want in the bank and he was to be denied this?

He hardly had time to get his head around that devastating news when the very next day he had a call from Crete. His beloved grandmother had been taken to hospital seriously ill. Without a second thought, Yiannis was on the first plane to Chania and by her bedside a couple of hours later. It broke his heart to see her so ill, teetering between life and death. He was wracked by guilt. He hadn't visited as often as he could have. There was always something happening in Athens which had seemed to be so very important. Christ, how his life had changed in the past two days, he thought. Things that had seemed so important, were now insignificant for him and things that he had taken for granted before, were all that really mattered. There was nothing he could do about the children issue, he knew. But now that he was back with his grandmother, he vowed that if she survived, he would take care of her, for as long as she needed him. She had been the most real thing in his life and he had neglected her. She had selflessly given up years to care for him. Now he would take care of her.

Once the decision was made, Yiannis felt happier than he had in a long time. Actually, as he sat by her bedside, he realised he wouldn't mind moving back to Crete permanently. Back to his roots. Back to the one place where he had always been happy. He prayed that she would be ok and that he would have a chance to talk to her again, to tell her about his plans. It felt right. Deep down in his gut he felt relieved. Just as his gut had told him the life he was leading in Athens wasn't right for him, his gut was now telling him that this was the right decision. He would leave Athens behind. His father's family seemed to want him mainly for his business acumen anyway. Everything that had ever been real and good in his life was right here, in Crete.

Eleni Mitsotakis rallied.

Good as his word, Yiannis left Athens to care for his grandmother. There was considerable fall-out in the company, of course, but Yiannis talked the family round. He made it abundantly clear he was very willing to hand over the reins to the next in line, which would keep one or other of his cousins very happy. And he assured them that he would always be available for advice or support if needed. They were under the illusion that it was a temporary arrangement, until his grandmother was well, but Yiannis felt deep down that once he left the city, he would never go back. It wasn't so easy to talk to Alexandra, his live-in girlfriend. She went ballistic. She would not give up her job and life in the city to move to some backwater, she said.

Eleni was overjoyed at the prospect of her grandson living near her again. Yiannis settled himself in the nearby town. The first thing he did was to get himself, a beautiful golden retriever. Something he had always wanted to do in the city, but it had never been practical. After that he was full of plans to renovate his grandmother's cottage. He wanted to modernise the house for her and make it more comfortable while at the same time convert an old shed on the property into an apartment, he or someone else could use if staying over. Eleni had never seen him so animated. He really loved this work. She had no interest in any renovations for herself. The joy of living near her grandson again was more than enough for her but she encouraged him to go ahead and refurbish the shed as he wished.

And so, for the next two years, they lived in close proximity on the peninsula, grandmother and grandson. Each with their own separate space and life, yet inextricably linked. Yiannis did an amazing job renovating the work shed into an apartment. Single-handedly, he threw himself into the job. It was what he knew and loved best.

By and by and totally unintentionally, the renovation grew into a small business for Yiannis. Someone saw what he was doing at the stone cottage and asked him to do some work for them. He ended up doing small jobs from his house. And very soon many small jobs became a fledgling business. Enough to keep one person fully employed. There was no business plan. No targets to be reached or aims to be achieved. Yiannis was happy to rely on word of mouth and his reputation.

In Crete he was Eleni's boy or the Mitsotakis grandson. No-one knew him as anything else and he was well pleased about that. He rejoiced in the ordinary life he led and very gradually he managed to shed the stresses and strains that go hand in hand with having led a false life. He took great pleasure in real relationships with people again; his old school friends, neighbours, Eleni's friends, people he crossed paths with in his line of work. Yiannis seldom brought any woman back to his house, aware he had swapped the relative privacy of city life for a microcosmic village life. He was discreet in his personal life. Every so often he would go to the mainland or disappear overnight, but he always made sure his grandmother's neighbour, Nikos knew how to contact him.

Yiannis loved the slow pace in Crete, the simple pleasures of a life he had nearly forgotten about. The company of good friends and his grandmother. Living in an area of stunning natural beauty. Leisurely meals and lively conversations. His loyal and faithful dog Zorba. A job he was passionate about once again. And making the best of every day. For the first time in years, he felt like he was really living.

Two years after Yiannis moved from Athens, Eleni Mitsotakis departed this life in the loving company of her grandson and dear friends. He was saddened but had known it was coming sooner rather than later. She had become frail in the last few months and was only able to live independently because he had moved to the work shed apartment to be close at hand and help look after her. She had been gifted two precious years since her last health scare and had been conscious right until the end. Something they were both extremely grateful for. Yiannis knew he would miss her very much. She had been such a powerful force in his life. A lady of great strength of character.

Once his grandmother had gone, Yiannis gave up the house in the nearby town and any notion of ever returning to Athens. He threw himself into the total renovation and redecoration of his grandmother's stone cottage. He took on a temporary apprentice while refurbishing, and six months later, it was done and dusted. He had created a beautiful home for himself in a beautiful location and turned the one-bed apartment into his very own work shed. He moved permanently to the stone cottage and moved his business base to the shed.

In the couple of years since moving back to Crete, life had been good to him. The business had become quite successful. Almost exactly what he had been doing in Athens – building and restoring, but he was determined it would stay small. He would do it his way and he only took on projects he was passionate about and could handle himself. Chania and further afield was awash with old venetian buildings that could do with renovation. This time around it was a one-man show. There were no employees, apart from the occasional helper, in times of need. And that's the way he wanted it. These days his phone was always ringing for a job here or there. His reputation had spread throughout Crete, by word of mouth, exactly as he had hoped for. He had full control. No one to answer to, only himself. The job could be on any part of the island. He bought himself a jeep to transport the tools of his trade and get himself and Zorba from job to job. He had never been more content.

Sometimes he went to Athens to catch up with the old friends, or real friends as he called them. They had kept in contact and were always glad to see him. He was amazed how many others had dropped him after he left his high-powered job. To his amusement, he discovered he was considered something of a recluse, living in the mountains, caring for some old relative. Sometimes when he was in Athens he saw his old girlfriend. Sometimes they slept together. Sometimes not. It was a very casual type of arrangement that suited them both. By and large Yiannis' life in Crete was exactly as he wanted it to be. Simple, stress free and uncomplicated.

Chapter Nine

THE EXHIBITION

They made a boisterous, happy group, their first night in Crete in the old harbour in Chania – all twenty-odd of them!

They were happy to settle on a restaurant at the waterfront and listen to the waves lap against the harbour walls and watch as the world slowly sauntered by. Large jugs of house wine and freshly squeezed orange juice got the evening off to a great start and they unanimously decided to go for food for sharing, Greek style. Before they had a chance to pour the drinks, baskets of warm crusty bread and *tzatziki*, the scrumptious Greek yogurt dip, had arrived at the table, followed not long after by plates of delicious looking Greek salads, grilled prawns, *souvlaki*, fried vegetables and homemade French fries. The smell and appearance of the food had them all watering at the mouth and unceremoniously they all tucked in. Everyone was in good spirits.

Kate looked on benevolently as her friends and family laughed and chattered excitedly about their different plans for the week ahead, and how much they were looking forward to the exhibition. She smiled and withdrew into her own headspace, marvelling at how lucky she was.

'What an amazing group of family and friends they were,' she silently observed as she inhaled the sights and smells of a city she loved.

Chania Harbour was quieter than it would have been at the height of the summer. The holidaymakers had left it to the locals, the odd tourist and the military personnel based at Souda. She sighed in contentment. Kate loved it at any time of the day, or year. But her favourite times spent there, had to be when the madness of the summer season was over. There was nothing as lovely as a long leisurely stroll out to the lighthouse to watch the sunset. Cafes, bars and tavernas were all lined up en route, tempting passers-by in for a coffee or something nice to eat. The sight of the old Venetian houses precariously perched on the ancient city walls thrilled her. You'd wonder how they didn't fall off as they looked down onto the harbour! And what about the beautiful historic mosque? Long since the hub of the harbour and only recently converted into a tourist centre. All the multi-coloured buildings seemed to squash in perfectly together and wrap themselves around the water. A little further out, her eye was once again drawn to the ancient shipping warehouses standing proudly erect, paving the way to the lighthouse. And then in the opposite direction, only a stone's throw away from where they were sitting, a maze of higgledy-piggledy, cobbled alleyways almost hidden from sight. With their exquisite craft shops and amazing restaurants, revealing further delights to anyone who cared to explore. The experience that is Chania, thought Kate lost in her daydreaming. Definitely so much more than the sum of its parts.

Hours had passed. Conversation had flowed. They had all enjoyed the delicious Greek cuisine. With their coffee, their thoughts turned again to the next day and plans for the week ahead. They agreed, in the various groups to do their own thing, using the list of attractions Kate had provided. Anyway, it wasn't as if they wouldn't meet each other, the harbour area was so small, the likelihood of them bumping into each other was very high indeed. They had five days. They would be meeting up again on Friday for Kate's exhibition. They booked the restaurant for the following Saturday night, their last dinner in Chania. And Kate warned everybody, to stay away from the exhibition space. She wanted no spies, she laughed.

She planned to be busy for the week. She had her paintings to organise, her catalogues to print off, and her opening speech to think about. And she needed to contact Yiannis. She didn't know when he would like to start hanging her paintings.

Tired but happy, they said their goodnights and headed off to their various hostelries with Kate, Jane, Molly, David and Jack the only ones staying out at her house. It had been a very long day.

Immediately after breakfast the next day, a nervous Kate rang Yiannis. Exhibition fever had started to kick in and she could feel the start of butterflies in her stomach. Friday night, she thought nervously as she punched out his number. When she reached him, he was away in the south of the island finishing off some job. He apologised as he had intended to be back that day and meet up with her. But as sometimes happened with him, the job he was on was taking longer than planned and he wouldn't be back until the following evening. He assured her the paintings were as perfect as when she had left them. "Fully dry and still looking spectacular," he laughed. God, she hoped so…

They arranged to meet on Wednesday at the exhibition centre, to discuss and plan everything then. After the initial disappointment of not getting to see her paintings that day, she realised that it suddenly afforded her a bit of breathing space. She hadn't expected to be so free, and with Molly, David, Jane and Jack gone off somewhere together, Kate was able to spend a pleasant day relaxing around the harbour with her friends. They chilled in one of the many cafés, walked the port, and used the extra time for a bit of retail therapy, just for good measure.

Before she knew it, it was Wednesday. Kate was hugely excited as she set off for the city once again. Driving the busy streets of the new town, she passed the bus station, and continued towards the old market building. Driving by the ancient Venetian walls, she tried as best she could to manoeuvre the car through crazy city traffic and on to the port. It was a skill in itself to drive anywhere on Crete, not to mention the manic city traffic of Chania. Kate exhaled, as she entered the cobbled courtyard, and parked directly outside the Exhibition Centre.

In Venetian times, The Exhibition Centre had been an old shipyard building constructed from beautifully cut stone. Only now it was skilfully restored and used as the perfect space for all types of exhibitions in the city.

When Kate cut the engine, there was a ferocious racket going on outside. Somewhere nearby, a dog was barking furiously. As she got out of the car, she spotted Yiannis striding out of the building in front of her, with a puzzled look on his face. She saw his jeep, saw Zorba and then put it all together exactly at the same moment as Yiannis did. Zorba had spotted Kate before she saw him. He was going mad – barking, wagging his tail and trying to free himself to get to her. Yiannis shook his head and grinned as they both arrived at his jeep together, greeting each other warmly in traditional Greek style.

"Yiannis, how are you?" Kate smiled at him as they kissed on both cheeks.

"I'm good but you'd better greet your number one fan, whatever else you do," he laughed nodding towards Zorba.

"Zorba," she called, going to him. He was so happy to see her, licking her hands, wagging his tail and yelping excitedly as she wrapped her arms around his neck and hugged him tightly, thrilled to see him again. It looked as if he was still as devoted and loyal to her as he had been in the summer. She hadn't seen Yiannis since August when he left for Athens. He looks well, she thought, tanned and relaxed. Even though they had spoken at length on the phone a few days before they stayed a while outside, making small talk, catching up on all the news allowing Kate to fuss over Zorba.

When things calmed down, they went inside to view the exhibition space and discuss how they might proceed. Kate was feeling a little off, with a considerable knot in her stomach. She was beginning to get really keyed up. She was disappointed when she saw that Yiannis hadn't brought any of the paintings with him. She had been dying to see them, touch them and feel them all over again. They were her babies after all. And as if he could read her mind, Yiannis explained that he had wanted to meet her first and talk things through if that was ok with her without the distraction of the paintings.

"Kate, I thought it better not to bring them today. There is so much to talk about. Maybe it wasn't such a good idea. I can see you're disappointed. I can always go back and get them…"

"No don't be crazy, Yiannis," gushed Kate, a little embarrassed her expression had given away so much. "I think I expected them to be here, that's all. I know we have lots to talk about."

So, they wandered around the space, discussing how many and which ones would fit where. Yiannis surprised her as he seemed nearly as familiar with the paintings as she was. They talked about how he would hang them, the lighting for the night and how to maximise that. He planned to start hanging the next day, Thursday and finish Friday.

As they were walking and talking, Kate was delighted at how good and professional he seemed. And his attention to detail was excellent. He was most definitely the right man for the job.

After a while, Isabella, her contact on the municipal arts council, wandered in. With her it was all about the logistics of the night. The format it would take. Publicity. The serving of the wine and *mezes*. The invitations, etc. Kate showed her the catalogues and price lists she had printed and took her aside to have a quiet word.

"Look, if Yiannis shows any interest in any of the paintings, please don't take any money from him," Kate explained. "I used his house for painting in the summer and I owe him big time." She circled Nikos' painting in the catalogue and asked her to put a red sticker on it. Other than that, she had no requests. Isabella assured her she would do her very best about everything. So, with business out of the way, a quick check on Zorba, the three of them went for a coffee in the adjoining café. And after a couple of hours they said their goodbyes, agreeing to meet up the following morning for the real work.

As she drove home, Kate felt both excited and a bit keyed up. She felt very much on the countdown now. It was still light. As soon as she got home, armed with pen and paper, she walked to the beach on her own, to have a go at composing her opening speech. Sitting on the promenade looking to the beautiful scenery in front of her for inspiration, Kate grew steadily more and more frustrated as she tried and failed to put clever words onto the page and write the perfect speech. She soon gave up, and as she mulled it over in her head, she realised she knew in her heart of hearts what she wanted to say. And that's exactly what she'd do, speak from the heart. She'd wing it and trust that with a bit of luck it would all come out all right on the night.

Thursday arrived. Kate made the same journey she had made the previous few days. She could hardly contain herself. This was the day the majority of the work was scheduled. The physical work would be up to Yiannis of course. Kate's job would be to express preferences about where she wanted her paintings to go, and which ones she wanted together. Although, totally trusting his opinion, knowing full well he could do the whole thing perfectly without her as he had two years ago. She still wanted and needed to be there, to have the final say – as any artist would.

The exhibition nerves were back again in full force.

When Kate first walked into the room that day and saw all her paintings neatly stacked in the laths, she felt goosebumps break out all over her body and the hairs stand up on the back of her neck.

"Oh my God! It's all happening," she declared excitedly. "Only a little more than twenty-four hours to go!"

"Yes, Kate, it's all happening," Yiannis looked at her. "They look pretty great all together, don't you think? But we'd better get going. We have a lot to do."

The two of them soon fell into an easy rhythm working together. It was a slow, painstaking and time-consuming job. There was no way you could rush it. Work was interspersed by general chit chat about their respective lives and a few laughs thrown in for good measure. Yiannis was extremely patient and thorough at his job, especially as Kate ended up changing her mind numerous times about the same painting. He was so relaxed he made it very easy to work with him.

It was almost a meditation watching him as he carefully and expertly placed the paintings into position. Then he would measure, stand back to check with the naked eye. And then he would repeat the same thing, over and over again for each painting, occasionally making a slight adjustment before he was satisfied. Some of the paintings naturally seemed to fall into smaller sub-groups. And then some demanded to stand out on their own. Kate followed Yiannis around, placing the special calligraphed titles she had made for all forty of her paintings. They broke for lunch when they had fifteen complete. Isabella, who was popping in and out all morning, joined them. It must have been the first time ever for Kate not to have a long leisurely lunch in Crete. And definitely no wine, they were back to business almost immediately. There was too much to be done. In the afternoon they finally got another fifteen finished and decided to call it a day. Yiannis and Kate agreeing to come in even earlier on Friday morning to finish the last ten.

Funnily, when Kate was back at home she noticed her nervousness and anxiety seemed to dissipate away from Chania and the exhibition area. She was very relaxed that evening, back at the house. Not a bit anxious, just terribly excited. They all turned in early that night, acutely aware of the hectic day ahead.

Friday dawned bright and clear and Kate was up first, long before anyone else. She sat on the patio hugging her knees to herself excitedly and thinking what a special day it would be. Her first solo exhibition in a foreign country and not just any foreign country, her favourite foreign country! She wanted to savour every single moment of the day. She set off down to the beach for some alone time before anyone else stirred. Sitting by the sea, she watched in a trance as the waves crashed to shore. Looking over at the beautiful peninsula she made a silent prayer of thanks to all the people who were in Crete, helping her and supporting her. She thanked Paul, for in some strange way facilitating the exhibition. It didn't hurt anymore to think about him. Actually, for a while now, she had noticed that whenever she did think about him, she would smile at the memory of the good times they had together and feel grateful for what they had shared. Life was definitely good and hopefully about to get better that night with a successful exhibition!! Happy and content she set off to Chania one more time. She was glad to be there first, even before Yiannis or Isabella. Delighted for the chance to enjoy a few minutes in the peaceful harbour.

"It must be my day for quiet reflective moments," she smiled to herself, "until tonight hopefully." She crossed her fingers

The city was very quiet, deserted even. She had never been there so early in the morning before and calmly observed the harbour slowly starting to come to life. She had gotten so used to being on her own, she reflected, had come so far from the dark times when she had hated being alone. Now she could honestly say she loved her own company.

A few minutes later Yiannis pulled in, putting an end to her quiet musings and without delay they started hanging the paintings straight away. Almost immediately Kate's stomach started with butterflies and cartwheels at full throttle. Once more they fell into an easy rhythm together, matching paintings and titles on the walls totally absorbed in their work.

They were about halfway through when Yiannis casually said to her, "Kate, remember when you asked if I could think of anything you could do in exchange for your time spent painting at the stone cottage in August?"

"Yes, sure." Kate stopped what she was doing. She was all ears now, looking at him expectantly.

"What about dinner when all this is over?" and he gestured to all the paintings.

"Oh!" she said taken aback. She thought he was going to say he liked one of the paintings. How self-centred is that? she quietly laughed at herself. "Oh, ok yes," she started to answer. And then as if having a rethink, "No. No. No way…"

Yiannis raised his eyebrows and looked amusedly at her. But Kate quickly continued on. "I mean yes to the dinner. I'd love to take you to dinner, but it would never be enough to thank you for all you've done."

"Look, let's have dinner first and then we can talk about that? When would suit you?" he asked with unusual directness.

"Well, they'll all be gone on flights Sunday, so I suppose any time after that." Kate had booked herself to go home a week after everyone else. She had hoped to be around to wrap things up regarding the exhibition and also to shut down the house for the winter. She didn't see herself being back before next Easter. And she still had a few bills and things to settle so the extra week had seemed like a good option.

"What about Sunday night?" Yiannis suggested

"Perfect," replied Kate, "and don't forget I'm paying!"

"As if!" he laughed.

They continued working amicably together.

By lunch time, it was all done. Paintings hung, with titles in place underneath. Catalogues stacked for the night. Wine glasses out and wine stored in the fridge. Plates ready for the *mezes*.

Kate felt very emotional as she stood back and took in the intensely colourful, finished room.

"My God," she whispered. "A year in the pipeline. Two months painting. And an ocean of emotions released..."

The room looked awesome. A sea of colour and vibrancy surrounded them.

It was almost unbelievable, Kate thought. These were all her paintings. A mix of emotions assaulted her all at once. Pride and joy and gratitude. She almost felt overwhelmed.

"My cup runneth over," she whispered to no-one in particular as a single tear ran down her face.

When she thought of the turns her life had taken over the last two years. How everything had changed and then changed again. Once again, Kate quietly marvelled at the resilience of the human spirit.

"Wow! It's amazing, Kate!" Yiannis interrupted her thoughts and put his arm around her shoulder, in a show of support.

"Life is amazing," replied Kate shaking her head in wonder.

Isabella wandered in just then.

"Oh my God Kate... it's so beautiful! So vibrant!" And she stood at the other side of her, putting another arm over her shoulder. And the three of them stood there for a minute or two in silence, admiring – each lost in their own thoughts.

Yiannis left first wishing her well for the night ahead. Kate stayed behind with Isabella, to have one final run through. To ensure things ran as smoothly as possible and they left together about twenty minutes later.

Once back at the house, it was all systems go then. A quick bite to eat, showers all round and then the real drama of getting ready. Hair, make-up and deciding what to wear. But of course, Kate knew what she was going to wear. She had forgotten about the dress all week, she had been so busy. But now it was a really nice thought to know she had something she loved and felt good in to wear. By six, the three girls were nearly ready to go, lounging in their dressing gowns, with hair and make-up done. All they had to do was slip into their clothes. She had arranged to meet Isabella at eight, so they were going to leave after seven to allow for traffic. Molly and Jack had bought a bottle of champagne and they popped it on the patio, toasting to a successful and enjoyable exhibition.

Feeling a little giddy from the excitement and the champagne, Kate went to get dressed. Emerging from her bedroom not long afterwards, to a chorus of whistles and wows. She looked stunning! The purple dress was as beautiful as it was the day she had bought it. It sat perfectly on her frame, accentuating her beautiful figure, in a very understated way. David was looking at her in astonishment as if he couldn't quite believe his eyes. He was dumbstruck and when he eventually found his voice all he could say was, "Mam, you look beautiful, but do you think maybe you should wear a shawl or something over it?"

They all laughed, teasing David. Clearly, he wasn't used to seeing his mother looking so 'hot', as Molly put it.

They set off in good spirits, laughing and joking on the drive and it was exactly eight o'clock as they pulled into the harbour car park in Chania. Isabella was there ahead of them, so Kate disappeared straight away. The others lingered a few paces behind, admiring the boats moored beside the centre, seeing as Kate had forbidden them to be anywhere nearby all week. When they arrived in, they all walked around the room in astonished silence, admiring as they went.

Molly kept saying, "Mam. Oh my god Mam, it's incredible."

David just as supportive, "Jesus Mam, they're class!"

Jane and Jack were equally admiring.

So, all six of them, were there together for a short while. Like the proverbial calm before the storm. But soon it was after nine and people had started to wander in, bit by bit. Her Irish friends were first, as it turned out. She got so many compliments on both the paintings, and her dress. Pretty soon the place was buzzing with the sound of excited chatter and glasses clinking. Kate was caught up in the whirl of it all. Mainly wishing for her Irish and Greek friends to mix. But they nearly all knew each other from previous trips here so that wasn't a problem. Kate felt quite giddy with the excitement of the whole evening. High on adrenaline. It was going perfectly. She was chatting away to her friends, when all of a sudden, her friend Aoife whispered quietly into her ear, "Jesus Christ, who's your man? He's gorgeous!"

Kate looked up in amused curiosity following Aoife's stare and it took her a few moments to realise that Aoife was referring to Yiannis. He had just come in with Katerina and Nikos and was walking towards her, smiling at something one of them had said. All of a sudden Kate looked at Yiannis as she had never looked at him before.

He was gorgeous, she thought. Typically Greek with his sallow skin, dark brown eyes, black hair and dark jaw. He had a kind, lived in face that comes with maturity and as he smiled his dark eyes twinkled in amusement. He was tall, well over six foot she guessed with a long lean body and looked naturally fit and in good shape. He was mid-forties, she knew that from bits of conversations with him. His hair was a little longer than the tight haircut men often wear and still looked completely black. He carried himself with an easy confidence and had the appearance of one who is very comfortable in his own skin. He was dressed casually in black jeans, and wearing a shirt, a shade somewhere between orange and pink that very few men could wear and carry off. Kate was momentarily flustered and realised with a shock, that she was staring at him, unconsciously of course.

How come she had never noticed it before? All the time they had spent together this past week… Her stomach was in a right knot. And now he was standing in front of her, with Nikos and Katerina, leaning towards her and she was standing there, frozen like a statue! She blushed thanking God he couldn't read her mind.

"Kate," he kissed her, "congratulations! It looks to be going brilliantly."

Quickly, she pulled herself together and beamed at all three of them.

"Hi Yiannis, thank you so much!" She could catch the whiff of his shampoo or something as she kissed him. "Nikos and Katerina, I'm so happy you came." She turned quickly to them, glad of the distraction, greeting them warmly, like the old friends they were. Having regained her composure, she introduced her friends, avoiding Aoife's eyes, and they chatted for a short while until Isabella came and whisked her away. Rescuing her in a way.

And that's how the night evolved. Kate, the artist, meeting and greeting as many people as possible. She was the common denominator, the link between her Greek and Irish friends. She was supposed to work the room. Make sure she met everybody and that they all felt welcome. Thus far, things couldn't be going any better.

Just after ten o'clock, as scheduled, Kate stood up on the step at the back of the room. It was her time to really take the limelight now, however brief. She had decided to officially open the exhibition herself. It wasn't the norm but who else was so familiar with the paintings and the process she had gone through. And of course, the people she needed to thank. The speech would be short and sweet, of that she was sure. She wasn't one for long speeches and egotistical ramblings.

As she surveyed the room, her heart felt full to overflowing at the sight of all her family and friends, Irish and Greek there together.

There was Sophia who had taken a night off, Yiannis, Nikos and Katerina, Costas with his wife Anna and their children, Maria who owned the beach taverna, Dimitri her paint supplier and his friends, the gang from Athens, not to mention her family and friends from Ireland – they were just something else. They were all chatting together, and they had all come for her, to support her. She fondly thought of all the fun times and trips to Crete she had shared with a lot of the people in the room. There were people there she didn't know either, but she had been introduced to every single one. Isabella was a very good networker. She caught Yiannis' eye and he smiled at her and raised his glass silently. She smiled back and shrugged her shoulders as if to say, well, here goes!

Kate clinked her glass a couple of times for quiet. The chatter gradually died down and a hush fell over the room as they all turned to look at her. She cleared her throat and smiled. She spoke clearly, confidently but most importantly from her heart.

"My dear family and friends, it gives me such great pleasure to welcome you all here tonight to the opening of *Letting Go*, an exhibition of forty abstract paintings. The idea for the exhibition came from a challenge I set myself about a year ago and while things were bubbling around in my head since then, the actual painting took place over a period of two months here, in Crete, in July and August. I can honestly say I went through the most turbulent, therapeutic and cleansing period of my life during those two months, as some of you may well know. (She looked directly at Yiannis, half apologetically) The paintings you may think are strangely named but that will give you an idea of what I was going through, at the time of painting.

This exhibition is dedicated to my two amazing children, Molly and David. (Kate touched her heart without thinking and looked lovingly at her two children, who were standing together and clearly chuffed. They had no idea this was her intention.) You are like rocks to me. Thank you for always supporting me. I love you with all my heart.

To my Greek friends, thank you so much for the kindness, friendship and hospitality you have shown to me, my family and friends over the years. Thanks to all the Athens gang who flew in today. Your support is evident by your presence here tonight. Isabella, thank you for organising everything so perfectly and to Yiannis, who opened his studio and his home to me during the summer. You helped me more than you will ever know.

And to all my Irish friends, who made the trip, and to those who couldn't. Thank you from the bottom of my heart, for supporting me always, but most particularly in the last two years. I feel so lucky to be surrounded by such good people here tonight. Thank you for your love and support. Enjoy the paintings everyone. And please raise your glasses to Molly and David and *Letting Go*.

Let the party begin!"

There was a huge round of applause in the room, with some cheers and whistles thrown in. The whole speech had taken less than five minutes. Kate was so relieved. She didn't particularly like speaking in public but if you were on the exhibition circuit like she was, you had to get over that. Actually, relieved was an understatement. Not for the first time she felt like some great weight had been lifted from her. She had a real sense of letting go.

Before she had a moment to let the speech settle, she was enveloped in hugs and kisses and good wishes. Everybody it seemed wanted to meet her again and congratulate her. And the night continued like that,

Isabella was repeatedly introducing her to potential buyers. She had organised for her to do a short radio interview, and also a reporter from the local paper wanted to ask a few questions. Typical Isabella, always thinking of the bottom line – sales. But that was her job and she was very good at it.

Kate's bottom line was light years away from sales. She didn't care if the paintings never sold. All that mattered to her was that all the important people in her life right now, were here in this room, chatting and talking and interacting. It was wonderful. She was the luckiest girl in the world. If she had hoped for a perfect exhibition night, this would definitely be it. She smiled to see her friends Emily, Orla and Marie chatting to Nikos and Katerina. And she was vaguely aware of Molly, David and Jack in deep conversation with Yiannis.

She barely got to meet her oldest friends from Athens before she was whisked away again by Isabella.

The remainder of the evening passed by rapidly and before Kate knew it people had started to drift away until all that was left was the core group of family and friends. They were moving to the taverna next door for more *mezes* and a few post-mortem drinks.

Yiannis, Nikos and Katerina found her to say *Kalinikta*. She pressed them to join the group at the taverna. But they declined. They were calling it a night.

"I'll see you all tomorrow," Yiannis said as he was leaving. Kate looked at him quizzically. "Molly and some others are coming out to see the studio and house. Around five I think?" Trust Molly to wangle herself an invitation, she shook her head, and laughed silently to herself.

Kate didn't sleep much that night. The excitement of the evening was still coursing through her veins. All night long she smiled and quietly laughed to herself as she tossed and turned in bed reliving the minute of the night.

The next day, she rolled out of bed at the last minute, still floating and high on adrenaline! She threw on a pair of black leggings, a long baggy white top, tied her hair up into a loose knot and wandered to the top of the road to catch the bus to Chania. For once she didn't feel like driving. She had arranged to meet the Athens gang for breakfast. They were also her oldest Irish and Greek friends. Before the advent of direct flights from Ireland to Crete, Kate and Paul and whoever was with them had generally travelled to Crete via Athens, combining holidays with a short stay in an ancient historic city.

Years before her distant cousin had married a Greek and settled in Athens so they had always delighted in using the stopover to catch up, enjoy the never-ending hospitality and explore the endless tourist attractions in the city. They had loved being taken to the Acropolis to take in the majestic Parthenon or revel in the architectural brilliance of the new acropolis museum, a profusion of glass floors and walls, housing priceless artefacts. A wander around atmospheric *Plaka* was a must, where artists and street vendors mingled with endless tourists. Kate fondly remembered the cable car rides up Lycabettus Hill for a panoramic view of the city and maybe something to eat. And what was nicer than a relaxing coffee in Syntagma Square to watch the changing of the guard outside the parliament, a place that in recent times seemed to have become synonymous with protests and street demonstrations. They had spent many years and many trips to Athens copper fastening relationships and making friends. No surprise then that she wanted to spend time with her dear friends who had travelled to Chania for one night only.

Kate used the bus journey to the city to blissfully relive the previous night's events again. It had been the best night ever, better than anything she could have imagined for herself. There were quite a few red stickers too! And what about the whole Yiannis thing, she wondered dreamily to herself. Despite the hectic pace of the night she had been acutely aware of him after Aoife had pointed out the obvious, even though she hadn't really been in his company. What was that all about?

Pushing it to the back of her mind, she strolled the short distance from the bus station to the harbour. It was unseasonably warm for the time of year and people were still wandering around in their short sleeves, enjoying the autumn sunshine.

Kate and the gang, as she affectionately liked to call them, spent breakfast rehashing the exhibition and catching up on all the news before they literally had to fly. But they arranged to meet in Athens airport for a short while, the following week when Kate would be passing through, on her way home. Before leaving the harbour, some of the other exhibition goers had started to surface for their morning coffee so she sat a while with them and was back home by four. Chania was definitely a bit like Dublin this week, she thought. You couldn't but run into someone you knew. Thank God she would have the following week to catch up on all the missed sleep, she thought as she yawned.

Three carloads of them turned up at Yiannis' house around five that evening.

"Typical Irish," laughed Kate. "All dying for a gawk."

She couldn't blame them though. She had gone on about the place so much, when she was back in Ireland after the summer. No wonder there were so many takers.

For Kate, it was a joy to be back after two months. It was every bit as beautiful as she remembered. Not so serene and peaceful now with fifteen chattering Irish. And an over-excited Zorba. But the essence of the place was the same. You could feel it. They were all wowed by its magnificence and uniqueness, the contrast of the contemporary living space with the stunning natural beauty had them all speechless. They walked down to the water's edge, up onto the cliff-tops where she used to walk with Zorba. And then Kate showed them the studio and her living space where a lot of the painting had happened. Yiannis seemed surprised when she was showing them where she had worked, ate and slept.

"I thought you ate and slept over in the house?" he looked at her curiously.

"No, I thought it would be more convenient to sleep here," Kate replied, not wanting to go into the ins and outs of not invading his personal space.

Even though she tried not to be, Kate was very conscious of him, all the time they were there. There were lots of butterflies and somersaults in her stomach. She quietly observed as he charmed each and every one of her family and friends. They spent a lovely hour or so at the cottage and in typical Yiannis fashion he insisted they all have something to eat or drink before they left. They all fell a little in love with the place that evening. But they had an arrangement for dinner in Chania later on, which was just as well, Kate really didn't want them to overstay their welcome. Greek kisses all round when they were leaving. Kate had asked Yiannis to join them for dinner, but he refused as she had expected.

"I'll see you tomorrow night. I'll pick you up at eight. Is that ok?"

"Perfect," she replied quietly hoping the others wouldn't overhear. She hadn't said anything about the dinner, hoping to avoid lots of comments and innuendo.

"What's this?" Molly smirked over at her when they were back in the car, on the way home.

"Just a thank you dinner, nothing else, Moll. We arranged it a few days ago. It went out of my head with all that was going on." Why did she sound so defensive? She wondered as she feigned total concentration on driving. She really didn't want to answer any questions.

"Wear the purple dress," was all Molly said in reply.

The dinner in Chania that night, was their last gastronomic experience together for a while. Everyone was nicely tired from all the comings and goings of the week. They had all had a great holiday, agreeing Kate's exhibition was the definite highlight, followed by their visit to the stone cottage.

"Don't forget to put back the clocks tonight!" Kate reminded them all as they said their goodnights. News that was greeted with much enthusiasm. "And for anyone who's interested, some of us are meeting here for a late breakfast/early lunch tomorrow before heading to the airport, say about half past twelve?"

The next day, as it happened, everyone turned up for a light lunch at the harbour and an hour later they were on their way to catch the flight to Athens.

Once again Kate was thinking how blessed she was to have a group of friends like them. They were laughing and slagging her about her dinner with Yiannis. It hadn't stayed a secret for long. She shooed them up the stairs at the airport to security and she nearly died of mortification when the last few of them turned at the top of the stairs and jokingly shouted to her (at the top of their voices of course!) "Wear the purple dress tonight!" The airport was so small, everybody stopped and turned to see what all the commotion was about. Kate turned on her heel and took off out the front door as fast as she could.

"Bitches," she laughed to herself.

Chapter Ten

SEDUCTION

All of a sudden, all her friends and family were gone. Kate was finally and completely on her own, as the airport receded into the distance. After the madness of the past week, the silence was deafening – apart from the sound of her thoughts. Unlike any journey she had ever made before, this drive was one of pleasurable preoccupation. This time her thoughts were firmly and fully on the night ahead, and her impending dinner with Yiannis.

Yiannis, she pondered. How little she knew about him. And yet, on another level, she knew everything she needed to know. He had trusted her with his home and dog for three weeks in the summer. She found him to be kind, thoughtful and charming. He was very easy to work with, interesting, great company and good fun. And now to add to that list, he was incredibly handsome, really gorgeous. You'd think it would have been the first thing she noticed about him, but she hadn't, not until Friday night. And suddenly, he had blasted his way right into her consciousness. Now she was very aware of him…

So, back to tonight, she thought

What should she wear? How should she behave? What if Colette had been right? What if he had been watching her on Friday night? No, Colette always exaggerated. Don't be ridiculous Kate, lots of people were watching you on Friday night. That's what happens at exhibitions.

But did she fancy him?

She liked him, yes… as a friend. But fancy? No, that was ridiculous…

Kate had thought a lot about Yiannis since Friday night. She had been very aware of him the day before, when they all went to the stone cottage. She had watched him out of the corner of her eye the whole time she was there. And in the last twenty-four hours or so, she'd caught herself thinking about him at really odd times. He'd definitely be on her sushi list now (A funny game herself and the girls used to play, taken out of a book by Marian

Keyes) actually he'd probably be at the top of her sushi list. Come to think of it, he'd be the only one on her sushi list! She hadn't been inclined to go down that road much lately. But now, driving back from the airport, she felt this sudden sense of freedom. Here she was, a single woman again after all. And, an interesting, handsome man had asked her out to dinner. Well, she was actually taking him out, but that was beside the point. It was nice to feel in demand, appreciated even. She felt giddy in anticipation of a pleasant evening ahead. The possibility of the possibility!

Mmm, thought Kate, what am I like? A teenager going out on a first date. Oh God, it's not a date. It's just dinner. I'm passing myself out here... She hadn't thought like this for years. She felt quite giddy and light-headed. I need to calm down and ground myself, she thought frantically. The entire journey passed like this. Kate in a world of her own lost in thought, conversing with herself the whole way home. She saw no landmarks on this journey. She most definitely had other things on her mind!

Once back at base, Kate did calm down – eventually and with great difficulty. A yoga session and before she knew it a good hour had passed and she felt half normal again. But she found it so hard to stop her mind from wandering and wondering...

A quick check of the mobile told her there was still plenty of time to get ready. So, she luxuriated in a long lavender bath. Followed that with an invigorating shower to wash her hair. Then she indulged her body with all the lotions and potions she had treated herself to in Chania. By the time she was finished, her golden tanned skin was so soft and smelled so divine she felt quite decadent. She dressed too with great care. Applied a little eyeliner and some lip-gloss and by seven thirty, she was ready to go, purple dress and all.

Well why not? All the girls thought she should.

She laughed out loud when she thought of them shouting at her in the airport and she realised she felt good! Really good!

Maybe a glass of wine, Kate thought and then decided against it. A glass of water would be fine. She settled on the patio with her drink and breathed in the night air. It was a balmy evening but dark since about five thirty or so. The bright evenings were long gone, so she lit a candle on the table and settled down to wait. There were no sights or sounds of life coming from any of the other houses. She seemed to be the only one around. Time passed slowly, as she sipped her water, idly wondering what the night might hold for her. A nice pleasant evening of good food, good company, interesting conversation, relaxed atmosphere. And yet she had gotten herself ready as if she were going out on a date. All those sensuous creams massaged into her body. Kate was confused. Her mind was confused but her body seemed to know exactly what it wanted. Did she want it to be a date? Was she ready? It was so nice to feel like a woman. And that's how she was feeling, like a woman... God it was well over two years since she had even thought like this. How come she hadn't thought like this last week? She had spent enjoyable days with him in Chania and never once thought of him in that way. What was happening to her?

At eight o'clock Kate got a little fidgety.

No sign of him. Breathe Kate, she reminded herself. Breathe!

Five past... ten past... still no sign...

Just as she was about to have that glass of wine, she heard a dog bark and a knock at the door.

And there he was, casually dressed in his denims and short sleeved shirt, smiling at her looking all male and gorgeous. His hair a little tousled and still damp from the shower she guessed. And her stomach did a flip.

Breathe, she thought. "Hi Yiannis," she got the musky scent of him as she greeted him with the usual kisses, fleetingly tempted to reach out and fix his hair.

"Sorry I'm late, Kate. Wow! You look great." He took her in, in one long look.

"Hey Zorba," she rubbed him to try and distract herself as he licked her hand. "Do you always bring him with you, wherever you go?" she continued out of genuine curiosity. Rarely had she seen such a close bond between man and beast.

"He generally comes with me to work," Yiannis looked at him good-humouredly, "but I usually leave him at home when I'm going to meet someone. For some reason, tonight he was waiting for me at the jeep. I think he knew I was coming to collect you!"

"Really! What a clever dog!" Kate smiled briefly wondering about the other someone Yiannis could be going to meet. And Zorba licked her hand again, excited to see her.

"Yes," laughed Yiannis, "he has good taste."

"So, where am I taking you?" she grinned at him.

"How about a little fish restaurant I know in the village?" he suggested.

"Perfect." She was glad he hadn't said Chania. For this one night, much as she loved the beautiful city, she had travelled that road so often in the past week, she needed a break from it.

Fifteen minutes later Yiannis parked the jeep near the tiny harbour in the small sleepy fishing village. They strolled down a narrow-cobbled alley-way, to the fish taverna, set right on the seafront. As they emerged from the alley, you could smell the sea air and hear the waves crashing to shore. It was a beautiful mild and humid night at the end of October and candles were flickering atmospherically on tables all around the restaurant. A full moon illuminated a glittering pathway across the sea. It was a clear starry night and the dark inky Aegean provided the backdrop. What a location, Kate thought.

"Wow! It's beautiful Yiannis!" was all she could say, very aware that you couldn't have ordered a more stunning or more romantic setting if you had tried. The beauty of Crete would never cease to amaze her.

Yiannis waved to someone inside the restaurant and then turned his attention to Kate.

"You seem different somehow tonight, Kate," he volunteered as he studied her carefully. He was perceptive.

"Really?" She half ignored his comment and smiled at him. He was right on the button though. She felt different, very different… Breathe! The seafront was busy with the last of the tourists out and about, making the most of the favourable weather.

"Inside or out?" He asked

"Definitely out," Kate replied, "if it gets chilly we can move in. It's too beautiful to sit inside."

They started the night with a jug of house wine at a table on the seafront, with unrestricted views of the bay and the moonlit night. Conversation flowed easily between them as it had for the past week. All Kate's earlier nerves evaporated as they chatted about this and that, mainly the exhibition, her friends and family, all now gone home. She filled him in on her connections with them all, right down to her massage therapist, Mary. He had met and charmed each and every one over the weekend. Very gently, he asked her about Paul. Truthfully, she was able to tell him how difficult it had been, (not the whole lot of it, of course!) and how she thought the painting trip to Crete had been part of some grand plan, something orchestrated by the universe to nudge her along. How she had found the summer so therapeutic in hindsight.

"Actually, Yiannis I know this sounds a bit weird, but I think the exhibition was somehow about letting go of it all. Friday night I felt like some weight had been lifted from me. I can think about my marriage now without being emotional or sad or guilty. I focus on the good times we had and I'm grateful for that. Look at Molly and David. I'm so proud of them and I know he would be too…"

He squeezed her hand lightly.

Jesus, she hoped that didn't sound a bit too much.

He entertained her then telling her about his former life in Athens. All the interesting places he had travelled to. It was amazing how he could make buildings and architecture sound fascinating and fun. Kate could tell from the way he spoke he was very passionate about it all. They were so engrossed in conversation; the waiter had come twice already, and they still weren't ready to order. The third time they decided to share lots of starters. Kate ordered orange juice and water to drink, that first glass of wine on an empty stomach had made her head feel a bit fuzzy. And she really wanted to keep a clear head.

Sitting in close proximity to Yiannis, for so long made her extremely aware of him, of his physical presence. She could almost feel the body heat emanating from him and she could definitely get the musky male scent of him. He was very tanned, and she noticed how the muscles moved in his arms as he spoke and gestured. Black hairs were visible near the top of his chest where his shirt buttoned. She absent-mindedly wondered if all his chest hair was as black as the hair on his head. When he looked at her, his eyes drew her in, almost hypnotising her, they were so dark and intense, like black velvet. Her mind had momentarily wandered, she gently chastised herself as she tried hard to focus on what he was saying.

The exhibition. He was talking about the exhibition.

Kate tried again to find out how much she owed him for hanging the exhibition. No joy. He just wouldn't tell her.

Kate found it so frustrating and said as much. "Yiannis, I'd prefer if you'd tell me what I owe. I don't like to have bills."

"But you don't have bills, Kate. I was happy to do it for you. I couldn't possibly charge you. You looked after Zorba for me in the summer. Accept it as a gift."

"A gift! Don't be crazy," Kate replied indignantly. "Look Yiannis, Zorba aside, I'm still trying to pay you back for the three beautiful weeks at your home. Sure that was what tonight and this dinner is about."

"Is that what it's about?" he smiled at her intently. His question was loaded, and he was watching her closely.

And there was a brief moment between them. She didn't quite know what to say. She didn't quite know what he meant, but she suspected.

'Thank God!' thought Kate, as the food arrived the very next moment, and the mood and the subject changed.

Hours passed as they shared a salad, grilled fish of the day and French fries along with the old reliable *tzatziki* for dipping their bread. There was something intimate about sharing food from the same plate as him. They continued to converse easily into the night albeit about safe subjects. But all too soon it was after one and when Kate finally looked around, they were the last two in the restaurant. She didn't want the night to end, but out of the corner of her eye, she saw the owner hovering at the bar.

"I'll get the bill," she volunteered reluctantly, as she signalled to him.

The owner chatted to Yiannis in Greek as he handed Kate the bill. They clearly knew each other. Kate could only understand a few words of the conversation. But typical of Yiannis, he reverted to English and introduced Kate to Stavros, the owner and an old school friend of his.

When Stavros was gone, Kate laughed out loud when she read the bill.

"Oh my God, Yiannis! Look, I know it's rude to talk about money, especially when I'm paying but do you know how much the bill is… for all the food we ate? And drinks? Thirty euro!" she continued. "Can you believe it? Jesus, I'd have to take you out for a whole month to put any dent into what I owe you."

Kate left forty euro on the table and they got up to leave calling out, "*Kalinikta*."

Yiannis put his hand lightly on her back as he steered her back out the alleyway.

'Christ…' thought Kate as she felt waves of heat pulsating downwards from where his hand lay.

He stopped halfway down the alley, turning to her as if a thought had just occurred to him, his eyes twinkling in amusement.

"Maybe that's not such a bad idea Kate. What do you think? Dinner for a week while you're here. How about it? I'll let you off the other three weeks. But I'd have to take my turn paying of course. Or maybe you have other plans?"

It took her a moment to twig that he was referring to her joke about the bill. Was he teasing or serious? Kate couldn't be sure.

She stopped dead in her tracks and looked at him, stunned into silence. She opened her mouth to speak and then closed it.

Dinner every night with Yiannis. Could she handle that? Of course she could, and she heard herself saying. "I'd love that, but I'd insist on paying or no deal." And as they continued back to the jeep, they jokingly argued over and back, about who would pay for all the meals. She still wasn't sure if he was serious or not. The only other plans she had for the week were a bit of tidying, a catch up on some much-needed sleep, and some financial things she had to attend to. She could easily fit dinner in around those.

At the jeep, poor devoted Zorba had sat patiently for almost five hours.

"Hey Zorba, time to go home I think," Kate patted him dreamily on the head.

"Actually Kate, there is something I'd really like to show you first. If you don't mind?" Yiannis suggested. "I would love you to see it. It's the perfect night for it and it won't take long, I promise."

Her curiosity was immediately aroused. "Of course," she agreed. Anything to prolong the night just a little longer.

Yiannis drove the jeep less than a minute away from the harbour, uphill towards his own place and then stopped suddenly at the side of the road. He hopped out, came over to her door, and took her by the hand.

"Mind your step."

His hand felt strong and solid around hers and it made her stomach do somersaults and cartwheels. His long fingers wrapped around hers and she could feel where there were tiny cuts and small calluses on his skin, probably from his work. Quite randomly an image of him placing the paintings for the exhibition popped into her head.

Yiannis led her in a large doorway at the side of the road and it took a few moments for her eyes to adjust to the night light. The first thing that struck her was the incredible tranquillity and stillness of wherever they were. The moon was high in the sky and as they emerged from underneath some kind of small shelter or building, she could quite quickly make out large dark shapes. Silhouettes of buildings she guessed. It seemed as if they were in some kind of courtyard because she could make out a wall around the edges with a smaller structure in the centre.

She looked at him curiously.

"Welcome to my new project," he smiled at her. "It's an old orthodox monastery. I intend to renovate it. Look there's the little church in the centre." She followed his arm as he pointed to a building in the middle. "And do you see, out at the side, set back against the wall – that's where the monks used to live." He was clearly passionate about it; she could hear it in his voice. "I haven't decided what I'm going to do with it yet. And you haven't seen the best bit!" He gripped her hand more tightly and led her all the way to the back of the courtyard, and out through a tiny doorway.

As they passed through the door, Kate caught her breath at the vista that was laid out before her. They were sky-high, perched on a cliff edge, or on some type of walled in veranda. Far down below in the distance she could hear the waves crashing against the bottom of the cliffs. It may have been dark, but the lights of the fishing village were just down from them, to the right. She thought she could even make out the restaurant where they had just been eating. But unsurprisingly her eye was drawn straight out in front. As far as the eye could see, the Aegean Sea by night and the lights of all the towns towards Chania twinkling, far off in the distance. An intensely starry night in the country. No city lights to detract. And if that wasn't enough, the full moon dominated the whole scene, sitting majestically in the sky, its reflection shimmering on the ocean making everything appear even more beautiful. It was truly breath-taking! Like her own private viewing of Crete by night. She felt she could almost reach out and touch the sky.

"My God Yiannis, it's magnificent," Kate whispered.

Humbled by the beauty that surrounded them, they both stood there, for what seemed like an age, not speaking, neither of them wanting to break the spell. Each lost in thought and yet fully aware of the other.

She could sense him just behind her. She could hear him quietly breathing. Eventually, it was Yiannis who broke the silence. Moving to stand in front of her, he looked her directly in the eye, and as if wrestling with a thought, said, "Ok, will I take you home now or would you like to come back to my house?"

Seconds passed…

There was no mistaking what he was asking, what his intention was. In that one question he had changed the whole night, while at the same time giving her a way out if she wanted it.

Kate stared back at him, holding his eyes with hers. Without hesitating, she said very softly, "I'd like to go to your house." And now there was no mistaking hers either.

He leaned over to her and kissed her very gently on the mouth.

Closing her eyes, she kissed him back, her whole body responding, goose bumps and stomach flips. God, he felt and tasted so nice, she thought, a mix of wine and mint. And there was that faint musky smell again. Breathe Kate…

He took her by the hand again and led her back out to the jeep, Zorba following.

They drove more or less in silence back to Yiannis' house. Every now and again he'd look over at her and smile, as if checking to see she was all right. Kate breathed down into her stomach for the short journey, appearing to remain unbelievably calm. She was anything but. Inside, her stomach was in a knot and her heart racing in anticipation. What was it she had said to herself earlier? Be in the present moment and let the night unfold. That's exactly what she was doing or trying to do.

Yiannis let Kate into the cottage and went to sort Zorba when they got back to the cottage. She stood alone in the kitchen for a few moments, her back to the sink, all of a sudden feeling shy and not quite sure what to do with her hands. The cottage was in total darkness, but the full moon was like subtle background lighting, shining in all the windows. Kate's body was on high alert now. Every nerve end was tingling, and adrenaline coursed through her veins in expectation, so much so, that when Yiannis came back into the room a couple of minutes later, she jumped.

"Are you sure?" he gently questioned her as he came to stand in front of her and took her hands.

She was never surer of anything. "Positive." She smiled at him. "It's just that," she attempted to tell him, "You know…"

"This is the first time since your husband," he volunteered his eyes full of understanding.

"Yes," she smiled at him. Of course, he had guessed.

And Kate closed her eyes as he kissed her hand so softly and so tenderly, she thought she'd imagined it. He kissed her other hand just as gently. Then her wrists. First one, then the other. When he kissed the side of her neck, her heart was thumping wildly in her chest. He was so close to her, she could smell his hair and feel his heart beating in rhythm with her own. There was no way Kate could move even if she had wanted to. She was enjoying every sensation surging through her. Her physical body taking over, and quietly surrendering to his kisses and caresses. Yiannis moved so subtly, she held her breath a part of her afraid that he might stop.

"Relax Kate," he whispered, perfectly in tune with her. Every movement he made was slow and deliberate. Kate leaned her body fully into his, wrapping her arms around his neck, kissing him back deeply with great longing. Their hands moved over each other, gently exploring. They were so close together, Kate could feel every bit of him against her. Goosebumps erupted all over her body again and she thought she would die with the feelings of pleasure that were coursing through her.

Finally, after what seemed like an eternity, he took her hand and slowly led her to his bedroom and his bed. Kate's limbs were weak with desire and she followed him as if in a trance. Slowly, slowly they undressed one another, quietly marvelling at the beauty of the human body. She loved the sensation of lying naked beside him, of their hands and lips touching and feeling each other, of his coarse chest hair rubbing against her soft breasts and his strong arms holding her. Bodies entwined, they were as close as two humans can get. Their lovemaking seemed to go on and on. Each instinctively knowing what the other wanted, communicating at some deep soul level. They moved together in perfect rhythm. The only sound, soft moans of pleasure and when they both climaxed, there was no need for words. There was nothing to say. Their bodies had said it all.

Kate, all at once felt physically drained and recharged. Her body felt sensuous and deliciously pleasured and she fell into a light sleep almost instantly, one arm across his stomach thinking what an amazing night it had been.

Yiannis held Kate in his arms thinking, What a great night! He couldn't remember the last time he had connected with someone at such a deep level. He gazed at her, until he too finally succumbed to a light sleep.

Chapter Eleven

SWEET NOVEMBER

Kate finally fell into a deep sleep, so peacefully and soundly that she never heard Yiannis get up. She didn't move when he lifted her arm from across his body. And she only barely stirred when he touched her cheek before he left the room.

When she eventually did wake, she stretched luxuriously, feeling as if every part of her body, inside and out, was smiling. It took her a few seconds to recall where she was.

In the stone cottage.

And what had happened.

A sense of pleasure and contentment washed over her. Without looking, she instinctively knew he wasn't beside her. And she was glad. It gave her a chance, to come to terms with what had happened the night before. The very thought of it now, brought goose bumps out all over her body and she smiled to herself again. What an incredible night they had! And what an amazing lover he was, considerate, so considerate. Every second of the night was well and truly hardwired into her brain and she felt herself blush when she thought about what they had shared. In the very next moment, she thought about Paul, and how he had been the last person she had made love to... but it was ok. A little bit of her felt guilty but she was also resigned now to the fact that he would never be a part of her life again.

Letting go and moving on, was what it was all about. Sleeping with another man was a sure sign she was moving on with her life.

Kate sighed as much in acceptance as in contentment. She went to retrieve her clothes and as she headed towards the shower she wondered dreamily to herself was this what they called a one-night stand?

She had never been in Yiannis' bathroom before but there were clean towels, toiletries and a new toothbrush left out – she presumed for her use.

He was obviously well used to this, she smiled half in amusement.

Kate loved the sensation of the warm water coursing over her body, en-hancing this new feeling of sensuousness emanating from her. She brushed her hair and teeth, and put on her clothes from the previous night, feeling a little overdressed in the purple lace creation. It was time to go find Yiannis to get a lift home. In a way she was stranded, no car. She hadn't thought about that the night before and she hoped there would be no awkwardness between them.

'How will it all play out?' she wondered a little uncertainly.

She really didn't know what to expect, having never been in the situation before. Truth be told, even though she was naturally affectionate, Kate had led a very protected life up until Paul died. A child of the sixties, she grew up through seventies and eighties Ireland. She married young, had two children very quickly and had slept with the same man for over twenty years. And she, like many others her age hadn't escaped the conditioning of her Irish Catholic upbringing. Of how things should or shouldn't be. A product of her environment as it were. So, being single in her forties was a sea change for her. The old conditioning was long gone of course but being with Yian-nis the night before was a whole new experience for Kate. One she wasn't quite sure how to handle.

As if on cue, Kate heard Zorba barking somewhere outside. From her vantage point she could see they were both on the beach so she called out the window, "*Kalimera.*"

Yiannis waved back and headed towards the house, Zorba bounding ahead. They met in the kitchen, Yiannis looked every bit as gorgeous as he had the night before.

"Good Morning," she greeted him as she petted Zorba gently.

"Not exactly morning," Yiannis shook his head and grinned at her. "It's four o'clock," and he leaned over and kissed her lightly on the cheek.

"Four in the afternoon!" Kate almost shrieked, "I must have slept four-teen hours!" Somewhere in her brain she logged the kiss and touched her cheek without thinking.

"A little less I would say," smiled Yiannis, a flicker of amusement in his eyes.

She blushed. Jesus, he was cool with the whole thing.

"Are you hungry, Kate?"

"Ravenous."

"Good, I got a few things from the bakery or I have oranges? Coffee, orange juice?" Yiannis asked. "Or a little yogurt and honey? What would you like?"

"Juice would be perfect," Kate smiled shyly at him.

And just like that, he went off and busied himself making the juice.

"Yiannis, have you a t-shirt I could borrow? I'm a bit overdressed for breakfast," she asked gesturing to the purple dress. The genius of Kate's lovely lace dress may have been that it could take her from 'exhibition first nights' to casual tavernas but morning-after breakfast was probably stretching it a bit.

"I'm not complaining," he grinned taking her all in, toying with her, but as if sensing her awkwardness, he said, "Look in one of the drawers," and he pointed towards the bedroom.

She went to look for a t-shirt, glad of something to do, however small. Her mind had switched to overdrive. He was acting totally normally, with some flirting thrown in and Kate was now feeling ever so slightly embarrassed in unfamiliar territory.

'Last night was wonderful, no, much better than wonderful. In fact, last night was amazing,' she thought, but now she was at his house, with no car, and dependant on him to get back to her own place.

Kate may have become very self-sufficient over the past couple of years and grown so used to fending for herself and to her own company that the thought of relying on a man for anything was almost alien to her. Unfortunately for her though, her personal growth had neglected the realities of new sexual relationships. Truthfully, she was feeling exactly as she had the night before, finding him totally irresistible. And while not wishing to put an end to their time together, she felt the need to put space between them. Get back to base as it were. It was difficult to think straight around him, especially with all the innuendo going on.

"Yiannis, I guess I really need to get home, change my clothes. Could you run me back to my house anytime soon?" Kate blurted more sharply than she intended, as she emerged from the bedroom looking a little silly with a t- shirt of his over her dress.

"Now, or after breakfast?" he looked at her quizzically sensing the sudden change in mood.

"Whatever suits…"

"And what about dinner tonight? Are you still happy for us to have dinner together?" he continued, his eyes studying her carefully now.

"Dinner…" she hesitated, "Yes, dinner would be great. I just need to clean up a bit." (Jesus. She had just gotten out of the shower!) And she had forgotten all about the dinners for the week joke, with all that had transpired between them. He clearly hadn't.

"Is everything ok?"

"Yiannis, you can probably tell, I'm really not good at this kind of stuff. I don't know what morning-after etiquette is. And, I'm finding it hard to think straight." She left out around you. "I just need my own space."

Yiannis stopped what he was doing. He walked over to her, shrugged his shoulders in that typically casual way and looked her in the eye.

"Whatever you like, Kate. I'm not sure what morning-after etiquette is either. But I do know I had a great time last night and I would like to do it again – the dinner that is. We're adults, Kate, and friends, I hope. We make our own decisions. Don't take it too seriously. Relax a little. Why don't I take you home and you decide what you want? If you want to have dinner again tonight, just drive back later and we'll take it from there."

Jesus I'm after making a right mess of this, she thought to herself. He had put it so well. She agreed with everything he said but his presence was a distraction to her. He was comfortable, she wasn't. Simple as that. She had a strong urge to run. Some little voice somewhere was telling her to take time out, to think. So that's what she'd do.

"Yeah that sounds like a plan," she smiled back, not committing to anything.

Without breakfast, they left for Kate's.

In the confines of his jeep, you couldn't but be acutely aware of him again, his arm on the gearstick, the scent of him, the faint smell of shampoo and the good-natured background chatter. When they reached her house, she jumped out of the jeep, calling over her shoulder as she ran up the steps, "I'll ring you later!"

Once home, Kate leaned against the door and let out a long, relieved sigh as she listened to the sound of his jeep receding into the distance.

Whew! What a night!

She sat on the veranda as daylight quietly changed to dusk, mulling things over in her head. Now she felt clear and calm again. Now that he was gone, and she was in her own space.

'Where had all this come from?' she puzzled. A week ago he was barely in her consciousness. She had liked working with him and they had spent three enjoyable days in the city hanging her exhibition. But since the exhibition it seemed as if he was camped inside her head. She was totally out of her comfort zone. It had to be a reaction to her solo existence for the last two years she thought. For as long as Kate could remember, she had constantly had a man in her life, mainly Paul, apart from a few flings during the college years. She had always enjoyed male attention, the flirtations, the intimacy. Then when he died, nothing for over two years – until last night.

'It had to be a reaction to the absence of all that in her life,' she decided. And yet there was something else she couldn't quite pin down… something she couldn't put her finger on… something about Yiannis…

So, what next? She could play it safe, call him later and politely decline dinner. But why would she do that? She didn't want to. She wanted to have dinner with him.

Anyway, he'd probably see right through that

Or she could go with the flow and go to dinner, stick to her old mantra, and enjoy every moment of this evening and any other evening as it unfolded?

With all the counselling under her belt, Kate thought she had become very philosophical about life in general, and her own in particular. Enjoying every day as it revealed itself. Not trying to force or manipulate any situation. All very easy when you're inside your comfort zone. She wasn't trying to force or manipulate anything with Yiannis, but something was telling her he was a threat. Not a threat exactly, a risk maybe or more of an unknown quantity?

She really liked him as a friend and he would be a great contact to have in Crete. Maybe she was afraid that she had sacrificed their friendship for one amazing night. And now, he was really pushing her outside her comfort zone, with the thoughts of more dinners and more nights. Challenging her to get out of her safe little world and live a little. How she wished Anne was there for a little counselling advice.

'That's it!' she thought. She was afraid. Afraid of being outside her comfort zone. Afraid of the unknown. And Yiannis on some level was definitely an unknown quantity.

'God, get me out of my own head,' Kate finally laughed out loud in frustration. She was overanalysing again. Feel the fear and all that, she thought.

Suddenly, the week she was to spend on Crete, on her own, was taking on a whole new energy. And she was starting to feel excited by it. She had never thought about the prospect of sleeping with another man apart from Paul. It just had never entered her head. Kate knew in her heart of hearts she wanted to have dinner with Yiannis that night. And that's what was being offered. If they happened to sleep together afterwards, that was fine too. More than fine if last night was anything to go by!

They were both adults with no ties. She had to keep reminding herself she was a single woman in her forties and so too was he single. How ridiculous to refuse because of a fear of being outside her comfort zone? Kate despaired sometimes she lived in her head so much. He had said not to take it too seriously and he was right. They were mature adults, good friends and well able to communicate. She got up from the table having made her decision. She felt so much better.

So Kate spent the next hour bathing, creaming herself, and throwing a few things into a bag, just in case…

Dressing very deliberately and with wicked intent, she put on the beautiful new lingerie she had bought in Chania. She covered them up with her comfy denims and a vivid fuchsia top she knew suited her dark colouring. A little face cream, lip gloss and she was good to go.

It was well after eight by the time Kate finally set off in the car towards the stone cottage, on her way to have dinner with a very interesting man. How lucky was she?

Zorba barked loudly and wagged his tail furiously as Kate pulled into the yard. She left her things in the car and turned to go into the cottage only to find Yiannis leaning against the doorway, watching her, his expression giving nothing away.

"Yiannis, I'm sorry about earlier," Kate smiled at him half apologetically. "I think I was a little overdramatic. I'd love to have dinner with you."

"I wasn't sure you'd be back," he said still studying her.

"I just got a bit frazzled. I'm sorry. I'm fine now obviously. Sometimes I get a bit ahead of myself." She didn't elaborate about why she was frazzled, hoping he wouldn't ask.

"What a funny, beautiful woman you are. Tell me the next time you're frazzled please!"

"You are such a patient man. Now can we go get something to eat? I'm starving. I haven't eaten since last night," pleaded Kate very aware of the compliment he had paid her.

"All this stress must make you very hungry," Yiannis teased, beside her now with his arms around her. He kissed her softly on the mouth and Kate's body reacted instantly.

"In lots of ways," she teased back.

Fifteen minutes later, they were in the jeep and on their way with Zorba in the back.

"So where are we going?" Kate asked not really caring where he suggested.

"How about Chania tonight? Is that ok?"

"Great, as long as I don't have to drive I don't mind where we go."

Chatting about this and that, the trip to Chania took less than thirty minutes. The roads were quiet. All the smaller tourist resorts were like ghost towns at the end of the season. No holidaymakers thronged onto the pavements. No lines of traffic holding things up

'How lovely to be back in the beautiful harbour so soon,' Kate thought. It was hard to believe it was only the day before she had lunched there with everybody from Ireland. So much had happened since, it actually felt more like a week. There was the same atmospheric buzz in the old port, not the same crowds, but it still had that lovely laidback feeling she adored. Nonetheless, somehow it seemed to surpass itself on this beautiful balmy night at the turn into November, full moon rising – perfect, just perfect.

The exhibition was closed by the time they parked, so they wandered along the harbour, down the tiny alleyways and in less than ten minutes, were sitting in a most exquisite Greek taverna.

Kate quickly discovered that when you were with Yiannis, you were really with him. He continually had his arm over her shoulder, held her hand or had his arm around her waist. He was full on, very physical, not in a possessive, clingy way but the opposite, in fact. In the most natural, relaxed, and pleasurable way. She loved it. She loved the feeling of his arm around her, or her hand in his. He was treating her with great care, she thought, like a precious jewel. As if protecting her somehow.

As usual, he was great company and Kate enjoyed chatting to him about almost anything, loving the beautiful stories he told of how his parents and grandparents had met. She told him about how she met Paul and why they had married so quickly. How and why they bought the holiday home in

Crete. Yiannis continued to entertain with stories of his time in the army, and some of the fascinating people he had come across while working and travelling. He was a very interesting man, and bit by bit he was revealing more of himself to her and she did likewise. She knew enough already, to know she trusted him wholly and completely. But the small details of a person's life, they both began to fill in. There seemed to be nothing they couldn't talk about, whiling away the hours, leisurely chatting as they shared a plate of *mezes*, salad and *souvlaki* washed down with a glass of the house wine. Simple, great tasting scrumptious food.

As they were eating, Kate was thinking to herself that she had almost spent the last twenty-four hours in his company and there wasn't one thing she disliked about him – not yet anyway. He was very much his own man which she liked. Very chilled, confident and comfortable in himself. And yet she knew there was a side to him that was sensitive and caring. He was great fun too of course, they always seemed to be laughing about something. He almost had an Irish sense of humour. And what a sensual man he was, if the night before was anything to go by. He was the most amazing lover.

"You look like you're studying me," Yiannis interrupted her thoughts, his eyes twinkling humorously. Sometimes he was so perceptive it unnerved her.

Kate blushed. "I was actually thinking what a nice man you are," she tried to cover up her embarrassment.

"Nice? I don't know if I like that word nice. Can you not think of another one?" He was playing with her now and she knew it.

She just shook her head and laughed.

"Kate, there is something I'd like you to think about…" Yiannis continued a little more seriously. "You're going back next Sunday, yes? If you don't have any big plans, I'd like to spend the week with you. Perhaps travelling around Crete, exploring a bit. What do you think?"

Kate straightened in her chair. Jesus, she was really taken aback now. Earlier she had thought that the week was changing by the hour. More like the minute now! He was definitely spontaneous, she'd give him that. Kate looked directly at him. The second time in twenty-four hours he had rendered her speechless. He was leaning back on his chair, watching her carefully. She could feel the weight of his eyes.

'This devastatingly attractive, interesting, man wants to spend the week with me, exploring his island. What do I say?' she wondered to herself.

In the next instant, she was beaming. She knew exactly what to say. Kate grinned at Yiannis. "That sounds like it would be really good fun. I'd love to!" she answered honestly.

As soon as she had it said, all the what-ifs came tumbling into her head, but Kate was having none of it. It seemed that when she had called the exhibition, *Letting Go*, the whole letting go thing had grown a life of its own. Now all the old conditioning of how things should or shouldn't be was literally being thrown out of her life. And so many new things were being laid out before her. To explore Crete by day with Yiannis would be enough in itself. Not to mention the thoughts of the next five or six nights.

For the second time that day, Kate felt really excited about the prospect of the week ahead. Here she was in her favourite foreign country, no friends or family to consult, no ties, no responsibilities only to herself. How free and liberated she felt! What a great decision it had been, to book the extra week. Never in her wildest dreams had she imagined that she'd be dining with this gorgeous man *and* planning to spend the week with him. At least now it seemed like they both knew exactly where they stood for the rest of her time in Crete.

Yiannis was clearly happy at her response. He took her hand and whispered softly to her, "You won't regret it. We'll have good fun."

"Leave me one day free?" she asked half- heartedly. "I have a bit of house-keeping to do. I need to shut the house for the winter and pay a bill or two, sort out my clothes. Actually, a couple of hours should do it, not a full day."

"If you want, I'll organise it when you're gone. That way you don't have to spend any of the week cleaning. The bills and clothes we can get any day you like. It's obviously up to you, of course..."

"That sounds great. If you really don't mind?" Kate was more than happy to let him handle things. It left her the full week to herself.

The simple act of knowing where they would be for the next few days, and a tension started to build between them again. The night before, Kate had been taken by surprise, by her own actions and reactions. This night, it was very different, it was inevitable. Yiannis seemed to sense it too, as he stood up rather abruptly and threw more than enough money on the table. He took her by the hand and they left.

They made love with an intensity that night, it seemed that whatever tenuous connection was between them had moved to another level. Kate felt alive when she was with him. Every cell in her body seemed to tingle with pleasure. She was in lust with him, she vaguely remembered thinking, as she drifted off to sleep hours later in his arms.

Once again, she slept soundly, but this time it was Kate who woke first. By the light in the room she guessed it was about pre-dawn. Ever so quietly she removed her arm from around him, picked up her clothes and made her way out of the bedroom. Zorba was awake in the kitchen as she slipped on her jeans and top and within five minutes they were both on their way up the hill to the cliff top, as they had done so often during the summer. Kate had a sudden desire to see the sunrise.

Herself and Zorba sat side by side, facing east, privileged to witness one of nature's daily miracles. It was so beautiful to observe the world change from darkness to light and watch as the astonishing pink sun pushed its way over the horizon. She sighed in contentment.

They sat there, probably for about an hour. Kate trying to take stock of how fast her life was moving. Naturally her thoughts settled on Yiannis. Despite her wobbler the day before, he was without doubt, sucking her in. She felt drawn to him like a magnet. She enjoyed his company. She liked him as a person. They laughed about the same things. And they were very compatible physically. Things were going at breakneck speed since their dinner two days ago. And if things went according to plan she'd be spending a lot more time with him this week too. She was having a ball! Nobody knew better than she how precious life could be. How it could be snatched away in a millisecond. This time next week she'd be back in Ireland and their brief fling or affair or whatever it was, would be over. Her old reliable mantra popped into her head empowering her once again: Take every moment as it comes. Accept everything. Resist nothing. It would work for her this week too, she vowed. Already it was worth it for the last two nights alone. She resolved she was going to have the time of her life and soak up every moment of the experience. "Pin your ears back, Kate, and enjoy the ride," she muttered to herself, "It'll be over in less than seven days."

Yiannis was up making breakfast when they arrived back.

"I was hoping you hadn't run away – again!" he laughed as she walked in.

"As if," she replied. "You were sound asleep when I left." And she kissed him, this morning.

He wound his arms around her waist and pulled her to him.

"I was adamant you were having breakfast this morning, whatever else!' he said softly. "And we have plans to make. The days are short, we need to make the best of them."

Over breakfast the two of them pored over a map of Crete and made out a rough plan for the week; listing all the places they would like to visit – way too many of course to squeeze into five days. They decided to stay away one night. Kate insisting the stone cottage was nicer than anywhere they could rent. The plans would evolve and change anyway, just as the week evolved and changed. They were both flexible. Several times that morning as they were making their arrangements, Kate felt like pinching herself. Imagine a road trip around Crete with a gorgeous companion when she had thought she'd be doing something else, something completely different, boring in comparison to what she was planning now. Wasn't life amazing sometimes?

An hour later they were en route. They had decided on a trip to, a beautiful, exotic, well-known beach at the south-western tip of Crete. Kate had been there before but only in the height of summer when it was packed full of tourists. Funnily enough Yiannis had never been there. They both welcomed the chance to visit at a quiet time of the year. They headed west along the highway branching off to take the route over the mountains. The sky was a vivid blue, and the sun was shining brightly as they passed through the sleepy villages dotted along the narrow roads. Most were deserted looking, even though now and again, you could see people in the coffee houses. The countryside looked as vibrant and alive as Kate felt. Sunglasses on, windows down, warm breeze blowing and music playing in the background, they laughed their way through the miles. You couldn't but be in good humour. The olive harvest was well underway as they passed the endless groves and every so often could hear the bells of the wild mountain goats from the sides of steep hills. Occasionally he would point out the beehives for the world famous Cretan honey.

Yiannis was the typical Cretan driver to Kate. Very confident and a little bit crazy. He saw no danger. And yet the funny thing was, she felt so safe with him. So glad he was driving and not her. Up and down hills and corkscrew roads they drove, enjoying the peaceful, rural countryside. He stopped the jeep at the side of the road before the descent to the coast to fully appreciate the panorama before them. Even from a height, the beach looked like a living breathing turquoise lagoon inviting them to visit and take a dip. Breathtakingly beautiful. As they continued, the mountains rolled back, the road widened out and revealed the sea. On a glorious day in early November, it seemed as if they were the only two out and about.

The beach itself was unspoiled and undeveloped, like several beaches masquerading as one. A few trees were randomly dotted near the entrance, and delicate pink sand defined the crystal-clear waters. Kate had never seen it looking so beautiful. She already had her bikini on and was in the water before Yiannis was even out of the jeep, the sea only up to her waist. It was heavenly and warmer than she had expected.

"Hurry up," she called back. "It's glorious." She had to wade out quite a bit before she could really duck down, but by then Yiannis had caught up with her and pulled her down into the water with him.

"I couldn't resist. You were begging to be ducked!" he laughed as Kate surfaced pretending to be offended.

They swam for a bit, waded out to the little island and explored around as much as possible. Later, relaxed and lying at the water's edge, Kate had never felt so lazy and so content in all her life. November sun beamed down on them, the waves were barely lapping. Yiannis was beside her chatting idly and casually stroking her skin. Kate wished she could freeze frame this scene in her brain forever.

They shared a light lunch at a small taverna and set off back via the coastal route. The plan was to make it to the northwest coast for sunset and dinner.

On the return trip they were literally driving along the side of the island, the whole western coast of Crete, from bottom to top. The views were so magnificent they kept stopping to take it all in. Infinite blue sea to the west with waves crashing to shore far below. Corkscrew bends winding along the cliff face, and dramatic drops to the ocean. Every cliff edge revealed a view more stunning than the one before. Kate felt her heart soar again and again, overflowing with the beauty and magic of the setting. Every so often she'd look at Yiannis, as if to prove to herself it was all really happening.

"Are you checking me out?" he laughed at her.

"Most definitely," Kate laughed back.

And that's how it was between them, an easy camaraderie, enjoying each other's company and loving the beautiful scenery along the way. Yiannis made no secret of the fact he found her desirable and Kate was basking in all the attention he was lavishing on her. He was spontaneous, and she still lived in her head a bit. A good balance, she thought. That's probably why they were getting on well.

By about five that evening they had made their way to a beautiful sandy beach at the most western point of the island. They stopped at the side of the road, high up above the beach with a clear view facing west. The landscape below them swept down to the sea, dotted everywhere with glasshouses, tunnels and solar panels. Kate sat on a wall with Yiannis in front, leaning against her and Zorba by his side. She had her arms around his neck.

What an awesome sight to see! The sun was disappearing into the sea. The sky illuminated with oranges, reds and pinks.

"How lucky am I? Today I saw the sun rise and now I get to see it set. Darkness to light to darkness again," she mused out loud. "Do you know we often miss this in Ireland because of the cloud cover. You are so lucky here. You get to see this nearly every day."

"I know," he smiled, helping her down off the wall. And somehow, she had the feeling he wasn't talking about the sunset.

After a long, relaxed dinner, they were back at the stone cottage by ten - even having swung by Kate's to collect a few bits and pieces. Without either of them verbalising it, it had been taken for granted that Kate would stay at the stone cottage. They could easily have stayed at her house but Yiannis didn't seem inclined. Funnily, the one or two times he was at her house she thought she noticed an uneasiness about him. Nothing she could quite put her finger on, but she sensed something all the same. He never delayed long and uncharacteristically always appeared impatient to go. Much as Kate loved her place in the sun, she knew it couldn't compare to the luxury of the stone cottage. Maybe he just preferred his own home, she thought. Simple as that. It didn't fit with the rest of his personality though.

Back at the stone cottage, Kate jumped into the shower to wash the remains of the salt water off her body. In two days she had gotten used to being in his space. Her toiletries and things were everywhere, and she'd have to borrow his robe after showering. He didn't seem to mind though. She had a feeling he didn't sweat the small stuff.

Later fresh and relaxed she joined him for a glass of wine, by the fire. He was showered too. He must have used the other bathroom. A little pang of guilt struck Kate. Oh God what must he think of her? She was taking over his home!

"Yiannis! Why didn't you ask me to use the other bathroom? I forgot I'm sorry!"

"Kate, a shower is a shower. It doesn't matter which one I use. Besides, I like you using my bathroom."

He never made her feel like she was a guest in his house, and at times it seemed like he was in her house not the other way around.

The wine, sea air and good food were all taking their toll on Kate. She yawned several times in quick succession.

"Tired?" he asked.

"Just a bit. How about an early night?"

"Definitely," Yiannis hopped up. "You go ahead. I'll sort Zorba out."

"Don't be too keen," she laughed at him. She had never seen him move so quickly.

He laughed at himself too and shrugged his shoulders, "See what you do to me?"

Kate felt a surge of excitement rush through her body as she headed off to the bedroom. The last thing she remembered thinking was that he was taking forever sorting Zorba and then – oblivion.

Yiannis, no more than five minutes behind her, at first thought she only had her eyes closed. As he got into the bed beside her, he could see she was breathing deeply and evenly, very clearly asleep. Not for the first time, he gazed at her in wonder. She looked so beautiful and so vulnerable all rolled into one. What kind of magic spell was she weaving? he wondered as he surrendered to sleep too.

The following morning, Kate was awake just before Yiannis. Stretching in the sumptuous surroundings, she was trying to recall the events of the previous evening when he stirred lazily beside her. *"Kalimera,"* he murmured as he kissed her on the neck and pulled her to him, still half asleep. *"Kalimera,"* Kate replied, surrendering to his arms and wrapping herself around him. She couldn't resist. He felt so nice. They were still in a dream-like state, somewhere between waking and sleeping. This was their first morning waking up together. And it felt nice – really, really nice. It surprised Kate how relaxed she was, as if she had known him all her life. Probably because he was easy-going and chilled out around her, always making her feel relaxed and at ease. Eventually disentangling themselves, they each went to shower and thirty minutes later were en route.

This was the day they were driving the whole way across Crete to the very eastern side of the island. Their destination was the famous sunrise beach, to catch the dawn the following morning.

They left the sleepy rural villages of Western Crete and turned onto the national highway only this time, headed east. The national highway spans the width of the island from west to east and vice versa. It runs along by the sea, so the views are continually breath-taking. Flying along with Yiannis and Zorba, Kate revelled in that lovely feeling of freedom she had gotten used to. She loved exploring and travelling around anyway, but it certainly added an extra dimension to be with an attractive male companion and all that that entailed. As usual, conversation flowed, no subject off limits. Kate listened in fascination as he told her all about the monastery and how he had come to buy it. "My grandmother used to bring me there a lot when I was a kid, on holy days and feast days. All the villagers would go, particularly for special occasions. When the ceremonies were over, we'd gather in the court-yard and there would be tables with food and drink for everyone. People would be talking and eating together while we played around the monastery. It was a happy time and I have very happy memories."

"Sounds idyllic," Kate responded genuinely captivated by the description of his childhood.

"Sadly though," he continued, "with the progress of tourism the monastery became so popular with holidaymakers, it seemed to distract the monks from the simple life they had signed up for. A few years ago, they decided to sell up and relocate to the original site of the monastery, to continue their lives in solitude. So, when it came up for sale, I was adamant the developers wouldn't get their hands on it. It all happened soon after I came back from Athens and I happened to be in a position to buy it. It's a prime location, and the architecture is fascinating, not to mention the history. There was a lot of interest but now that I have it, I don't quite know what to do with it…" his voice tapered off as if he was thinking out loud.

"So, a man of principles and integrity too." Why was she not surprised? She didn't ask how he could afford to buy it, presuming he was now in debt to the hilt.

"I'd love to see it again another day," Kate said, grinning at the memory of her first time there. "Maybe in daylight this time!"

"Sure, whenever you like," he smiled at her.

Flying along the highway, they weren't in any particular hurry but Yiannis still wanted to cover as much ground as possible. The east coast was hours away at the other side of the island.

Passing the big cities, the great White Mountains were left behind as they moved eastwards, where Kate had been eons ago and she recognised a lot of the old familiar names on signposts.

"All the times I've been in Crete and I've missed some of the most obvious places like Knossos. I'm almost embarrassed to say I've never been there, have you?" Kate asked him.

"But of course," he answered. "Crete has lots of historical, archaeological and scenic sites. We won't even begin to scratch the surface this week. And you know the nicest places are probably not on any map or tourist guide. Places you just happen to come upon, or real gems, like the church out on the peninsula."

"Maybe we could go there too if there's time," Kate asked hopefully, knowing she'd love to see the place where his grandparents had met.

They pressed on to the next town and took a break; another beautiful town set well into eastern Crete. Zorba was taken for a walk and given some water, and then the three of them sat in a taverna, looking out at the boats moored near the bridge. The days continued unseasonably hot and sunny and their senses were assaulted by the beauty of the picturesque harbour. The gentle lapping of water, the low murmuring of voices, cooking smells, warm sun on their faces, and of course the taste of their delicious lunch lulled them into a feeling of total pleasure and relaxation.

But they had to press on. An hour or so later, they were back on the highway. At this stage Kate was thanking her lucky stars Yiannis was doing the driving. The narrow road was hairy to say the least. A lot different than the cliff road they had been on the day before. One minute they seemed to be hanging onto cliff edges and the next they were coasting along the sides of very steep mountains. The views were magnificent, of course, but Kate gradually became quieter and quieter much to Yiannis' amusement. He twigged something was wrong when she stopped talking and gently teased her. Her logical brain was telling her he was a good confident driver, used to travelling for his work. Nonetheless he slowed to ease her discomfort, and the views were stunning anytime she allowed herself to look. Much to Kate's relief though, they arrived in the last city, not far from their final destination. A quick coffee and a short drive to their base for the night. It had been a long day!

Kate was excited when they finally reached a traditional Greek village in a rural area. It was near the sea and the perfect place from which to visit Vai in the early morning – if you were to believe all the signs around. Yiannis had pre-booked their room so she wasn't quite sure what to expect. He drove on through the village and she kept expecting him to stop at any of the signs for accommodation, but he continued an extra two or three kilometres towards the coast puzzling Kate a little. All of a sudden, he stopped the jeep right at the water's edge, at a tiny beach.

"Here we are, Kate. This is where we're staying tonight," Yiannis declared looking over at her.

Not for the first time, Kate found she was pleasantly surprised. They were parked beside a beautiful whitewashed bungalow, set right at the edge of the water. A veranda wrapped itself around the bungalow. It was all alone, on its own private beach, not another house in sight. Kate smiled in delighted anticipation as Yiannis let them in through a vivid blue door. As they walked inside, Kate took it all in – the high ceilings, the whitewashed walls, beautiful stone features, a modern kitchen with all mod cons. She felt as if she had seen it all before. In fact, it reminded her of Yiannis' home. All the front windows had stunning views, directly facing the beach. It was fabulous! Even the two en-suite bedrooms, had French doors, leading onto the sand. Beautiful fittings everywhere and subtle lighting screamed elegance. Both bedrooms had their own wet room while the main bathroom was again stylish and contemporary, tiled top to bottom. It had everything you could ever want in luxury accommodation and still maintained a unique Greek style and cosy feel. It was very like the stone cottage, with a few obvious differences. In fact, it had him written all over it.

"This is like the stone cottage. Did you have something to do with it?" Kate turned to him questioningly. "It has your stamp all over it. It's amazing!"

He smiled. "A few years ago, I took it on. It was one of my first renovation projects on Crete after my grandmother's cottage. You like it?"

"I love it. It's really beautiful, Yiannis. You are so gifted," she answered honestly

"When I realised we were coming this way, I rang the man who owns it to see if it was free. Luckily it was, and here we are."

He really was so very good at what he did she thought. And not a bit vain. He went to get the bags, leaving Kate to mull things over.

Kate realised the places they had visited so far were on her wish list, not his. Without overdoing it, she felt Yiannis was very much indulging her over the last couple of days. Picking such a beautiful place to stay. Driving across Crete with her and generally spoiling her. She had seldom felt so pampered. She was having an amazing time and she casually wondered if he treated all his women like this.

Zorba was barking excitedly, glad to be in the fresh air again after being cooped up for most of the day. Kate took him for a walk along the deserted beach leaving Yiannis to his siesta. He was shattered. There wasn't a sound anywhere except for the waves, the birds and Zorba barking. No sound of cars or traffic. The hills around were green and lush looking and the fields full of crops for a late harvest. She spent about an hour on the beach walking and exploring and it was almost dark by the time she got back.

'No light, so he must still be asleep,' Kate thought to herself. Not wanting to disturb him she found a few candles and placed them here and there, made herself a drink and went to sit on the patio. She couldn't resist a peek in at Yiannis as she passed the bedroom door. It was only his silhouette she could see now. He lay on his back on the bed, one arm behind his head, his chest rising and falling slowly and rhythmically, in a light slumber. His features weren't clear, but Kate could still sense his dominant presence.

Despite the long drive, they had had great fun that day. Kate smiled to herself, spending about five minutes or so looking at him, lost in thought – half tempted to go and cuddle up beside him, but deciding against it knowing where that would lead.

An hour later he appeared, all showered and gorgeous, as he usually did. "Come on, the sooner we go get dinner, the sooner we will be back," he whispered suggestively into her ear, pulling her gently out of the chair and into his arms.

"Hold that thought," Kate smiled. "Give me five minutes." And she went off to change and freshen up.

They had a beautiful night together. Their dinner was long and leisurely and pleasurable like all of the others they had shared to date. Good food, good conversation, just in a different location. What more could you ask for. But also like every other dinner she had with him, there was an underlying tension. An anticipation of what was to come later. She wondered could he sense her desire. He amazed her sometimes he was so in tune with her. Sometimes he would know what she was thinking before she had the thought fully formed in her head. Deep down in her belly, Kate could feel her stomach flip and butterflies fluttering, and the occasional missed heartbeats. Never wanting time to move faster than it did, she was still always nervously excited when the bill was paid, and they were on their way home for a night of passionate lovemaking. And this night would be no different to any of the others.

She was in a deep, dreamy sleep when Yiannis woke her the following morning. He was already fully dressed.

"Come on sleepy head," he coaxed, "we need to go if we're going to make sunrise."

It was pitch dark and Kate was warm and cosy where she was.

"Are we mad?" she said as she reluctantly crawled out of the cosy bed to dress. It was chilly so early in the morning. They grabbed a blanket, a couple of other things and before long, were on their way.

The beach was a short drive, so well before sunrise the two of them were settled with Zorba beside them. Kate was wrapped in a blanket still not fully awake, snuggled into Yiannis.

As she sat there she noticed the light gradually change. Things had gone from dark silhouettes to lighter silhouettes and she could make out the outline of some trees. Little by little she could see more and more of her surroundings. There were lots of palm trees, and soon she could see where the beach began and ended, the rocky sides to it, and the hills and road behind it.

"Look this way, Kate," Yiannis nodded his head. She followed his eyes and looked out to the horizon. She could barely make out the start of a pink sun over the top of the grey sea. Gradually, the sun pushed up higher and higher and all around them the light was steadily changing. The silver sky was tentatively lit up by soft pastel shades of lilac, pale orange and pale pink. The landscape took on a softer version of its own colour. And when you looked away and back again, the colours had intensified just a little more. There was a haziness… Everything was bathed in gentle, early morning delicate light and quiet – everywhere was so quiet. They must have sat for an hour or so not wanting to move, lost in their own private space and feeling very fortunate to witness it. When they did eventually stir themselves, and go for a swim, the sea wasn't as cold as Kate had expected. It was holding onto the summer heat. In the full morning light, Kate could appreciate the beauty of one of the most famous beaches on Crete, with its backdrop of palm trees surrounding it. The water was clear and calm, and the swim made an exhilarating start to another beautiful day.

Back at the bungalow, showered and changed, they decided to get on the road early and stop for breakfast somewhere.

"How about the south coast for breakfast?" suggested Yiannis.

He was indulging her again. She was fairly sure it was out of their way.

"Well if you don't mind driving, I'm happy to be your co-pilot," she shrugged her shoulders at him.

"South coast it is," laughed Yiannis, and off they went.

She was getting used to the breath-taking scenery – much to his amusement she had stopped saying Wow!. Kate soaked it all in and filed it away in her mind under Beautiful Memories. From stunning sea views, to lush agricultural land, it was all there, as far as the eye could see.

Breakfasting on the tree-lined seafront looking out at the Libyan Sea was almost surreal. Next stop Africa… For the past few days Kate had been intermittently pinching herself, to try and keep in touch with some kind of reality. It felt like she was having a very long, very beautiful dream, as if she had stepped outside of reality. And she really didn't want to wake up.

Yiannis was sitting across from her, smiling studying her as he often did, with intense eyes.

"What are you thinking?"

"I'm sitting here, looking out at the Libyan Sea, sun on my face, in the company of a lovely man and waiting for someone to bring me my breakfast. What more could I possibly need?" she laughed at him

"I know exactly what you mean, Kate," he grinned, "only I'll switch the lovely man for a beautiful woman."

A couple of hours later, they were back on the road, heading cross-country to link with the national highway and start heading west. Finished their whistle-stop tour of eastern Crete. It had been short, but most definitely very sweet. Once they got to the main road they brought Zorba inside the jeep and Yiannis sped off towards Chania. It was the same road as the day before, the same beautiful scenery only from a different angle. By dusk they were a little peckish again and Zorba definitely needed a stop, so they pulled into a harbour for a late lunch. This day like all the others was punctuated by stops for food and coffees. And to be honest, at this stage Kate had lost track of who had paid for what. Apart from the first night, Yiannis always tried to, unless she absolutely insisted.

Who cares? He would say when she said it to him. All that matters is that we're having a good time. And he was probably right.

The last leg of the trip was the most tiring. Bellies full and nicely relaxed, Kate dozed off near enough to the cottage. They both felt so tired they decided to sit in and not even attempt to go out later for dinner. Anyway, they weren't hungry. They cosied up on the couch with a bottle of wine, and Zorba at their feet.

"Yiannis, thank you for a really beautiful trip. I know I'll never ever forget it," Kate whispered quietly to him, "It was very special."

"It was special to me too," he murmured pulling her close.

You'd think we'd be sick of each other at this stage, Kate mused to herself, but she was finding the exact opposite to be the case.

Friday dawned bright and clear and they lazed in bed for a long time. The days were racing by now. The last two had been a bit hectic so they decided to relax. Kate made Yiannis stay in bed while she made him breakfast, wanting to pamper him for a change. Without speaking about it, she was very aware it was getting nearer to Sunday. It was funny how things had happened so naturally between them. From what she could see they were well balanced. She liked the fact that he was so chilled. They liked a lot of the same things and both had a great sense of humour. It was all very easy.

When they eventually did get up, they set off for the mountains and the starting place for the world-famous Samaria Gorge. Kate had never walked the gorge, but it was on her future list of things to do now, along with Knossos and Spinalonga.

Once more they passed through the olive groves, orange groves and small sleepy villages of Western Crete and started to climb uphill on the narrow country roads. The higher they went, the more breath-taking the scenery became. And funnily once they got nearer to the gorge, it surprised Kate how suddenly the land flattened out, as if they were on some great wide-open prairie. Amazingly Yiannis told her they were in the middle of the *Lefka Ori*, the great White Mountains. They drove through the village as far as the gorge but as expected it was shut for the winter. But you could still get a sense of its magnificence, from the sheer cliff faces and huge drops. All they could see was the little wooden staircase disappear down, down into the gorge below. They didn't delay but made their way back, enjoying the views all the more, from the high vantage point, stopping at some random taverna tucked away in the hills not because they were hungry or thirsty but because of the panoramic view it offered. From the veranda, they could see the whole way from the *Lefka Ori* to Hania Bay. Another stunning vista on the long list of stunning vistas they had seen all week.

On the way back, Kate got Yiannis to stop at her house and brought him to the beach for sunset. He had never seen it from her point of view. Kate laughed when she suddenly remembered that this was the place she had first met him.

"You were very difficult that evening," he teased her.

"I know," she agreed unashamedly

"That's probably why I found you interesting," he grinned at her.

"Because I was difficult?" she asked uncertainly.

"No, because you were honest. You held nothing back that day," he shrugged at her.

Looking west towards the peninsula, they tried and failed to make out where all the landmarks they knew were. The clear view was gone soon after sunset.

Kate packed her bag and threw it into the jeep. She had given up all effort at even attempting to stay in her house and with only two more nights, she knew she wouldn't be back before she left. She was enjoying the adventure too much. On Monday the week had stretched out endlessly before her, and now the days were flying alarmingly fast. She desperately wanted to hit the pause button but unfortunately that wasn't possible.

Enjoy every moment, she reminded herself again. She most definitely was.

They ate in the fishing village on the way back. The same place they had eaten on Sunday night, they even sat at the same table and there was the same anticipatory nervous energy inside Kate. High uphill on the cliff edge she could see the monastery towering over the village.

"Funny I never noticed it last time," Kate mused out loud.

"Tomorrow we'll go and hopefully get you out to the church on the peninsula," Yiannis suggested.

"I'd love that," she said.

Saturday was supposedly a day off. No long trips anywhere. Both of them wanted to spend a relaxing day at the cottage and Yiannis had volunteered to cook dinner for their last night. They were up early, swam in the sea and walked along the cliffs. Later he took her into the village, to the monastery and to do a little shopping. He had to get food for dinner and Kate wanted to browse in the beautiful craft shop, she had seen and maybe get some oil and honey to take home.

The monastery was every bit as beautiful as she remembered, probably even more so in daylight. Kate hadn't realised how big it was, there were at least three levels to it, but most definitely the top floor where they entered had to be the most spectacular. They may have been without the effect of the full moon, but the blue sky and sea were ample substitutions. In broad daylight you could fully appreciate its magnificence. The simple wooden doorway gave no hint as to the wealth of treasures within. Once again, the first thing that struck Kate was the feeling of tranquillity and peacefulness that hung in the air. You could sense the spirituality, you could even imagine generations of monks there.

They entered a very large, very pretty courtyard to the left and to the right of which were what looked like two lime trees, surrounded by terracotta pots, the plants long since dead. Either side of the yard she could clearly make out two floors of rooms or accommodation, by the regularly spaced doors and windows. The top floor had a wooden balcony overlooking the courtyard and the bottom floor had marble benches running the length of the walls, broken only by wooden doorways and stone surrounds. A timber trellis between the floors offered shade from the sun and was laden down with grapes.

"That's where the monks used to live," offered Yiannis pointing to the rooms.

Kate slowly walked the courtyard, touching everything as she passed in acknowledgement of a reverent past. In the centre of the yard was the old Orthodox Church, the entrance to which was by a hand carved wooden door. Surrounded by an elaborate sculpted architrave it led to the teeny tiny cool interior. Everywhere she looked there were stone features and beautifully calligraphed Greek inscriptions on the walls. Kate was at a loss to know which way to turn next, so overawed was she by the beauty of her surroundings.

"I imagine every time you come here you find something new to admire," she looked at Yiannis.

"Every time," he confirmed.

And of course, the *piece-de-resistance* was the veranda overlooking the sea. Separated from the courtyard by a modest doorway, it was exactly as she had remembered. It was as if the whole Aegean Sea and sky above, was laid out before them. A clear view as far as the eye could see, only broken by the headland in the distance. Her heart swelled in appreciation. She felt almost moved to tears by the beauty before her. Yiannis was behind her now and he put his arms around her and held her. The two of them gazed in wonder. Kate thought she could have stayed like that forever. One thing she was sure of, Yiannis was the right man for the job. Whatever he did, he would restore it passionately and with great skill.

"You know," said Kate thinking out loud, "it would make a great yoga centre or a healing centre or something like that… in keeping with the energy of the place."

"That is an idea," Yiannis answered thoughtfully.

Shortly afterwards browsing in the craft shop, Kate found the perfect gift for Yiannis. It wasn't expensive but to her it symbolised the week. Two sculpted ceramic hearts, about the size of her hand. One overlapping the other, and glazed patchily in a vibrant shade of red. When she first saw them, she thought of him instantly. What they had shared, this past week… The fun. The friendship. The passion. He had helped open her heart again and for that she would always be truly grateful. Maybe they were a bit much, but she didn't want to leave them behind. She'd buy and decide later.

They lunched in a fish taverna and on the way back called to Nikos and Katerina. Kate wanted to say her goodbyes. Of course, they were delighted to see her. They gave no indication whether or not they knew she had stayed all week at the stone cottage. Nikos usually called every day to Yiannis but this week, for some reason, he hadn't. His very absence spoke volumes to Kate. Nikos was a father figure to Yiannis. He had been a good friend to his grandmother and when she passed away, he had kept up the habit of calling to Yiannis, in a way looking out for him. They spent a pleasant couple of hours, talking about this and that, and having light refreshments. When they were saying their goodbyes, Nikos discreetly said to Kate that he had never seen Yiannis so content and when would she be back again? He wanted to know.

He knows well, thought Kate. Proper little matchmaker. She hadn't the heart to fill him in. "Next year, Nikos. Maybe Easter? I don't know," she answered honestly.

Because they had spent more time than planned socialising, there was no time left to visit the church on the peninsula.

"We could go now, Kate, but we'd have to rush it," Yiannis said, "and it's too beautiful to be rushed. We wouldn't even get to see it in the daylight. Maybe we'll go there another time?" he casually suggested.

"Yeah maybe," said Kate a bit disappointed. Somehow, she couldn't imagine herself ever going there without Yiannis. She would have loved to have seen it.

What little time was left was spent lazing at the cottage with Zorba. Everything had been kept very light and fun all week. There had been no declarations of like or love. No empty promises. Up until that morning Kate had fully intended to drive to the airport as she normally would have and leave the car to be picked up by Costas. But Yiannis was adamant, he would drive her. In fact, he was quite cross about it and she had never seen him cross about anything before. He told her to ring Costas and arrange to have the car collected at her house instead. No discussion.

"Don't go all male and chauvinistic on me," she tried to tease him. But he didn't see the funny side, so she just let it be.

While Yiannis was cooking dinner, Kate went off to do her last few bits and pieces. She had a small bit of packing to do and she wanted to pamper herself and look nice for their last dinner together. She soaked in the bath, lathered cream on herself and for the last time put on her beautiful purple dress. She would never be able to wear it again without thinking about her time in Crete, the exhibition and particularly Yiannis. Even though Kate was trying to push it to the back of her mind, the next day was looming large. She dreaded the thought of leaving this beautiful place again. For one short week, she had been on a rollercoaster of a ride and that would be over. Without doubt she had the time of her life. Happy to go with the flow all week. She had discovered lots of new things about herself and for that she had Yiannis to thank. But she knew it couldn't last forever. Maybe it was just as well she was going. Tomorrow they would both go back to their old lives and carry on as normal. She sighed. But they did have one more night to go. So, stop thinking about tomorrow and live in the moment she reminded herself.

Much later, all glammed up and dressed for dinner, she went out to the kitchen. Yiannis was deeply absorbed with his food preparation and looking like he was far away somewhere in thought. When he saw her, his expression softened immediately, and he smiled at her admiringly.

"You look beautiful! And smell beautiful too," he said as he kissed her and wrapped his arms around her. He smelt of onions and spices and cooking food smells but behind it all Kate could still get that distinct musky masculine smell from him. One kiss and he could reduce her to a quivering mess and make her want to forget everything, except him, she laughed to herself as she remembered how she had behaved all week.

"Have a glass of wine while I have a quick shower. Dinner's under control. No need to do anything," and he left her on her own.

Kate poured herself some wine and lay back on the sofa. The smells coming from the cooker were making her mouth water. He had the table beautifully set, with candles lighting and lamps on in the background. There was music on somewhere even though it was only barely audible and a small fire in the grate gave a lovely cosy feel to the room. It all added to the atmosphere. They were all set for a very romantic dinner. Kate closed her eyes wanting to memorise every single detail. She wanted to remember this always. She wanted to be able to remember it, when she was far away from here and Yiannis. When blue skies and strong arms were a dim and distant memory.

A few minutes later when she opened her eyes again, Yiannis was back in the room, his hair damp and ruffled, his clothes changed.

Dinner was an absolute delight. Why was she not surprised that he turned out to be a superb cook, to add to his many other talents?

He had made delicious grilled vegetables, a salad from mountain greens, figs and toasted walnuts. He knew she really liked the vegetarian food, so he had made stuffed vegetables and grilled enough fish for a small army. Home-made wedges complimented the food and he had chilled a bottle of the local wine to round it all off. Kate was touched he had gone to so much trouble for her. As usual conversation flowed, and he entertained her with the old war stories he had heard from his grandmother. They talked and talked and talked long into the night. From his work, to her work, to the meal, to his old life in Athens. The only reference to the future was when he talked about keeping any unsold paintings from the exhibition until she returned. Before they knew it, four hours had passed.

Yiannis got up suddenly, held out his hand to her and simply said, "Come on Kate, it's time for bed." She took his hand and they went to his bedroom blowing out the candles on the way, leaving everything else as it was.

A quiet desperation entered their love-making that night. They were like two restless souls unwilling to surrender to the inevitable. Afterwards unable to sleep, Kate dared him to a moonlight swim.

"Are you crazy?" he teased, "It's too cold."

"Well, you've obviously never swam in the Atlantic," she challenged, "now that's cold!"

Laughing and joking they swam in the cool clear water at the stone cottage and later lay on the beach wrapped in soft blankets underneath the stars. They showered the salt water from their bodies and Yiannis tenderly wrapped Kate in his robe and took her back to bed. The last time they made love, Kate could have cried it felt so exquisitely beautiful. A short while later Yiannis felt the dead weight of her body relax onto his as she lay her head on his chest and finally succumbed to sleep, curling her leg around his and throwing her arm across his stomach exactly as she had done every other night before.

The next thing Kate knew, it was morning and Yiannis was no longer beside her. She sighed in resignation and went to shower. Gathering up all the last few bits and pieces, she threw them into her case. She scribbled a note and threw the ceramic hearts under his pillow before she changed her mind. She knew she would need to be strong.

When she was dressed and ready to go, she went to find him. He was on the beach playing with Zorba. She went towards them both and knelt behind Yiannis putting her arms around his neck. They stayed like that for a few minutes, until he attempted to break the silence, "Kate, when..."

But Kate cut across him a little prematurely, lost in her thoughts of what may or may not happen next, she put her hand to his mouth to stop him from speaking. The most important thing now was that they remain friends. It had been an amazing adventure and she had had the most fantastic week of her life.

"Yiannis," she blurted, "promise me we'll always be friends, no matter what?"

There was silence for a few minutes before he replied. "Is that what you want Kate? Friends? You want us to be friends?"

"More than anything in the world..."

"Then we'll always be friends, Kate. I promise," he answered solemnly

They said their goodbyes at the cottage, and as they kissed the desire almost overwhelmed them again.

Some friends we are! she heard him mutter under his breath to no-one in particular.

The drive to the airport was difficult, to say the least. He picked her up at her house and Kate made small talk for a short while, gradually letting it peter out, noticing he wasn't saying much. In fact, he was quiet, eerily quiet, staring straight ahead, not even glancing in her direction.

When he pulled up at the airport, Kate gave Zorba a hug and leaned over to Yiannis kissing him tenderly on the lips, lingering a little longer than she had intended. She touched his face, puzzled by his silence.

"Yiannis, thank you for everything," she whispered, "For the most amazing week…" she stopped herself saying of my life, even though she wanted to. She frantically searched his eyes for some kind of response or reaction from him. He just looked at her coldly with his dark intense eyes. As if he was thinking about saying something but changed his mind. She wanted *him* to say the same thing back to her. That he had had a great week that he had loved it too. But he didn't. He just sat there and said nothing.

So much for his promise to be friends, she thought wryly

Kate didn't wait, she couldn't. Grabbing her bag, she hopped out and quickly walked away from the jeep without a backward glance. She couldn't do it any other way. Inside the airport, Kate could feel tears behind her eyes. She was being silly and sentimental she thought as she busied herself with her bag. Luckily there was no queue, so she moved quickly from check-in and went upstairs to security.

An amazing week and it had ended like that? Kate was puzzled, annoyed and hurt as she walked to her gate for the flight. Why had he insisted on driving her to the airport? Why had he ruined it all? Why could he not bring himself to say anything? Anything at all? His behaviour over the last few hours contradicted everything she had thought about him over the past week. He had her fooled. She certainly hadn't seen that coming. Maybe she was just naïve in these situations. But before she knew it, she was airborne to Athens and as luck would have it, the plane flew directly over the peninsula as if rubbing more salt into her wounds.

That whole Sunday travelling passed in a fog for Kate. She was torn between missing Yiannis' physical presence and total confusion around what had happened at the airport, *or* rather what hadn't happened. They had practically been together for a whole week and now he was no longer beside her. She actually felt physically cold.

In Athens her cousin Emma met her flight. Kate found it hard to focus on anything and Emma asked her several times was she ok. Kate couldn't concentrate on what she was saying, continually thinking about Yiannis, finding it hard to get her head around the goodbye. Wondering what had gone wrong. It was like he became a different person. Maybe she had just been another in his long line of conquests, she thought sarcastically to herself and that's how he ended things. So much for the chilled and confident Yiannis Theodorakis. That was a bit too chilled for Kate.

It was with relief then that she finally said her goodbyes in Athens and boarded the plane to Dublin. She desperately wanted to get home and lick her wounds. She had four uninterrupted hours to pull herself together and stop thinking about him.

When Kate turned her phone on in Dublin, the first thing she did was to text Yiannis and say that she was home safely, and to thank him again. It was something she always did out of habit, no matter where or with whom she had been. She didn't expect it but there was a text back almost immediately saying that that was great, and he'd ring her later in the week.

Like that was going to happen. She was tempted to text back, *Don't bother!*

When Molly picked her up she was all questions and all excited. How did the dinner go? What did she do for the week? Did she meet Yiannis again? Was she ok? She looked different, somehow?

How could she tell Molly that she had just had the most amazing week of her whole life. A passionate affair. That she had thrown caution to the wind and had virtually moved in with Yiannis. And that it had all ended a little disappointingly. Something she couldn't fathom. She wasn't ready to start answering questions about him just yet, so she lied to her daughter, to put her off the scent and buy herself a bit of time. She had to come to terms with it herself first. She needed to find a way to let it all go now. Chalk down the whole week to experience. Remember the good times and let go of the disappointment.

Chapter Twelve

THE DANCE

It was 2.30 a.m. when Yiannis' phone beeped. He had been in the workshop for hours and had lost track of time.

To be honest, he had wanted to lose track of time...

Since he came back from the airport, he couldn't settle at any one thing and needed the physical release of the workshop. There was a backlog of jobs he had put off over the past two weeks, and he was glad of the distraction they offered now.

Earlier, the airport had been a disaster, to say the least. He felt he had hurt Kate and he never intended to do that. But by the time he had figured out something to say, she was gone. It all happened so quickly, he was still a bit stunned.

She had made it clear at the house earlier that she did not want a long drawn out goodbye. He could respect that. But this friends thing was a bit much. He had been about to suggest that they see could they make something work between them long distance. He assumed they would naturally progress to some kind of a relationship, given how they had gotten on all week. That it was the next step for them. That's what he wanted anyway. But she had cut him off, before he got to say anything. He was taken aback when she said she wanted friendship. She wanted them to be friends. He still couldn't quite believe it. Then she had kissed him, like she had kissed him all week. Like the lovers they were. Talk about mixed messages! Maybe it was for the best? Maybe it wasn't meant to be...

Yiannis checked his phone. It was Kate.

Just arrived safe and sound in Dublin. Thanks for everything, Kate.

He stared at the text for a few moments, lost in thought, and then text back, *That's great. Will ring later in the week.*

That would buy him a bit of time until he figured out what to do next.

Zorba and himself strolled to the cottage. Zorba looked a bit like he felt – miserable and confused.

Yiannis was really tired, as if everything was suddenly catching up with him. Even though he had cleared and tidied earlier, he could feel her presence everywhere in the house. Things moved or little bits she had forgotten, a sense of her in the air. And when he went to get into bed, he could smell her distinctive perfume on the sheets...

Frustrated, he pulled them off, and as he went to make a fresh bed, the two ceramic hearts fell out from under his pillow. Yiannis wasn't quite sure what to think when he read the note.

Thanks for helping to open my heart again K x

He smiled despite himself. They were beautiful, the two hearts and typical of her. He threw them into a drawer with the note.

'Mixed messages again,' he thought shaking his head. He'd deal with that later too.

He was physically exhausted by the time he finally got into bed but sleep only came in fits and starts. All night long, he tossed and turned, not able to settle in any position. Feeling cold. Once, he even reached out for her, like he had on other nights, only to remember she was gone...

Sleep came no easier to Kate in Molly's. She too tossed and turned, welcoming first light when it finally arrived. Now, she could get up early, head for home and get on with her life... The remnants of the Cretan sun may still have warmed her skin. Unfortunately, no Yiannis to warm her body...

What a pity, she thought for the millionth time. What a pity it had ended the way it had.

Kate half dreaded the thoughts of going home, knowing full well she would have to field all the questions from her friends, just like she had with Molly the night before. Of course they would ask her about Yiannis. They all knew she was having dinner with him, the night they had left and she couldn't fob them off as easily as she had Molly. There was probably no point in doing anything but being perfectly honest with them.

She had an amazing week in Crete. A passionate affair, but now it was over She didn't regret one second of it. She was just disappointed at how it had ended. But that's life and now it was time to move on… She hadn't been straight with Molly the night before. She really couldn't have faced that conversation straight after flying home.

Kate usually found it therapeutic talking to her friends. This time it was both therapeutic and exhausting. One half of her wanted to talk about Yiannis and their parting and the other half wanted to forget about him and move on… The girls were thrilled to hear they had gotten together and what's more, they seemed none too surprised. They reckoned they had seen it coming. Each of them had their own opinion to offer. It seemed they all liked him, from the short time spent in his company. He had charmed them all, each and every one. Kate knew that. But what she really needed to know was where to go from here. Talking about him was partially reliving the whole experience. At some stage she would have to meet him again, he had keys to her holiday home, and would have her paintings…

How would that go? she wondered. It doesn't matter, she answered her own question.

She wouldn't have to deal with all that, until the following year. And he'd be a dim and distant memory by then, she hoped. At least the affair would. But like her, the girls couldn't fathom the airport bit. They chewed on it and dissected it over and over, desperately looking for some reason to excuse his behaviour other than what Kate thought – that he was moving on – very quickly. It hurt just a little to think of him moving on so quickly.

"It doesn't fit with his personality to behave like that! He's not rude." they kept saying.

Kate was inclined to agree but what other excuse was there? The one thing she didn't want to do was turn the whole week into a negative experience when it had been anything but.

"Look it's all academic!" Kate finally exclaimed in exasperation. "For a week, I had a ball. And now it's over. So that's that!"

Kate didn't convince anyone, not even herself.

Anxious to get back on track and put Yiannis to the back of her mind, Kate followed this mad urge she had to clear and declutter her house. Starting with a vengeance, she cleaned out every wardrobe and press. She hired a skip and dumped a load of stuff she had been meaning to get rid of for years. Copious amounts of black sacks found their way to charity shops. She got a painter and launched herself into the complete redecoration of the house, to give it a fresh new feel.

She wasn't even remotely aware but somewhere in her consciousness Kate had latched onto Yiannis' text. At some level she was waiting for a call. She became fixated with having her phone nearby – just in case. And every now and again she'd check it, as if somehow willing it to ring. Days later when she finally saw his name flash on the screen, her heart jumped in her chest!

It wasn't awkward like she thought it might be. It felt really nice to hear his voice again. Safe somehow, but much to her dismay, it accentuated a deep ache of longing for him. In spite of all this, she couldn't help but feel a little sceptical as they spoke at length about the happenings in Crete and Ireland. Which Yiannis was she speaking to, she wondered, the friendly one or the rude one?

He told her the weather had changed dramatically the day after she left. They were now having one of the coldest Novembers on record. He asked her lots of questions about the yoga centre she was attending. Thanks to her suggestion, he said he hoped to go ahead with a similar type centre at the old monastery. He had shut down her house. And the exhibition was due to wind up in about a week. He congratulated her, as all the paintings were sold, so there would be nothing for him to pick up. Isabella would be in touch with her in due course to sort out the finances. When they were all up to speed on each other's lives, Yiannis awkwardly said to her, "Kate I'm sorry about the airport. About letting you go without saying anything. I was on another planet. You left so quickly… It all took me by surprise!"

He didn't tell her that he had waited at the airport for a long time, thinking illogically that at any minute she'd walk back out. That he eventually followed her in, only to find the flight was checked in and there was no sign of her. She had long since gone through security.

"Don't worry about it," Kate replied a little thrown he had even brought it up. "I know it wasn't your style. I'm sorry too. I didn't exactly hang around to give you a chance to say anything."

And that was that, conversation over. They both clicked off and Kate promised to ring a couple of weeks later.

As soon as the call finished, Kate was all over the place. She felt sick to her stomach and she wished she could rewind the clock and be back in Crete again. She had loved hearing his voice, with his perfect English and Greek accent. She was so happy that he had rung her and not faded into oblivion like she thought he might. His apology had sounded so genuine that maybe the airport hadn't been about him moving quickly on. It was still strange though. Something still didn't sit right with her. Regrettably, there was only the smallest of connections between them now – a set of keys. Part of her wished all the paintings hadn't sold so she would have to go back to the stone cottage.

'God! What was wrong with her?' she scolded herself. But at least they were friends. Maybe, maybe she could move on.

On the outside things looked good for Kate. She appeared healthy and content. She was busy with the house, attending her yoga classes and having regular massages. Out and about meeting people. But only the closest people to her knew that there was a spark missing since she had returned from Crete. The glint was gone from her eye and her natural sense of good fun was in short supply. A sense of fun that had taken so long and lots of therapy to rekindle after Paul. She wouldn't admit it to anyone, not even herself, but Kate was missing Yiannis terribly. They all quietly guessed.

In Western Crete, Yiannis threw himself into his work. He took on way too much and soon found himself snowed under, welcoming the fact that he was so occupied. It didn't leave him much time to think. He was up every morning first thing. He would spend the day in the monastery, on the road travelling to the next job or was to be found in the workshop late at night. Nikos found it hard to catch up with him, as if Yiannis was avoiding him somehow. When he eventually did, Yiannis looked tired and drawn.

Nikos casually enquired about Kate, and knew immediately from the reaction, therein lay the problem. He just muttered he didn't know when she'd be back.

Yiannis worked hard for weeks and weeks, anxious to go full steam ahead renovating the monastery. The plans were nearly drawn up and ready to go. And then one night, when he was home late, exhausted and with all his defences down, he thought about Kate and had her name pressed on his phone before he could talk himself out of ringing her.

She sounded happy, like she was in the next room, but he couldn't see her face, to tell how she was really feeling. It was hard to know where it had gone wrong, given that they had such an incredible week together. Both of them had been acting more like polite strangers over the last couple of calls. There was a lot left unsaid, at least on his part… He missed her. He missed everything about her, their long talks and chats and how they laughed about everything. She sometimes had a different perspective on things and was refreshingly honest with him. Not to mention how he missed her at night. He felt he wanted more than friendship with her. He had felt that after their first night together. And he was sure she had felt it too. Bodies don't lie.

In Ireland Kate continued with the painting and redecoration of her house. She got rid of some older fixtures and fittings. Put in new floor length windows to maximise the lush green views she had, and treated herself to new furniture, a luxurious new bed and some to die for accessories. Unintentionally she had completely updated her house in a warm inviting style all with a creative twist.

By Christmas, both Kate and Yiannis had decided the new year would be a good time to put it all behind them and move on with their lives. Not too easy of course when there's some lingering contact with the other person. Kate was thinking at this stage, she wouldn't go to Crete at Easter and let the calls dwindle. The calls unsettled her and made her think about him more and more. She knew she was avoiding the issue. A part of her wanted more than friendship with him. She felt so confused. Anyway, it was all too late now. At least in Ireland, she wouldn't have to see him.

Yiannis spent Christmas with Nikos and Katerina.

Kate was with Molly, David and Jack.

It should have been a nice relaxing day, a day spent doing nothing. Just what the doctor would have ordered for both given that they were each working so hard, trying to forget the other. Naturally their thoughts drifted across Europe, wondering. They had shared a short phone call Christmas week, to wish each other season's greetings. But to be honest Kate was finding it a strain, trying to keep up the happy small talk with him

Once the New Year was rung in, Kate was adamant she was going to put a whole new plan into action for herself. God knows she was good at that. She needed a distraction, something totally different. Maybe she'd give online dating a go and amuse herself for a while. And she wanted to seriously look at getting a new exhibition up and running in Ireland, she needed to have a focus to work towards. Besides which at forty-three the menopause had kicked in and she needed to look after her body.

By mid-January Kate was feeling better, she thought, much more positive in herself. She had taken up a salsa class with the girls and was back painting furiously in the studio, having put out a few feelers about an exhibition. She had made a real conscious effort to not think about him all the time. And there was progress, she was sure of it. She had even been asked out to dinner by a nice man in her dance class. And she had taken the plunge and signed up to an online dating agency. She definitely felt more upbeat in herself and more in control. So much so, she decided to test her theory. To prove to herself, she was getting on with her life, she decided to ring Yiannis in January, one last call, she vowed – to wish him well for the year ahead and finally let things drift.

When she reached him, he sounded relaxed and happy to hear from her. She was genuinely full of the joys, chatting away to him about the news in Ireland until she discovered he was in Athens. Kate was stabbed by such a feeling of jealousy, it nearly took her breath away. She almost couldn't breathe. As quickly as she could, she wished him well and wound up the conversation.

Yiannis in Athens on a social visit usually meant one thing. He would most likely hook up with his ex-girlfriend. He had told her that himself during one of their many chats. There was nothing wrong with that of course, but what really surprised Kate, was the depth of her jealousy. What did she think, for God's sake! This was exactly what she had hoped to avoid by herself and Yiannis remaining friends. The feelings, resulting from intruding into each other's lives.

What a load of crap! she thought. So much for progress. Well, that was that.

It was the final kick she needed to move on from him. She would cut Yiannis out of her thoughts and her life. He certainly had, so why couldn't she? She resolved she wasn't going back to Crete until summer at the very least, and definitely no more calls. It was more than time to file away her amazing week in November under happy memories. Time to finally let it go.

Yiannis had hooked up with his ex-girlfriend. He had gone to Athens for a break, in the hopes of lightening his mood. Himself and his friends had a very relaxed dinner and enjoyable evening. And as had happened so often in the past, Yiannis found himself heading home with Alexandra, his ex-girlfriend. They had lived together for a few years in his Athens days. They were part of the same circle of friends even though Yiannis was seldom with them now.

Back at Alex's apartment, she was puzzled by his behaviour. He is in a funny mood, she thought, he is behaving very strangely. Earlier he had been all over her. Then after a phone call, his mood had completely changed. Now, he was a cold fish, yet it was he who had initiated the whole evening.

This wasn't like him at all. Yiannis didn't play games.

Alexandra was no fool. Over the last few years they had been in a similar situation, lots of times, depending on whether either one of them was with someone or not. It was an arrangement that suited them both. Friends with benefits and all that. No strings. If they met a few times a year that was it. It was generally a memorable night.

Tonight though, Yiannis was behaving so out of character it really baffled her. In fact, it worried her a bit.

"Yiannis, are you ok? I'm getting mixed signals from you all night. One minute it's like you want to be with me and the next, you're far away – somewhere in your thoughts. What's wrong with you? Do you want to be here or not?"

"Sorry Alex. Do you mind if we talk for a while?"

"What is it, Yiannis? You're not yourself tonight."

Alexandra had a real soft spot for Yiannis and was probably over-protective of him. Living with him for three years had been one of the highlights of her life to date. But she was a smart girl and knew that his heart hadn't been in it. It wasn't what she had wanted but they had split amicably when he left to live in Crete.

"What is it, Yiannis?" she probed again.

He just shrugged his shoulders at her. And something in his gesture, his tired expression or her woman's intuition prompted her to say,

"Yiannis, you've met someone haven't you?" she hazarded a guess, as her heart sank in her chest.

He looked at her wearily and confirmed, "Yes and No."

"What do you mean yes and no? Who is she? And why are you here with me?"

Yiannis shrugged his shoulders again as if to explain. "She phoned earlier tonight."

And then rightly or wrongly, he poured his heart out to Alex. Glad to finally offload to someone. He told her about Kate. The exhibition. The affair. And the leaving. They talked through the night. Alexandra listening patiently, offering the woman's perspective even if she wished it was her. She had had her chance with him and it hadn't worked out. Truth be told, she was still a little in love with him. Who wasn't? He was every girl's dream man – kind, thoughtful and generous to a fault. Not to mention handsome and passionate. You always knew where you stood with him.

Lucky thing whoever his latest woman was.

She had seldom known Yiannis to behave like this about anyone before. And she had known him a long time. She couldn't help but feel a little sad and just a teeny bit envious. So she decided to play the long game and take a gamble. She advised him to go after her. He seemed smitten so maybe a bit of reverse psychology would work.

"Go to Ireland. Surely, it's worth a try. I know she said she wanted to be friends, but from what you've told me, she has no idea how you feel. See her face to face. You can't tell anything from a phone call. Worst case scenario, she's not interested. What have you got to lose? You know the saying, better to have loved and lost, than never to have loved at all."

Deep down Yiannis knew she was right. He decided there and then, that's exactly what he'd do. Somewhere in his mind he could hear his grand-mother's words echo Alex's. Follow your heart, no matter where it leads you, she had said to him, the day she died. And it looked like his heart was leading him to Ireland.

Yiannis took the first flight home in the morning.

Back in Crete, he sorted out his work, made a few phone calls. He had a few jobs to finish before he cleared his calendar for a week mid-February, organising Nikos to look after Zorba. He had nothing to lose, he knew. He could handle it if she refused him face to face, but it was the wondering and waiting that was killing him. Unfamiliar territory and all that.

In early February, Kate finally got to the doctor. She tested her hor-mones for the menopause, took samples and was very thorough. Basically, she gave her a full medical. It was as she was leaving the doctor's office, that her phone beeped. Lost in a world of her own, Kate absentmindedly checked to see who was looking for her. She almost laughed out loud when she saw Yiannis' name.

'Oh God! The universe is conspiring against me,' she thought ironically. It had been several weeks since the phone call when he had been in Athens.

Meet me in Dublin?? Her stomach did a ginormous flip.

He was coming to Dublin? How weird was this. Why was he coming to Dublin now? Must be something to do with work… Probably the yoga centre, he had asked so many questions about it. Could she handle seeing him? They could talk face to face.

She sent a text back straight away.

Of course. When?

Tomorrow!

Tomorrow? Jesus Christ! TOMORROW!

Great, text on your flight details and I'll pick you up….

Later that night, Kate was still reeling and went to have a glass of water. She threw it away and poured wine instead. She abandoned that too. She turned the tv on and mindlessly watched as the images flickered across the screen. Lost in her imaginings. She was in a right predicament and it was all her own fault. What to do? She needed to think this through.

A little less than twenty-four hours later. Kate was sitting in Terminal 1 waiting for his flight to come up on screen. She couldn't stop herself wondering and playing things over in her mind.

How would it go? How would she greet him? Why was he coming? What would he say? What would she say? How would he react? She nearly drove herself crazy, visualising the different scenarios.

She saw him then, before he saw her. Walking confidently out in that easy relaxed way of his. It had to be one of her favourite things about him. He was so comfortable in his own skin, he made everybody around him feel relaxed. Smiling and chatting to someone near him, all the while, his eyes skimming the crowd, seeking her out. In his denim jeans, dark sweater and jacket. He looked gorgeous, of course, all six foot four of him. Whatever about out of sight, out of mind, there wasn't a hope of that now. Now he was very much in her sight and in her mind.

Instantaneously her physical body reacted. All at once, she had this really nice, warm, safe feeling, mixed with a strong feeling of desire.

He saw her then. For two seconds it was like they were back on Crete, in early November. The intensity between them… It was as if the intervening months had never happened. Her heart pumped hard in her chest.

Yiannis thought Kate looked as beautiful as ever. Maybe just a little tired. She looked tired. She was smiling at him but intuitively he knew there was something different about her. What that was, he didn't know, but something was different.

How he had missed her…

Not sure of her ground, Kate kissed him on both cheeks mumbling how nice it was to see him again, and really meaning it. They chatted, making small talk about safer subjects as they set off to her car. She had booked him into a nearby hotel. They could go, drop his bag and get something to eat, she suggested.

"We need to talk, Yiannis. We really need to talk."

"I know," he agreed.

By the time they collected Kate's car, got to the hotel and to his suite, things were strained. If he thought it strange she had booked him into a hotel, he said nothing. And he could clearly see she had no bag with her. She obviously had no intention of staying in Dublin. More and more he could sense her awkwardness.

Maybe he should never have come. And yet, as soon as the door to the suite closed behind them, Kate slowly turned to him.

"Yiannis, I'm pregnant," Kate spoke softly and she could feel the tears well behind her eyes. It was as if she was affirming it to herself, as she was telling him.

A silence descended between them, in contrast to all the small talk since the airport.

Yiannis looked at Kate shell-shocked. He took a step away from her. He went to say something, and then stopped.

'This changes everything,' he thought.

Finally, after what seemed like an eternity, he said, "Congratulations, Kate. I didn't realise you were dating someone."

"Oh God! Yiannis, no… No, I'm not dating anyone! It's yours. It's your baby…" she barely whispered.

She waited for her words to sink in.

Seconds passed.

'She would never be that cruel,' he thought shaking his head slowly.

"Kate, you know it's not possible."

"But it is, Yiannis. It has to be! I know it's my fault! Remember in Crete, we didn't… at least I stopped you…" She didn't finish her sentence, desperately looking at him for help, thinking back on how she had thrown caution to the wind in lots of different ways. How she, they, had gotten carried away making all kinds of assumptions. Thinking there was no need. Ultimately it had been her decision.

"How could I forget," he answered her just barely audible, a frown across his brow. For a second the same image flashed through their minds.

"Yiannis," Kate continued uncertainly, "think how your life changed when you left the city. You told me yourself how you swapped a very stressed life for a stress free one. You started to live a really contented life in Crete. Maybe that's got something to do with it too. I don't know! Look, I don't know why this has happened now for you or me. But you know it only takes one…" Kate's voice tapered out. She felt like she was pleading with him to believe her. She didn't have all the answers. All she knew was that it was happening to her, to them, now…

Yiannis stared at her as if in some kind of daze, shook his head and walked away from her. He was finding it hard to take in. He had to process this. Kate let out a sigh and sank into the nearest chair. She would give him time.

This was big for him. Very big. It was big for her too, of course. Huge. But very big for Yiannis. He looked overwhelmed, a bit like she had been the evening before. At least she had had the night to think about it.

Ten minutes passed before Kate followed him. She found him sitting on the bed in the other room, his head in his hands, for once looking a bit lost. Her heart went out to him. Unsure of herself and of what to do, she knelt down on the floor in front of him, took one of his hands and spoke very, very gently.

"Yiannis? I know this is really big for you… It's big for me too. I only found out yesterday. But it's good news. Somehow, we managed to make a baby, between us in Crete."

At least he was looking at her now.

Kate nervously continued, "I'm terrified Yiannis. I'm in my forties and it's twenty-two years since David… I'm afraid. I'm really afraid. But I've been given this amazing chance. No matter what happens, we'll always share this bond now. The baby can travel over and back between us, spend time in both countries. We'll make it work somehow. We'll make something work." She was still nervous. He hadn't said anything, not one thing. He appeared to be totally dazed. Just looking at her.

Yiannis knew, just like he always knew when Kate was speaking from her heart. He shook his head, gazing at her with the intensity of the world in his eyes.

"Kate," he whispered, "wherever did you come from? You blasted your way into my life like a shooting star, and then you were gone, in a week. And now you tell me we're having a baby… A baby! The impossible becomes possible…"

She gently wiped a tear from his eye with her hand.

He put his arms around her and buried his face in her hair. Kate closed her eyes, inhaling him to the very depths of her being. And they held onto each other for a long time.

Eventually, it was Kate who pulled away, as if suddenly remembering. "Yiannis, if you're with someone else now, that's ok too. It's all good. Nothing will change the fact that we're having this baby."

"Is that what you think, Kate?" he interrupted. "That I'm with someone else? I'm not. Why do you think I'm here now?"

Kate looked confused, not knowing what to think.

"I don't know. The yoga centre, I suppose? All our conversations have been about the yoga centre. It's just that when I rang in January, you were in Athens. I thought you were back with your old girlfriend…"

It sounded like she was questioning him, and she didn't want to do that. They were free agents after all. No ties.

Suddenly a few things made sense to Yiannis. He thought about their last phone call. How he had sensed her mood change from one sentence to the next. She had assumed he was with Alex in Athens. She was half right after all. Had she been jealous? And she thought he was in Ireland about the yoga centre.

"Kate, I'm not here about the yoga centre. I came to Ireland to see you. To see if we could make something work between us. You and me. Miracle baby aside, I want something with you. Since the week in Crete I've wanted something with you. That's why I've come. For no other reason."

Kate was silent. She was looking at him now with a puzzled look on her face. Like the dots were joining up for her. All the bits falling into place. All except his behaviour at the airport. "But what about the airport, Yiannis? Why didn't you say anything that day? Why didn't you even speak to me? I thought it was your way of finishing things."

"Kate," he sighed, "I'm sorry about the airport. You wanted us to be friends! Friends was the last thing I wanted. By the time I thought of something to say, you were gone."

"So you came to Ireland, to see if we could start something together? You and me?" she repeated slowly.

"To continue where we left off… I hope."

He let the idea sit for a few moments before he pressed her, "What about it, Kate? The two of us? Will you give us a chance? See where this goes?" Yiannis asked, watching her face carefully for reaction.

Kate sighed and her face broke into a slow resigned smile. She was tired. Tired of missing him. Tired of wondering about him. Tired of wanting him.

"I think maybe I'd like to give it a go. I don't think this friends thing is working for us!"

"I could have told you that in Crete!" Yiannis smiled taking her gently back into his arms, sensing the intensity in the room finally lifting.

"You are willing to try us, Kate, the two of us?" he asked again, to make sure.

"Let's try it for a while and see how it goes…" she answered a little cautiously. "Slowly… Slowly…"

"Are we really having a baby, Kate?" he asked still a little unsure and emotional.

"It appears as if we are," Kate nodded her head, beaming at him. And then, as if suddenly having a thought, before she even kissed him, she hopped up and said, "Yiannis don't move! I'll be back in five minutes. I have to go downstairs. I think I saw a chemist." Kate grabbed her bag and was gone before Yiannis even had a chance to react.

"What is she up to now?" he asked himself.

Good as her word, she appeared back a few minutes later, with something in her hand.

"Two more minutes, Yiannis," and she disappeared into the bathroom…

Kate emerged from the bathroom and went to him. He was standing by the window.

"Look!" And she held out something towards him. "It's a pregnancy test. Look here," and she pointed to the important bit.

"Pregnant, 12-14," it said.

Yiannis wasn't exactly sure what he was looking at, and it took him a minute to realise what was going on.

"Kate! I don't know what to say… Have you any idea what all this means? It's almost too good to be true. I know it doesn't work like this but if I could have picked anyone to have a baby with, it would have been you…" he sighed with relief, happiness, pride. He gently pulled Kate into his arms kissing her softly on the lips.

That was it, she was lost to him. Being with Yiannis was like going home. They made love tenderly, in some hotel room, near the airport. Crete all over again. Bodies and souls uniting. They had missed each other so much.

"Kate, this is like some crazy destiny thing." Yiannis whispered to her afterwards. "In the blink of an eye, you have given me what I want most in the world. A chance to be a father and a chance with you. It couldn't have worked out better."

They decided to lock themselves away for a couple of days, just the two of them, somewhere quiet, with no distractions. They had a lot to talk about and get their heads around. Two different countries. Two different lives. A baby on the way. Their fears, reservations and hopes. And they had a lot of catching up to do. Then, they would tell everybody together.

They found a beautiful old country house just south of Dublin, the perfect place to talk and discuss their plans. Unwittingly, with so much else on their minds, they had checked in on Valentine's Day. Yiannis decided that it was a good omen for them. Mind you, he seemed to have no worries or fears. He was crystal clear. He knew exactly what he wanted.

They agreed that he would stay for two weeks. Kate would go to Crete for a month at Easter. And Yiannis would fly over the last week in July for the birth. They just had to work out the in-between bits. And they'd see after that.

"Marry me, Kate?" he asked her the next morning as they lay in bed.

"Wow! Yiannis!... Where did that come from?" Kate replied rather quickly, a little shocked.

"I want this baby to have a mother and father to love him or her. Who'll be there for him. All the time."

"This child will have parents who love him. Let's spend some time together first. See how we get on. No matter what, I will always want you to be part of the baby's life. You're the father, that will never change whether we're together or not. Look at you and Alexandra? That was like a marriage. You were together for three years and you still broke up, it didn't work out." Kate was full of angst and what-ifs.

"Kate, I never asked Alex to marry me. I never talked to her and laughed with her the way I do with you. And we never, ever made love the way we do."

Yiannis silenced Kate for a few moments but he couldn't stop the thoughts inside her head. Kate had feelings for him and that's all she could commit to. She had no doubt that she wanted to be with him, but marriage? No way, there was no way she would ever marry again. The whole scenario reminded her of getting pregnant with Molly so young and marrying so quickly. It was a step too far for her now. She couldn't go there in her head. It was all too soon. She hadn't even got her head around the baby bit.

"Yiannis, I'll never marry again, ever. I just can't..." Kate said more ferociously than she intended to. She had to be straight with him. How could he be so confident? she wondered. She was the one who thought of the uncertainties. All the things that could go wrong. All the ways she could get hurt. The week in November had been a far cry from this. An affair she had thrown herself into it, body and soul, holding nothing back. Thinking it would be over in seven days. But this was very different. She needed to tread cautiously. She had been hurt before. She didn't want to go through all that again. She couldn't, and somehow, she had the feeling that Yiannis would have the capacity to hurt her if she let him.

Yiannis let it go. He knew she was frightened and even guessed why. To him, Kate epitomised everything that was good and right about the world. She was kind and compassionate. Funny and confident with a strong sense of her own worth. She had an open, warm heart. Not to mention the fact that she was beautiful and passionate. And now she was going to be the mother of his child. He was crazy about her. But there was no point in trying to force the issue. He was happy to be with her.

After two beautiful days in Wicklow, they went back to Dublin to break the news to Molly and David. Both of them were thrilled, even over-protective David. They both liked Yiannis and only wanted to see their mother happy. Anyone could see he was crazy about her and there was huge excitement when they realised there would be a new addition to their family too.

"Will you try and make it down tomorrow night for the dinner?" she asked them, "I'd love you both to be there."

"We'll be there, Mam!" they chorused. "We wouldn't miss it for the world!"

Kate had text all her friends and asked them to dinner on Friday night. Not one of them had a clue Yiannis was even in the country. They thought it was a good way of breaking the news to them all, together.

The dinner at Kate's became a celebration. A new relationship and an unexpected pregnancy. The wine flowed while Yiannis wowed them all with his cooking skills. Everyone was thrilled for them, and not too surprised that they were together again. The good news lifted all their spirits.

Yiannis and Kate slipped back into their old easy way of being together. Kate liked being the other half of a couple with him, someone to share the small stupid stuff with, to laugh with, to eat with, someone special to make love to, to feel safe with. And what a breath of fresh air it was to see everything in Ireland through Yiannis' eyes. Her home, her studio and her beautiful location, he loved it all. He continually marvelled at the views out every window whether lying in bed with her or at the table. She had exactly what he had, he said, only hers was a lush green and his a vibrant blue.

They travelled only a little, already a week nearly gone with all the drama. They made a few trips to the yoga centre, spent time with Molly and David, and Kate's friends. David even took him to the pub for a pint, the seal of approval from him. His second week evaporated with all the comings and goings. But without doubt, a magical moment was being able to go to the ultrasound together. Suddenly it became very real indeed. He held her hand the whole time and said very little. It was only the second occasion she had seen him stuck for something to say. Quite quickly Kate had learned that when Yiannis went quiet, he was generally processing something or mulling something over in his head exactly as had happened at the airport.

It was miraculous for them both to see this tiny new life, its heart beating on a screen. It put everything into perspective and neither of them wanted to know the sex. A surprise for the birth, they agreed as Kate gave him the photo to take back to Crete.

A couple of days later, as she dropped him to the airport, he slipped something into her pocket.

"Open it when I'm gone," was all he said.

He had bought her a delicate neck chain with two hearts centred on it. One white gold, one rose gold and had written a note:

I may have helped open your heart Kate, but you have mine. Y x

Kate was touched. He had never mentioned the ceramic hearts before, and she had forgotten all about them. Obviously, he hadn't…

They spoke every night on the phone when he was gone, sometimes for over an hour. Trying to find a way of being together they could both live with. And before they knew it, weeks had flown by and Kate was on her way to Crete to spend the entire month of April with him. It was a totally new experience for her to land in Chania and have Yiannis waiting there to pick her up. She actually felt a little shy and strange at first, embracing him when she landed. It felt very different, and very nice.

Before April, Kate had been a little apprehensive about how things would work out for them. A whole month together as a real couple. It would be their first real test. She need never have worried, so many amazing things happened.

The weather was delightful. Gentle sunshine the whole time she was there. Vibrant colours and new growth everywhere. An island in the full throes of a beautiful spring after a long hard winter. Yiannis joked it was a bit like himself!

Along with the monastery, renovations were well underway at the stone cottage. Yiannis wanted to extend before the baby arrived so they split their time between the work shed and Kate's house. She spent hours with him at the yoga centre, giving her opinion, suggesting a few things she thought might help and then back at base amusing and entertaining him with her new postures for pregnancy yoga. Or on the odd occasion he had to travel anywhere, he didn't have to try too hard to get Kate to travel with him. She enrolled in an intensive Greek class in the city and met up with Sophia every couple of days for coffee, to practice her fledgling Greek.

Whenever she could, she spent enjoyable hours in Nikos's vegetable garden, tending what he had already sewn or sometimes planting new seedlings and then getting Nikos or Yiannis to do the heavier manual work for her, mainly Nikos as Yiannis was so busy. Kate dabbled only a little at painting, ending up with one small canvas for the cottage. It wasn't the same tranquil place it had been the previous summer, with all the work that was going on.

They visited the church on the peninsula where Yiannis' grandparents had met, which in hindsight was one of the highlights of the trip. She had loved it. The ruggedness and beauty of the place. The remote windswept location perched on the edge of the world. She could almost picture his grandmother finding her one true love.

They lunched together almost every day, either at Kate's or she would meet up with him somewhere. And in the evenings when he was finished work, one of them would cook or they would go out to eat, continuing on their tradition of long leisurely, pleasurable meals and she got to meet and love all his Cretan friends from the village.

They celebrated Easter in both the Christian and Orthodox Greek style – a real community celebration. Kate was enthralled with all the religious processions, fireworks and lamb on the spit and of course a few *rakis* thrown in for good measure, the ultimate village experience.

Easter was also the time when Kate realised that Yiannis was wealthy, very wealthy. Not that it mattered to her in any way. But it inadvertently became the cause of their first row.

Yiannis had a car almost bought for her when she first arrived. Just like that, no discussion. He told her straight up he had more money than he would ever need and wanted to do this small thing for her. But Kate who was fiercely independent, stuck to her own arrangements with Costas, to rent a car for the entire month. Yiannis wouldn't let it go too easily

"Kate, it's dead money."

"I know, but it's my dead money."

"Kate, don't waste your money. Let me do this for you. Let me buy you a car."

"No, Yiannis. Thank you, but no."

"It makes sense, Kate."

"Maybe so, but the answer is still no!"

"Why?"

"Stop pushing me, Yiannis. I don't want your money. I have my own."

"I know that, Kate. I only want to do one small thing…"

"Yiannis No. You can't buy me… I'm not for sale," she finally shouted at him, wanting to put an end to the conversation and the feelings of discomfort she had.

Yiannis shrugged his shoulders, "I'm not trying to buy you. Kate, you know that," and he walked away from her into the work shed.

As soon as the words were out, Kate knew she was out of line. That was below the belt, she thought. Why had she said that when all he ever did was be good to her, pamper her and spoil her and look out for her. He didn't deserve it. She sat for a few minutes with her own thoughts, pondering.

Before long she followed him. He was at the table in the work shed, banging at something. Kate put her arms around him and held onto him tightly.

"I'm sorry, Yiannis. I'm really sorry… I know you weren't trying to buy me. You frighten me sometimes, you do so much for me. What would I ever do without you?"

"Don't be crazy, Kate," he answered her, "You won't ever have to do without me, unless you want to that is." He turned around taking her into his arms not sure where this had come from.

"I know you mightn't mean to, but you might leave me…" Kate retorted quietly.

"I'm positive, I'll never leave you, Kate."

"You never know, Yiannis, you mightn't mean to… You might die…" she whispered quietly.

And in that moment Kate showed her vulnerability. There it was, her one big fear and she hadn't even known herself until that instant. She almost felt naked in front of him, stripped bare, down to her very soul.

"Kate." Yiannis held her more firmly in his arms. How could he promise her this one thing he had no control over?

It was a learning curve for both of them. That same evening, she cried in his arms as she finally felt able to tell him the full extent of how things had been between herself and Paul before he died. How they had been struggling with the relationship despite perceived notions to the contrary. And the guilt she felt after he died. A huge overwhelming selfish guilt, for wanting a better life for herself and for burdening Paul for the last few months of his life.

Yiannis didn't judge her, he just held her and told her it was ok. Everything was ok. There was no need for her to feel guilty anymore. Things were the way they were back then. It wasn't her fault. It wasn't Paul's fault. It wasn't anyone's fault. It was just one of those things. He was the only person outside of her counsellor she had ever confided in. They didn't speak about it again but there was an understanding between them. Yiannis finally appreciated exactly where she was coming from and Kate realised what was holding her back.

Kate may have kept her car but Yiannis continued as always to spoil her in other ways. He was wonderful to be around, spontaneous, always making impractical gestures. The days were long and leisurely for her while he was working. Zorba at times abandoning his master to stay with her and accompany her no matter what she was doing.

Kate loved to watch Yiannis in his own environment, observe him as he interacted with people. How he carried out his business affairs. He had this gravitational pull, people were drawn to him, like a magnet – just like she was!

And he whisked her away to the mainland for a long romantic weekend. It was probably the other highlight of the whole trip for Kate. He brought her somewhere she had never been before, a small town on the mainland, in an ancient, historic part of the Peloponnese, overlooking The Gulf of Corinth. A place that was so steeped in history Yiannis said it could easily trace its roots back thousands of years. It was just the two of them, lazing the days away, exploring exactly like they had their first ever week together. One of the nights randomly stumbling across an open-air classical concert in the charming town square. Yiannis swore he hadn't known about it but Kate suspected differently. It was nearly too good to be true. They spent a delightful couple of hours, sitting on a stone step in the square, arms around each other, listening to the enchanting music. In their hearts, transported to another place and time. Kate had never experienced anything like it before.

Without doubt all the pampering was seductive but they both knew they would never have lasted the pace if there wasn't a connection between them. Yiannis was an amazing man, never making any demands on her or expecting anything from her, content to be with her. She knew he loved her, because he had told her so many times. She couldn't reciprocate, not yet anyway. But Kate found the more time she spent in his company, the more time she wanted to spend with him. The relationship was working. They were so in tune at times, they actually finished each other's sentences or had the same ideas about something. And then other times, sparks flew because they had such differing opinions and it gave them both a whole new perspective. Always respecting and learning from each other.

Kate got her own house repainted and bought a few new bits of furniture. Even though they were staying between both places, she couldn't even think about getting it ready to rent. It was like her safety net, her 'just in case it doesn't work out' place. She didn't think too far into the future, just trying to take every day as it came. Anyway she told herself, friends or relatives travelling out might need it sometime. Typical Yiannis though, he continued full steam ahead with the renovations at the cottage, adamant they would be finished by the time the baby arrived.

Two bedrooms were being added to the cottage. He was thinking of Molly or David wanting to visit. "If this is your home, it's their home too," he would say to her matter-of-factly. "Besides," he added suggestively, "What about you and me, don't you want us to have a bedroom to ourselves? Just the two of us…"

Kate laughed at him. The way he said things sometimes and looked at her could almost instantly turn her into a pulsating ball of desire.

He had taken on an apprentice to help him out and give him breathing space seeing as he planned to be travelling quite a bit over and back to Ireland. She envied him, his total confidence in them.

Kate's body was changing at an alarming rate, nearly six months pregnant now. She felt full and ripe and in her prime. Her fears about giving birth at her age had receded, just a little. Yiannis continued to reassure her and say that whatever life threw at them they'd handle together. He was fascinated how pregnancy could make her more beautiful and more desirable. Kate loved waking up beside him in the mornings and going to bed with him every night. When she left Crete after Easter, having already changed her ticket to stay an extra week, she felt recharged, relaxed and vibrantly healthy. This was to be their longest separation, until nearer the birth. Kate knew she would miss them all – Yiannis, Zorba, Nikos, Katerina, the place, everything. She was hardly on the plane when she knew she couldn't wait to be with him again.

Back in Ireland, barely a month later at the end of May, Kate learned that she amongst other artists was to be honoured with an award for artistic endeavours. She guessed she had been chosen because of the success of the exhibition in Chania. She knew there had been talk about it in artistic circles in Ireland and it had even made an article in one of the papers. It was a very big honour for her and everybody of course was thrilled.

In a way though, Kate dreaded the thought of the night. Not the award, of course. She was chuffed about that but the type of night she assumed it would be. A prestigious formal function, a black-tie and evening gown affair, probably a forgettable meal, lots of speeches and having to make small talk to people she didn't even know. Everything she disliked in a night out. And of course, it didn't help that she was seven months pregnant and suddenly feeling large and hormonal. Yiannis was in Crete and not due to travel over for another month, so busy he was well out of the picture. Definitely one of the down sides to a long-distance relationship, Kate thought to herself. To not go would have been unbelievably rude and ungracious. Feeling just a little vulnerable, she decided to go the whole hog, pampering herself luxuriously ahead of the night; hair, nails, new dress, etc. to give herself a well-deserved boost. They had taken a table at the function. Molly, Jack, David, Jane and a few other friends. All the usual suspects, supporting her as always. Kate was the only one to be put up at the hotel courtesy of the awards. She had splashed out on a red, strapless chiffon full-length dress that flowed over her curves. "It even makes my bump look respectable," she laughed to herself. And the colour suited her to perfection, intensifying her healthy Cretan tan. She looked stunning. Putting the final touches to her make-up, Kate answered the hotel-room door to Molly and the rest of the gang.

And there he was… large as life, in full technicolour, stood Yiannis, with a big grin on his face, complete with dress suit, ready to take her to the ball.

Kate stood in the doorway, shaking her head trying to take it in, not fully believing her own eyes. A myriad of emotions crossed her face. Disbelief and gratitude warred within her that this man had flown across Europe to be with her. Relief that she wouldn't have to go on her own. And most importantly, the dawning realisation that she truly loved him. Not because he had made the grand gesture. No, she realised that she had probably loved him from the start but hadn't admitted it to herself. She hadn't asked for a knight in shining armour, but by God had she got one!

Transfixed, it was as if she was staring at her other half. Kate had always felt full and complete in her own right, but she realised she was a better person by merely being around him. With Yiannis life was vivid, intense and amazing. Without him, it was a little less vivid. Overwhelmed she just managed to mumble, "Oh my God, Yiannis!" and fling herself into his arms, before giving into the tears. He held her without saying a thing until she stopped crying, finally asking, "Could I come in now?" Both of them dissolved into laughter. One ruined white shirt later and a make-up overhaul and they were sitting at the table with the others. They had all known he was coming of course, everyone except her.

All night long at the function, in between the official demands, Kate was curiously quiet, not her usual talkative self, calmly observing Yiannis. Smiling to herself, as if she was silently processing something. Wondering why it had taken her so long to realise she loved him. She kept looking at him.

"Are you still checking me out, Kate?" he teased her, looking directly at her bump. "See where that got us last time?"

"Always, Yiannis. I hope I'm always checking you out," she laughed back.

He sat next to her all night long, his arm casually slung over the back of her chair, even his body language confirming his presence. For Kate, it was a defining moment in their relationship. She could clearly see a future for them now. Life was almost unimaginable without him. And as luck would have it, it seemed the moment her personal life was on track; her career was on an upward curve in tandem. New connections were made that night copper-fastening Kate as the emerging artistic in Ireland. How she managed to bag herself a personal assistant she wasn't sure. Everybody it seemed wanted a piece of her, but she had eyes only for Yiannis.

Later that night, as they made love, it was the first time she ever told him that she loved him. Yiannis knew that for Kate to admit she loved him was a big step. Deep down he had known it. He may have joked that the trip was worth it, just to see her face. But he knew what it really meant to her.

He stayed a week.

Carried along, on this wave of spontaneity and positivity, Kate travelled back to Crete with him for a further week. And Yiannis did the same thing all over again, a few weeks later, out of the blue, just because he missed her. And then, as planned, towards the end of July, Yiannis bought a one-way ticket to Ireland. And they settled down to wait for the impending arrival.

On the first of August, Seán Yiorgas Dimitris Theodorakis, named after his father and grandfathers before him, was born in Ireland. A healthy nine-pound baby boy. A big shock of black hair and dark sallow skin. Everything went perfectly. Kate was exhausted and exhilarated, all rolled into one. All her fears disappeared with the relief of safe delivery. And Yiannis, he looked like someone who had been hit by a truck with his rapid introduction to childbirth. He stayed with her through every ache and pain. When it was all over, he stood there quietly staring at the two of them, like someone not quite sure what to do with himself, momentarily insecure. Very quickly Kate passed Seán to his dad to hold and within minutes, he was back suckling at his mother's breast. They both laughed. He was a hungry child. Why were they not surprised seeing as the simple pleasure of food played such a large part in their lives.

Yiannis was truly overcome. Their miracle child. He couldn't express how he felt that day. There was a huge swelling of his heart, like it had tripled in size. The arrival of his son Seán… His son… Something he thought would never happen and he had never seen a more natural or more beautiful sight than Seán being fed by his mother. They marvelled at the wonder of nature and how privileged they felt to have played a part in bringing a new life into the world. Yiannis was completely happy. Himself and Kate. And now, Seán, his son to complete the picture. He asked her again to marry him but she quietly reassured him they were perfect just as they were.

They spent four weeks in Ireland allowing Seán to settle into some kind of routine and get to know his Irish family, most particularly his big brother and sister, Molly and David, who took it all in their stride. But as soon as Seán's passport arrived they booked their flights. Kate knew Yiannis was dying to bring Seán home. This would be their first taste of the reality of being in Crete with a baby, all three of them together.

Just as in Ireland, everybody in Crete was dying to see their little bundle of joy and celebrate his safe arrival into the world. Nikos and Katerina, were beside themselves with excitement, the unofficial grandparents, doting on little Seán, just as they had always doted on Yiannis and more recently Kate too.

It was funny to watch Zorba as he assumed the role of guardian. He would sit by the door of their bedroom all day long and only move when Seán was moved. Cock his head at Yiannis or Kate as if to say, I'm in charge now.

Life settled into blissful, disorganised chaos at the stone cottage. The place was a bomb site, with baby stuff everywhere. Kate hadn't even time to take in all the new renovations. Sometimes she smiled to see Yiannis scratching his head, looking a little bemused as if he wasn't quite sure what had happened. He looked a bit helpless but supported Kate as best and in whatever way he could. He had to get back to work, so everyday Katerina came to prepare food or wash some clothes or do whatever was needed.

Yiannis tried to work as much as possible from home, reluctant to be away from either of them. Seán was still awake at night so Kate slept when Seán slept. Sometimes Yiannis was awake with them but mostly he'd just put his arm around Kate and fall back to sleep. She insisted there was nothing he could do, there was no point in the two of them losing sleep. Kate loved this precious time she had with Seán. She knew once it was gone, it was gone forever. She loved holding him close in her arms and cuddling him. Or the feel of his baby soft skin against hers and the warmth and smell of him and the strong bond she felt while feeding him. But gradually, little by little, the hours between feeds extended, things improved and one night, miracle of miracles, he slept through.

The odd day, Yiannis got to have Seán all to himself while Kate went out to do some errand or other. On this particular day, it was hot, very hot for September. A beautiful breeze was blowing on the peninsula cooling everyone down.

When Kate arrived back from the doctors, the only sound to be heard was the crickets making the usual deafening racket. No sign of Yiannis or Seán or Zorba.

When she finally found them, they were in the bedroom - all three of them asleep. Seán was lying across his father's chest, skin on skin, their breathing perfectly synchronised and Yiannis' arms were around him, protectively. Zorba was asleep on the floor at the end of the bed. Kate touched her heart and looked on for what seemed like an eternity.

A magical sight. Father and son, they looked so perfect together. Imagine if she had never met Yiannis that evening on the promenade? Imagine if he had never followed her to Ireland? The different turn their lives could have taken… Now thank God, she had two new men in her life whom she adored. Kate felt an inexplicable feeling of expansion. It melted away her reservations, her fears and her doubts.

She made up her mind in that moment.

She gently lifted Seán, kissed him softly and put him into his cradle. Then she knelt on the bed beside Yiannis.

He stirred, instinctively reaching out his hand to her. "Hi, you weren't long. Is everything ok?"

"Yes, perfect…" she whispered. "Yiannis? Yiannis, will you marry me?"

He was suddenly wide awake and took her into his arms. "Yes, of course I'll marry you! Yes! What brought this on?"

"I don't know. You and Seán asleep together. It seemed so perfect. So right somehow. I know I'm a part of this. But it's like I want more. I want to marry you. I want you to be my husband. It's like all my doubts and fears have vanished. We're good together Yiannis, the two of us. You know I love you."

"I've always known you love me, Kate. We will make it up as we go along. We've no big decisions to make until Seán starts school. We'll fly over and back until then. I don't know what the future holds, Kate. All I know is I love you and Seán. I know you were badly hurt when Paul died. I don't plan on going anywhere but I don't control the future. I can't guarantee anything. I want to grow old with you. I want to spend whatever time I have with you and Seán. We'll be ok, Kate. Actually, we'll be better than ok. We'll be great together. We are great together." He hesitated a little. "Speaking of ok. Are we ok? Can we… you know?"

Kate just laughed and answered him by kissing him full on the lips, so there could be no doubt.

PART 3

TEXT GATE

It was 6 p.m. when her mobile beeped.

She recognised the number immediately and opened her messages to read the full text.

It's time to put the plan into action

Leaving soon

Text now

M

***

Ok

When?

Flight details??

***

Next day or 2

I'll let u know

Rem protocol with db

***

Yes Tiny amount – same as prep

***

Be careful
Has to be EXACT MEASURE

***

Yes I know
Never done before
Bit unsure

***

His hand froze in mid-air about to compose the next text and his jaw clenched. He wasn't fully sure about her. But it had to be done straight away or they could both kiss their plans goodbye.

Do you want out?

***

No

***

Rem why - K bleeding him dry

***

I know! No second thoughts

I'd love a mon too!!

***

Send the 1ˢᵗ text now or 2 late

***

She calmly composed the text and pressed the send button before she got cold feet. It was all for the best. He was being played for a fool and she had to stop it.

OK Done

I'll let u know as soon as I have news

***

Heard back from Y

He's on

***

Gr8! Arrange for tom nite

Last flight to X

OA344

Ring u later to confirm all

***

Done
All hell broke loose
Made it look good!
Feel guilty…

***

??
No need
I'll pick up the pieces this end, Y all yours

***

Chapter Thirteen

BETRAYAL

The reality of weaving two independent lives, two different countries and raising a small child kept their nuptial plans on hold for a couple of years. Life was good but continually busy, busy, busy.

Kate often thanked her lucky stars that she now had her very own personal assistant, acquired the night of the awards ceremony in Dublin. Thank God for Matthew.

She appreciated this relative newcomer into her life. He helped her organise the details of her busy comings and goings, leaving her time to focus on painting and Seán. If it wasn't for Matthew, she would have missed many of the flights to and from Ireland. It had taken herself and Yiannis, (well really Yiannis) two years to get their act together and organise the civil wedding the previous November. That in itself had forced them both into thinking about where they wanted to settle. They were a bit of a disaster sometimes allowing things to drift along and unfold organically. But before Yiannis left after Christmas, they decided that by the wedding party in late spring they'd have a decision made one way or another.

After a near perfect Christmas in Ireland, Yiannis returned to Crete a couple of weeks ahead of Kate and Seán. Before that, they had spent the holidays with Molly and David but Yiannis had work commitments in Crete and Kate needed to stay in Ireland to attend to some exhibition stuff. Matthew had organised a major exhibition in New York in the early summer and they had to draw up a plan of painting action and sort out all the logistics.

Randomly, just before he left Yiannis had said that maybe it was time they sort something more permanent out, that maybe it was time he moved to Ireland. Kate was quite taken aback when he had said it, and quite delighted if she was honest. They had been mullacking along as best they could over the last couple of years, but she hadn't realised he was thinking along those lines. She always thought, it was mainly her who did the missing. At least she was the one who vocalised it the most these days.

Unwittingly, Yiannis had given Kate plenty to think about when he went back to Crete. Aside from Molly and David and her friends, Kate had no real reason for basing herself or her career in Ireland. Her two older children had their own lives and homes. They ended up travelling to Crete so often for holidays she saw even more of them, especially since Seán was born. Moreover, she couldn't imagine Yiannis living full time in Ireland. Whatever way she turned it over in her head. He was Cretan to the core. She realised she wouldn't mind making the move herself. All along Kate had been lucky enough to do exactly what she loved. From the first day at art college, she took to painting like a duck to water, always following her instincts about career choices. And ultimately of course it had led to a successful and prosperous livelihood for her. There was no way she would ever turn her back on Ireland or her friends, but Kate thought a more permanent move to Crete might be a very good idea. The light was amazing and it was always so easy to paint there. All week long while working alongside Matthew, she had been preoccupied, tossing all the different scenarios around in her head. And then quite suddenly at the end of the first week, she made her final decision. They may have had fulfilling separate lives, but Kate missed Yiannis to distraction when they were apart. Time didn't seem to be improving anything in that regard. Enough was enough! She was tired of the separations, the goodbyes and the continual dragging of Seán from Ireland to Crete and vice versa. He missed his Dad when he was with Kate and missed his Mum when he was with Yiannis.

Now that fame and a lucrative career beckoned, Kate realised it wasn't what she craved at all... A successful career flying here and there to exhibitions, living the so-called good life? To be further separated from Yiannis or Seán? Nothing fulfilled her as much as chilling on the peninsula, working in the studio there or being with a man she adored and mother to their miracle child. No, life was good and more than enough to fulfil her at every level of her being. Seán needed to put down firm roots and Kate finally decided it would be on the peninsula. She wanted him to have the same happy childhood his father had before him. Kate could easily move her artist's base to Crete and keep her home in Ireland, but she would cut out a lot of the toing and froing. So, much to Matthews's disgust, she cancelled out of the New York exhibition, cut her holidays short by a week and headed back to Crete to surprise Yiannis and pin down their future.

It was after midnight when their flight touched down in Chania Airport and well after one by the time they were in the taxi, en route to the peninsula. Seán was grouchy and overtired but Kate didn't mind she was so excited at the prospect of seeing Yiannis and filling him in on her new plans.

The cottage was in total darkness when the taxi pulled in and she smiled when she saw his jeep parked in the usual haphazard way, in front of her car. Good, he's in bed, she thought and as soon as Seán was settled she'd be joining him. A little quiver of anticipation brought goosebumps out all over her body as Kate let them in through the unlocked door.

Thankfully Zorba remained asleep in his basket and barely opened an eye as she tip-toed for the stairs. He could have barked the house down and ruined her surprise she chuckled to herself, but even Zorba seemed to be conspiring with her. With little or no hiccups, Seán sank into his soft comfy bed and turned straight over to fall fast sleep sucking his thumb and snuggling up in his blankets. Kate crept back down the stairs, thankful that Zorba had stayed asleep. Maybe it was all the decisions that had made her so giddy she thought as she padded from the bathroom to their bedroom or maybe it was that she was dying to see him again.

From the doorway of their bedroom the moon shone through curtainless windows and cast soft shadows over the room. Despite the dark she could easily make out Yiannis lying on his back breathing deeply and evenly, his chest exposed and his arm behind his head. As she edged closer towards him, she was momentarily puzzled by the space he was taking up in the bed.

He hadn't bothered to make it properly, she grinned to herself. She moved closer and then reversed quickly to the wall. Confused she flicked on the light switch to check out what was the strange shape in the bed.

From the door Kate's hands flew to her mouth and she gave a loud cry when she realised the scene she had walked in on.

There was a woman in the bed. Their bed.

A naked woman with blonde hair lay turned away from her.

Kate stood stunned, her throat dry and her heart pumping wildly in her chest as she swallowed several times in quick succession, her eyes glued to the woman's back.

Her cry stirred Yiannis. She looked on in disgust as he stirred and smiled at her.

"Kate...?" he said reaching out his hand.

He had the cheek to look confused when he took in the horror on her face. How stupid was he? Had he forgotten there was a naked woman beside him?

A shocked Kate stood frozen and watched aghast as her hopes and dreams for their future were disintegrating before her very eyes.

Suddenly real time kicked in and Kate sprang into action. She reversed out of the room to the sound of Yiannis' voice.

"Kate! Kate, wait... Please!"

And then a chillingly familiar voice purred, "Yiannis, what's going on? What are you doing? Come back to bed."

Kate was sick to her stomach and broke into a cold sweat when she heard that voice. A voice she thought she recognised. Yes, she did. It sounded just like, Yiannis' old girlfriend from Athens. The woman he had lived with for three years. The woman she had first met only the year before. The scene was playing out like a bad movie, but she had to go back and see for herself. To witness the sad sordid scene, to at least see her face.

She almost collided with Yiannis at the bedroom door.

"You bastard," she spat at him. "You complete bastard."

"Kate," he pleaded lamely, a hand on her arm. "Please don't go... I don't know..."

Even through the haze of emotions Kate could think rationally at some level. She looked through him with icy eyes and looked down at his hand.

"Don't you ever put your hand on me again. Ever. Now get out of my way!" she interrupted him and pushed him with such force he stumbled backwards, and she had a clear view to the bed.

As she had guessed. It was Alexandra, sitting up, clutching a sheet across her breasts. The beautiful Alexandra with her svelte, model like figure. An image she would never forget.

Up until that moment if someone had tried to tell Kate that Yiannis would ever be unfaithful to her, she never would have believed it. But there was no denying the picture in front of her eyes.

Jesus, she had to get away…

She stormed her way to the kitchen.

"Don't go, Kate! Please don't go!" Yiannis followed her, repeatedly imploring her to wait.

"Where are my keys? Where are my keys?" Kate ignored him as she frantically searched the worktop, desperate to get away from the house of horrors. She fumbled around the kitchen in anger looking in the most obvious places. She couldn't think where she had left them. Their wedding invitations landed on the floor, a casualty of her rage.

"Here, I have them," Yiannis held the keys. "Don't drive, Kate, you're not in a fit state. At least let me drive you please?" he pleaded.

"And whose fault is that. Give me the fucking keys…" Kate snarled and snapped them out of his hand. She gulped down the heartbreak and stoically tried to maintain some kind of composure. She would not cry. He would not see how devastated she was.

A little more steadily she barked at him, "Has it slipped your mind we have a son and he's in his bedroom? Or maybe you'd like your girlfriend to mind him? I certainly wouldn't!" and she stormed out the front door. She was in the car, leaving a shocked Yiannis behind before he had a chance to answer, but not before she noticed a third car in the yard partially hidden by the jeep.

Once Kate was in the car and on the way, she could feel the hurt and heartbreak course through her whole body, but she was determined she would not cry, not yet. Not until she was safely inside her own house.

Twenty minutes later, she slammed the door against the world, leaned against the back and sank to the floor. Two seconds later she was in the bathroom vomiting the contents of her stomach down the toilet. The steely composure she had maintained for the last thirty minutes deserted her and she ended up a crumpled mess on the bathroom floor. Kate sobbed her heart out and kept shaking her head not wanting to believe what she had just seen.

Yiannis from hero to zero in a second, and all her hopes and dreams for their future were gone with him. Almost immediately her phone started to ring, his name lit up the screen in the dark room. Viciously she switched it to silent and flung it away from her.

Had that all just happened?

How could her life have changed so utterly, in such a short space of time?

How could he have done that to her? How long had it been going on?

Only that she had seen it with her own eyes, she never would have believed it of him. Never! What a spectacular fool he had made of her and what a bad judge of character she must be. Jesus all the times he had been in Crete without her since they got together.

Kate steeled herself. She had been down a similar road before, grieving over a man and as she surrendered to the tears again, she knew somewhere at her deepest subconscious level, she would survive this. She would come out the other end. She had before, and she would again but Jesus Christ how it hurt.

"You bastard!" she cried out loud. "You fucking bastard!"

How long was it going on? How did she not see the signs? She thought again of all the times Yiannis was on his own in Crete. All the opportunities he would have had. Was Alex the only one? She wondered tormenting herself with all the unanswered questions. She had never suspected a thing. For all his faults Paul had never betrayed her in such a cruel heartless way. Yiannis Theodorakis had played her for a fool. How naïve he must think she was.

And the worst bit, the worst bit was that she had been about to give up her whole life for him. Move to Crete so that they could be a proper family, the three of them. That would really have ruined his plans. He probably had it all arranged. He'd keep her in Ireland and then move the beautiful Alexandra to Crete to be near when he travelled back. She was such a fool. None of it made much sense to her. How she hated him in that moment. He had sucked her in so brilliantly, persuaded her to marry him, and she had fallen for it all – hook line and sinker. Up until an hour ago she never would have doubted him. Never. Now? Now, it was all a huge mess. Kate bawled again.

All night long the image of Yiannis and Alex in bed together kept coming into her mind. There was no way around it. He had shattered her heart into a million pieces in their bedroom at the stone cottage.

Every so often her crying was distracted as the screen of her phone lit up somewhere in the dark room.

"Why did you ever ask me to marry you if you wanted to play the field?" she screamed at the phone. And then she remembered how it was actually her who had asked him in the end. How naïve of her! No, not naïve, just plain stupid. Maybe he had been going off her at that stage. Maybe… But they had always seemed so compatible, or so she thought. There was no need for him to stray. And then she wondered whether there were others besides Alex. Kate shivered when she thought about the last time he had touched her the morning he left Ireland, barely a week ago. Jesus, maybe he was one of those sex addicts or maybe he was just a cheating bastard.

Oh God, why had he ever come into my life, she thought.

In the very next instant she thought about Seán and felt guilty. Wishing Yiannis away was like wishing Seán never existed and she could never do that. All the joy he had brought into her life.

A horrible thought suddenly struck Kate. Things between them had happened so fast, too fast. Maybe he had only married her because of Seán. A bit like Paul when she had gotten pregnant with Molly. She had heard of patterns repeating themselves. That had to be it. That made her cry even harder. Did he think he was doing the right thing? In his warped world of screwed manliness did he think she couldn't cope, a woman on her own? For

God's sake she had practically raised Molly and David on her own. Or much more deviously, was he just guaranteeing his paternal rights?

Out of the whole sad and sorry mess she had Seán, the only good thing out of her time with Yiannis. And she'd hang onto that.

Thinking about Seán made her feel strong again.

Yiannis was a good father. There were no complaints on that score and Seán worshipped the ground he walked on. Whatever happened between them, she was not going to use the relationship against him, but she could feel her beautiful life in Crete slipping away from her. Who knew what would happen next? All she knew was there was no way she could be near Yiannis again. She certainly didn't want to be in the same country as him. Horribly, history was repeating itself. She was alone in her house in Crete sobbing her heart out over a man.

Even though Kate lay on the bed to sleep, every time she closed her eyes an image of Yiannis and Alex making love appeared before her eyes. It sickened her to her stomach. She couldn't bear it. She needed to think, and fast. She needed to take some action. She wasn't going back to Ireland. She couldn't. Not yet. Without thinking about it too deeply, Kate retrieved her phone and looked through her texts. More than anything she needed space and distance. She started to formulate a plan and though she didn't make any definite decision, she had a fair idea what she would be doing in the very near future.

One thing she was sure of. She had no intention of ever telling anybody what she had walked in on. Her lips were sealed, if only to protect Seán.

Kate didn't sleep a wink that first awful night. Her mind was racing and her thoughts hopping between Yiannis and Alex and what she was going to do next. There was absolutely no hope of a restful sleep so at about eight am she roused her sore stiff body and went about opening up the house. She hadn't turned on the water and electricity the night before, so the place was a mess. She was a mess.

Bleary-eyed she pulled open the shutters. The bright January day dazzled her but not before she caught sight of a lone dark figure in the garden. Her stomach lurched. An intruder was all she needed now to finish off the night of all nights. The other houses were empty, so she knew she was alone and was more than a little concerned as the figure started to walk towards her house. Suddenly recognition dawned. It was Yiannis.

A fragile exhausted Kate didn't feel like having that conversation, but if she didn't let him in, it would have to be done the next day or the day after that. She may as well get it over with. She hardened her heart.

"Where's Seán?" she demanded as she let him in the patio door, glad that he looked as rotten as she felt. It looked like he didn't get much sleep either.

"With Katerina," he answered awkwardly. "Kate, I'm sorry about last night. It never happened before. I don't know what happened. She was here working, and we went…"

"Look, spare me the details," Kate cut across him fairly sharpish. "I'm not interested. Why are you here?"

"I thought maybe we could talk about last night?" Yiannis was struggling and Kate could almost say she enjoyed his discomfort. His confident swagger had temporarily deserted him and his body language screamed guilt. What she had previously mistaken for confidence was actually arrogance, she realised.

"Are you for real?" She bit back at him. "I have no interest in talking about last night! All you need to know is I'm bringing the American trip forward. Quite a bit forward," Kate continued very business-like. "There's nothing booked but I plan to go as soon as possible. I've spoken to Matthew already." As she watched his reaction to her news, she was thinking what a devious man he was. She knew he didn't like Matthew. He pretended to look crestfallen. And imagine he had the cheek to advise her over a year ago whom she could and couldn't trust.

Yiannis had no idea she had planned to move to Crete permanently and now he never would.

"All we have to do is decide about Seán," she pressed on.

He looked at her questioningly.

"Will I take him with me to America or do you want him to stay here?"

"I don't know, Kate," he sounded unsure. "What do you think is best?"

She didn't answer. She could honestly say she didn't know either. Their common ground was Seán. Thankfully neither of them was rushing to use him against the other.

It was Yiannis who finally said deflated. "He's an innocent victim in all this. His welfare must come first."

"I agree," replied Kate, but she wanted to scream at him, it's a pity you didn't think about that last night, but instead she bit her tongue

"Think about it and let me know asap." It was the first and only sign of any softening on Kate's part. "I'm going to stay here until I go to America. Seán can stay with you. But I would like to see him every day."

"Please Kate come back to the cottage? Don't go to America. Stay and work things through with me…"

Kate raised an eyebrow at him scathingly, "Are you for real?"

"She's gone," he volunteered. "She left last night after you."

Kate ignored his half-hearted plea and reiterated what she had just said to him only this time more slowly and more loudly as if she was speaking to a small child.

"I will stay here until I go to America and I will not be going to the stone cottage. Maybe you could organise for Seán to be dropped here for a while every day?"

Yiannis got the message loud and clear.

"Of course," he answered, "I'll bring him over myself."

With that Yiannis got up to go. He went to say something but stopped and just ended up saying, "I'm sorry Kate," before he walked out the door.

As good as his word he was back with Seán that afternoon and checked with Kate before he left about picking him up. Seán stayed two hours before Yiannis was back for him. As he left that evening he turned back before he went to his jeep.

"Kate, I think Seán should go with you to America. He should be with you. Will you let me book the flights? May I travel to Athens with you both? To see Seán off?"

"Fine," Kate replied deadpan. "But he might be gone for two months, maybe three. The exhibition isn't scheduled until early summer at the very least."

"That's ok. I'll come and see him, if that's alright?"

"Fine," she answered curtly.

And then they were gone out the door and Kate knew that her life would never be the same again. The events of the last twenty-four hours had changed things forever.

Chapter Fourteen

LIMBO

The days Kate spent on her own settled into a boring repetitive routine. The only light relief was her time with Seán. She found herself in a place she seldom was, a limbo of powerlessness. Other people, as in Yiannis, seemed to be controlling her life. Events that she had no hand act or part in were dictating her daily activities. And she had overlooked the fact that allowing him to book their flights to America was effectively giving him even more power. He could book the flights or not. Kate was way too stubborn and too proud to inquire. She ended up waiting and waiting. Waiting for news of a departure date. Desperate to flee.

Apart from the short conversation with Yiannis on the first day back, she had little or nothing to do with him. Ordinarily they would almost have known what the other was thinking. Big mistake, she realised. Huge miscalculation, to have given so much of herself to another man. Kate was an all or nothing person. And she had given him all of herself. What a fool she was to think it was the same for him too. Some women she knew could turn a blind eye or even forgive the indiscretion, but she wasn't one of them. There was no way she could ever be with a man she didn't trust. She despised his deceit. She was lucky to have had her own place to escape to. How many other women or men were stuck in bad relationships with nowhere to go?

Kate came to the conclusion that she really didn't have much luck with men. Paul and herself hadn't been in a great place either. But at least he hadn't slept around, well, not that she knew of… She felt the all too familiar tears ready to spill. Blocking the bad thoughts as best she could and putting on a brave face was the only way of getting herself through the limbo days.

Kate was sleeping badly so an early morning start became part of the day. It was January and thankfully all the other houses were deserted so there would be no socialising with the neighbours. They were in the middle of a Cretan winter which paled in comparison to an Irish one. It may have been cold, but it was nothing like the freezing cold rain and grey skies she had left behind. A rainy day in Crete blew quickly away and left no hangover of low grey skies. It would nearly always be possible to get out into the fresh air if that's what she wanted, which she didn't. Not this time. There would definitely be no walking anywhere. No chance of bumping into any of the locals in the village.

In the mornings, Kate set off for the anonymity of the city and for some form of normality or contact with human beings, even if it was only to ask for a coffee from a random stranger. The first morning she found a small cafe in the old harbour. She deliberately picked somewhere she had never been before and ordered a strong coffee to keep a pep in her step. Almost everywhere, outdoor dining had moved indoors, with patio heaters and pull-down canopies offering a cosy refuge. Kate scanned the café and was a little alarmed to recognise a couple of faces. Thankfully no one she really knew, so she just smiled and nodded her head in acknowledgment across the room.

Before she had taken the first sip of her coffee, another group entered the café. This time she wasn't as lucky.

Shit, she thought as she pretended complete absorption in the newspaper on the table.

"Kate! How are you?" a loud voice called out.

"Isabella, it's lovely to see you," Kate replied tightly as she watched the attractive lady make her way across the room and kiss her on both cheeks. Isabella was an acquaintance from the Municipal Arts Council who had been very helpful when Kate had the exhibition a few years back. But Kate was very aware she knew Yiannis a lot longer than she knew her.

"How's that gorgeous man of yours? I heard he was back!" Isabella gushed asking a million questions at once. Not waiting for a reply. "When did you get back? Are you taking the exhibition in Athens?"

"Only the day before yesterday. I'm passing through, Isabella, on my way to New York," Kate replied poker faced choosing her answers and ignoring the questions about Yiannis and Athens.

"Oh? Where's Seán?"

"With his Dad," Kate answered truthfully.

"I must phone him. There's something I need him to do for me."

"You do that," Kate smiled indifferently, viciously wondering what Isabella could need from Yiannis. Anything was possible.

"Ok, we'll talk later." And thankfully Isabella took her leave.

Was she imagining it or had Isabella seemed a little uncomfortable? The whole exchange had felt awkward.

I bet she knows, thought Kate

Kate gulped the rest of the coffee and made good her escape. She should have known the chances of meeting people she knew in the harbour were high. Winter often brought many of the villagers into the old port until the new season began. She was in no mood for socialising or making small talk.

After the first disastrous trip to the harbour, Kate stayed away from the port and stuck to the busy new town where she knew nobody. For her daily fix of normality, she would pick the most obscure, out of the way café to be doubly sure of not bumping into any acquaintances. And she went to a different one every day. It was the same ritual every morning. She'd order a coffee and despite herself end up people watching, zoning in on couples, feeling sorry for them and then herself. They had no idea what was in store for them, she thought. She knew the ultimate betrayal had turned her thoughts into bitter hard thoughts. It was so unlike her. A miserable wander around the shops followed the coffee and Kate would find herself back at the house, generally with things she didn't want or need. But at least the morning would be over. She'd leave time to make herself a coffee and a quick freshen up to look nice for Seán.

Everyday Yiannis dropped Seán off and everyday he asked what time should he pick him up. He never seemed to be in a hurry, but Kate never asked him in. He could go rot in hell as far as she was concerned.

The few hours Kate had with Seán became the most precious to her. Her days revolved around his visits. She bought him toys in the city that she knew would distract him. All the paraphernalia for a creative stay were purchased – paints in every possible colour and a load of the air-drying clay he loved to play with, along with the latest gimmicky thing she hoped would distract him. When Yiannis dropped Seán, everything was put on hold as Kate flopped down onto the floor beside him, her phone on silent. On a fine day they might potter down to the beach. There was nothing that would disturb her from her time with her son. Despite all the colourful toys he spent all his time babbling about his papa and his mama and one of the days Kate nearly fell away when he looked thoughtfully at her and said very clearly, "Mama sad, Mama sad…"

Kate almost broke down in front of Seán as she realised he was just like a sponge, soaking up the atmosphere between herself and Yiannis, despite all the distractions she had put in place. It rattled her, and she vowed to try and make a better effort with his Dad. But it was hard.

By the third day Yiannis had news, offering her two different options for getting to America. Kate didn't think too deeply about it.

"Whichever is the soonest," she answered him flatly.

"Are you ok to stay overnight at the apartment in Athens?"

"Fine."

"I'll book it."

"Fine."

Once Seán was collected, the long evenings were filled with endless house work, needless decluttering and occasionally a little cooking. Kate never went out to eat, again loath to bump into anyone she knew. She couldn't face Sophia's, her favourite taverna. That would involve excuses and explanations as to why she was in the village and not with Yiannis. She wasn't ready for that. The best she could do was a text to Molly and David telling them she was in Crete, explaining that the exhibition in New York had been brought forward and herself and Seán would be leaving for America soon. It was the truth. They wouldn't question it, they were so used to her travelling. She had a one-word text back from David, Cool. Molly text back asking about Seán and Yiannis, saying she would ring her in America. More breathing space until they got to New York.

She really hoped America would bring clarity of thought and the space from Yiannis she so badly needed. She'd leave all the big decisions until then.

She couldn't even consider painting, so her house ended up spick and span. The cooking and cleaning filled that never-ending stretch until the small hours when there might be some chance of a few hours' sleep.

A day later Yiannis handed her a few printed sheets. It was booked. He had sorted it all, flights, visas, everything. It was all there in black and white. Once the flights were booked there was an air of finality about Kate's time in Crete. They were going. She would be leaving this place behind. The place that had once nourished her body and soul. Now, she couldn't wait to get away. She couldn't wait to leave her shattered heart behind and see what America would bring

Chapter Fifteen

LAST NIGHT IN ATHENS

The last few days dragged painfully but before any of them knew it, Yiannis, Seán and Kate were together on a plane for a flight to Athens, en route to New York.

Despite the minimal extra room business class provided, Kate was sickeningly aware of Yiannis sitting only one seat away from her. It was bizarre to be sitting so near him and not to be talking to him or holding his hand or touching him in some way. Thank God for Seán she thought the buffer in a strained atmosphere. All their energy was directed towards him. From complete and utter separateness for over a week, to the miniscule world of a fifty-minute plane ride was weird, very weird. A part of Kate wanted to physically hurt Yiannis and yet she knew there was a bit of her that wished it could all go back to the way it was before she had walked in on him and Alexandra. They were in a strange place, not together and not separate. He was on his best behaviour and Kate was full of hurt and resentment, trying not to show it for Seán's sake. Every time he spoke or asked a question she tried to respond civilly. Why he had thrown away everything they had together, she'd never know. It was going to be a long evening and night. And Kate was very aware it would most likely be their last.

They landed in Athens shortly after six and Yiannis had a car pick them up from the airport. The flight to New York wasn't until the following morning so they were staying overnight in his apartment in Athens, his most beautiful apartment at that. It was a huge penthouse apartment in downtown Athens. Kate had been there quite a few times and it definitely was a toss-up between that and the stone cottage for the most beautiful building she had ever seen. It was so near to the ancient acropolis, you could pick out the tourists on the Parthenon.

The building dated from the mid-nineteenth century, was an unusual curved shape building and had full length shuttered windows on each floor and wrought iron balconies. When you entered the traditional front door even the communal interior was understated and stylish with its marble floor and cream stone architraves around the windows and door – Yiannis style, of course. His apartment comprised the whole top floor of the building and just like the cottage it had retained all the style and elegance of the period. He had his own distinctive style, a great way of marrying old and new together. He told her he had found the building years before when he was working in Athens and fell in love with it, with the location and views more than anything else. The firm bought the whole building, renovated it into separate apartments and Yiannis kept the penthouse for himself.

A claustrophobic ride in the lift and they were at the apartment. Before he even let them in the front door, memories of their last stay there started to flood Kate's mind. She could remember every little detail of the trip because it had been so amazing. Their first trip away anywhere on their own since Seán's birth. Katerina and Nikos had taken Seán and packed them off. It had been so last minute, they were lucky to make the last flight to Athens, and with no plan went straight to the apartment. They had slept, talked, ate and made love, barely stirring outside the apartment all weekend. Now like every other memory she had of him, she wondered how tainted it was by Alex or any other woman. How many times had he brought her there? Kate hardened her heart.

The apartment was as beautiful as always. No matter how many times she was there she never failed to catch her breath as she walked in the door. The views through the windows were spectacular and she had to stop herself from rushing over like a child to admire Athens by night. Yiannis, with great foresight, had converted a portion of his massive roof terrace into a master bedroom, one whole wall of which was glass. So, it not only had incredible views over the city and the famous acropolis, the glass doors opened fully on those hot sultry nights in the city. You could lie in bed and count the columns of the Parthenon or star gaze the night sky. And with no high-rise neighbours, it led to extreme privacy.

Kate was suddenly struck by all the things she would miss in a life without Yiannis. She had gotten used to all the pampering. Never having to think or wonder about money and to be able to drop everything and take off at a moment's notice had its advantages. He was a very generous man. But she could do without all of those in a heartbeat. It was the simple things she would really miss. She always thought they lived a very privileged life on the peninsula. Doing what they both loved and raising Seán as best they could. She, painting the days away looking forward to him coming home. Eating together or with friends. Putting Seán to bed. Making love. Yiannis had been the other half of a very blessed life for her. Kate sighed. Was anything ever as it seemed?

Once in the apartment, Seán immediately jumped out of Yiannis' arms and ran off towards his bedroom.

An unreadable Yiannis turned to Kate

"Where would you like to sleep?"

"I don't care. It makes no difference to me," she lied hoping he would take the master bedroom. There were too many memories there.

"You take the main bedroom so and I'll sleep in the other bedroom," he gestured.

"Perfect," she lied. He had given her the room with the view. The room full of memories.

Kate busied herself getting ready for dinner and freshening up. There were clothes left from the last trip in the wardrobe. And she had forgotten about her beautiful silk negligée that she hadn't got a chance to wear. The negligée that had almost caused them to miss their plane she remembered sadly, as she thought about how she had made Yiannis stop at her favourite shop en route to the airport laughing at him and promising him the moon. Memories, she exhaled holding the exquisite fabric to her face and staring into the far-off distance thinking of another time.

Kate dressed carefully for dinner. Yiannis had booked a table somewhere within walking distance. Kate was going to look her best, leave him with a lasting impression. With that in mind she put on the best clothes she could root out of the suitcase. She refused to play the role of the poor helpless wife whose husband had cheated on her. She pulled on her tight fitted jeans with a vengeance and teamed them up with a black lace top she had bought in Chania for the trip to America. They were travelling light. She had refused his offer to pack a bag for Seán, pleading a growth spurt. They would buy new clothes in America. It was literally going to be a brand-new start in every way.

Dinner was pleasant enough despite the circumstances. Yiannis had picked well. A small family run taverna where the food was great and the staff friendly. They even managed to laugh a few times in unison at Seán. Occasionally they locked eyes, but Kate looked away immediately, feigning complete indifference. She was able to park her resentment over dinner and even though she remained slightly detached, she couldn't help but notice how women in the restaurant looked at Yiannis. Even the waitress was flirting with him. Then they would look at her nervously, enviously and he would pretend to be completely unaware. If only they knew, Kate sighed to herself. Well they were welcome to him. Maybe she was being melodramatic but a part of her was a little lonely, their last night together, probably ever.

Back at the apartment the pretence continued and it was all very civilised as they said their goodnights and went to bed. She left Yiannis putting Seán to bed and headed upstairs. That extra glass of wine made sure she fell into a deep sleep for the first time in over a week.

In the dead of night, Kate woke from her slumber, parched with the thirst. The apartment was still and peaceful, they were both clearly asleep. She tossed and turned and flapped around in the bed for a while, unable to go back to sleep, her head full of the next day and the emotional wrench she knew it would be. Leaving behind a place she loved and the huge uncertainty of not knowing what her future held. She tiptoed down stairs to the kitchen for a drink of water. On her way back, she passed by Yiannis' door. On the rare occasion she got the chance, she liked to look at him as he slept, stretched out on his back, with one arm thrown over his head. When they slept together, it was so different. They would be wrapped around each other their limbs intertwined. She felt the weight of her decision. Never to be with him again. Never was a very long time.

Yiannis had the strangest of dreams that same night. It wasn't so much that it was strange, just more unusual given the circumstances. He dreamt that Kate was beside him in bed. She was running her hands over his body and kissing him gently as if she wanted to make love to him. It felt good, really good. But he needed to talk to her. He tried to tell her that he was sorry and that it was a mistake. A huge mistake. But she didn't say anything, as if she couldn't hear him. She was distracting him with her slow lingering kisses and sensual touches. She moved on top of him and he could feel her soft naked skin against his. He missed Kate so much. Her body was warm and inviting, yet her open eyes were cold and distant. She was making love with her body and not her heart. She stroked his body, her hands all over him making her intention very clear. He wanted her too, but something wasn't quite right. She was moving away from him, saying goodbye. He was losing her. Yiannis couldn't resist. He took her into his arms and held her the way he knew she liked to be held and kissed her back. He'd talk to her later. They made love then with a quiet ferocious passion.

All of a sudden Seán was in the dream. Crying.

Kate was lying still beside him, her eyes closed but awake. She was breathing deeply. He was confused. He walked to Seán's room in a trance and held him until he fell back to sleep. He had to get back to Kate. When Yiannis returned to the room, his bed was empty. No Kate and no sign of Kate. He should have known. It was too good to be true. He had dreamt it all. But making love to her had felt very real. And Seán?

Yiannis walked quietly up the stairs to where Kate was sleeping.

He opened the door and whispered her name.

"Kate?"

No response.

He whispered her name again. "Kate?"

Nothing.

The room was still and peaceful and Kate was clearly fast asleep.

Yiannis walked back down to the spare room puzzled. He was disappointed. It had been a dream.

The next morning as soon as Kate and Seán disappeared through security and were out of sight, Yiannis felt a huge emptiness engulf him. They were gone. How had he fucked up so badly? The last two weeks had been torture. Self-inflicted torture. Walking on eggshells around Kate and wondering how in the hell he had slept with Alex. What had possessed him? He remembered so little about that night. It reminded him of the days at the height of his career in Athens. His pre-Alex days. At times waking up beside a woman and not even knowing her name. Trying to figure out how he got there. Trying to piece together the events of the night before. He had thought those days were well and truly behind him. Now here he was again, in the same place. Not exactly in the same place, now he was in a much worse place. He had betrayed the trust of his wife and son and left the two of them, mainly Kate, with a whole other set of decisions to make. He had no idea what was going to happen next? He had never seen Kate so angry and disgusted. He was angry and disgusted with himself.

He had given her ample reason to walk away from him.

He'd have plenty of time to ponder that while they were in America.

Yiannis had a flight booked back to Crete but he made a snap decision there and then to stay in Athens. He wanted to go and find Alex and talk to her about the night in question. She was the only other person who knew anything about it and he hadn't been in touch with her since. He hadn't the stomach for it.

Over an hour later he was back at the apartment. The place was a bit of a mess, they had left in such a hurry that morning. He'd get the cleaners to come in the next day. Yiannis was drawn to the master bedroom. Kate was everywhere. The wardrobe was full of her clothes. Even the clothes she had worn the night before were thrown on the floor. He lay on the bed and took small comfort from the slightest remaining body warmth underneath the duvet. He picked up the delicate silk negligée and held it to his face.

Yes a major fuck up, he thought. He looked at his watch. He'd ring Alex, arrange to meet her, see what she had to say.

Yiannis tried Alex's mobile a couple of times without any luck.

He gathered up his phone and keys and called a taxi to where she worked. Alexandra worked for a large high-end, hotel chain. Her specialty was luxury corporate breaks. That was how he first met her. And that's why she had been in Crete ten days ago. Checking out the corporate standards in the five-star hotels in the area.

He'd surely meet her at the headquarters. He felt bad knowing he must have used her the night she was in Crete. When Yiannis asked for Alex at reception, he was sure it would only take a couple of minutes. The receptionist told him to take a seat and she'd call her. She never asked him his name and smiled at him knowingly, as if she knew him or was privy to some personal information about him.

He had spent his former working life in places like this, but now he and his denims looked so out of place.

Ten minutes later, the receptionist approached him quite apologetically. "I'm very sorry Mr. Theodorakis, but Ms. Batavanis is not available. She's away on business. I'm afraid she's out of the country."

"And you will tell her that I called and would like to get in touch with her please?"

"Certainly, sir."

He'd have to put that plan on ice for a while. He got up to leave.

"By the way, how did you know my name? I didn't give it to you."

The receptionist blushed and looked a little shy and Yiannis thought he saw unease in her eyes. "I remember you from before," she said. "from when you used to come here."

"Oh!" he said puzzled. He must have been there more than he thought. "Have you a number I can contact her on."

"I can give you her mobile number."

"No, it's ok. I have that." Nothing for it, only go back to Crete, and then he was gone.

Chapter Sixteen

THREE LONG MONTHS

Kate let out an exhausted sigh and sank back into her comfortable seat for the long flight to JFK. Seán had finally fallen asleep and with nothing or no one to distract her, the thoughts she had been fighting to keep at bay came rushing in.

The long goodbye in Athens had prolonged the agony for her but the dice was well and truly cast in her mind. She'd leave him. She had no choice. He didn't know it yet, but he wasn't stupid, and he'd surely guess it might be her intention. Why else did he say to her at the airport, "Don't give up on us, Kate," as he kissed her goodbye, his treacherous black eyes beseeching her.

Far away across one large sea and one very large ocean, thousands of miles, a not too dissimilar dark, sallow skinned man waited patiently for Kate O'Shea.

He was pleased with himself. He had finally persuaded her to come to New York, something he had been trying to do for a while now.

A few years earlier Matthew Ryan had flown to Dublin for an artistic awards ceremony, to check out new talent in Ireland and Kate O'Shea had been the name on everyone's lips. She had been voted best new artist, up and coming artist or some title to that effect. He liked her the minute he met her. He could see her artistic potential. Her work was very new, very energetic, something completely different and he knew it would go down a treat stateside. He had hounded her that night. You could say he head-hunted her. She was half-heartedly looking for an assistant at the time and he had all the right connections. So he talked her into signing with him. All he had to do after that was convince her to exhibit in New York. For two years he worked tirelessly in the background, synchronising his trips to Ireland with hers and before long becoming indispensable. When Kate O'Shea became the next big thing in America, she would be a very valuable asset for him.

Matthew's Colombian mother and Irish father made sure he inherited a very interesting gene-pool. His parents' union had not been a happy one and they only stayed together for his sake. As a result he grew up to a background of continual shouting matches, coupled with an overuse of alcohol. By the time he was nine or ten, his mother had left New York for Colombia taking him with her. There he swapped an acrimonious home life for the complete and utter freedom Colombia offered. His mother worked to play. She spent most nights in the bars near where they lived, drinking or hooking up with anyone who'd buy her a drink. Matthew spent a lot of time with his Colombian uncles who made sure his education was complete in every way.

The wild child, *Matheu*, yo-yoed between Colombia and New York continually seeking an elusive security and validation from his estranged parents. His father was a distant man who tried but failed to fulfil the inner yearnings Matthew so desperately needed. And the child saw so little of his mother, he may as well not have had one. Somewhere in his teenage years, the Colombian wild child Matheu, transformed into Matthew Ryan, Irish American entrepreneur, serious mover and shaker on the New York art scene. Nobody quite knew where he came from, but he used his dark sallow features to charm and his father's Irish name to open doors for him. A childhood spread between Colombia and New York made him very resourceful and very adaptable. By the time he was eighteen, he had it pretty well figured out. Money talked. It bought you everything you ever wanted, and people treated you differently, very differently if you had money. Matthew knew exactly what he wanted out of life, so he left Colombia and moved to New York where anything and everything was possible.

A flickering screen caught Matthew's eye and he could see her flight had landed. He got ready to welcome Kate O'Shea to New York.

Kate and Seán were in the first group of people to exit the plane and pass through immigration. They were physically rested. Seán had slept for most of the eleven-hour flight in his luxurious first-class bed. Typical of Yiannis, Kate thought cynically as she had boarded the plane at the other end, did he really think booking them first class seats would soften the unpleasantness between them? Kate may have been rested but she was an emotional mess.

She had to pull herself together. This was the first day of the rest of her life and she resolved Matthew would not know anything about what she had left behind in Crete.

There were people milling everywhere in the arrivals hall. All races. All ages. All types of luggage in tow. All dressed differently and all going about their business, looking like they knew exactly what they were at. The energy of the place was palpable. In spite of everything she couldn't help but feel a little distracted by the thoughts of being in New York, the sleepless city.

It was a relief to see Matthew in the arrivals hall waiting patiently for them. They had an easy working relationship and she almost burst into tears to see his smiling, welcoming face as he wrapped his arms around her in a big hug.

Thank God it wasn't family or friends. She couldn't have handled that. The anonymity of New York was exactly what she needed.

Matthew's piercing blue eyes looked momentarily puzzled as he took in the sight of Seán sitting on top of the luggage trolley.

With all the drama in Crete, Kate had forgotten to tell Matthew that Seán was coming with her.

Without batting an eyelid, Matthew bent down to Seán and joked, "I forgot you were coming too young man, so we better go and make up a bed especially for you!" and he caught Seán up onto his back to give him a piggy-back. "Now let's get to the beach! What am I saying? Silly me!" he laughed at Seán mimicking a frozen body. "It's too cold for the beach! To the beach house – the next best thing." He had the confused child laughing in seconds.

"You can look out at the sea…" he cajoled.

Bless him for trying so hard, thought Kate as she looked at him gratefully. He was going to make her temporary transition into American life a whole lot easier.

They chatted as they left the arrivals hall and exited the terminal building. Nothing could have prepared Kate for the biting New York cold. But of course, Matthew to the rescue again. Within five minutes he was back and had them sorted with winter woollies to counter the harsh temperatures. "They're not designer but they'll do until tomorrow!" he quipped as he handed over the jackets.

Kate hadn't bothered asking for any details about where she would be staying or working while in New York. She didn't really care. She had left that completely to him when she rang from Crete. So once Seán was strapped in the car, she sat back and prepared to embark on a new journey. Kate stared out the window, somewhat detached as the iconic New York skyline receded into the background.

It was supposed to have been herself Yiannis and Seán doing the American trip together. They had been talking about taking a long honeymoon in America after the wedding party that would take in the exhibition as well. It should have been a thrilling adventure for the three of them, but of course it never got past the talking stage. Kate sighed and gazed idly at the scenery as they discussed a few work details and the car headed for god knows where. She told Matthew again about her sudden change of heart with regard to the exhibition.

"I don't know if I'll ever get this chance again. Who knows where it will lead," she smiled at him hoping he accepted her explanation, feeling a little guilty that she was lying. He didn't blink but replied, "I'm thrilled, Kate. I'm glad you changed your mind, again. It was a great decision. I think the exhibition will go down a treat. You know how long I was trying to get you here. Watch this space as they say!"

Seán quickly fell asleep so the journey passed remarkably quickly. Most of it on a motorway and only later in the trip was Kate aware they had left the motorway and were passing through small pretty towns. The place names meant nothing to her.

Two hours after leaving the airport they arrived into another pretty village, only this time she felt from Matthews's body language this was their destination. Kate perked up. It may have been dusk but there was the glimpse of seascapes out the car window. Site after site along the road they were driving on was filled with massive beach houses, a lot of them in total darkness with the odd boat stashed at the side. Where there were people home, the lights were as cosy and welcoming as a coal fire in December. Each house seemed nicer and more luxurious than the one before. They probably all had amazing sea views.

"Where are we?" Kate asked distractedly.

"Welcome to the Hamptons!" was Matthew's delighted reply.

Matthew drove down another small sandy side road and stopped the car outside a house a little more modest than the ostentatious neighbours.

"This is your home for the duration," Matthew announced.

"Wow," sighed Kate. "It looks lovely. I can only imagine what the views are like."

"Come on, let's go in," Matthew replied as he led the way, looking pleased.

Kate got Seán out of the car as quickly as she could and hurried after Matthew. A blast of warm air hit them as they stepped inside the pristine house. They had stepped into an immaculate cream paneled space, typically American – at least what Kate imagined was typically American. They were in a big open-plan kitchen with all of the modern conveniences in place and a glass porch at one end. It was like a large dolls house, it looked so perfect. A quick guided tour showed Kate the house had three spacious bedrooms and three bathrooms. Kate thought an annex off one of the bedrooms would be a perfect painting space. And Matthew said there was lots of outdoor space but of course they couldn't see a thing in the pitch dark. Seán was funny babbling about the sea and pointing out the windows. Matthew stayed about an hour with them and then he took off to give them time to settle into their new home. He said he'd see them the next day.

Once Matthew was gone Kate suddenly felt wiped. By ten o'clock in their new time zone they both hit the sack. She gave in to Seán and let him sleep in her bed for his first night in a strange country, stroking his face and whispering softly to him as his eyes closed. They could do all the unpacking and organising the next day, she thought wearily to herself as she quickly followed him into the bed snuggling beside his soft warm body, but not before silent tears of heartbreak had a chance to flow down her cheeks.

Small soft chubby hands woke Kate the next morning.

"Mama! Mama! Wake up, wake up!" Seán was shouting at her and point-ing to the window. It took her a few seconds to remember where she was. The room was bright and warm, but Kate had no idea what time of the day it was. Her mobile was in a jacket pocket somewhere. It must be morning she decided. She padded to the window, lifted Seán into her arms and raised the blinds. They were looking out onto a very long – as far as the eye could see long, sandy beach. The sky was crystal clear blue. The sea stretched out before them and down below she could see a little sandy pathway that led onto the deserted beach from their garden. Kate sighed. It was very beau-tiful. They could do worse than spend the next couple of months in such a lovely location.

Seán wriggled down onto the floor and began pulling on his shoes de-terminedly. She smiled because she knew exactly what was in his head. He was mad to get outside and play in the sand just like he did at home. Indulg-ing him, she dressed quickly, brought him downstairs, got their jackets and gingerly opened the porch doors onto the decking. An icy wind took Kate's breath away and she immediately retreated trying to distract Seán as she did. No wonder the beach was deserted! They needed scarves and hats and gloves and warmer jackets.

"Later, Seán," she promised. "We have to get some new clothes. Come on, let's unpack your toys!" Kate sidetracked him and led the way back up-stairs. Her mobile was in her jacket pocket and when she turned it on to check the time she duly noted two missed calls from Yiannis, a call from Molly and one from Matthew. And it was eleven a.m. American time.

Kate quickly realised that the few clothes she had brought were totally unsuitable for their new environment. A winter in Crete or Ireland it seemed was completely different from a winter in New York. Fine if you wanted to stay indoors all day long but she planned to go out and about in the fresh air every day and more than anything, Seán loved to play on the beach.

She made up his bed, and they explored every nook and cranny of the house. The annex off one of the bedrooms looked even better in the daylight as a painting space, except for the cream carpet but they could get around that. Every window revealed another beautiful sea view. There was no visible sign of a town centre, so Kate started to make a few notes. The fridge was packed with every kind of convenience food imaginable, but Kate longed for fresh fruit and vegetables. She'd have to source a good market nearby, another scribble.

After a while Kate returned Matthew's call. They made all the small talk and then she asked his advice about the things she needed. A car was a must, she said.

"Look out the front door," he laughed. "I had it sent over this morning, but you must have been in bed. The keys should be in the post box. I'll be there later so we'll go for a drive – explore the village and do a few other things too."

Thank God! thought Kate as she clicked off. What would she have ever done without him?

Seán and herself spent the rest of the morning getting organised, until Matthew arrived and took the two of them off in the rental car to explore the area.

The house was on the outskirts of a small quaint town. The heart of it was a big wide street. Bare trees on either side were still festively decorated. The shop fronts were well-kept, almost old-fashioned as if stuck in a time warp. Some were in sale mode after the holiday season. Fairy lights and pretty window displays were everywhere. It made the bitter January day just that little bit more bearable. They stopped at a clothes shop and Kate kitted herself and Seán out against the freezing January weather and the expected snowfalls. After a trip to a local food store, they all went to a small tea shop overlooking the sea before Matthew showed Kate all the local landmarks. On the drive home he brought them on a tour of the most expensive beach houses.

All in all, it was a good afternoon. Seán's cheeks were flushed from the fresh air. The daylight was suddenly gone, and he was happy to play indoors with the new toys Matthew had bought him. Later, he ordered a take-away dinner for them and it was only in the course of conversation that it transpired Matthew owned the beach house she was renting. He also had an apartment in the city where he was mainly based, he said. Hence, she realised a little uncomfortably a visit entailed a four hour round trip for him.

"Sometimes I might stay in the spare room if that's alright with you," he stated rather than asked a little later, as Kate tried to express her gratitude.

"Of course," she replied anxious to make his commutes a little easier. He had been so good to them both.

They ticked a lot of boxes on their first day. She was anxious to get stuck into the painting even though Matthew wasn't putting any pressure on her. He hadn't even mentioned the exhibition and was vague on the details when she asked him.

"You paint whenever you're ready, Kate. Leave the rest up to me," he had laughed when she asked him about it.

On their second morning, they got up a little earlier and at about ten a.m. Kate heard the doorbell ring. Curiously she opened the door to find a sallow skinned lady smiling at her. She looked quite a bit older than Kate.

"Hello, I'm here to work. My name is Maria. Matheu – Mr. Ryan said you might need someone to clean or cook or look after the child?"

"Oh…" Kate was taken aback. It wasn't her intention to leave Seán with anyone. Funny he never mentioned that the day before. Thinking quickly, Kate decided he was right. Of course she'd need someone to help her. When she was in the full throes of painting she couldn't ignore Seán and hope that he would be ok. She sighed, she'd always had someone to fall back on before, whether in Crete or Ireland. The sooner Seán got to know Maria, the better. She was well and truly on her own now, well, regarding Yiannis she was. Molly and David were none the wiser in Ireland and that's the way she wanted it to stay for the moment. Good thinking on Matthew's part again and it really helped that Kate warmed to Maria the minute she opened the door to her.

Later, thinking about Molly reminded her to return the call. Doing a quick time calculation, she dialed her number.

"Well, hello there. Did ye arrive safe and sound? I was about to ring the police!" Molly's laughing voice came down the phone.

"Well, of course we arrived safe and sound. Didn't I tell you I'd ring at the end of the week?"

"Yes, I know that but Yiannis was on to me to know did I hear anything. I guess he couldn't get through to you either."

Kate had to think quickly. "Typical Yiannis," Kate laughed. "You know how he gets if he doesn't know exactly where Seán is!"

She swiftly changed the topic and regaled Molly with all the details of their new surroundings, distracting her, making sure to steer her clear from asking anymore questions about Yiannis.

Maria it seemed was the perfect balance between babysitter, mother-figure and housekeeper. She arrived first thing the next morning and didn't leave until she had cooked them dinner and the place was spick and span in the evening. Seán took to her instantly and even though her background was Latin American, her English was more than perfect. The arrangement would allow Kate to focus entirely on her painting.

Inevitably Matthew was an invaluable resource when it came to ordering the necessary art supplies. He knew all the best suppliers and he even pressed her to paint in New York or at the very least take a painting space in the local arts centre. But Kate had her mind made up. She was adamant. There was no way she was leaving Seán during the daytime to further add to the upheaval in his short little life. "There is a perfect annex to a bedroom at the beach house," she reassured a surprised Matthew. Then she saw his face pale at her suggestion. "Professional cleaners or painters will be well paid to leave the house as good as new when I'm finished. It will be perfect for painting."

Once all the household and paintings tasks were organised, Kate finally took out her mobile to ring Yiannis in Crete. She had ignored a few calls from him. She had been putting it off for days but ever since she had spoken to Molly, she knew it was only fair to let him know they had arrived safely and fill him in on Seán. Even with all the distractions he had asked about his papa every single day since they arrived, and bedtime had become a challenge – for both of them.

Once she heard the international ring tone, Kate handed the phone to Seán and watched with a heavy heart. The child went from puzzlement to bewilderment to frenetic excitement as he realised he was talking to his papa. The words changed to Greek and she couldn't help but smile as she watched Seán disappear into the other room, plonk himself on a rug and babble excitedly to his daddy. After a long time, Seán came running back and handed Kate the phone.

"Papa, Papa!" he said pointing to the mobile. She didn't want to talk to Yiannis but the calls were going to be very much part and parcel of their future, at least until Seán reached a certain age.

"Yiannis?" she said in a clipped tone.

"Kate! how are you?"

"Fine, thank you."

And they continued in a formal, terse vein. It was awkward. She filled him in matter of factly about Seán and a little about where they were living. All she felt was resentment simmering inside her but Seán was beside her hanging on to every word, so she remained as civil as she could. They agreed to set up skype as soon as possible for Seán's sake and she handed the phone back to him to say his goodbyes. All in all, it was a difficult call. Kate wished she didn't feel so angry, but it gladdened her heart to see how happy Seán was after talking to his papa. She knew she'd have to suck it up and find some way of communicating with Yiannis.

One week in America and Kate was good to go. She had paid to get the annex room covered in plastic and was ready to embark on her new painting venture. Every day when Maria arrived, Kate disappeared to her new studio. She ate all her meals with them, took a break mid-morning to take Seán for a walk and then finished painting for the day when Maria left to go home. She was glad she had stayed put at the house. Seán was so unsettled he was sleeping with Kate every night. The skype calls were making him very lonely for his daddy and as a knock-on, clingy with her. He couldn't understand where Yiannis went once they hung up and he needed to see him every day. Skyping became the norm and after a while Seán could almost set it all up on his own. It was no surprise to Kate when after a few weeks Yiannis asked if he could visit them in America, sooner rather than later.

The only thing that surprised Kate was her absolute determination not to be around when he arrived. There was no way she wanted to meet him. She thought she was being adult and generous by offering him the beach house for his stay, which he graciously accepted. Matthew had asked her a million times to go to New York, on his frequent visits. Kate had never felt like it, but she knew it would be a good place to escape to once Yiannis arrived. The only problem was his imminent arrival, she'd have no choice but to confide in Matthew and Maria about herself and Yiannis. She had managed to avoid it thus far. She could always go somewhere on her own but she didn't feel like being alone. She felt a little vulnerable. She knew she wanted company. So, without going into any of the gory details she merely said that they had separated, and she'd love to go to New York.

The dreaded weekend turned out to be the greatest non-event ever. There was the inevitable emotional wrench when Kate was leaving Seán with Maria, right about the same time Yiannis' flight was landing in JFK. Only then could she be persuaded to leave for the city having checked he was en route. The only thing she had deliberately neglected to tell Yiannis was that she would be in the city. Matthew, like Maria was a brick. He said nothing when she filled him in but said she could stay with him or he'd book her into a small hotel in the city. He must have driven past every famous landmark and site in New York City that weekend. And taken her to different cafés to distract her, but Kate's heart wasn't in it. She spent the few days wondering how Seán was and what they were doing.

How pathetic of her then to pump a toddler for information when she returned.

It emerged during the following week that Yiannis had spent only one night in the house. Maria told her that after the first night, he had paid her well and sent her home. Kate could feel Maria's eyes staring hard at her full of unasked questions. But Kate couldn't go there. He had obviously won her over. Maria somehow knew they had stayed in a hotel for the other two nights. And when Kate went to the tea rooms with Seán the following week, she was surprised to find the normally reserved waitress knew Seán by name and had the welcome of the world for him. Kate felt she was overfamiliar and it irked her beyond comprehension.

After Yiannis' first visit, the phone relationship worsened over the next few weeks. She avoided speaking to him as much as she could. On one of the few occasions they did speak he actually had the cheek to ask her if she needed money for Seán. Kate took a certain delight in replying that she had more money than she could ever possibly need. Something he had once said to her in Crete. How dare he think she needed money from him. She continued to be so angry towards him, mostly spitting fire as she painted. Even though the painting was going reasonably ok, she wasn't enjoying one single minute of it. It wasn't exactly flowing, more like short sharp bursts of angry inspiration. Her heart wasn't in it.

A disintegrating relationship most certainly motivated Kate into taking the step she had been putting off since her arrival in America. An appointment at the family law offices. Maybe it was the painting but six weeks on she felt she had to explore all her options around disentangling herself from Yiannis. Bracing herself Kate took a deep breath and pushed open the front door of the luxurious law offices of *Robinson and Associates, Family Law Firm.*

'No-Fault Separation' was printed on the doorway underneath the name. In a perfect world that's what most people would seek out she thought ironically, wishing she was in that enviable position, a no-fault divorce. She liked the sound of it. But the short time she had spent in Yiannis' confusing world of deception and betrayal was in danger of making her bitter and cynical, permanently. There were other details printed on the door which Kate ignored as she single-mindedly made her way to the reception area and announced she was there for a consultation with Marcia Brown. She hadn't just gone to the firm raw. They had come highly recommended by Matthew who boasted they got him the very best deal possible when he was in a similar situation. It couldn't hurt. The first consultation was free.

Kate felt nervous as she was shown into a plush office and found herself sitting opposite a small fair-haired mousey looking girl. Never in a million years had she expected to or wanted to be talking to a stranger about separating from Yiannis and what her options were.

"Mmm, that's a bit of an inconvenience," was Ms. Brown's comment when she told her about the three-month-old civil marriage.

Inconvenience would have been the last word she ever thought she would have been using to describe that day. It had been one of the most perfect days in her life to date. Low key, no fuss. Molly and David, Nikos and Katerina their witnesses. Just the seven of them in the city, eating out celebrating the occasion. Barely three months ago. "Yes, a big inconvenience," she heard herself agreeing.

Marcia Brown looked like she was too young to even know what incomes and assets were, but boy did she quiz Kate about everything to do with Yiannis' finances, earnings and possessions. She acted shocked when Kate looked at her blankly as she mentioned pre-nuptial agreements. A part of her wanted to run away and ignore the invasive questions about the circumstances of their marital strife, their incomes and assets. Instead she answered anything she was asked as truthfully and matter-of-factly as she could. But when Marcia brought up about custody of Seán, Kate abruptly stood and left the offices muttering she would think about it, her head buzzing with all the legal jargon. Custody of Seán was a bridge too far.

Kate shed bitter tears when she got to the car, unsure if she really wanted to go down such a cold harsh pathway all the way to divorce. Surely there had to be another way?

Life in The Hamptons continued in the usual fashion. Every day Kate went through the motions, somewhat detached, but doing the best she could. At some level she knew she was lucky to be in such a beautiful place, by the sea but she could not connect to it. Her life had become joyless except for Seán. The complete opposite of the life she had led in Crete. Then again that life was based on a lie, a lie she had fully embraced and believed. If it weren't for Maria during the day and Matthew calling in the evenings, she would have been lost for the want of adult company.

Seán seemed content during the days but every night he kicked up stink to sleep with Kate. She had no problem giving into him knowing the phase wouldn't last forever. Her whole focus now was around him and making sure he was OK on a day-to-day basis.

Kate found herself forcing every brushstroke onto the canvas. She would have twenty canvasses ready for the exhibition no problem, but to her they were soulless pieces. By her but not of her. She had a lot on her mind. Her few phone calls to Ireland were becoming difficult, putting on a front and trying to appear as if it was her choice to be in America painting and wondering when the time would be right to tell Molly and David the full story.

Before any of them realised it, another few weeks had passed and Yiannis was on his way to America once again to see Seán. This time Kate had no choice. She knew she was going to have to meet him, at least once and possibly twice. Maria had asked for the weekend off ages before they even knew of his trip and Matthew was gone to South America. All her allies had unintentionally absented themselves and she was not looking forward to the first meeting with her husband in two months.

When the doorbell rang, Kate quickly gathered up Seán and his bag, her body tense before pasting on a fake smile and opening the door.

"Yiannis," she greeted him as she stood in the doorway.

"Kate?" He looked surprised. "How are you?" he asked easily, holding her eyes as if he really cared and it was the most natural question in the world, as he leaned forward to kiss her on the cheek.

"Fine," she quipped placing Seán into his arms and stopping any kind of physical contact between them.

"Hey buddy," Yiannis was momentarily distracted by his son and hugged him affectionately and ruffled his hair.

Kate took the milliseconds to study his features. He looked the very same, maybe a little tired. Burning the candle at both ends, now that you've no ties in Crete, she thought sarcastically,

"What time will you have Seán back on Monday?" she almost snapped at him, at a loss to know what else to say.

He was staring intently at her now his black eyes boring through her. "First thing, if that's ok," he answered calmly. "I have to catch an early afternoon flight."

"Perfect," Kate grimaced as she waved goodbye to Seán firmly closing the door in Yiannis' face. She could tell they made no move to leave but her heart still managed to jump when the doorbell rang again almost immediately.

"Kate, what are you doing this evening? Why don't you come with us for a coffee?" Yiannis was smiling and looking at her expectantly.

Kate was clearly taken aback by the direct question and became flustered. "No, thank you... I have plans," she managed to stutter, her face flushed red with the lie.

She leaned back against the door once they were gone and sank to the ground her head in her hands. She was so angry with him, swanning around the world, jetting into New York when he felt like it, to play the doting dad to his son. She was the one who had to pick up the pieces and deal with the fall-out from his betrayal on a nightly basis. It was hard to feel upbeat and she was exhausted from putting on a show for Seán. The audacity of him to assume she had nothing to do. She would not be seen in Southampton over the weekend for fear of bumping into him. And she would make damn sure Maria was the one to meet him on Monday morning.

Without question or comment Maria shook her head compassionately at Kate and took Seán back from Yiannis the following Monday.

Unexpectedly she had become a strong ally for Kate. She looked after almost everything in the house and spent more and more time there with them, encouraging Kate to take time-out for herself more and more. At times she'd hand her little leaflets about things she thought Kate might like and then she'd insist on minding Seán while she sent her off. It was as if she could see how stressed Kate had become and was trying to help. And little by little Kate found she was confiding things in Maria. Woman to woman stuff. Little bits about the separation but none of the finer details, not yet. They had become friends.

Funnily it seemed to Kate at times as if Matthew didn't particularly like Maria. He was impatient around her and she had overheard him on occasion putting her down, verbally. She didn't like it and definitely didn't understand why Maria allowed it. After all it was Kate who paid her wages, not Matthew. He continued with his frequent visits from the city, generally a few times a week, always when Maria was gone and always on the pretext of something he had to discuss with her. They were more than two months stateside and Kate was getting the feeling that Matthew's interest in her was more than just professional. She was picking up certain vibes from him. A touch lasting a fraction too long. A knowing look. Things she couldn't quite put her finger on. Kate didn't reciprocate. The last thing she needed was the complication of another man. Anyway, she didn't like him in that way. He may have been thoughtful and handsome, but she was not attracted to him, at all.

Once Kate had gotten over the shock of a face to face meeting with Yiannis, she decided to take a day off, alone and get the train to New York. God knew she needed a bit of a diversion and Matthew had been asking her for ages to go to the city again to see his office. So, not long after Yiannis' visit, Maria had taken Seán and practically beat her out the door. Kate was looking forward to negotiating New York City on public transport and finding her way to Matthew's office, all on her own. She wanted to surprise him and the worst thing that could happen was that he wouldn't be at the office and she'd have to lunch on her own. Plus she badly needed a change of scene, hopefully to distract her from the million and one decisions she knew were hurtling her way sooner rather than later.

It was a cold dry March day when Kate left The Hamptons and set off for New York City, buoyed by her decision to make a solo trip. She had spent way too long hibernating by the sea in the relative safety and security of Matthew's beach house. It was time to get back out and live a little. Kate negotiated New York's public transport and walked the final few blocks to Matthew's building. There was a spring in her step as she walked down the corridor to his office. She had asked his secretary not to alert him of her arrival. "A surprise," she smiled at her conspiringly.

Kate's hand was poised ready to knock when she heard voices from inside. She froze on the spot. The door was slightly ajar and one of the voices was Matthew's but the other voice, the other voice was so distinctive it immediately evoked old memories. She would recognise it anywhere, even though she seldom heard it. Alex. And the last time she had heard it, was on that awful night in January in the stone cottage.

"It's becoming very, very difficult," a strong foreign voice was saying, "Everywhere I go, he's there. It's like he's stalking me. Athens, Cyprus, not to mention phone calls!"

"And that's a problem, why?" was Matthew's response.

"He's a very persistent man, I don't trust myself with him. Yiannis knows me too well. The last time we were together..."

"Listen to me. Make sure..."

Kate's heart sank, and she felt sickened to her stomach when she realised who they were talking about. How pathetic of Yiannis to be following Alex around like a lapdog? And why was she confiding in Matthew about her love life?

All this heartbreak and hurt could have been spared if only he had been up front with her from the beginning. She never would have married him if she thought he wanted to play the field.

She must have sighed or gasped or something because suddenly the conversation was over, and a panicked looking Matthew was stood facing her.

"Kate! How long have you been standing there?" he asked.

"Long enough to know that my husband has it bad for his ex-girlfriend – girlfriend, and he's obviously making a fool of himself. Jesus Christ! I have to do something for myself!" Kate muttered. "Maybe it's time for another visit to the lawyer."

"Kate, I'm sorry you had to hear all that," Matthew said after a long time. He was by her side with his arm around her shoulders pulling her into his arms.

"It's not your fault." She felt suddenly deflated standing in the doorway of his plush office in New York City.

"I have to go home…" She had a longing to get back to Seán, hold him in her arms, bury herself away again.

Was there no escaping Yiannis Theodorakis? She wanted to scream. She hated that everything now was pointing to the fact that it was time she grasped the nettle and made some firm decisions about her future.

Matthew wouldn't hear of her escaping back to The Hamptons. They were going for lunch he insisted kindly, as he led her away from his offices. She heard him cancel all his appointments for the afternoon and berate the secretary who had allowed Kate in unannounced.

"It's not her fault," Kate tried to explain to Matthew. "I talked her into it." But he was already guiding her out the door towards the elevators. Some serious pampering was in order, he declared. Bless him but he managed to salvage something out of a rotten day.

It seemed to Kate that every time she took a positive step forward, Yiannis was there lurking in the background waiting to remind her of his betrayal. It was definitely time to firm up on the separation. It was only later on the train home that Kate realised she had forgotten to ask Matthew how he even knew Alex.

As soon as Kate got back from the city, Maria could tell something was up. Kate barely said hello but walked straight to Seán, picked him up and held him tight in her arms until he squirmed to get back to his toys. The house may have been warm and inviting with a roaring fire in the grate, but Kate looked cold and drained. Seán seemed contented playing on the floor so Kate had plonked herself down beside him and joined in his mindless chatter and self-absorbed games, looking like she was waiting for any opportunity to touch him or kiss him, to comfort him. But Maria could clearly see, it was Kate who needed the comfort. A mug of steaming hot tea was placed beside Kate and Maria sat on the couch in silent support. Before long Kate started to mutter to no-one in particular. It flowed out of her and she quietly told Maria of Yiannis' betrayal and how it had prompted her to end up in America, right up to the phone conversation she had so recently overheard.

"Oh I've met your husband. He seemed a nice man," Maria countered softly full of compassion for this lady who had so recently become her friend. "You know sometimes things aren't always as they appear to be…"

"Yes, I agree," Kate's tone was icy. "But this I saw with my very own eyes."

Maria saw the hurt still burning so strong in Kate's expression.

"I thought he was for keeps. I really loved him. But it's over, definitely over."

They talked long into the night and Kate filled Maria in on her whole life story, her first marriage and then how Yiannis had swept her off her feet so much so that she had nearly ended up in Crete permanently.

"The thing is, I feel a bit lost now, Maria. I'm not sure what to do next…"

The question of what to do next took on a life of its own in the following weeks. Things seemed to almost resolve themselves. The unburdening to Maria prompted Kate to move to the next level with regards to Yiannis. After a lot of thought and reflection, an assertive Kate was back at the offices of *Robinson and Associates*, this time as a full, fee paying customer.

Once they were seated in the plush office, Ms. Brown seemed to find it necessary to give Kate the full blurb regarding divorce, rights entitlements and assets all over again. Kate let her speak, and calmly listened until the lecture appeared to have naturally concluded.

"Ms. Brown? Marcia? I get that this is the way things are done in America with regard to divorce. But I'm not American and I would like things done my way." Kate's voice had a steely edge to it, and she knew she had her lawyer's full and undivided attention. "I'm not interested in Mr. Theodorakis' money," she simply stated. "The most important thing now is how we handle all this for Seán's, for my son's, sake – our son's sake."

"Firstly, I would like custody is to be shared equally between myself and Mr. Theodorakis and any major decisions regarding Seán's future to be agreed by both of us until he is old enough to make his own decisions.

Secondly, the monastery in Crete that was gifted to me at our civil wedding is to revert back to Mr. Theodorakis and be held in trust for Seán until he comes of age.

And thirdly, I do not require any financial assistance or maintenance from my husband. I am financially independent, Ms. Brown.

Formalise it all please. I'd like it to go in the post to Mr. Theodorakis before the end of this week. And send copies to my addresses here and in Ireland please. The bill can be sent to my address here in The Hamptons. It's not negotiable." Kate paused, "I don't anticipate any objections from my husband."

"Well, I should think not," retorted Ms. Brown.

Kate handed over the short, hand-written sheet to her lawyer who quickly skimmed over its contents; her eyes darting over and back as she read through the list. Finally, she looked at Kate who was sitting opposite her.

"Are we done?" Kate frowned at her

Several times Ms. Brown went to say something but stopped. Finally, she stood up and held out her hand to Kate. "Yes, we're done, Ms. O'Shea," she smiled. "It was a pleasure doing business with you. We'll be in touch."

"Thank you."

Kate took her hand in hers and then walked out of the office, her head held high knowing she had finally put some course of action into place. She knew it was time to let it go before she ended up hating Yiannis altogether. She had to salvage a working relationship with him, for Seán's sake. Kate had just drawn a line in the sand under it. If only it were as easy to disentangle her heart… But a phone conversation with Yiannis the next day copper fastened the need to move on.

"Hi Yiannis, how are you?" Kate's tone was the nearest thing to being civil it had been in over two months.

A surprised silence seemed to greet her from the other end. "I'm good, Kate," he replied. "And you and Seán?" he rushed. Without waiting for an answer, he continued, "Look I'm ringing to let you know our flight is due to land at four p.m. tomorrow, so it'll be earlier by the time we get to your house – in case you want to make plans...' He hesitated a little, "We're staying in The Village Inn Resort just up the coast from you if you need..."

Yiannis' words faded into the background and Kate became enveloped by a mind fog. She replayed the conversation in her head. Alarm bells were going off. Everyone locally knew that The Village Inn Resort was the most expensive place to stay, and it was marketed as an exclusively romantic get-away. Matthew had once brought her there for a look. The last two times Yiannis had visited he had stayed in a small boutique hotel in Southampton. She knew that by deduction. This time he was going all out. Something in what he had said didn't add up or rather added up to a little too much. Kate tried to recall his exact words. Yes, that was it... he had said 'our flight' and by the time 'we get to your house'.

He's bringing Alex with him, thought Kate. That's the reason for the lux-ury resort. Yiannis had never before given as much information in a phone call. He was letting her know that Alex was travelling with him. They had obviously made up and Yiannis was bringing her to the luxurious Village Inn Resort along with Seán.

Kate sighed. She didn't like it. Not one little bit. Yiannis and Alex was hard enough to take. But now Yiannis, Alex and Seán?

Kate managed to be civil as she said that was lovely, but that she would be in New York, with Matthew, she added. He could get her on the mobile if he needed to.

When they had clicked off, Kate suddenly realised. This was the new way of being for Seán. This was what she had tried to put in place, only the day before at the lawyers. This was what she wanted for the two of them. To be grown up and mature about the circumstances they now found them-selves in. The hard bit, of course, was to suck it up and try and get on with her own life. With that thought firmly at the back of her head, Kate looked up her contacts and pressed call. She'd go to bloody New York for the week-end and have the time of her life. Fuck him!

When exactly Kate decided to sleep with Matthew she wasn't sure, but it was most definitely influenced by the few glasses of wine she had with her meal. Who was she kidding, she had her mind made up right after the phone call from Yiannis. A pounding at the side of her head, and dryness in her throat had woken her early. She didn't move but kept her eyes closed, feigning sleep. She could sense Matthew beside her. Kate almost shivered at the thoughts of what had happened the night before. Things were moving too quickly for her now.

Yiannis was clearly with Alex. The divorce was well underway, and papers would be delivered in the next week sometime. She would soon be booking her flights home to Ireland. As and from last night the exhibition dates were set. The only mistake she had made was sleeping with Matthew. Kate knew she had knee-jerked her way through her time in America. Reacting and over-reacting to every perceived transgression of Yiannis'. Sleeping with Matthew had been her crowning glory. He had groped and fumbled his way through the coupling, in no way aware of Kate squirming at his touch. Kate had hated every minute of it. Matthew had appeared puffed up and over-confident in his abilities as a lover. There would be no repeat performance she thought.

She could lie still for hours, if needs be.

"Kate," Matthew mumbled, "are you awake?"

She didn't move a muscle.

She heard the bed creak as Matthew got up, and only then chanced peeking through her eyelashes. He dressed quickly, smiling to himself, scribbled on a piece of paper, grabbed his keys and phone from the locker. A few seconds later the front door of the apartment clicked shut.

As soon as she heard the door click, Kate sat upright in bed and groaned loudly shaking her head to herself. She reached out for the piece of paper he had left on the locker.

10.00a.m. Going to make a few calls. I'll get breakfast.

Be about 40 minutes.

See you when I get back.

Matthew.

The note was a bit like himself, precise and factual.

What had she done? That had to be one of the most disastrous nights of her life. In fairness to Matthew, it was all her doing. She had initiated it. She had made her intentions very clear the night before while they were at dinner. And he had been the willing co-conspirator. In fact, he had behaved like the cat that got the cream. Kate cringed again. Obviously, you couldn't have everything in life. Yiannis was proof of that. She felt a sudden strong urge to get back to Ireland. At Christmas, America may not have been her choice of residence but whatever way you looked at it she had gotten through the first few horrendous months of separation from Yiannis.

Kate sighed. She went and showered and dressed as quickly as she could, made the bed and left the bedroom pristine, trying to erase evidence of her presence. Waiting for him to return she nosed around the apartment quite uninterested. It was a huge ultra-modern apartment located somewhere in the city, Manhattan, she thought he had said. It had a massive living room space dominated by a giant TV screen. In the corner of the room a large computer was set up on a table. Sleek leather couches, modern bookshelves filled the living space, and a shiny brightly coloured modern kitchen finished the room. Everything was neat. The cushions were perfectly plumped up and placed on the couches. The books neatly filled the shelves, not a millimetre out of place. She had to tug hard to get one out. *David and Goliath by Brandon Stanton,* Kate had never heard of the author. The pages were crisp and clean as if no-one had ever read them. She recognised John Grisham's name on a few spines. Again, it looked like the books had never been opened. She was surprised there weren't a few art books.

As she looked around Kate realised everything was perfect and in its place. There wasn't even a glass out of place. It was a bit clinical. Last night Kate had made sure they had gone straight to the bedroom for no other reason than she thought she wanted to get on with it. Her favourite part of the apartment was the artwork on the walls. All modern art. She recognised a Miro, a Pollock even a Rothko. Two of them were prints, but the Miro, it could hardly be an original? Kate checked the time. If only she knew where exactly in the city she was, she could leave. She could write Matthew a note and be back at the beach house by afternoon. Probably not such a good idea, he'd probably follow her to The Hamptons and she didn't want that.

As she was deliberating over her next move, the rhythmic sound of a mobile phone came from the bedroom. She had hers in her hand. He must have forgotten his phone. Kate instinctively followed the sound. But wait a second, thought Kate. Matthew took his phone – she saw him. How odd. He must have two. She had come to that conclusion by the time she reached the source of the ringtone. It was coming from a drawer in a desk in Matthew's bedroom. Kate looked furtively around and then opened the drawer exactly at the moment the caller rang off. She picked up a phone still attached to a charger and stared at the screen in shock. It read, *Alex 1 Missed call.*

Jesus, she was ringing him from The Hamptons. He obviously knew her well.

Kate's heart jumped a mile as a loud beep from the phone signaled an incoming message.

Need to talk ASAP

Under pressure from Yiannis + need to get rid of db

Googled scopolamine - Nothing

Help

Desperate

What a strange text, thought Kate. Why would she be under pressure from Yiannis? She wondered sadly, deep down knowing the answer.

Who was db? And Kate had never heard of something called scopolamine. She had so many questions after reading the text. It sounded a bit weird. Like something strange was going on. The sound of a key in the lock made Kate put the phone straight back into the drawer and quickly leave the room as she pushed the text to the back of her mind. All she wanted to focus on now was making her escape and giving herself time to mull over what had happened.

Much later, safely ensconced back at the beach house, Kate had time to reflect on all the goings-on. Matthew had insisted on driving her back when she had told him how ill she was. Kate felt guilty at how easily the lies flowed out of her mouth when he came back with breakfast. He didn't look one bit happy. It was awkward enough without having to try and spend any more time with him. It had never been said outright the night before, but the implication was that she'd spend the weekend in New York. He knew Seán was gone for two nights. Kate knew she had used Matthew, mainly because she was reeling from Yiannis' phone call. It was all well and good to say she was ready to move on, but the reality was different, very different indeed. Sleeping with Matthew was a mistake and one not to be repeated. How could she communicate that to him without hurting his feelings or taking advantage? Thinking about Matthew reminded her about Alex and the text. Funny thing, it had been on the tip of her tongue to tell him about the phone ringing in his apartment, but something had stopped her.

All alone in the beach house with the night stretching out in front of her, Kate's curiosity got the better of her and she turned on the computer. She tried hard to recall the text...

Need to talk

Pressure from Y

Get rid of db

What was the word again? she wondered. Scopa something, Scopaline, something like that.

She Googled *scopaline*.

Hours later an exhausted confused Kate got up from the computer. She must have got the word wrong because a word very like it kept coming up every time she searched *scopolamine*. That had to be it. Kate read hours of articles and watched documentaries. It was all very coincidental. It was definitely the right word because a few little pieces fell into place. She now knew who or rather what db was. The connection to Colombia. The second phone seemed a bit strange. Matthew and Alex were into something funny and Kate's big question was what Yiannis had to do with it. Was it something to do with drugs? Yiannis would never be involved with something like that, would he? Not with Seán?

A little nagging doubt crept into her head and reminded her about his time in Athens. He had told her about that himself. He had been adamant that it was just for a very short while. But then again Yiannis had told her a lot of things that weren't true. Seán was her only concern now. If his father was going to have him half the time, she needed to know he was in a safe place. Whatever Matthew and Alex did was up to them. How could she ever find out?

Kate spent a restless sleepless night tossing and turning, with the same question going around and round in her head. How could she find out? How could she possibly confirm her suspicions about Alex, Matthew and Yiannis' involvement in it all?

By morning Kate really did feel ill but nothing could stop her from getting back onto the computer and re-reading all the stuff from the night before. She ignored calls from Matthew and just text him that she was still feeling terrible and needed time to herself. This time she knew what she had to do. She had to get to Matthew's phone again. She only had to figure out how.

The following week, the answer to how became apparent fairly quickly. What a rapid escalation of events! A bit disheartened by the weekend, Kate was further devastated to learn that it was Nikos and Katerina had been in The Hamptons with Yiannis, not Alex and she hadn't gotten to meet them. Maria was able to tell her that there were two elderly people in Yiannis' car when he dropped Seán back on Sunday and Seán arrived back with a photo of himself with the two of them, taken locally. Alex hadn't been with Yiannis at all. She had jumped to the wrong conclusion completely. Of course, she would have gone and met with them. They were so good to her in Crete. They were Seán's unofficial grandparents and she loved them dearly. But she resented the fact that he hadn't even given her the choice. And she wouldn't ring him to challenge him about it, she was so angry. A small little voice from somewhere whispered in her ear, When the separation papers arrive in Crete, they won't be part of your future either, Kate. They're Yiannis' and Seán's family, not yours. A stab of pain caught Kate's breath in her chest as she realised another loss she would have in her life when she left Yiannis. She had brought Seán too far away from his roots. Both of them were. She thought sadly.

Her copy of the separation papers arrived on Tuesday. That was another shock. To see it officially in black and white. To see Seán's future laid out so clinically almost broke her heart. She imagined Yiannis receiving them in Crete.

Kate finally confided in Maria what had happened at the weekend.

"I wondered," laughed Maria. "I'm only surprised it took so long. He's had his eye on you for ages."

When she went on to tell her about the text, Maria became quite serious and thoughtful for a long time.

"Kate, I know Matthew, Mr. Ryan, for a long time. I can honestly say I don't know if he's involved in drugs but most people from Colombia have heard of Devils Breath and he has lots of connections in Colombia. I've never seen him high or anything like that and I've worked for him a long time. He has a strong mind. He generally gets what he wants. I've watched…" Maria suddenly stopped. "It's a pity you can't find out more," she continued shaking her head, looking at Kate very thoughtfully.

Even though Kate was more interested in what Yiannis' role was, she ended up with a valuable insight about Matthew from a loyal employee. At the back of her head was the gnawing worry that Yiannis was involved in something underhand. She had to find out for definite, for Seán's sake. And then she'd re-evaluate.

Kate was at the end of her painting and it came as no surprise to her when the very next night Matthew showed up in the beach house unannounced, with a humongous bunch of flowers, on the pretext of discussing the exhibition. He virtually swaggered in the door with a self-assured smile on his face. The phrase 'the cat that got the cream' jumped to Kate's mind again. She had been trying to put off meeting him since Saturday morning, using illness and Seán as her excuses but all to no avail. Incredibly, he came assuming he could stay the night, but Kate put her foot down firmly, and immediately softened the rebuttal with the suggestion of a day out in Manhattan at the weekend. She had to get back into his apartment. She had to get a look at that phone again… Kate shivered involuntarily.

Kate was cautious and on her guard around Matthew. She watched him closely all the time he was at the beach house, noticing things she hadn't noticed before. Was it a flaw in her personality, she wondered, that character traits she had failed to see before became very obvious once she paid attention. Yiannis would have been a typical example of that, Paul even and now Matthew. He was a super confident man and quite liked to be in control, judging by the orders he barked to Maria. How did she stand for it?

There may have been a grey area between Maria and Matthew – his house, her employee, but Kate was the one paying Maria on a week to week basis. Come to think of it, she was paying him a considerable sum to rent the beach house. Maria seemed a different person around him. Not the wise sympathetic Maria who had given her advice on numerous occasions. There was an underlying unspoken negative atmosphere between them. Probably what bothered Kate the most was the fact that he interacted with Seán very little, who in turn seemed to ignore him completely. How things had changed since they first arrived in JFK when he had Seán eating out of the palm of his hand. He even suggested to Maria at one stage, she put Seán to bed. Kate could see Maria dithering, her eyes darting between Kate and Matthew, looking as if she was going to do his bidding. How dare he think it was ok to interfere with Seán, Kate fumed silently as she intervened diplomatically. Something told her she would need to keep Matthew on side, at least for the foreseeable future.

Were all men controlling bastards, she wondered in exasperation.

The minute the exhibition was over she was going to book flights to Ireland and tie up all the loose ends. She had been deliberately evasive and vague over the last few months on calls to Ireland. It was time to tell Molly and David about what was going on. Her children were her priority more than ever now.

By Thursday it hadn't escaped her notice either that four days had lapsed and Yiannis hadn't skyped. The separation papers would have made their way to Crete. Maybe that's what had happened. Punishing Seán wasn't fair even though it was the first and only week Seán hadn't kicked up to talk to his papa. At least not yet. The very next time they spoke it should be to organise getting Seán to Crete or at the very least discussing it. Yiannis had been on her mind a lot this past week.

It was time to find out for definite what, if any involvement he had with Matthew, Alex and scopolamine. She considered confronting Matthew, but Maria had advised her against that. If there was no Seán, Kate didn't think she would have cared at all but Seán's father possibly involved with drugs? That was a whole other ball game. Finding out the truth necessitated a return trip to Matthew's apartment and at this stage it looked like there was only one way that was going to happen. Ironically Yiannis rang in the middle of it all asking about exhibition dates and wondering about his next trip to see Seán. Was he fishing for an invitation to the exhibition? He never mentioned separation papers or Nikos and Katerina and he caught her at a relatively good time. Kate was still empowered both by her recent decisions about them, and thoughts that soon she would be in Ireland. Kate was civil to him on the phone. Nothing he could say to her now could shake her. The truth would out.

Thursday afternoon Kate asked Maria to mind Seán, and she took a long walk on the beach to think things through and plan the next move. She had arranged to visit Matthew in the city the very next day. She had to move quickly, or she may not get another opportunity like it. In a couple of weeks the exhibition would be over and she planned to be back in Ireland. Things were at a crucial point. The phone could be gone, or the texts deleted, she surmised. It was definitely a risk, albeit a very calculated one. Kate had no way of knowing for sure. She just had to see if Yiannis was in cahoots with Matthew.

It was all or nothing time. Could she go ahead with the plan in her head? She had nothing to lose anymore. But she had to know what was Yiannis' involvement with drugs if any, and what scopolamine had to do with any-thing. Kate's heart sank. A part of her knew the answer. It would change the whole custody thing for sure. Maybe she had been a bit hasty sending out the separation agreement. She would do anything for Seán if needs be. Once she had even thought like that about his father she remembered wistfully. Kate fisted her hands and steeled her body. She would go through with the plan. All she needed was a little help from Maria and the job was as good as done. On Friday, Kate had organised for Maria to be available all weekend if needs be, principally for Seán but a little for herself too. She had a feeling she might need some moral support when she got back from the city.

Things could not have panned out better. Matthew rang to say he had a meeting on Saturday morning that he couldn't miss and straight after that he was meeting Mr. Ferris for lunch. Mr. Ferris was the patron of her exhibition and Matthew was thrilled to have brought him on board. He wanted to change their dinner date to Saturday night. Kate lied, saying she had organised something with Seán for Saturday evening. The business meeting was no problem, she said she could relax at his apartment and then meet them afterwards. He didn't know Kate had no intention of meeting either of them irrespective of what she found out on Friday night.

With the details falling into place, Kate found herself at a very nice table in a very nice restaurant sitting across from Matthew, not quite sure how she got there. She remembered saying goodbye to Maria and Seán at the station but other than that, the journey was a blur. Matthew was on his best behaviour and dressed impeccably, she noted cynically. She mentally debated whether to have wine or not. She was on a mission and needed all her wits about her. He didn't even notice she had barely touched her glass. They made the mindless small talk and eventually impatient, Kate pushed her agenda and suggested they leave.

God, he was so gullible thought Kate as they got a taxi back to his. He hadn't a clue about body language or he would have known she resented being there with every fibre of her being. Her words and face were saying one thing, while her body was telling a whole other story and he was acting like the proverbial child in the candy store.

Back at his apartment there was no opportunity for Kate to search. He was by her side all the time so there was nothing for it only go ahead with the plan. She couldn't let him undress her so she faked shyness and made him get into bed before her with the lights dimmed. Kissing him was the worst part. It was such an intimate connection with another human and it was all she could do not to openly shiver. As she lay there pretending she was interested she realised she was no better than a prostitute selling her body in exchange for a commodity. Actually, she was worse than a prostitute. At least they were honest about their profession she had lied the whole night through. The tears trickled silently from Kate's eyes as she wondered what had brought her to this point in her life where she was ashamed of herself and what she was doing to fool another person.

Once the deed was done, Kate pretended to fall asleep. It was the best plan. Matthew seemed all set for talking, but she gave him no option as she turned away and lightly snored. She heard him go to the bathroom, saw the bright light as he checked his iPad or phone. Then she felt him toss and turn a bit before he eventually settled down and fell off to sleep. Kate finally let out a long breath. Thank God it was over. Why had she taken such a sudden dislike to him? Probably because she felt forced into doing something she would never have done in a million years. Sleep with someone for a very specific outcome. And nothing was written in stone. It's quite possible the second phone wouldn't even be where it had been last week. Kate didn't sleep a wink. She spent all night thinking things over in her head.

She didn't really care what the phone revealed about Matthew and Alex. She'd soon be out of there and once the exhibition was over have nothing to do with Matthew again.

But what might it reveal about Yiannis?

How would she react if it pointed to him being involved with drugs?

Would she confront him?

Would she get locked in a custody battle with him?

How could she look after Seán's best interests?

All night long she tried to imagine every possible scenario that might arise. It weighed heavily in Kate's head as she lay wide awake in Matthew's bed, praying for morning to arrive, praying for him to leave for his meeting.

Chapter Seventeen

THE TRUTH WILL OUT

The minute Kate heard the apartment door click behind Matthew, she jumped out of bed and ran to the bathroom and scrubbed every inch of herself in the shower. She felt sick with dread and fear because she was so near to discovering the next part of the phone story. Fear of what she might find out about Yiannis and dread about what she might have to do about it.

She hurriedly dried herself and got dressed. She took a deep breath before walking to the press where she found the phone a week before. She slowly opened the drawer, tense with expectation.

Shit no phone! she thought as she quickly scanned the drawer. She closed the first drawer and tried the next. Nothing. And then the next. Nothing. She cringed at the thoughts that the night before might have been for nothing.

"Don't panic," she whispered out loud as she retraced her movements and tried the first drawer again. Holding her breath, she moved a few papers and heaved a sigh of relief as she spotted the phone. Kate gave a quick glance around; irrationally afraid she was being watched. She carefully lifted the phone and studied it. It was still plugged into the wall, but this time there was no message on the screen. It was an iPhone, the same as her own and Kate broke out in a cold sweat, suddenly remembering she was snookered if Matthew had a passcode on it.

She unplugged the charger, carefully placing it into her bag before sinking to the floor to start her investigations.

Thank God, no passcode. Kate shook her head and quickly got into messages. For a second before she even started she closed her eyes in silent prayer, knowing that what she might find out could change her son's life forever and hers as a consequence.

She gave a quick flick into contacts. It wasn't hard to find Alex's name, it was nearly the only name in the phone. In fact, she noticed there were quite a few calls between them. Kate shrugged and switched to messages. An extra message from the previous weekend was the first text that came up.

RING U TOM

TOO LATE NOW

***

Need to talk ASAP

Under pressure from Yiannis +need to get rid of db

Googled scopolamine - nothing

Help! Desperate

***

Like a bee to honey...

***

K heard u on phone

All ok now

Text in future

***

M ring me

Need to talk badly

Under pressure here
Y stalking me

***

Need to talk
Can you ring me please??

***

Need to talk
Ring me

***

K+1 Brat in tow

***

Y in Athens
Turned up at work
Sec put him off

***

???

***

Can't face Y yet

***

I'll pick up the pieces this end
Y all yours

***

??
No need…

***

Job done
All hell broke loose
Made it look good!!
Feel guilty

***

Done

***

Gr8 Arrange for tom nite

Last flight to X

OA344

Ring u later to confirm all

       ***

Heard back from Y

He's on

       ***

OK

Done

I'll let u know as soon as I have news

       ***

Send the 1st text. NOW

or 2 late.

       ***

I know.

No second thoughts

I'd love a mon too!!

***

Rem why
K bleeding him dry…

***

No

***

Do u want out??

***

Yes I know
Never done before
Bit unsure

***

Be careful
Has to be EXACT MEASURE

***

Yes Tiny amount…as prep

     ***

Next day or 2

I'll let u know

Rem protocol with db?

     ***

OK

When?

Flight details??

     ***

It's time… put the plan into action

Leaving soon

Text now

M

***

Kate waded through reams and reams of texts. She was able to load ear-lier messages, read them over again and then go back to try and make sense of it all. At least she knew what scopolamine was now. How did Matthew and Alex even know each other? It seemed they were the ones to have used the drug, but she wasn't quite sure how. There was nothing to implicate

Yiannis in anything except stalking Alex. But straight off a few other things screamed at her and made her pay close attention. She scrolled back to the beginning of the texts and read them all over again and again focusing on times and dates. It was only then that a possible explanation began to dawn on her.

It couldn't be… Could it?

Kate re-read them again. She could tie in the dates of the texts to significant events.

She was assuming K referred to herself and the Y to Yiannis. The thing that stung was the bit about Yiannis stalking Alex.

Last flight to X – the exact date of her flight to Crete coincided with a text.

The night she found Yiannis in bed with Alex. What had Alex texted? JOB DONE. MADE IT LOOK GOOD.

Flight to New York on the exact date of her flight to New York coincided with *K+1. BRAT IN TOW.* That had to be herself and Seán, a shocked Kate realised. He referred to Seán as a brat.

Oh my God, thought Kate, that's how he thinks of Seán.

What kind of a man was Matthew that he could send such cruel texts? And be involved in what she was starting to suspect. Ever since they had started to work together, she had trusted him completely and he certainly had access to lots of her private details. He was in a prime position to do something like this, Kate thought shocked to the core.

She continued to scroll over and back, over and back shaken, that the phone seemed to be revealing so many unpleasant secrets.

The previous week Matthew had texted, LIKE A BEE TO HONEY. What did that mean? Was it what she thought? She knew by the date, she was with him. It was the first night she had slept with him. In fact, the text was timed only hours after she had… Oh Jesus!

The reference to the mon she thought was a spelling mistake first. She thought it should read man but then if mon was right, it could be short for monastery and then it would fit in with the tone of the other texts. Few enough people knew about the gift of the monastery in Crete and Matthew was one of the few. No doubt about that but she didn't understand, *she's bleeding him dry...* unless...

Kate had answers and then some more questions when she finished reading the texts. At least she had a heads up on the scopolamine and how it worked. Matthew and Alex didn't appear to be selling drugs, but they had very obviously used the devil's breath at least once.

But why?

She went back and read everything again, this time with a crazy viewpoint in her head. It was all a bit coincidental. Too many pieces would fall conveniently into place if... Was she looking at it the wrong way or was there a different slant she could take?

It was beginning to look like Matthew and Alex had engineered her trip to New York but again she had to ask why? Why would Matthew and Alex want her in New York? It was too creepy to even think about.

Kate shook her head and glanced at the clock. An hour or so had passed since she first started reading the texts. She continued to stare at the phone in her hand. A phone full of strange messages.

Was she adding two and two and getting twenty-two?

No, she didn't think so.

If it was true then, Yiannis... she couldn't bear to think it

Before she reached any concrete conclusion she carefully put the phone into her bag, next to the charger, knowing the only proof she had of anything were the texts she had just read.

What am I going to do about any of this? she wondered. Decisions will have to be made and quickly.

It was still very early, and the morning stretched out in front of her, giving her time to make a dash to The Hamptons if she wanted. There was no way she could rely on public transport to get her there and back. First, she'd empty her bank account and then she would have two hours travelling time to put some plan into action. She grabbed her bag and banged out through the apartment door, lost in thought.

Kate spent the journey to The Hamptons online researching and booking a few things. She had drafted a rough plan in her head of where she was going to be in the afternoon. Everything hinged on Maria now. If she wasn't on board, there was precious little Kate could do. When Kate landed back at the beach house mid-morning, Maria was more than surprised to see her. Kate went straight to the bedroom, grabbed a couple of things and then sat Maria down. The simplest thing to do was show her the texts and see if Maria agreed with what she believed had happened. Had she been wrong about Yiannis?

Less than an hour later Maria, Kate and Seán were in the cab on their way to the city. Maria had filled in a few more pieces of the puzzle and Kate was convinced her instincts were right. A text had been sent to Matthew to alert him she was running late. Maria had agreed to look after Seán and meet her later. It was all systems go to implement her crazy half-baked plan.

When Kate strode into the restaurant thirty-five minutes behind schedule, Matthew and Mr. Ferris were already at a table chatting and sipping drinks. Kate smiled inwardly as she remembered how ecstatic Matthew had been to have Mr. Ferris on board. How he kept saying it was a huge feather in his cap, for the exhibition but also for his own business. It wasn't only the financial boost, but it was the prestige that Mr. Ferris' name carried in New York. She had his permission to charge what she liked for the paintings, he had arrogantly bragged. They were both in line for a big windfall.

It was that same egotism that Kate was now gambling on. The two men rose as Kate joined them and Matthew started the introductions, but Kate jumped the gun and beat him to it.

"Mr. Ferris, I presume?" Kate held her hand out to the elderly gentleman smiling at her.

"Please sit," she inclined her head ignoring the seat Matthew held out for her and sat herself next to Mr. Ferris across the table from Matthew.

"I apologise for my late arrival but I assure you I had very good reason. You could say a family crisis."

"Nothing too serious I hope, my dear," Mr. Ferris added kindly.

Kate smiled, shook her head at them both but looked directly at Matthew. "Nothing I can't handle, Mr. Ferris. Nothing I can't handle," she barely drew breath and continued on. It was all or nothing. "I don't know if Matthew has had a chance to fill you in, Mr. Ferris, but we have discussed the exhibition at length, the price point of the paintings and how we would like to show our appreciation to you, our patron..." Both men were looking at her in anticipation. "There is nothing like a family crisis to put things in perspective," she continued quietly, appearing to talk to no-one in particular at this point.

Kate took out the two phones she had in her bag and placed them on the table. "Apologies, I am expecting a very important call."

Matthew didn't blink but raised an eyebrow as Kate placed the phones on the table beside Mr. Ferris.

"This part, Mr. Ryan doesn't even know yet but I'm afraid the family crisis will not permit me to be at the opening of my own exhibition, next weekend. As we speak, my husband is flying into JFK and I need to leave shortly, to meet with him. I hope you both understand..."

Kate saw Matthew pale, and he sat up straight in his chair as if to hear her better.

'Independent of this, Mr. Ryan and myself were talking only recently about how we would like in some way to repay your kindness, Mr. Ferris. We appreciate your willingness to be associated with the exhibition. It has already led to lots of media interest and as you know, Mr. Ferris, there is no such thing as bad publicity, particularly with opening night looming.

For my part to make up for my absence on opening night, I would like nothing better than to donate all the proceeds from the first night to the charity you are linked with in the city. I believe it's the NYSPCC? Whether that happens in a week's time or a month's time or even in a year, it doesn't matter – it's up to you. Perhaps somebody from the charity could handle this, Mr. Ferris? I think it would be better if myself and Mr. Ryan had no personal involvement with the finances except perhaps to sign things over to you. And I'm sure Mr. Ryan will waive his hefty commission," Kate smiled directly at Matthew, openly challenging him. "I am returning to Europe with my husband and I don't think I will be exhibiting in America in the near future. Actually, Mr. Ryan and I have naturally come to the end of our... our association."

Matthew had stopped smiling and was openly frowning now, not sure what Kate was going to say next. She knew she had him over a barrel, but it still didn't stop him reaching across the table to her phones.

"Is that my phone, Kate?" he asked using his cold blue eyes to try and intimidate her, aware Kate had stumbled onto something.

She was one step ahead of him again though and held the offending phone up as she replied, "Matthew, I always have a second phone with me to keep a record of texts and phone calls that are significant to me. Texts that are very private, that I wouldn't like other people to read." That was as blatant as Kate wanted to be, letting Matthew know she was on to him.

Thank God, she thought, that neither man challenged her as to how in reality a second phone for texts and calls actually worked. She hadn't a clue how to explain that.

Matthew didn't speak. She was gambling on the fact that he didn't want to ruffle Mr. Ferris' feathers. He had to live and work in New York. She didn't.

Kate stopped talking and the normally reserved Mr. Ferris took the chance to gush his appreciation. "My dear, I cannot tell you what a fine thing you and Mr. Ryan are doing on the charity's behalf. You know the publicity alone will catapult the charity into New Yorkers consciousness. It looks like it could be win-win all round. And, if it helps a cause very dear to my heart, all the better! I hope your family emergency is, well, not too bad. You know things are never as bad as they seem, Kate?"

"I know, Mr. Ferris. I know. I have learned that things are never as they appear. I have learned that to my own personal cost." She left that comment hang.

Matthew continued to stay silent, a smile pasted onto his face.

"Now, I must go," Kate laughed, "if I'm not at the airport to meet my husband in a few hours, I'm afraid he may scour New York looking for me." Kate looked at Matthew pointedly. "I'll leave you two gentlemen to work out the finer details. All the paintings are in The Hamptons and ready to go."

Kate stood and slowly picked up the two phones off the table and placed them into her bag. Matthew got up with her, "Let me drive you to the airport, Kate. I'm sure Mr. Ferris won't mind."

"Absolutely not, Matthew!" Kate dismissed the offer. "I have a taxi waiting outside. You two get the whole thing underway. One last thing Mr. Ferris here is my phone number. Will you ring me after the exhibition opening, if only to reassure me that everything goes according to plan and that all the monies end up where they are supposed to end up?"

"Of course, my dear. Of course!" Mr. Ferris beamed at Kate taking the number, very pleased at the upturn in events and for the unexpected boost the NYSPCC would get. He was also fully aware there was an unexplained undercurrent at the table he didn't entirely understand, and that Kate O'Shea was purposefully warning him to be cautious about something.

"Leave it in my capable hands, my dear, and I will be in touch sooner rather than later."

Kate shook his hand warmly, a little disappointed she wouldn't have the chance to get to know him better and she ignored Matthew as she swept out of the restaurant before either of them noticed she was trembling all over and sick to her stomach.

Kate flagged a taxi to keep her meeting with Maria, collect Seán and implement the next part of her plan. She knew she wouldn't be able to relax until herself and Seán were safely on the plane out of New York as far away from Matthew Ryan as they possibly could be.

Chapter Eighteen

THE MONASTERY

By the time their third flight landed in Chania Airport, Kate could hardly speak, she was so exhausted. Her head was reeling, full of texts, stupid reactions and months of self-imposed exile not to mention the clanger, the two clangers Maria had landed on her in JFK. On top of which they had been travelling almost a full twenty-four hours and Seán had only fallen asleep on the last leg. She hadn't the heart to wake him, so she struggled down the plane steps holding the sleeping child in her arms. Heavy as he was and exhausted as Kate was, inhaling the sights and smells of being back in Crete energised her in a way that a night's sleep would never have. They had finally come full circle. Kate had a spring in her step as she exited the airport and went to get a taxi. Hopefully they were on the last leg of a marathon journey, a journey that had taken in New York, London and Athens.

As the taxi flew along the familiar route to the peninsula, Kate knew the next few hours would be vital to salvaging any kind of relationship with Yiannis. They had left New York so rapidly all their stuff was left behind. Split-second decisions meant she had only gone back to Southampton for Seán, their passports and some dollars. None of that mattered now, only that they had made it safely. God how she hoped he'd forgive her, or at least give her a hearing. She couldn't really blame him if he didn't. She had been deliberately cold and emotionless in all their dealings over the last three months. If only he knew. If only he knew the half of it...

By the time the taxi reached the stone cottage, the initial excitement at being back had diminished a little, replaced by slight apprehension. She was surprised to see that her car was back parked in the yard and disappointed that Yiannis' jeep was nowhere in sight. No sign of Zorba either. It was afternoon. The working day was on a break and he would always have been home at this time when she was there. Where was he? For the briefest of moments, she thought about getting the taxi to take them to her own house, but that would defeat the purpose of being back. She had to talk to him face to face.

So, she put on a brave face, smiled at Seán and as gently as she could, roused him and paid the taxi driver.

Certain he wasn't there, Kate still knocked on the door and called out his name before she let herself into the cottage, feeling a little like a trespasser. The door was unlocked as always. Kate slowly walked the house she hadn't set foot in for nearly three months. The place she had called home for two years. It looked the same. It smelled the same. It felt the same. Comfortable, cosy and home. It had the same tranquil feeling it had the first time she had ever gone there with Yiannis, nearly three years ago now.

Lost in her reminiscing Kate was distracted by Seán, finally fully awake and running through the house shouting, "Papa, Papa!" as he realised exactly where he was. She had forgotten it would have to be the same for him too. He hadn't been home for three months either. And now she could see his excitement at being back written all over his small chubby face. Kate sighed deeply. She regretted her hasty departure and knee-jerk reactions.

In the living room, Kate's eyes took in the familiar space, the cushions scattered on the sofa, a lingering smell of coffee, a cup on the table, her car keys where she always used to leave them, the wedding invitations now neatly piled on the worktop beside a distinctly familiar large brown envelope, addressed to Yiannis. She knew exactly what that was. With a sinking heart she picked it up. It clearly had been opened. She could picture Yiannis reading its contents. Unable to resist her fate, Kate looked inside, a morbid curiosity gripping her. Her heart sank when she saw his familiar signature as she flicked through the pages. So, he had signed the papers. He was willing to let her go.

She had moved at lightning speed once she got to New York and Kate felt her eyes fill up as she stared out the window desperately hoping that she hadn't left it too late, hoping they could salvage something, at the very worst an amicable working relationship for Seán.

From her vantage point Kate saw a familiar figure ambling down the lane towards the cottage and the months of emotional turmoil sought an escape. She ran outside to greet Nikos, Yiannis' nearest neighbour, unofficial granddad to Seán and father-figure to them all. Nikos opened his arms as

Kate threw herself into his comforting embrace and sobbed her heart out. He held her without speaking for a long time.

"Hush child," he eventually soothed. "Are you back to stay?"

"I don't know," she sobbed, "I think I might have left it too late."

"Kate, it's never too late."

Please God let him be right she thought in desperation.

"Where is he, Nikos?"

"Try the monastery. He's been there a lot lately."

How fitting that he would be there, when the monastery had figured so much in their past. A place that meant so much to them both. It was symbolic, it had marked the beginning of things between them and of course it was the place they had planned to have the wedding party, before she abruptly left. Yiannis had gifted it to her on the day of the civil wedding ceremony, before all the shit hit the fan, until she had thrown it back in his face. Let's hope it wouldn't mark the end now. With all that she had to tell him and the fact that she had seen the divorce papers, she wasn't hugely optimistic about reconciliation.

Seán tugged at Nikos' pants reminding them that he was there too.

"Seán? Will you…?" Kate pleaded as she made to get her car keys.

"Go…" Nikos gently pushed her towards the car. He already had Seán up in his arms, playing with him as he headed out the road.

"Let's go see Katerina. She will be so happy to see you!" Kate heard him say as she started the ignition and set off out the lane towards the monastery.

Kate drove the short distance to the monastery her mind teetering somewhere between hopeful anticipation and dreaded fear.

Sure enough, as she pulled into the car park, Yiannis' jeep was there, and Zorba raised his head from the back, wagged his tail furiously and barked when he saw her.

"Oh Zorba!" Kate jumped out of the car and buried her face in his soft fur, taking small comfort from the fact that at least he seemed happy to see her.

As soon as she let herself into the monastery a familiar peace and calm wrapped itself around her. It was what she loved about the place. No matter what was going on, a short time spent there always made her feel better. It was the one place in the whole world where she felt closest to Yiannis. Everything always felt so right there, so perfect. Like they were meant to be. If they had any chance of getting back together, it was in this beautiful place they both loved so much. She hoped that wasn't going to change as she was about to have the hardest and most important conversation of her life.

A dragging noise distracted her, and she made her way slowly towards the open door at the back. As she edged closer to the door, she could hear the rhythmic sound of the waves breaking against the cliffs somewhere down below. Kate saw him then out on the veranda, his back to her, fully absorbed in the task at hand. Her heart thumped in her chest and she couldn't fully catch her breath. She watched him in a sort of trance, half hidden by the door sad and guilty that she had not stayed and fought for him. What an amazing man he was. He had to be the kindest man she had ever come across in her life. He was the same with everyone; unflappable, strong and sometimes vulnerable.

He had been wronged so badly this time. Why had she found it so easy to believe he had betrayed her? Probably because the plan had been so very well devised and executed, a voice answered back from inside her head. She had Matthew to thank for that. She longed for Yiannis to take her into his arms and tell her that everything was ok, and that he didn't want a divorce either, that he forgave her for what she had done. But there was a lot of water under the bridge now. So many things had happened. The one thing she couldn't forgive him for three months ago was the one thing she needed him to forgive her for now. There was a time not too long ago when he would have sensed her presence, when he would have looked up the moment she entered a room and smiled at her in that slow sensual way of his. Now she could study him uninterrupted and watch mesmerised as he moved a large rustic pot into place beside others.

Slowly Yiannis stood up and appeared to take stock of his work. He took a few steps back and tilted his head. With no warning he swung around, and her heart turned over as he looked directly at her, taking her completely by surprise.

"Kate…" he stared at her. "I had a feeling it was you."

She swallowed a lump as she held his gaze.

In the few short weeks since they had met in New York, he appeared just that bit older or greyer or was she imagining it? Why could she not have stayed and worked things through with him like he had asked? Everything she had ever felt for him was there, and more besides.

"We need to talk," she all but whispered as she walked towards him.

"Where's Seán?" he looked a bit apprehensive.

"He's fine. He's with Nikos."

"I signed the papers, Kate," he sighed. The words, what else do you want from me were left unspoken.

Kate deliberately gazed out to sea over his shoulder, wanting things to be different, looking for some divine inspiration, briefly wanting to be any-where but where she was having this conversation.

"I'm sorry. I'm so sorry," she blurted. "Yiannis, there's so much you need to hear, good news, bad news… We were both fooled by people near to us!" Kate took a deep breath.

Yiannis frowned and looked at her curiously and she could see that she had his full, undivided attention. She had desperately wanted to not cry, hold her composure talk rationally and calmly, but she found that all the hurt and devastation she had felt when she thought he had slept with Alex was finding its way out. The feelings of broken-heartedness and betrayal she had swapped for detachment and coldness in New York, would have their moment. Please God let him not want a divorce when she told him the full story of what had happened. Let him not resent her for the speed at which she had sent the divorce papers from New York. Things had come full circle. It was a big ask.

"It's hard to know where to even begin… You didn't sleep with Alex," she shook her head at him. "At least, I don't think you did… She drugged you. It was a set up. They wanted me to find you in bed with her."

"Who did? Who's they?" Yiannis looked at Kate incredulously.

"Matthew principally, and I think Alex too. They were in it together." Her voice petered out. She knew the story sounded farfetched.

"Look I think – No, I'm fairly sure, between them they set the whole thing up."

"Go on," replied Yiannis.

"Matthew texted Alex with my flight details the night I arrived back in Crete. I can prove that. I'm guessing she texted you sometime before then."

"Yes…"

"Without your knowledge, I think she gave you or somehow got you to take a drug called scopolamine or devils breath. It wipes your memory, so that you do things and then don't remember them…"

"Why on earth would she do that? How…?" Yiannis asked impatiently not sure where the hair-brained story was going.

"So she could get you to take her back to the stone cottage and sleep with her. And I'd find you and…"

"That's ridiculous, Kate! I think I'd remember if I invited…"

"But that's just it, you don't remember! You said so yourself after that night. The drug makes you forget. He got it in Colombia, I think. Matthew engineered the whole thing. I have his phone. I have the proof. All the texts are on it… Look!" She almost shouted at him willing him to believe her and she took the phone out of her bag and held it out to Yiannis. "Look… Start from the beginning. The beginning is the end… please. There's the first… And look at the dates as well…" she leaned over to show him where the texts were.

For the next thirty minutes Yiannis said nothing, only read and reread the texts on Matthew's phone.

"Do you know how farfetched this whole thing sounds," he finally raised his eyebrows at her, but she could see a spark of belief.

"Let's just say Alex did, Kate, why on earth would she do such a thing? Why?"

"Jealousy? I don't know. This bit I'm guessing, but I think Alex has always loved you, Yiannis. I think she never wanted to let you go when you left Athens but went along with your plan and was happy with your arrangement for a long time until..." She didn't want to say, until I arrived on the scene. "And then when she met Matthew, I really don't understand why but it's like they discovered they had something in common or at least had a common purpose! Matthew knew about the monastery from me. I was excited, and I told him when I went back to Ireland after the wedding. He was privy to all kinds of information from me, about me. He even booked the flights to Crete for myself and Seán. The proof – only he and I knew the flight number."

"But what about America?" Yiannis looked confused, "I booked those flights."

"I think he gambled on the fact that after I found Alex in bed with you, sooner or later I'd rethink the American exhibition. I don't know if he realised it would be as soon. And I know he wasn't expecting Seán to be with me."

"He took a gamble that you'd go to America and he'd have you all to himself." Yiannis said slowly, as if something else had dawned on him. "Remember Kate, we argued last year, over him. He was pushing you to go to America back then and you weren't ready."

"Yes, I've thought of that a million times since yesterday. He really wanted me to go and then he was doubly disgusted when I pulled out after Christmas."

Yiannis looked at Kate curiously, "At Christmas? What are you talking about?"

She had totally forgotten he didn't know that bit. "Yiannis, there's so much you don't know! The bit I don't get, is how they even knew each other.

I've gone over it and over it and I can't think. Even I only ever met her a couple of times."

The words lingered in the air between them for a long while and then Yiannis quietly spoke.

"I was the one who introduced them. Matthew and Alex. Remember that time he surprised you here to see your studio and flew back to New York from Athens? You were here with Seán and I was in Athens. He ate with us that night, with Stavros, Dimitri, Michalis – Alex included. None of them liked him, only Alex it would seem. I think they may even have spent the night together.

Funny thing is she has been elusive over the last few months, ever since the night in January. Something didn't feel right about that night – apart from the obvious. I remember so little, only that we arranged to meet for dinner, her picking me up and then being in the restaurant. After that it's fuzzy. Next thing I knew, you were in the room and Alex was in the bed and you know the rest…" he broke off.

"I don't remember sleeping with her, Kate. I really don't. I thought it was funny when she turned up to collect me. And I've tried to get hold of her several times since. She was the only person who was there, who could tell me what happened. I've tried to track her down over the last few months but could never seem to catch up with her."

"Oh no! All the pieces are falling into place. I overheard Alex tell Matthew on the phone that you were stalking her. I thought it was because you wanted to be with her."

"No, I wanted to talk to her."

"Matthew, it seems, is really not a very nice person – and that's being generous. Yiannis, I trusted him with so much. He's evil. Messing with our lives. Giving you drugs. He's dishonest and greedy, shallow and dangerous. And I didn't see it! He could have wrecked our lives. He did. He was the one pulling all the strings."

"Kate, the first time I met Matthew, I didn't like him. I knew he liked you, but I just didn't realise how much. Your career had taken off and you'd just won the award in Ireland. I think he had some weird notion of you two together as a team, him managing your lucrative career and then you keeping him through your painting sales. He wanted you for himself. Literally."

"I never knew that," Kate retorted, "I never thought like that!"

"It was in my head, Kate. I thought it was me, but it makes sense now if what you say is true. The whole thing is so farfetched it's off the scale. Only that we have the phone as the proof, we'd never believe two people could be so devious. It's crazy stuff!"

"What do you want to do about all this?" she tensed her body feeling angrier and angrier. "About Matthew and Alex? He could have killed you, in a roundabout way. I don't think it would have cost him a thought."

"I don't know," Yiannis replied, "they've already taken three months of our lives. Are we going to let them take up more? I don't want that. They shouldn't get away with it."

"Indirectly I confronted Matthew in New York. He knows I have the phone," Kate filled Yiannis in on the meeting with Matthew and Mr. Ferris and herself. "I know it's cold comfort but business wise, Matthew's sorted. We no longer work together. The money from the exhibition will be channelled to a charity. I have a feeling his work will dry up in New York thanks to an astute Mr. Ferris. And Maria," Kate gulped, "filled in the final piece in the puzzle at the airport yesterday. Can you believe it? She told me she's his mother? She's Matthews's mother! She wasn't hugely surprised. She thinks he's manipulative and capable of lots of things. He's horrible to her and she just takes it. They seem to have a strange dysfunctional relationship. It's like he's punishing her for something. It's the only thing I feel a bit guilty about, leaving Maria behind to deal with Matthew on her own." Kate thought back on her final conversation with Maria at the airport. It chilled her a bit to think that she had trusted Seán with Maria all along not knowing what was going to unfold. And then yesterday, without realising it, she had asked Maria to choose them over her own son and Maria had come up trumps.

"I can't think straight anymore," Kate fisted her hands in frustration. "I have no appetite for revenge. The thing that most gets me in all this, is Seán.

He was separated from you for months! I know I had my part to play. I fell for it all hook, line and sinker..."

"Come on, Kate. Let's not beat ourselves up. I don't know what I would have done if I found you with someone. And Alexandra? I have a feeling she knows what she nearly did. I think she has more of a conscience than Matthew. Let's sit on it all for a while. Let's see if either of them tries to get in touch? Where does that leave us? How did you find out all this? How did you get his phone?" Yiannis looked at her quizzically.

A silence descended.

"There's more," she held his gaze sick to the stomach.

Everything Kate had planned to say to him that night months ago came out in a garbled mix of words interspersed with the exhibition in New York, Seán and how they had missed him, how she had been coming back on that fateful night to tell him they were going to move to the peninsula permanently. The only time in all the ranting that she lost eye contact with him was when she told him about sleeping with Matthew.

"The weekend you brought Nikos and Katerina to America with you, I thought it was Alex. I thought you had brought Alex with you. I..."

Eventually Kate realised she had been wittering on and on and half crying, he was just standing there saying nothing, so she stopped and stared at him.

Finally, he spoke. "Am I right in thinking you don't want a divorce?"

Kate shook her head not trusting herself to speak anymore.

"And, I didn't sleep with Alex?"

She shook her head again.

"But you slept with Matthew..."

She nodded.

He looked away again and said nothing for a long time.

Eventually he spoke, "I can't pretend that I'm ok with it. There's a part of me that wants to kill him and there's a part of me..." He didn't finish his sentence but looked away again. "Everything has changed and yet nothing has changed," he murmured to himself.

Eventually he asked, "Are you ok? And Seán?"

"Yes," she managed to whisper.

"Are we ok, Kate?"

This time she nodded. "God, I hope so!"

"Then it'll take time, but everything will be ok. Do you trust me, Kate?" he asked her.

"I should have trusted you three months ago."

"Do you trust me now, Kate?"

"With my life."

"Then give me the phone."

She handed it over.

"It's our only proof..." she started.

"Are you planning on taking them to court," he asked.

"No, but..."

He didn't let her finish but caught the phone and threw it as hard as he could over the veranda and out towards the sea.

"That's it, Kate, it's gone. Let it go. Let's put it behind us. I just hope I never see that man again or..." Yiannis didn't finish.

It was the measure of the man he was that he didn't fly into a rage with his wounded male ego. He merely took her into his arms and held her. She marvelled at his touch and how the energy seemed to flow from him to her. Such a simple gesture and it always had a profound effect on her. Kate inhaled his smell and relaxed into his arms. She was home at last. Neither of them moved, surrendering to the stillness, and the feelings of complete and utter relief that the last few months were hopefully over.

"Don't you ever be unfaithful to me again," Kate finally laughed pulling away from him trying to make light of it.

"I won't. I promise," he laughed back.

"There's something else I have to tell you," Kate continued

"There's more?"

"Just a bit more."

This had nothing to do with Alex or Matthew now. It was all about them. It was the last thing Maria had pointed out to her before she left them in JFK. Something she had noticed over the few months in America.

"Remember the night before we left for America? Remember the night in Athens?" she asked mischievously grinning at him.

"Of course, I do…"

EPILOGUE

Easter in Crete, probably the most beautiful time of year to be on this bewitching island. An island bathed in gentle sunshine. The weather as pleasant as a good Irish summer and the tourist season not yet in full swing. Everywhere was overflowing and abundant with wild flowers and spring growth. And the promise of a great summer hung in the air.

It was the perfect day for celebrating.

Yiannis had Seán on his shoulders, at the newly refurbished yoga centre. Nearly three years old now and the light of his parents' life.

At first glance, he appeared to be just like his dad, with his jet-black hair and sallow skin, but on closer inspection, when he fluttered those long black lashes, his eyes were a carbon copy of his mothers, distinctively almond shaped and stunningly green.

The scene was set.

In the courtyard, long rectangular tables were in place alongside the lime trees. They were covered with pristine white cloths, simply and artistically decorated with spring flowers, awaiting only the food. Patio heaters had been placed here and there, in case of chill night temperatures and barbeques were already lit in the background. Bottles of chilled champagne were stored and ready to be popped once the ceremony was over.

A small crowd had already gathered. Everyone they cared about, Molly, David and Jack, Nikos and Katerina, Jane, friends and relations from Ireland, Athens and the village, Sophia and her new partner, Costas and the family. And of course, Zorba. Kate had even hoped Maria might have taken up their invitation but there was no word back from her.

As he surveyed the gathering, Yiannis thought how his life had grown and changed since Kate's appearance in it more than three years ago. Days definitely didn't come much better than this.

Stubborn and strong-willed she had steadfastly refused to marry him when he first asked. He never once doubted her commitment to him. He knew she loved him. He probably knew that before she did. She just didn't want to marry after being widowed and he could understand that. So, it took him completely by surprise, when she had asked him after Seán was born.

The intervening few years had been filled with the busyness of looking after Seán, trips over and back to Ireland and of course the debacle in America which very few knew about.

They found their personal lives enhanced by the love and support of the other. They missed each other while separated but had recently decided that's the way it would remain for the moment at least, continuing to negotiate a life that suited, split between their two countries. Yiannis knew that even though Crete was part of Kate's soul, she was Irish to the very tips of her fingers and always would be. A lot of their time together, apart from a couple of Irish Christmases' had been spent on the peninsula, and in a way, they were living an idyllic existence. In some ways cut off from officialdom and the real world. And in more ways than either of them could even comprehend, living a life fuller and more real than anything that had gone before.

Perfectly imperfect.

Over the last few weeks it had been all systems go getting ready for the christening/wedding party and many official documents had winged their way from Ireland to Crete, some with great urgency. Unbeknownst to everyone except a few, they had had a small civil wedding ceremony in the town hall last November with Molly and David, Nikos and Katerina as their witnesses. Just the six of them and Seán. It had all been kept very quiet. And no one knew about America except the same trusted few.

But this day was about celebrating with family and friends. It was a small semi-religious ceremony and gathering. Most thought they were there for Seán's christening and an early holiday on the Aegean. What a surprise it would be when Kate and Yiannis exchanged rings! A school friend of Yiannis', a long time orthodox priest, was more than happy to officiate. It was more of a blessing than anything, to be witnessed by everyone they loved. A prayer of gratitude for the gift of Seán, a simple ceremony and an exchange of rings, followed by a big party.

Kate was wearing a loose cream lace top over her black leggings and flat sparkly sandals. The top she had picked up at a local craft market and it was the perfect mix of chiffon and hand-stitched lace. Yiannis was wearing his trade mark denims and a cool white linen shirt Kate had bought for him.

The previous November they had gone all out and dressed up for the official ceremony. Kate had even rescued her purple dress from semi-retirement and added a shawl to take the bare look off it, and Yiannis had worn a classic dark suit from his Athens days. The image perfectly captured on camera and given pride of place in the stone cottage amid the other family photographs.

But today was low-key and casual. There was no fuss or formality. Even the footnote on the invitations had said, *It's Crete, wear what you like.*

Kate made her way over to Yiannis and Seán. He put his arm around her shoulder, drawing her into his embrace.

"I think it's time we got the celebrations underway, don't you?" she smiled at him taking Seán from his shoulders.

"Can I call you, Mrs. Theodorakis, when it's all over?" he joked with her. He may have loved the fiercely independent streak in her, but he never missed an opportunity to tease her about it.

"Not if you expect me to answer!" she laughed back at him.

Funny thing was, for all her independence, she would have changed her name in a heartbeat. She loved the sound of Kate Theodorakis and she loved the way he had jokingly called her *Kyria Theodarakis* after the civil ceremony.

"Did I tell you how beautiful you look today?" Yiannis looked at her admiringly.

"Yes, you did," she grinned at him. "Have you got the rings?"

"Of course." He touched his pocket to reassure her.

Kate had spent hours sketching a rough draft of the rings and had taken her sketches to a local jeweller to have them replicated. Bands of silver were framed with rose gold, decorated with intertwining Celtic spirals and Greek keys. Their names and the date were inscribed on the inside. The finished products had turned out to be exquisite, more beautiful than she had imagined in her head. Yiannis suggested they wear them on their right hands, in Greek tradition, seeing as Kate had already done it the other way. And even though they had officially exchanged them at the civil ceremony, they had left them off in the meantime to avoid unnecessary questioning.

"So… where are you taking me after the party?" She pressed him, knowing he was sure to have something special up his sleeve. Going away for a few nights on their own would be a real luxury.

"Wait and see!" was all he would say, smiling and winking at her. For once, resisting her charms.

All of a sudden Yiannis' demeanour changed from one of tenderness to intensity as he looked at her quite seriously for a moment and gestured with his arm out.

"Kate, I hope you know that despite everything, despite the last few months. I really want all this to be yours. The monastery. From me to you… again."

She could see by his face, he was in earnest. He was deadly serious. They hadn't spoken about it since she came back from America. Nothing had changed for him it seemed. She touched her heart.

"Yiannis, I don't know what to say only that I accept it gladly, and hopefully will turn it into something wonderful."

"You've already done that," he answered softly

He tried to make light of it, "At least you have the contacts. Run it any way you like. Or hire someone to do it. I don't mind… Besides I always think of you when I'm here."

"I would do it anyway, Yiannis. You don't have to give it to me."

"I want to."

"You crazy man! I love you," she whispered kissing him as she gripped his hand tightly with her free one, shaking her head in disbelief, too overcome to be mad with him.

Was he for real, she sometimes wondered. He never ceased to amaze her. Earlier that morning in one of their more intimate moments he whispered his vows to her, for their life together. For her ears only, he said. He wouldn't be repeating them for all to hear.

"Kate," he had said, "I promise to love you and make love to you for as long as we both can. When we can no longer make love, I promise to hold your hand and take you in my arms, and talk and laugh with you and watch as Seán and the world grow a little older…"

She was very moved and though her words to him were maybe not as eloquent, the feelings behind them were just as passionate.

Kate wanted in some strange way to reciprocate, her heart bursting as she gripped his hand even tighter. They were both thrilled she was pregnant again and she was positive it had happened the night before she left for America. She had wanted it to happen, ever since Seán was born. But with all the trauma of the last few months it had almost happened unbeknownst to herself.

The blessings of the gods, again!

They stood together, the three of them, for a few moments. Words unnecessary. Both feeling blessed.

Seán finally forcing them apart.

Kate kissed them both tenderly.

"Now come on," she grinned at Yiannis, "I want to marry you again! Maybe a bit late but every bit as special."

Anyone who ever saw them together knew they were witnessing something beautiful. Electricity crackled between them. What had started as a fling or affair had morphed into something wonderful, a palpable connection for all to see. And had proven itself against the test of outside interferences.

Yiannis, for his part, loved Kate and Seán with every fibre of his being. There were no half measures. He had often wondered about this great passion that his grandmother had spoken about. He never quite got it. Until he met Kate, of course. Now he knew first-hand. He was living it. Now he understood when she had spoken about her beloved Dimitris and how she knew instinctively he was the one for her. Kate was the one for him. "Always follow your heart," Eleni Mitsotakis had said to Yiannis on her death bed. Yiannis knew he would have followed Kate to the ends of the world and back.

Kate smiled at them both, father and son. Her life, one long rollercoaster since first meeting him. Once she had ditched her fears and surrendered to her deep feelings for Yiannis, things had flowed more easily in her life, despite the last three months. Because of that they were stronger than ever. He touched that place in her soul where magical things happen. She loved him with all her heart. She loved everything about him. He was kind and confident, loyal and loving. A wonderful father. And boy could he make her pulse race!

And Seán, their miracle child. A child never more loved. Like millions of children, in millions of homes across the world, adored by their parents. She was so fortunate. To have had something once with Paul was a blessing. But to have found a love as passionate and intense as theirs was truly a miracle.

Kate calmly reflected on the path her life had taken to this point in time. It had been a very ordinary, yet extraordinary one, traumatic and blessed. Good times and bad times. All the major happenings had overlapped and interspersed with each other, making her the person she was today, her marriage to Paul, the gift of her daughter and son, the joy of painting, her place in the sun, bereavement, grieving, exhibitions and traumas. And now her new family with Yiannis, Seán, and their unborn baby along with Molly and David. She had no idea what life had in store for them but right now on this day, in this year, she knew she was with her soulmate where she was supposed to be. After that, life would unfold according to some grand plan, and everything would be ok.

As Kate stood on the cusp of a new life with Yiannis and Seán, she felt all the possibilities of life wrap around them and dissolve into the atmosphere to be reincarnated another day.

About the Author

Siobhán Curran lives in a small town in rural Ireland. She is married and has two daughters. She trained as a primary school teacher, has a degree in education and worked happily in the same school for twenty-one years.

After a devastating health diagnosis in 2000 the course of her life changed dramatically. She retired from teaching in 2004 and embarked on her own journey of self-discovery.

Along with maintaining a healthy lifestyle, she is blissfully involved in all things creative. She is a long-time attendee at yoga and meditation classes and frequently travels over and back to Crete.

This is her first novel.

Please Review this Book

Dear Reader,

Thank you for taking the time to read this book. If you enjoyed it, please visit Amazon to write a review. A review can also be left on Goodreads. This matters because most potential readers first judge a book by what others have to say. An honest review would be most appreciated. Thank you!

59308767R00179

Made in the USA
Middletown, DE
11 August 2019